TRANZLATY

Language is for everyone

语言属于每个人

Folk Tales of Bengal

孟加拉民间故事

Part One
第一部分

Lal Behari Day

1 / 2

English / 普通话

Folk Tales of Bengal
孟加拉民间故事

Life's Secret
生命的秘密

Once upon a time there was a king.
从前，有一位国王。
This King had married two Queens.
这位国王娶了两位王后。
The two queens were called Duo and Suo.
两位皇后分别叫多和索。
Both of the queens were childless.
两位女王均无子嗣。
One day a Faquir came to the palace gate.
有一天，一位法基尔来到了宫门口。
The Faquir had come to ask for alms.
法基尔来乞讨。
Queen Suo went to the door.
索皇后走到门口。
And she gave him a handful of rice.
她给了他一把米。
The mendicant asked her a question.
乞丐问了她一个问题。
"Do you have any children?"
"你有孩子吗？"
The queen had no children.
女王没有孩子。
"I wish had children, but I have none"
"我希望有孩子，但我没有"
The holy man refused to take alms from her.
圣人拒绝接受她的施舍。
In these times there were different traditions.
在那个时代，存在着不同的传统。
And the people believed many different things.
人们相信许多不同的事情。
Don't take charity from the hands of a childless woman.

不要从没有孩子的女人手中接受施舍。
Such hands were ceremonially unclean.
这样的手在礼仪上是不洁净的。
The mendicant offered her a drug.
乞丐给了她一剂药。
This drug was to remove her barrenness.
这种药物可以治愈她的不孕症。
She expressed her willingness to take the drug.
她表示愿意服用该药。
The mendicant told her how to take the drug.
乞丐告诉她如何服用这种药。
"This is the potion you must swallow"
"这是你必须吞下的药水"
"Prepare the juice of a pomegranate flower"
"准备石榴花汁"
"Swallow the drug with the juice"
"将药汁一起吞下"
"If you do this, you will soon have a son"
"如果你这样做，你很快就会有一个儿子"
"Your son will be exceedingly handsome"
"你的儿子一定会非常英俊"
"His complexion will be beautiful"
"他的肤色将会很漂亮"
"He will have the colour of pomegranate flowers"
"他的肤色将像石榴花一样"
"And you shall call him Dalim Kumar"
"你就给他起名叫达利姆·库马尔吧。"
"But he will also have enemies"
"但他也会有敌人"
"They will try to take your son's life"
"他们会试图夺走你儿子的生命"
"But there is a secret to his life"
"但他的生活中有一个秘密"
"And I will tell you this secret"

"我会告诉你这个秘密"
"In front of your palace is a pond"
"你的宫殿前有一个池塘"
"In that pond there is a big Boal fish"
"那个池塘里有一条大博尔鱼"
"Your son's life is connected to that fish"
"你儿子的生命和那条鱼息息相关"
"In the heart of the fish is a small box"
"鱼的心脏里有一个小盒子"
"This small box is made of wood"
"这个小盒子是木头做的"
"In the box of wood is a necklace of gold"
"木盒子里有一条金项链"
"That necklace is the life of your son"
"那条项链就是你儿子的生命"
The mendicant gave her the drugs.
乞丐给了她药。
And they said their farewells.
他们便告别了。

Soon all in the palace whispered of an heir.
很快，宫殿里所有人都在悄悄谈论继承人的事情。
Great was the joy of the King.
国王非常高兴。
He had visions of an heir to the throne.
他梦想着能有一位王位继承人。
A never-ending succession of powerful monarchs.
强大君主的继承永无止境。
He dreamt of how they perpetuated his dynasty.
他梦想着他们如何延续他的王朝。
These ideas floated before his mind.
这些想法浮现在他的脑海里。
It made him the happiest he had ever been.
这让他感到前所未有的幸福。

Many ceremonies were performed for the occasion.
为了这一时刻，人们举行了许多仪式。
The people of the kingdom played loud music.
王国的人民演奏着响亮的音乐。
The birth of a prince was a truly special event.
王子的诞生确实是一件特殊的事件。
Soon queen Suo gave birth to a son.
不久索皇后就生了一个儿子。
He was more beautiful than anyone had imagined.
他比任何人想象的都要英俊。
The King saw his son's face.
国王看到了儿子的脸。
And his heart leaped with joy.
他心里高兴极了。
Soon the child ate his first rice.
不久，孩子就吃了他的第一顿米饭。
Mukhe bhaat was celebrated with great joy.
人们非常高兴地庆祝了 Mukhe bhaat。
And the whole kingdom was filled with gladness.
整个王国都充满了欢乐。

Dalim Kumar grew up to be a fine boy.
达利姆·库马尔长大后成为了一个优秀的男孩。
There was one activity he particularly liked.
有一项活动他特别喜欢。
He loved playing with the pigeons.
他喜欢和鸽子玩耍。
However, the pigeons often flew to Queen Duo.
然而，鸽子却经常飞向Queen Duo。
Nobody knows why they did this.
没有人知道他们为什么这么做。
And they flew into her apartment.
它们飞进了她的公寓。
So Dalim Kumar often met Queen Duo.

所以Dalim Kumar经常会见到Queen Duo。

At first, she happily gave the pigeons back.
一开始，她很高兴地把鸽子还了回去。
But later she wasn't as willing to return the pigeons.
但后来她不太愿意归还鸽子了。
She gave the pigeons up with some reluctance.
她有些不情愿地放弃了鸽子。
She felt she could use this to her advantage.
她觉得她可以利用这一点来为自己谋利。
She naturally hated the child.
她自然是恨这个孩子。
Since Dalim's birth the king had neglected her.
自从达利姆出生以来，国王就一直忽视她。
And the King idolized the mother of Dalim.
国王非常崇拜达利姆的母亲。
Somehow, she had heard of the mendicant.
不知何故，她听说过这个乞丐。
She heard he had given queen Suo a medicine.
她听说他给了索皇后一剂药。
She had also heard about what he had said.
她也听说了他所说的话。
There was a secret to the prince's life.
王子的生活中有一个秘密。
She had heard his life was bound to something.
她听说他的生命与某种事物息息相关。
But she did not know what his life was bound to.
但她不知道他的人生将走向何方。
She was determined to get the secret.
她决心要得到这个秘密。

Of course, the pigeons came back to her.
当然，鸽子又回到了她身边。
And the pigeons flew into her room again.
鸽子又飞进她的房间。

This time she refused to give the pigeons back.

这次她拒绝归还鸽子。

"I won't just give you your pigeon back"

"我不会直接把鸽子还给你"

"First, you have to tell me something"

"首先，你得告诉我一件事"

"What do you want, aunty?" the boy asked.

"阿姨，你想要什么？" 男孩问道。

"Oh, my darling, do not worry"

"哦，亲爱的，别担心"

"It's just a small thing I want"

"这只是我想要的一件小事"

"I want to know where your life is hidden"

"我想知道你的生命隐藏在哪里"

The boy was very confused by this.

男孩对此感到非常困惑。

"What is that, aunty?"

"那是什么，阿姨？"

"Where can my life be, except in me?"

"除了我自己，我的生命还能在哪里？"

"No, child, that is not what I meant"

"不，孩子，我不是这个意思。"

"A holy mendicant told your mother a secret"

"一位圣僧告诉了你母亲一个秘密"

"Your life is bound up with something"

"你的生命与某些事物息息相关"

"I wish to know what that thing is"

"我想知道那是什么东西"

The boy was confused by what she said.

男孩对她说的话感到困惑。

"I never heard of any such thing"

"我从未听说过这样的事"

But Queen Duo insisted it was true.

但女王杜奥坚称这是真的。

"Promise to find out from your mother"
"答应我向你妈妈打听一下"
"Ask her where your life is hidden"
"问问她你的生活隐藏在哪里"
"Then I will let you have the pigeons"
"那我就把鸽子给你。"
"Otherwise, I will keep the pigeons"
"否则，我就把鸽子留下来"
The boy wanted his pigeons back.
男孩想要回他的鸽子。
So he agreed to get the information.
因此他同意获取这些信息。
But first she made him promise.
但首先她要他做出承诺。
"Promise me you won't tell your mother"
"答应我，你不会告诉你妈妈"
And the boy promised not to tell her.
男孩答应不告诉她。
"I promise I won't tell my mum"
"我保证不告诉我妈妈"
Queen Duo freed the prince's pigeons.
杜奥王后释放了王子的鸽子。
Dalim was overjoyed to have his birds again.
达利姆很高兴能再次拥有他的鸟。
And he forgot the entire conversation.
他忘记了整个谈话内容。

The next day Dalim was playing again.
第二天，达利姆又开始比赛了。
You can imagine what happened again.
你可以想象又发生了什么。
The pigeons flew to Queen Duo's apartment.
鸽子飞到了杜奥女王的公寓。
And they flew into her room again.

然后它们又飞进了她的房间。

Dalim went in to his stepmother's apartment.

达利姆走进了他继母的公寓。

And he asked her for the pigeons.

他向她要鸽子。

Of course she asked him for the information.

当然，她向他询问了这些信息。

Dalim could not tell her where his life was hidden.

达利姆无法告诉她他的身世究竟隐藏在何处。

"I promise I will ask her today"

"我保证今天会问她"

"But please can I have my pigeons"

"但是请问我可以把我的鸽子还给我吗？"

She didn't give the pigeons back so quickly.

她没有这么快就归还鸽子。

But, in the end, he got his pigeons again.

但最终，他还是再次得到了他的鸽子。

After playing, Dalim went to his mother.

玩完后，达利姆去找妈妈。

"Mamma, please tell me where my life is hidden"

"妈妈，请告诉我，我的生命藏在哪里"

"What do you mean, child?" asked the mother.

"孩子，你是什么意思？"母亲问道。

She was astonished at the question.

她对这个问题感到很惊讶。

Why would her child ask her this?

她的孩子为什么会问她这个问题？

"Yes, mamma," replied the child.

"是的，妈妈，"孩子回答道。

"I have heard of a holy mendicant"

"我听说过一位圣僧"

"He told you something about my life"

"他告诉你一些关于我的生活"

"He said my life is hidden in something"
"他说我的生命隐藏在某种东西里"
"Tell me what that thing is"
"告诉我那是什么东西"
"My child, my darling, my treasure"
"我的孩子，我的爱人，我的宝贝"
"My golden moon," his mother pleaded.
"我的金色月亮，"他的母亲恳求道。
"Do not ask such a question"
"不要问这样的问题"
"Cover my enemies' mouths with ashes"
"用灰烬盖住敌人的嘴"
"Let my Dalim live forever," she begged.
"让我的达利姆永远活下去，"她恳求道。
But the child insisted knowing the secret.
但孩子坚持要知道这个秘密。
He refused to eat or drink until he knew.
在他知道之前，他拒绝吃喝。
Queen Suo had no choice but to tell him.
索皇后只好告诉他。
Eventually she told him the secret of his life.
最终她告诉了他人生的秘密。

The next day Dalim was playing again.
第二天，达利姆又开始比赛了。
You can imagine where the pigeons flew.
你可以想象鸽子飞到哪里。
Dalim chased after the birds into the apartment.
达利姆追着鸟儿进了公寓。
His stepmother told him many sweet words.
他的继母对他说了很多甜言蜜语。
And finally, she got his secret from him.
最后，她从他那里得知了他的秘密。
She wasted no time to start her wicked plan.

她立即开始实施她的邪恶计划。
And she gave orders to her servants.
她又吩咐仆人说：
"Get some dried stalk from the hemp plant"
"拿一些大麻干茎"
"Make sure the stalks are very brittle"
"确保茎秆非常脆"
Brittle hemp stalks make a cracking sound.
脆弱的麻杆发出噼啪的声响。
The sound is similar to the cracking of joints.
这种声音类似于关节断裂的声音。
And it sounds like the bones of old people.
听起来就像是老人的骨头。
She put the brittle hemp stalks under her bed.
她把脆弱的麻杆放在床下。
And then she lied on her bed.
然后她躺在床上。
She wanted to test the hemp stalks.
她想测试一下大麻秆。
The stalks cracked just as much as she wanted.
茎秆按照她想要的程度断裂。
She was satisfied with how her plan was going.
她对计划的进展感到满意。
She gave more orders to her servants.
她向仆人们发出了更多命令。
"Tell the King I am very ill"
"告诉国王我病得很重"
"He must come to see me immediately"
"他必须马上来见我"
The king did not love this queen.
国王并不爱这位王后。
But he still had a duty to care for her.
但他仍然有照顾她的义务。
If she was ill, he had to look after her.

如果她病了，他就必须照顾她。
The King came to her bedroom.
国王来到她的卧室。
She rolled on the bed in pain.
她痛苦地在床上翻滚。
The King heard the cracking of her bones.
国王听到了她骨头断裂的声音。
He ordered his best physician to attend her.
他命令他最好的医生去照顾她。
But the queen had thought of this.
但女王却想到了这一点。
She had already spoken with the physician.
她已经和医生谈过了。
"There is only one remedy," he told the king.
他告诉国王："只有一个办法。"
"There's a pond in front of the palace"
"宫殿前面有一个池塘"
"In the pond there's a large Boal fish"
"池塘里有一条大宝鱼"
"The remedy is in that fish"
"解药就在鱼里"
So the king let the physician catch the fish.
于是国王就让医生去抓鱼。
Meanwhile Dalim was busy playing.
与此同时，达利姆正忙着玩耍。
He knew nothing of his aunt's illness.
他对于姑姑的病情一无所知。
The fish was taken out the water.
鱼被捞出了水。
Dalim fell to the ground immediately.
立刻倒在了地上。
He flopped around on the floor.
他倒在地上。
And he could not breathe.

他无法呼吸。
The guards immediately noticed.
守卫立刻注意到了。
Dalim was taken to his mother's room.
达利姆被带到他母亲的房间。
And the King was informed of his son.
国王得知了他的儿子的消息。
He couldn't believe his son's illness.
他简直不敢相信儿子的病。
The fish was taken to Queen Duo.
这条鱼被带给了Queen Duo。
Queen Duo was being saved.
女王杜奥正在被拯救。
At the same time Dalim was dying.
与此同时，达利姆也濒临死亡。
The fish was cut open.
鱼被切开了。
And they found the wooden box.
他们找到了木箱。
In the box lay a necklace of gold.
盒子里放着一条金项链。
Queen Duo put on the necklace.
女王朵朵戴上了项链。
And Dalim died at the very same moment.
而达利姆也在同一时刻去世了。

News of the tragedy reached the king.
悲剧的消息传到了国王的耳中。
He was plunged into an ocean of grief.
他陷入了悲痛的深渊。
News of Queen Duo's recovery did not help.
女王杜奥康复的消息并没有起到什么帮助作用。
He wept painful and bitter tears.
他流下了痛苦而辛酸的泪水。

No one thought he would recover.
没有人认为他会康复。
He could not bear to bury his son.
他不忍心埋葬自己的儿子。
Nor did he allow his body to be burned.
他也不允许自己的尸体被焚烧。
He could not accept that his son had died.
他无法接受儿子已经去世的事实。
His death was so sudden and senseless.
他的死是如此突然和毫无意义。
He had the dead body moved to a garden-houses.
他把尸体移到一座花园房屋里。
This garden-house was in the suburbs.
这座花园洋房位于郊区。
Here his son was laid in state.
他的儿子被安葬在这里。
All sorts of provisions were put there.
那里摆放着各种各样的物品。
Although everyone knew it was unnecessary.
尽管大家都知道没有必要。
The young boy did not need food anymore.
小男孩不再需要食物了。
The house was kept locked day and night.
房子日夜都锁着。
Dalim had had one very close friend.
达利姆有一位非常亲密的朋友。
Only this friend was allowed to visit.
只有这位朋友被允许探望。
He was the son of the prime minister.
他是首相的儿子。
He was entrusted with the key of the house.
他被委托保管这所房子的钥匙。
Once a day he could visit his dead friend.
他每天可以去看望一次他死去的朋友。

Queen Suo retired after the loss of her son.
索皇后在丧子之后便退隐江湖。
Now the King spent the nights with Queen Duo.
现在国王和多奥王后一起过夜。
The Queen wanted to avoid suspicion.
女王想避免引起怀疑。
So she took the necklace off at night.
所以她晚上就把项链摘了下来。
But Dalim's life was tied to the necklace.
但达利姆的生命却与这条项链紧密相连。
And his death was not so simple.
而他的死，却没有这么简单。
He was dead when the queen wore the necklace.
当女王戴上项链时他已经死了。
But when she took the necklace off, he returned to life.
但当她摘下项链时，他又复活了。
And so he returned to life every night.
就这样，他每晚都恢复了生机。
Every morning she put the necklace on again.
每天早上她都会戴上这条项链。
And so, he died again every morning.
就这样，他每天早上又死去。
At night he ate whatever food he liked.
晚上他吃任何他喜欢的食物。
Because there was plenty of food for him.
因为那里有足够的食物给他。
He walked around in the premises.
他在屋内四处走动。
And he meditated on the strangeness of his life.
他沉思着自己生活中的奇异之处。
Dalim's friend only visited him during the day.
达利姆的朋友只在白天来看望他。
So he always saw him as a lifeless corpse.

所以他总是把他看作一具没有生命的尸体。
But his body never seemed to change.
但他的身体似乎从未改变。
There was no sign of putrefaction.
没有腐烂的迹象。
The body was lifeless and pale.
尸体毫无生气，脸色苍白。
But there were no symptoms of death.
但没有死亡症状。
It all seemed too strange for him.
这一切对他来说都太奇怪了。
So he decided to watch the corpse more closely.
于是他决定更仔细地观察尸体。
And he visited his friend at night.
晚上他去拜访了他的朋友。
He was astonished at what he saw that night.
那天晚上所见的景象让他大吃一惊。
His dead friend was walking about in the garden.
他死去的朋友正在花园里散步。
At first he thought Dalim might a ghost.
起初他以为达利姆可能是个鬼。
So he went to see if he could touch him.
于是他去看看是否可以触摸他。
And then he saw it was really his friend.
然后他发现这确实是他的朋友。
Dalim told his friend everything that had happened.
达利姆把发生的一切告诉了他的朋友。
He told him all the circumstances of his death.
他向他讲述了自己死亡的全部情况。
And soon they solved the mystery.
他们很快就解开了谜团。
They understood why he revived only at night.
他们明白了为什么他只在晚上苏醒过来。
Every night the king came to see Queen Duo.

每天晚上，国王都会来看望多奥王后。
When the King visited, she took off her necklace.
当国王来访时，她摘下了项链。
The life of the prince depended on the necklace.
王子的生命取决于这条项链。
So the two friends worked on a plan.
于是这两个朋友制定了一个计划。
Night after night they consulted together.
他们夜复一夜地一起商议。
But they could not think of any feasible scheme.
但他们想不出任何可行的方案。

Eventually the Gods must have taken pity.
最终，诸神必定会怜悯他。
And they decided to free Dalim.
他们决定释放达利姆。
But we must understand how the Gods work.
但我们必须了解神的运作方式。
These things are planned long before.
这些事情都是早就计划好的。
The sister of Bidhata-Purusha had had a daughter.
Bidhata-Purusha 的妹妹有一个女儿。
Bidhata-Purusha was a great fortune teller.
Bidhata-Purusha 是一位伟大的算命师。
He had written something on the child's forehead.
他在孩子的额头上写了一些东西。
"This child will marry the dead bridegroom"
"这个孩子将嫁给死去的新郎"
Her mother was very saddened by this.
她的母亲对此非常伤心。
She did not want this destiny for her daughter.
她不希望自己的女儿遭遇这样的命运。
But she could not argue with him.
但她无法与他争论。

He never changed what he had written.
他从未改变过他所写的内容。
The child became exceedingly beautiful.
这个孩子变得非常漂亮。
But the mother could not take any pleasure in this.
但母亲对此却并不感到高兴。
Because she knew the destiny of her child.
因为她知道孩子的命运。
Eventually the girl came to marriageable age.
最终，女孩到了适婚年龄。
She had to find a way to avoid her fate.
她必须找到一种方法来逃避自己的命运。
So the mother fled the country with her child.
于是母亲带着孩子逃离了这个国家。
Perhaps she could avoid her dreadful destiny.
也许她可以避免可怕的命运。
But what was written was written.
但写下来的东西已经写下来了。
And fate cannot be overruled like this.
而命运是不能被这样推翻的。
Together they journeyed through the land.
他们一起游历了这片土地。
You can imagine how fate was working.
你可以想象命运是怎样运作的。
They wandered past Dalim's resting place.
他们漫步经过达利姆的安息之地。
The shade of the evening was approaching.
夜幕即将降临。
"Mother, I am thirsty," said her child.
"妈妈，我渴了，" 她的孩子说。
"Sit at this gate," replied her mother.
"坐在这扇门口，" 她母亲回答道。
"I will search for water in the village"
"我要去村里找水"

The girl was curious about the garden.
女孩对花园很好奇。
And in the garden she saw strange house.
在花园里她看到了一座奇怪的房子。
She pushed the gate, which opened itself.
她推了一下门，门就自己打开了。
When she went in, she saw a beautiful palace.
当她进去的时候，她看到了一座美丽的宫殿。
But she had an uneasy feeling about the palace.
但她对这座宫殿却有一种不安的感觉。
However, the door had shut itself.
然而，门却自己关上了。
So she had no way of getting out.
所以她没有办法出去。

When night came the prince revived.
夜幕降临，王子苏醒了。
As usual, he walked around in the garden.
和往常一样，他在花园里散步。
But this time he saw a female figure.
但这次他看到的是一个女性的身影。
The figure was standing near the gate.
那个身影正站在大门附近。
Soon he saw that it was a girl.
很快他就看出那是一个女孩。
And he saw she was of unsurpassed beauty.
他发现她有着无与伦比的美丽。
"Who are you?" he asked her.
"你是谁？" 他问她。
She told Dalim everything that had happened.
她把发生的一切告诉了达利姆。
All the details of her little history.
她这段小历史的所有细节。
"My uncle is the divine Bidhata-Purusha"

"我的叔叔是神圣的 Bidhata-Purusha"
"He wrote on my forehead at birth"
"他在我的出生时就在我的额头上写下了"
"This child will marry the dead bridegroom"
"这个孩子将嫁给死去的新郎"
"My mother did not want that life for me"
"我妈妈不希望我过那样的生活"
"So we left our house and city"
"所以我们离开了家和城市"
"And we wandered through the country"
"我们在这个国家流浪"
"We had come to the gate of your palace"
"我们已经来到了你的宫殿门口"
"After our journey I was thirsty"
"旅途结束后我感到口渴"
"So my mother went to look for water"
"所以我妈妈去找水"
"And now I am standing here before you"
"现在我就站在你们面前"
Dalim Kumar knew the meaning of the story.
达利姆·库马尔知道这个故事的含义。
"I am the dead bridegroom," he told the girl.
"我是死去的新郎，" 他告诉女孩。
"It is me who you will marry"
"你要嫁的人是我"
"Come with me to the house," he asked of her.
"跟我进屋吧，" 他向她请求道。
But the girl wasn't so easily persuaded.
但女孩却没那么容易被说服。
"You are standing and speaking to me"
"你站着跟我说话"
"How can you be the dead bridegroom?"
"你怎么会是死去的新郎？"
The prince understood her objection.

王子理解她的反对意见。
"You will understand it afterwards"
"你之后就会明白的"
The girl followed the prince into the house.
女孩跟着王子进了屋。
She had been fasting the whole day.
她已经禁食一整天了。
So the prince gave her wonderful food.
于是王子给了她美味的食物。
Meanwhile, the girl's mother had come back.
与此同时，女孩的妈妈回来了。
She was standing at the gates of the garden.
她正站在花园门口。
But her daughter was not there anymore.
但她的女儿已经不在了。
She cried out for her daughter.
她大声呼喊她的女儿。
But she got no reply from her daughter.
但她没有收到女儿的回复。
So she went looking for her in the village.
于是她就去村里寻找她。

As usual, Dalim's friend came that night.
和往常一样，那天晚上达利姆的朋友来了。
Dalim was still entertaining his guest.
达利姆仍在招待他的客人。
He was not expecting to see a stranger.
他没想到会看到一个陌生人。
And the girl retold him her story.
女孩又向他讲述了她的故事。
You can imagine his surprise when she told him.
你可以想象当她告诉他时他的惊讶。
He was able to confirm Dalim's story.
他证实了达利姆的故事。

Soon they had all accepted destiny.
很快他们都接受了命运。
That night they fulfilled their fates.
那天晚上，他们实现了自己的命运。
They decided to unite the couple in matrimony.
他们决定让这对夫妇结婚。
It was going to be impossible to get a priest.
找到一名牧师是不可能的。
So Dalim's friend performed the hymeneal rites.
因此达利姆的朋友举行了婚礼仪式。
The friend of the bridegroom left the palace.
新郎的朋友离开了宫殿。
The newly-weds had the palace to themselves.
这座宫殿只属于这对新婚夫妇。
The happy couple did not sleep much that night.
那天晚上这对幸福的夫妇没怎么睡。
So it was long after sunrise that they woke up.
所以他们醒来时，天已经亮了很久了。
Of course it was only the young wife that woke up.
当然，醒来的只有年轻的妻子。
The prince had become a cold corpse again.
王子已经重新变成了一具冰冷的尸体。
The queen had put on her necklace.
女王戴上了项链。
And life had departed from him again.
生命又一次离他而去。
You can imagine how the young wife felt.
你可以想象这位年轻妻子的感受。
She shook her husband to try and wake him.
她摇晃丈夫试图唤醒他。
She kissed him on his cold lips.
她吻了他冰冷的嘴唇。
But all her efforts were in vain.
但她的一切努力都白费了。

He was as lifeless as a marble statue.
他就像一座大理石雕像一样毫无生气。
The young wife was stricken with horror.
年轻的妻子惊恐万分。
She smote her breast with her fists.
她用拳头捶打自己的胸部。
She struck her forehead with her palms.
她用手掌拍打额头。
And she tore her hair from her head.
她把头发都拔掉了。
She ran through the garden like a mad woman.
她像一个疯女人一样跑过花园。
Dalim's friend did not come during the day.
达利姆的朋友白天没有来。
He did not want to see his friend this way.
他不想看到他的朋友这个样子。
The poor girl did not know what to do.
这个可怜的女孩不知道该怎么办。
Time could not pass quickly enough.
时间过得真快。
The day seemed as long as a year.
这一天仿佛像一年一样漫长。
But the even longest day has its end.
但即使是最长的一天也有结束的时候。
The shades of evening were descending.
夜幕渐渐降临。
Her dead husband was awakened into consciousness.
她死去的丈夫被唤醒了。
He rose up from his bed again.
他再次从床上起来。
And he embraced his new wife.
他拥抱了他的新婚妻子。
Again they ate, drank, and became merry.
他们又吃又喝，过得很快乐。

His friend made his usual appearance.
他的朋友像往常一样出现。
And the whole night was spent celebrating.
整个晚上都在庆祝。

They spent the next seven years this way.
他们就这样度过了接下来的七年。
During the day Dalim was lifeless.
白天，达利姆毫无生气。
But at night he came to life.
但到了晚上他又活了过来。
And their life was quite usual.
他们的生活也很平常。
The princess gave her husband two lovely boys.
公主给她的丈夫生了两个可爱的男孩。
They were the exact image of their father.
他们和他们的父亲一模一样。
Of course the king and Queens did not know.
国王和王后当然不知道。
They did not know they were grandparents.
他们不知道自己是祖父母。
And they did not know Dalim was alive.
他们并不知道达利姆还活着。
To be precise I should say he was alive at night.
准确的说，他晚上还活着。
They all thought he had long been dead.
他们都以为他早已死了。
They assumed his corpse would now be gone.
他们以为他的尸体现在已经不见了。
But the heart of Dalim s wife was yearning.
但达利姆的妻子心里却充满着向往。
She wanted nothing more than her mother-in-law.
她只想要她的婆婆。
Over the years she had come up with a plan.

多年来她已经想出了一个计划。
Perhaps she could see her mother-in-law.
也许她能见到她的婆婆。
Maybe they could get hold of the necklace.
也许他们可以得到这条项链。
She asked for the consent of her husband.
她征求了丈夫的同意。
And he allowed her to disguise herself.
他还允许她伪装自己。
She took on the appearance of a female barber.
她看上去就像一名女理发师。
Like every female barber, she needed equipment.
像每个女理发师一样，她需要设备。
She took the following tools;
她带了以下工具；
An iron instrument for preparing finger nails.
用于修整指甲的铁制器械。
Another iron instrument for scraping the feet.
另一种刮脚的铁器。
A piece of burnt jhama brick.
一块烧焦的贾玛砖。
For rubbing the soles of the feet.
用于揉搓脚底。
And paint for the edges of the feet.
并画出脚的边缘。
She took all her tools with her.
她把所有的工具都带走了。
And she stood at the gate of the King's palace.
她站在国王宫殿的门口。
I forgot something else she brought.
我忘了她还带了一些东西。
She had come with her two sons.
她和她的两个儿子一起来了。
She spoke with the guards.

她与警卫交谈。

"I work as a barber"

"我是一名理发师"

"I have come to offer my services"

"我来提供服务"

"I desire to see Queen Suo"

"我想见索皇后。"

Queen Suo quickly gave her an interview.

索皇后赶紧对她进行了采访。

The queen was quite fond of the two little boys.

女王非常喜欢这两个小男孩。

They strangely reminded her of her own son.

奇怪的是，他们让她想起了自己的儿子。

And she remembered her lost treasure.

她想起了她丢失的宝藏。

Tears fell profusely from her eyes.

泪水从她的眼眶里涌出。

She had not the remotest idea who they were.

她根本不知道他们是谁。

Of course we know who they are.

我们当然知道他们是谁。

The two little boys are her grandsons.

这两个小男孩是她的孙子。

She spoke to the barber.

她和理发师说话了。

"My son died when he was young"

"我的儿子很小就去世了"

"I have given up these vanities"

"我已经放弃了这些虚荣"

"I stopped having my feet ceremoniously dyed"

"我不再隆重地染脚了"

"But I would be glad to see your two fine boys"

"但我很高兴见到你的两个好儿子"

The barber agreed to let Queen Suo see her boys.

理发师同意让索皇后见见她的儿子。
But she had one question before she went.
但她去之前有一个问题。
"Are there other ladies in the palace?
"宫里还有其他的宫女吗？
"Someone else I could provide my service to"
"我可以为其他人提供服务"
She was told there was another queen.
有人告诉她还有另一位女王。
And she was also allowed to go to that queen.
并且她还被允许去见那位女王。
Queen Duo allowed her to prepare her nails.
Queen Duo 让她准备指甲。
And she was allowed to scrape her feet.
她被允许刮擦她的脚。
She painted her feet with alakta.
她用阿拉克塔（alakta）涂抹她的脚。
And the queen was very pleased with her skill.
女王对她的技能非常满意。
She also enjoyed the sweetness of her disposition.
她也享受着自己性格的甜美。
So she booked to have more of her services.
因此她预订了更多她的服务。
The female barber had come for something else.
女理发师来是为了别的事情。
And she quickly noticed the necklace.
她很快就注意到了那条项链。
The necklace was around the Queen's neck.
这条项链戴在女王的脖子上。

The day of her second visit had come.
她第二次来访的日子到了。
She gave her eldest son the instructions.
她向大儿子发出了指示。

"We are going into the palace again"
"我们又要进宫了"
"When in the palace you have to cry"
"在宫里就得哭"
"Say you would like the queen's necklace"
"说你想要女王的项链"
"Don't stop crying until you have her necklace"
"拿到她的项链之前别停止哭泣"
The female barber went to queen Duo's apartment.
女理发师来到了多奥王后的公寓。
Soon the elder boy started to cry.
不久，大男孩就开始哭了。
The boy acted his role well.
这个男孩很好地演绎了他的角色。
Nothing would console the boy.
没有什么能够安慰这个男孩。
"What is wrong?" Queen Duo asked.
"怎么了？" 女王朵朵问道。
They boy could hardly speak.
那个男孩几乎说不出话来。
"Your necklace is so beautiful"
"你的项链真漂亮"
And he continued to sob.
他继续抽泣。
"Can I please hold the necklace?"
"我可以拿着这条项链吗？"
Queen Duo did not want to let him.
朵女王不想让他这么做。
"I cannot part with my necklace"
"我不能丢下我的项链"
"It is my most valuable jewel"
"这是我最珍贵的宝石"
But the boy did not stop crying.
但男孩并没有停止哭泣。

So she took the necklace off her neck.
于是她把项链从脖子上摘了下来。
And she put the necklace into the boy's hand.
她把项链放到了男孩的手里。
The boy quickly stopped crying.
男孩很快就停止了哭泣。
And he held the necklace in his hand.
他手里拿着项链。
The female barber had finished her work.
女理发师已经完成了她的工作。
She was packing up her tools.
她正在收拾工具。
And she was about to leave the palace.
而她也正准备离开宫殿。
So the queen wanted the necklace back.
因此女王想要回项链。
But the boy would not let her have the necklace.
但男孩不让她拿走项链。
His mother attempted to snatch the necklace from him.
他的母亲试图从他手中抢走项链。
But he wept bitterly when she tried.
但当她尝试时，他却痛哭流涕。
And he cried as if his heart would break.
他哭得心都碎了。
The female barber politely asked the queen;
女理发师礼貌地询问女王；
"Please let the boy take the necklace home"
"请让男孩把项链带回家"
"He will fall asleep after drinking his milk"
"喝完牛奶他就会睡着"
"And then I will bring your necklace back"
"然后我会把你的项链带回来"
She could see she had no choice.
她明白自己别无选择。

The boy would not allow her to take the necklace.
男孩不允许她拿走项链。
So she agreed to the proposal.
于是她同意了这个提议。
"Dalim must now be long dead," she thought.
"达利姆肯定早已死了，" 她想。
And she had nothing to worry about.
她没什么可担心的。

The princess had the prized necklace.
公主有一条珍贵的项链。
The treasure bound to her husband's life.
与丈夫生命绑定的宝藏。
She rushed back to the garden-house.
她冲回了花园小屋。
And she gave the necklace to Dalim.
她把项链送给了达利姆。
Dalim had been alive all morning.
达利姆整个上午都充满活力。
It was the first time he saw the sun again.
这是他第一次再次看到太阳。
Their joy of his life knew no bounds.
他们对他的生活感到无比的喜悦。
Their friend advised them to go to the palace.
他们的朋友建议他们去宫殿。
"Go to the palace tomorrow"
"明天去宫里"
"Present yourselves to the King and Queen"
"向国王和王后致敬"
"Let them know you're alive and well"
"让他们知道你还活着，而且很好"
The couple accepted their friend's advice.
这对夫妇接受了朋友的建议。
And they prepared everything for their arrival.

他们为他们的到来做好了一切准备。
An elephant was brought for the prince.
有人给王子带来了一头大象。
A pair of ponies were brought for the boys.
他们给男孩们带来了一对小马。
And there was a grand chaturdala.
并且有一个盛大的 Chaturdala 活动。
It was furnished with curtains of gold lace.
房间里装饰着金色蕾丝窗帘。
Word was sent to the king and the Queen Suo.
消息传到了国王和索皇后那里。
"Prince Dalim Kumar is alive and well"
"达利姆·库马尔王子还活着，而且很健康"
"And he is coming to visit you"
"他要来看你"
"Now he has a wife and two sons"
"现在他有妻子和两个儿子"
The King and Queen Suo could hardly believe it.
索王和索王后简直不敢相信。
But they were assured that it was all true.
但他们确信这一切都是真的。
Queen Duo quickly realized her predicament.
女王朵奥很快就意识到了自己的困境。
And she became overwhelmed with grief.
她陷入了深深的悲痛之中。
A band of musicians followed the prince.
一队乐师跟随着王子。
Prince Dalim Kumar approached the palace-gate.
达利姆·库马尔王子走近宫殿大门。
The King and Queen Suo went to the gates.
国王和索皇后来到城门口。
And they welcomed their long-lost son.
他们迎来了失散多年的儿子。
You can imagine how happy they were.

你可以想象他们有多高兴。
Dalim told his parents of his death.
达利姆将自己的死讯告诉了父母。
He told them of the pond by the palace.
他向他们讲述了宫殿旁边的池塘。
And he told them of the fish in the pond.
他向他们讲述了池塘里的鱼。
He told them of the wooden box in the fish.
他向他们讲述了鱼里面的木盒子。
He told them of the necklace in the wooden box.
他向他们讲述了木盒子里的项链。
And he told them the secret of his life.
他向他们讲述了他人生的秘密。
He told them how he died each night.
他每晚都向他们讲述自己是如何死去的。
Of course he also mentioned his new wife.
当然他也提到了他的新婚妻子。
The king was inflamed with rage at the news.
国王听到这个消息勃然大怒。
He ordered Queen Duo into his presence.
他命令女王杜奥到他面前。
A large hole was dug in the ground.
地上挖了一个大洞。
The hole was as deep as the height of a man.
这个洞深约有一人高。
Queen Duo was made to stand in the hole.
女王杜奥被要求站在洞里。
Prickly thorns were heaped around her.
她的周围堆满了带刺的荆棘。
The thorns went up to the crown of her head.
荆棘一直长到她的头顶。
And in this manner she was buried alive.
就这样，她被活埋了。

Phakir Chand
帕基尔·钱德

There was once a king, who had a son.
从前有一位国王，他有一个儿子。
The king's minister also had a son.
国王的大臣也有一个儿子。
The two sons loved each other dearly.
两个儿子彼此深爱着对方。
And they did everything together.
他们一起做所有事。
The two sons sat and stood up together.
两个儿子一起坐下，一起站起。
They walked together to the same places.
他们一起走到同一个地方。
They ate their meals together.
他们一起吃饭。
They slept and got up together.
他们一起睡觉，一起起床。
They spent years in each other's company.
他们在一起度过了多年的时光。
One day they both felt a new desire.
有一天，他们都感受到了新的渴望。
They wanted to see foreign lands.
他们想去看看异国他乡。
And so they set out on their journey.
于是他们踏上了旅程。
One of them was the son of a king.
其中一位是国王的儿子。
One of them was the son of his chief minister.
其中一人是其首席部长的儿子。
So of course they were both quite rich.
所以他们当然都很富有。
But they did not take any servants with them.

但他们没有带任何仆人。
They went by themselves, on horseback.
他们独自骑马前往。
The horses were beautiful to look at.
这些马看上去很漂亮。
They were Pakshirajes horses.
它们是 Pakshirajes 马。
Such horses are known as the kings of birds.
这种马被称为“鸟中之王”。
The two sons rode together for many days.
两个儿子一起骑马出行了很多天。
They passed through extensive plains.
他们穿过广阔的平原。
And the plains were covered with paddy.
平原上长满了水稻。
And they passed through strange cities.
他们穿过陌生的城市。
And they passed through towns, and villages.
他们穿过城镇和村庄。
They passed through treeless deserts.
他们穿过了没有树木的沙漠。
And they passed through forests.
他们穿过了森林。
And the forests were dense with trees.
森林里树木茂密。
These forests were the abode of the tiger.
这些森林是老虎的居所。
And the bear also lived in these forests.
熊也生活在这些森林里。
One evening they were overtaken by the night.
一天傍晚，夜幕降临了。
They had not seen any human habitations.
他们没有看到任何人类居住的地方。
But it was getting darker and darker.

但天色却越来越暗。
So they dismounted beneath a lofty tree.
于是他们在一棵高大的树下下了马。
They tied their horses to the tree.
他们把马拴在树上。
And then they climbed up the tree.
然后他们爬上了树。
They covered the branches with thick foliage.
它们用茂密的树叶覆盖着树枝。
So that they could sit on the branches.
这样他们就可以坐在树枝上。
The tree had grown near a large body of water.
这棵树生长在一大片水域附近。
The water was as clear as the eye of a crow.
水清澈得像乌鸦的眼睛。
The two friends made themselves comfortable.
两个朋友让自己感到舒服自在。
Of course it wasn't very comfortable in a tree.
当然，树上并不太舒服。
But it wasn't uncomfortable in the tree either.
但在树上也并不感到不舒服。
They had decided to spend the night there.
他们决定在那里过夜。
They sometimes chatted together in whispers.
他们有时会低声聊天。
They felt whispering was better than talking.
他们觉得低声说话比说话更好。
Because the region seemed very strange to them.
因为这个地区对他们来说非常陌生。
And soon they were falling into a doze.
很快他们就进入了瞌睡状态。
But their attention was suddenly jolted.
但他们的注意力突然被吸引了。
From the water they heard a noise.

他们听到水里传来一阵响声。
It sounded like the rushing of water.
听起来就像水流奔腾的声音。
In front of them was a terrible sight!
呈现在他们眼前的是一幅惨不忍睹的景象！
A huge serpent came from under the water.
一条巨蛇从水下冒出来。
The snake swam ashore and slithered around.
蛇游上岸，四处爬行。
But something else attracted their attention.
但其他事情引起了他们的注意。
The crested hood of the serpent was shining.
蛇的冠冕闪闪发光。
The snake had a brilliant manikya embedded.
蛇身上嵌有一颗璀璨的玛尼基亚（manikya）。
The jewel shone like a thousand diamonds.
这颗宝石像一千颗钻石一样闪闪发光。
The crystal lit up the water in the tank.
水晶照亮了水箱里的水。
The embankments and trees were irradiated.
堤岸和树木均受到辐射。
The serpent doffed the jewel from its crest.
蛇从它的冠上摘下了宝石。
And the serpent threw the jewel on the ground.
蛇把宝石扔到了地上。
And then the serpent went in search of food.
然后蛇就去寻找食物了。
They could not believe what they had seen.
他们简直不敢相信自己所看到的一切。
They stayed in the safety of the tree.
他们待在安全的树下。
But they greatly admired the jewel.
但他们非常欣赏这颗宝石。
The ruby shed an ineffable luster.

红宝石散发出难以言喻的光泽。
Everything had a magical glow around it.
周围的一切都散发着神奇的光芒。
They had never seen anything like it.
他们从来没有见过这样的事情。
Although, they had heard of this treasure.
虽然，他们听说过这件宝物。
The jewel equaled the treasures of seven kings.
这颗宝石的价值相当于七位国王的财富。
But their admiration soon changed to fear.
但他们的钦佩很快就变成了恐惧。
The serpent came to the foot of their tree.
蛇来到了他们的树脚下。
The serpent had found their horses!
蛇找到了他们的马！
The poor horses had been tied to the tree.
可怜的马匹被拴在树上。
The animals had no way of escaping.
动物们没有办法逃脱。
One by one the serpent ate their horses.
蛇一只接一只地吃掉了他们的马。
But the serpent's appetite did not seem satisfied.
但蛇的胃口似乎并没有得到满足。
They feared they would be the next victims.
他们担心自己会成为下一个受害者。
But their fears were soon relieved.
但他们的担忧很快就消除了。
The gigantic cobra had not seen them.
巨大的眼镜蛇没有看到他们。
And eventually the snake left again.
最后蛇又离开了。
The minister's son saw an opportunity.
部长的儿子看到了机会。
This was his chance to take the gem.

这是他夺取宝石的机会。
But there was one problem they had.
但他们遇到了一个问题。
The jewel shone incredibly bright.
这颗宝石闪闪发光。
The serpent would know what had happened.
蛇会知道发生了什么事。
But there was a way to overcome this problem.
但有一种方法可以解决这个问题。
And the minister's son knew the solution.
而部长的儿子知道解决办法。
He had to cover the stone with horse-dung.
他不得不用马粪盖住石头。
And there was some horse-dung by the tree.
树旁边还有一些马粪。
He quietly came down from the tree.
他悄悄地从树上下来。
He picked up the horse-dung off the floor.
他把地上的马粪捡起来。
And he threw the dung upon the precious stone.
他把粪便撒在宝石上。
And then he climbed up into the tree again.
然后他又爬上了树。
The serpent noticed something had happened.
蛇注意到有事发生了。
The light of the jewel had vanished.
宝石的光芒已经消失。
The serpent rushed back with great fury.
蛇愤怒地冲了回来。
The serpent returned to where it had left the stone.
蛇回到了它离开石头的地方。
The serpent let out a frightful hiss at the night.
蛇对着夜空发出可怕的嘶嘶声。
The snake's groans and convulsions were terrible.

蛇的呻吟和抽搐十分可怕。
The snake went round and round the jewel.
蛇绕着宝石转了一圈又一圈。
But the stone was covered with horse-dung.
但石头上却覆盖着马粪。
This way the serpent could not see its treasure.
这样，蛇就看不到它的宝藏了。
Finally, the serpent breathed its last breath.
最后，蛇吐出了最后一口气。

The two friends did not sleep much that night.
那天晚上，两个朋友都没怎么睡觉。
In the morning they came down from the tree.
早上，他们从树上下来。
They went to where the crest-jewel was.
他们来到了宝石所在的地方。
The mighty serpent was still laying there.
那条强大的蛇仍然躺在那里。
But now the snake's body was perfectly lifeless.
但现在蛇的身体已经完全没有生命迹象了。
The friend of the prince stepped over the dead snake.
王子的朋友跨过了那条死蛇。
And he picked up the dung covered jewel.
他捡起了那颗覆盖着粪便的宝石。
Both of them went to the bank of the water.
两人便来到了水边。
And they washed the precious stone.
他们洗净了宝石。
Finally, all the dung had been washed off.
最后，粪便全部被洗掉了。
And the jewel shone as brilliantly as before.
这颗宝石依然像以前一样闪耀着光芒
The jewel lit up the entire bed of the tank of water.
这颗宝石照亮了整个水箱水床。

Now they could see the innumerable fishes.

现在他们可以看到无数的鱼。

But the light also revealed something else.

但光线也揭示了其他的东西。

This astonished them more than all the fishes.

这比所有的鱼都更让他们惊讶。

In the bottom of the water there was something.

水底有东西。

They could see there were lofty walls.

他们看到那里有高耸的城墙。

The walls were from a magnificent palace.

这些墙壁来自一座宏伟的宫殿。

The prince's friend was feeling venturesome.

王子的朋友感到很有冒险精神。

He convinced the king's son to follow him.

他说服了国王的儿子跟随他。

And then they wanted to swim to the palace below.

然后他们想游到下面的宫殿。

The prince's friend took the jewel in his hand.

王子的朋友把宝石拿在手里。

And they both dived into the waters.

然后他们双双跳入水中。

Soon they stood at the gate of the palace.

很快，他们就站在了宫殿门口。

To their surprise the gate was open.

令他们惊讶的是，大门是开着的。

They saw no being, human or superhuman.

他们没有看到任何生物，无论是人类还是超人。

So they decided to venture inside the gate.

于是他们决定冒险进入大门。

Inside the walls there was a beautiful garden.

墙内有一个美丽的花园。

In the middle of the garden was a house.

花园中央有一座房子。

No one had ever seen so many flowers.
没有人见过这么多的花。
There were roses of all imaginable varieties.
有各种各样的玫瑰。
There were endless numbers of yellow jessamine.
有无数朵黄色的茉莉花。
And there were numerous white bell flowers.
还有无数的白色风铃草。
These flowers were the king of smells.
这些花是气味之王。
The most scented lily of the valley.
香气最浓郁的铃兰。
There were the flowers from the champaka tree.
那是金香树的花。
And a thousand other sweet-scented flowers.
还有一千种芳香的花朵。
Acres covered with the delicious jessamine.
大片土地上开满了美味的茉莉花。
All the plants were gemmed with flowers.
所有的植物都开满了鲜花。
And all the flowers were in full bloom.
所有的花都盛开了。
So the air was loaded with rich perfume.
因此空气中充满了浓郁的香气。
A wilderness of sweet scents everywhere.
到处都是甜美香气的荒野。
They went through this paradise of perfumery.
他们穿过了这个香水天堂。
And eventually they reached the house.
最后他们终于到达了房子。
The house was surrounded by lofty trees.
房子周围环绕着高大的树木。
Soon they stood at the door of the house.
很快他们就站在了房子门口。

Now they could see it was a fairy palace.
现在他们看清楚了，这是一座仙宫。
The walls were of burnished gold.
墙壁是抛光的金子。
Here and there shone diamonds of dazzling hue.
到处都闪耀着璀璨夺目的钻石。
But they did not see any beings.
但他们没有看到任何生物。
So they went inside the palace.
于是他们就走进了宫殿。
The palace was richly furnished.
这座宫殿装饰华丽。
They went from room to room.
他们从一个房间走到另一个房间。
But they did not see anyone.
但他们没有看到任何人。
It seemed to be a deserted house.
这似乎是一所废弃的房子。
At last, however, they found a special room.
但最终他们找到了一个特殊的房间。
In this room there was a young lady.
这个房间里有一位年轻的女士。
She was sleeping on a golden bed.
她正睡在一张金色的床上。
The young lady was of exquisite beauty.
这位年轻女士容貌绝伦。
Her complexion was a mixture of red and white.
她的肤色是红白相间的。
She seemed to be about sixteen years of age.
她看上去大约十六岁。
The two friends gazed upon her.
两个朋友注视着她。
They were enchanted by her beauty.
他们被她的美貌迷住了。

But they could not admire her for long.
但他们无法长久地欣赏她。

Because the young lady opened her eyes.
因为小姑娘睁开了眼睛。

Her eyes seemed like the eyes of a gazelle.
她的眼睛就像瞪羚的眼睛。

On seeing the strangers she said;
看到陌生人时，她说；

"How have you come here, ye unfortunate men?"
"你们这些不幸的人怎么会来这里？"

"Be gone, be gone! I beg of you two"
"走开，走开！求求你们了。"

"This is the abode of a mighty serpent"
"这是一条巨蛇的居所"

"The serpent which has devoured my parents"
"那条蛇吞噬了我的父母"

"And my brothers, and all my relatives"
"还有我的兄弟和所有亲戚"

"I am the only one that he has spared"
"我是他唯一放过的人"

"Flee for your lives while you still can"
"趁还能逃命的时候赶紧逃吧"

"Or else the serpent will eat you both"
"否则蛇会把你们两个吃掉"

The prince's friend told her what had happened.
王子的朋友告诉了她所发生的事。

"The serpent has breathed his last breath"
"蛇已咽下最后一口气"

"The snake's body lies lifeless on the floor"
"蛇的尸体毫无生气地躺在地板上"

"We took the head-jewel of the serpent"
"我们取走了蛇头上的宝石"

"The jewel's light showed us to the palace.
"宝石的光芒指引我们来到宫殿。

She thanked the strangers for their bravery.
她感谢陌生人的勇敢。
"You have freed me from the infernal serpent"
"你把我从地狱之蛇的魔爪中解救出来了"
"Please live with me in my palace"
"请和我一起住在我的宫殿里"
"But please promise never to desert me"
"但请答应我永远不要抛弃我"
They gladly accepted the invitation.
他们欣然接受了邀请。
The king's son was smitten with the princess.
国王的儿子深深地迷恋着公主。
He adored the charms of the peerless princess.
他崇拜这位绝世公主的魅力。
And he married her after a short time.
不久之后他就和她结婚了。
There was no priest at the palace.
宫殿里没有牧师。
So the hymeneal knot was tied by other means.
因此，婚姻线结是通过其他方法打结的。
A simple exchange of garlands of flowers.
简单的交换花环。
The king's son became inexpressibly happy.
国王的儿子感到无比高兴。
He delighted in the company of the princess.
他很高兴与公主相处。
The prince's friend also had a wife.
王子的朋友也有妻子。
Of course she was living in the upper world.
当然，她生活在上层世界。
But he participated in his friend's happiness.
但他分享了朋友的幸福。
The time they spent together passed merrily.
他们在一起度过的时光非常愉快。

But they could not live here forever.
但他们不可能永远住在这里。
The prince had to return to his kingdom.
王子必须返回他的王国。
But he knew the return would require some planning.
但他知道回归需要一些计划。
The occasion would come with a lot of pomp.
这次活动将会十分隆重。
There were going to be many ceremonies.
将会有很多仪式举行。
Because there was a lot to be celebrated.
因为有很多值得庆祝的事情。
First the prince's friend was going to go.
首先，王子的朋友要去。
And then he was going to return with the attendants.
然后他就要和侍从们一起返回。
Horses, and elephants for the happy pair.
幸福的一对将拥有马和大象。
The prince accompanied his friend.
王子陪伴着他的朋友。
Together they went back to the surface.
他们一起回到了地面。
And they saw the upper world again.
他们又看到了上面的世界。
The two friends bid each other adieu.
两个朋友互相告别。
The prince returned to his lovely wife.
王子回到了他美丽的妻子身边。
Before leaving everything had been organized.
离开之前，一切都已安排好。
The prince's friend arranged his return.
王子的朋友安排了他的回程。
He said when he was going to go the embankment.
他说他正要去堤岸。

He was going to have the horses that they needed.
他将得到他们需要的马匹。
Elephants were going to be there too, and attendants.
那里也会有大象和侍从。
They were going to wait upon the prince and princess.
他们要去拜访王子和公主。
The snake-jewel gave them the rights to this.
蛇宝赋予了他们这个权利。
The prince's friend went back to his country.
王子的朋友回国了。
To prepare for the return of his friend.
为朋友的归来做准备。

One day the prince was sleeping.
有一天，王子正在睡觉。
He had just had his midday meal.
他刚刚吃过午饭。
The princess had never seen the upper regions.
公主从未见过上层地区。
She felt the desire to see the upper world.
她渴望看看上面的世界。
For this she needed the snake-jewel.
为此，她需要蛇宝石。
Only this could help her through the water.
只有这样才能帮助她渡过水面。
The jewel was shining its bright light in the room.
这颗宝石在房间里闪耀着明亮的光芒。
She took the snake-jewel into her hand.
她把蛇形宝石拿在手里。
And then she left the palace and the garden.
然后她离开了宫殿和花园。
She successfully swam to the upper world.
她成功游到了上层世界。
No mortal had caught sight of her.

没有一个人见过她。
At the edge of the water were some steps.
水边有一些台阶。
The steps were for the convenience of bathers.
这些台阶是为了方便沐浴者。
And this is also where she sat.
这也是她坐的地方。
She scrubbed her body with the sand.
她用沙子擦洗身体。
She washed her hair with the fresh water.
她用清水洗了头发。
And she played with the water for fun.
她还玩水玩得很开心。
She walked about on the water's edge.
她在水边走来走去。
And she admired all the scenery around.
她欣赏着周围的一切风景。
But finally she returned back to her palace.
但最终她还是回到了自己的宫殿。
Her husband was still deep in sleep.
她的丈夫还在酣睡。
But eventually he had slept enough.
但最终他还是睡够了。
She did not tell him about her adventures.
她没有告诉他她的冒险经历。
The next day her husband fell asleep again.
第二天她的丈夫又睡着了。
And again she paid a visit the upper world.
她又一次造访了上层世界。
And she remained unnoticed by mortal man.
而她仍然没有被凡人注意到。
Her success was starting to give her courage.
她的成功开始给予她勇气。
So she repeated her adventure a third time.

于是她第三次重复了她的冒险。

The rajah's son was out hunting that day.

那天，拉贾的儿子出去打猎了。

He had his tent not far from the water.

他的帐篷距离水边不远。

His attendants were cooking his meal.

他的侍从正在为他做饭。

So, he wandered about along the water.

于是，他沿着水边徘徊。

Nearby an old woman was gathering sticks.

附近有一位老妇人正在收集木柴。

She was collecting dried branches of trees.

她正在收集干树枝。

She needed the sticks for kindling wood.

她需要木棍来引火。

This was when the princess came out the water.

就在这时，公主从水里出来了。

She gazed around and she saw a man.

她环顾四周，看到了一个男人。

And then she saw there was also a woman.

然后她看到那里还有一个女人。

The princess knew she didn't want to be seen.

公主知道她不想被人看见。

So she went back down to her palace.

于是她回到了宫殿。

But the rajah's son had caught a glimpse of her.

但拉贾的儿子却瞥见了她。

And the old woman gathering sticks saw her too.

那个捡柴的老妇人也看到了她。

The rajah's son stood gazing on the waters.

拉贾的儿子站在那里凝视着水面。

He had never seen such a beautiful woman.

他从未见过如此美丽的女人。

She seemed to him to be a deva-kanyas.

在他看来，她是一位天神。

Heavenly goddesses he had read of in old books.
他曾在古书中读到过的天上的女神。

They are said to visit the upper world.
据说他们要去往上层世界。

And the upper world is honored to have them.
上层世界很荣幸能拥有它们。

But it is said to happen only rarely.
但据说这种情况很少发生。

The way that angels only visit rarely.
天使很少来访。

He had seen the princess' unearthly beauty.
他见证了公主超凡脱俗的美貌。

She had made a deep impression on his heart.
她在他的心里留下了深刻的印象。

Although he had seen her only for a moment.
尽管他只见过她一瞬间。

But her beauty distracted his mind.
但她的美貌分散了他的注意力。

He stood there like a statue, for hours.
他像雕像一样站在那里好几个小时。

All he could do was gaze into the waters.
他所能做的就是凝视着水面。

In the hope of seeing the lovely figure again.
希望能够再次见到那可爱的身影。

But all his time was spent in vain.
但他所有的时间都白白浪费了。

The princess did not appear again.
公主再也没有出现。

The rajah's son became mad with love.
拉贾的儿子因爱情而疯狂。

He kept muttering, "now here, now gone!"
他不停地嘟囔着："一会儿来，一会儿走！"

He refused to leave the water's edge.

他拒绝离开水边。

His attendants had to forcibly remove him.

他的随从不得不强行将他带走。

They took him to his father's palace.

他们把他带到了他父亲的宫殿。

But he was in a state of hopeless insanity.

但他已经陷入了无可救药的精神错乱状态。

He couldn't be made to speak to anyone.

他无法与任何人说话。

And he spent his days sobbing heavily.

他整天都在悲痛地哭泣。

No others words came out of his mouth.

他嘴里再没有说出别的话。

"Now here, now gone!"

"一会儿在这里，一会儿又消失了！"

"Now here, now gone!"

"一会儿在这里，一会儿又消失了！"

You can imagine the rajah's grief.

你可以想象拉贾的悲伤。

"What could have deranged my son's mind?"

"什么事情会让我儿子精神错乱？"

"'Now here, now gone,' what does it mean?"

" '一会儿在这里，一会儿又走了' 是什么意思？"

He could not unravel the words' meaning.

他无法理解这些话的含义。

His attendants couldn't decipher the words either.

他的侍从也无法理解这些话。

The land's best physicians were consulted.

他们咨询了国内最好的医生。

But their consultation had no effect.

但他们的咨询并没有什么效果。

The sons of æsculapius were not able to help.

埃斯库拉庇俄斯的儿子们却无力提供帮助。

No one could ascertain the cause of the madness.

没有人能够确定这种疯狂现象的起因。
Without knowing the cause there was no cure.
不知道病因就无法治愈。
The physicians tried to ask the prince.
医生们试图询问王子。
But all he said was, "now here, now gone!"
但他只说了一句："一会儿在这里，一会儿又走了！
"

The rajah was distracted with grief.
拉贾悲痛欲绝。
Day and night he worried for his son.
他日夜担心儿子。
He wished for his son's intellects to return.
他希望儿子的智力能够恢复。
A proclamation was made in the capital.
首都发布了一项公告。
Town criers were sent into the city.
城镇公告员被派往城里。
And they beat their drums for attention.
他们敲响鼓声以引起注意。
"The rajah's son has lost his mental faculties"
"拉贾的儿子失去了心智"
"The rajah seeks a cure for his son"
"拉贾为他的儿子寻求治愈方法"
"A reward is offered for the cure"
"治愈者有赏格"
"The hand of the rajah's daughter"
"拉贾女儿的手"
"Her hand comes with half his kingdom"
"她带来了他半个王国"
The drum was beaten around the city.
鼓声响彻全城。
But no one felt they could touch the drum.
但没有人觉得自己能碰到鼓。

No one knew the cause of his madness.
没有人知道他疯狂的原因。
At last an old woman came forward.
最后，一位老妇人走上前来。
And she stepped up to touch the drum.
她走上前去触摸鼓。
"I will discover the cause of his madness"
"我要找出他疯狂的原因"
"And I will cure him from his disease"
"我会治愈他的疾病"
She had seen what happened to the boy.
她看到了男孩身上发生的事情。
She was at the water's edge that day.
那天她在水边。
It was her who was gathering up sticks.
原来是她正在收集木棍。
This woman had a crack-brained son.
这个女人有一个精神失常的儿子。
Her son was named of Phakir-Chand.
她的儿子名叫 Phakir-Chand。
So she was called Phakir's mother.
因此她被称为 Phakir 的母亲。
The woman was brought before the rajah.
这位妇女被带到了拉贾面前。
And the following conversation took place.
随后发生了如下对话。
"You are the woman that touched the drum"
"你就是那个敲鼓的女人"
"You know the cause of my son's madness?"
"你知道我儿子发疯的原因吗？"
"Yes, oh incarnation of justice!"
"是啊，正义的化身啊！"
"I know the cause of your son's madness"
"我知道你儿子发疯的原因"

"But I will not say the cause of his madness"
"但我不会说出他疯狂的原因"
"First I will cure your son of his madness"
"首先我要治好你儿子的疯病"
"How can I believe you are able to?"
"我怎么能相信你能做到呢？"
"The best physicians of the land have failed"
"国内最好的医生都失败了"
"You need not now believe, my king"
"国王陛下，您现在不必相信。"
"Wait till I have performed the cure"
"等我把病治好"
"Many an old woman knows many secrets"
"许多老妇人知道很多秘密"
"Secrets wise men are unacquainted with"
"智者所不知的秘密"
"Very well, let me see what you can do"
"好吧，让我看看你能做什么"
"In what time will you perform the cure?"
"您什么时候进行治疗？"
"It is impossible to fix the time"
"不可能确定时间"
"Ff course I will begin work immediately"
"当然，我马上就开始工作。"
"But I need your lordship's assistance"
"但我需要大人的帮助。"
"What help do you require from me?"
"您需要我帮什么忙？"
"Your lordship will please order a hut"
"请大人订一间小屋。"
"Have the hut raised on the embankment of the water"
"把小屋建在水堤上"
"Where your son first caught the disease"
"你儿子第一次感染这种疾病的地方"

"I mean to live in that hut for a few days"
"我打算在那间小屋里住几天"
"And please order some of your servants"
"请吩咐你的仆人。"
"They have to be in attendance at a distance"
"他们必须保持距离"
"Tell them to be about a hundred yards away"
"告诉他们离我们大约一百码远"
"That way I can call them over when we need them"
"这样，当我们需要他们的时候，我就可以叫他们过来。"
The king had listened attentively.
国王认真地听着。
"I will order that to be immediately done"
"我会立即下令"
"Do you want anything else?"
"你还想要什么吗？"
"Those are all the preparations I need"
"这就是我需要做的全部准备了"
"But let me remind you of the agreement"
"但是让我提醒你一下协议"
"You promised the hand of your daughter"
"你答应嫁给你的女儿"
"And you promised half your kingdom"
"你还承诺给你半个王国"
"But I can't marry your daughter"
"但我不能娶你的女儿"
"Because your daughter has to marry a man"
"因为你的女儿必须嫁给一个男人"
"But I also have a son of marriageable age"
"但我还有一个适婚年龄的儿子"
"Allow my son to marry your daughter"
"让我儿子娶你女儿"
"Allow him to have half of your kingdom"

"让他拥有你一半的王国"
The king was agreed with the terms.
国王同意了这些条款。
"If you find a cure, he marries my daughter"
"如果你找到治愈方法，他就娶我女儿"
"And half of my kingdom shall be his"
"我的王国一半属于他"
A temporary hut was quickly erected.
一间临时棚屋很快就搭建起来了。
The hut was built on the embankment of the water.
小屋建在水堤上。
And Phakir's mother took up her abode.
法基尔的母亲就在这里居住。
An outpost was also erected at some distance.
在一段距离处还设立了一个前哨站。
Because the woman might require some attendance.
因为这位女士可能需要一些照顾。
Strict orders were given by Phakir's mother.
法基尔的母亲下达了严格的命令。
No one was allowed to go near the water.
任何人都不被允许靠近水。
Only she was allowed to stay by the water.
只有她被允许留在水边。

But let us leave Phakir's mother at the water.
但是让我们把法基尔的母亲留在水边。
Let us hasten down the subterranean palace.
让我们赶紧前往地下宫殿吧。
To see what the prince and the princess are doing.
看看王子和公主在做什么。
The princess did want to go up again.
公主确实想再上去。
But she now knew that it would be dangerous.
但她现在知道这很危险。

And she had given up the idea of a fourth visit.
她已经放弃了第四次访问的想法。
But women generally have greater curiosity.
但女性一般有更大的好奇心。
And the princess was no exception to the rule.
公主也不例外。
One day her husband was asleep.
有一天，她的丈夫正在睡觉。
He always slept after his noonday meal.
他总是在午饭后睡觉。
She took the snake-jewel in her hand.
她把蛇形宝石拿在手里。
And she rushed out of the palace.
她冲出了宫殿。
And she came up to the upper world.
她来到了上层世界。
There was an upheaval in the waters.
水域发生了剧烈波动。
And Phakir's mother was on high alert.
而 Phakir 的母亲也处于高度警惕状态。
She was hiding in the hut.
她躲在小屋里。
And she was looking through the chinks.
她正透过缝隙向外张望。
The princess saw no human being nearby.
公主没有看到附近有人。
So she came to the bank of the water.
于是她来到了水边。
Phakir's mother showed herself outside the hut.
法基尔的母亲出现在小屋外面。
And she addressed the princess politely.
她礼貌地对公主讲话
"Come, my child, thou queen of beauty"
"来吧，我的孩子，你是最美丽的女王"

"Come to me, and I will help you to bathe"
"到我这里来，我帮你洗澡"
So saying, she approached the princess.
说着，她向公主走去。
The princess saw she was just an old woman.
公主发现她只是一位老妇人。
So she made no resistance to her offer.
所以她没有拒绝她的提议。
The old woman was washing the princess' hair.
老妇人正在给公主洗头发。
And she noticed the bright jewel in her hand.
她注意到了她手中那颗闪亮的宝石。
"Out the jewel here till you are bathed"
"把宝石放在这里，直到你沐浴完毕"
Now the jewel was in the hands of Phakir's mother.
现在这颗宝石在法基尔母亲的手中。
She wrapped the jewel up in a cloth.
她用布包住了宝石。
And she wrapped the cloth around her waist.
她用布裹住腰。
Now the princess was unable to escape.
现在公主已经无法逃脱了。
And Phakir's mother gave the signal.
法基尔的母亲发出了信号。
The attendants rushed to the water.
侍从们赶紧冲到水边。
And they took the princess captive.
他们把公主俘虏了。
The news soon reached the city.
消息很快就传到了城里。
"Phakir's mother had captured a water-nymph"
"法基尔的母亲捕获了一位水仙女"
And the people rejoiced at the news.
人们听到这个消息都很高兴。

All came to see the"daughter of the immortals"
大家都来看望这位 "神仙女儿"
She was brought to the palace.
她被带进了宫殿。
And she was brought to the rajah's son.
她被带到了拉贾的儿子面前。
The rajah's son was still of impaired intellect.
拉贾的儿子智力仍然有缺陷。
But that cloud on his brain soon dissipated.
但他脑中的阴云很快就消散了。
"I have found you! I have found you!"
"我找到你了！我找到你了！"
His eyes had been vacant and lusterless.
他的眼神空洞无光。
But now his eyes had the fire of intelligence.
但现在他的眼中闪烁着智慧的光芒。
He had almost lost the use of his tongue.
他几乎已经无法说话了。
"Now here, now gone!" was all he had been able to say.
"一会儿在这里，一会儿又走了！" 他只能说出这句
话。
But this sense too was restored.
但这种感觉也恢复了。
The joy of the rajah knew no bounds.
拉贾的喜悦无以言表。
There was great festivity in the city.
城市里充满了欢乐的气氛。
The people praised Phakir-Chand's mother.
人们赞扬了 Phakir-Chand 的母亲。
And everyone soon expected the marriage.
很快每个人都期待着这场婚礼。
The rajah's son was to wed the water-nymph.
拉贾的儿子将要娶水仙女。
The princess, however, had made a promise.

然而，公主已经做出了承诺。
She told Phakir's mother of her promise.
她将自己的承诺告诉了法基尔的母亲。
"I won't as much as look at another man"
"我不会再多看其他男人一眼"
"For one year my vows shall last"
"我的誓言将持续一年"
"The marriage cannot happen in that time"
"这段时间内不可能结婚"
The rajah's son was somewhat disappointed.
拉贾的儿子有些失望。
But he readily agreed to the delay.
但他欣然同意延期。
"Delay enhances the sweetness of the pleasure"
"延迟增强了快乐的甜蜜"
Of course the princess spent her time in sorrow.
当然，公主是在悲伤中度过的。
She spent her days and nights sighing.
她日日夜夜都在叹息。
And she lamented her idle curiosity.
她对自己毫无意义的好奇心感到悲哀。
The curiosity that led her to the upper world.
好奇心驱使她来到上层世界。
The curiosity that separated her from her husband.
好奇心使她与丈夫分离。
She thought of her unfortunate husband.
她想到了她不幸的丈夫。
She had left him all alone below the waters.
她把他孤身一人留在水下。
And she wept bitter tears each day.
她每天都会流下痛苦的泪水。
She wished that she could run away.
她真希望自己能够逃跑。
But that would have been impossible.

但那是不可能的。
Because she was immured within walls.
因为她被囚禁在墙内。
And there were walls within the walls.
墙内还有墙。
And what use was getting out the palace?
离开宫殿又有什么用呢？
She couldn't get to her husband anyway.
无论如何，她都无法找到她的丈夫。
She didn't have the serpent jewel.
她没有蛇宝石。
The ladies of the palace tried to comfort her.
宫中的女官们尽力安慰她。
And Phakir's mother tried to divert her mind.
法基尔的母亲试图转移她的注意力。
But their efforts were in vain.
但他们的努力都是徒劳的。
She took pleasure in nothing.
她对任何事都不感到快乐。
She hardly spoke to anyone.
她几乎不和任何人说话。
She wept throughout the day.
她哭了一整天。
And she wept through the night.
她哭了一整夜。

The year of her vow was drawing to a close.
她宣誓的那一年即将结束。
But she was still disconsolate.
但她还是很沮丧。
The marriage, however, had to be celebrated.
然而，这场婚礼还是要庆祝的。
The rajah consulted the astrologers.
拉贾咨询了占星家。

The day and the hour had been decided.
日期和时间已经决定了。
The nuptial knot was to be tied.
即将举行婚礼了。
Great preparations were made.
做了充分的准备。
The confectioners were busy day and night.
糖果制造商日夜忙碌。
They prepared all sorts of sweetmeats.
他们准备了各种各样的甜食。
Milkmen supplied the palace with tanks of curds.
送奶工向宫殿提供一罐罐凝乳。
Great quantities of gunpowder were manufactured.
制造了大量的火药。
There were going to be grand fireworks.
将会有盛大的烟花表演。
Stages were erected everywhere.
到处都搭起了舞台。
And musicians were selected to play music.
并选出音乐家来演奏音乐。
All the city assumed an air of mirth.
整个城市洋溢着欢乐的气氛。
All looked forward to the festivities.
大家都在期待着节日的到来。

We must return out attention to the minister's son.
我们必须重新关注部长的儿子。
He had left his friend in the subterranean palace.
他把他的朋友留在了地下宫殿里。
And he had gone to his country.
他已经回自己的国家了。
He was bringing horses and elephants.
他带来了马和大象。
And he had with him many attendants.

他身边还有许多侍从。

For the return of the king's son.

为了国王儿子的归来。

And for the return of his lovely princess.

以及他可爱的公主的归来。

So that the ceremony had due pomp.

以使典礼有应有的盛况。

The preparations took him many months.

准备工作花费了他好几个月的时间。

But eventually all was prepared.

但最终一切都准备好了。

And the minister's son started on his journey.

于是牧师的儿子开始了他的旅程。

He was accompanied by a long train of elephants.

一长队大象陪伴着他。

And behind the elephants were horses.

大象后面是马。

And all the horses had their own attendants.

所有的马都有自己的侍从。

He reached the water ahead of schedule.

他提前到达了水边。

So he had two or three days to spare.

所以他有两三天的空闲时间。

Tents were pitched in the mango slopes.

芒果山坡上搭起了帐篷。

So the men and cattle had accommodation.

这样，人和牲畜就有了住处。

The minister's son kept his eyes on the water.

牧师的儿子一直注视着水面。

The sun of the appointed day sank below the horizon.

指定日期的太阳已沉入地平线以下。

But there was no sign of the prince.

但没有王子的踪影。

Nor did the princess come to the surface.

公主也没有浮出水面。
He waited two or three days longer.
他又等了两三天。
Still the prince did not make his appearance.
王子仍然没有出现。
What could have happened to his friend?
他的朋友可能发生了什么事？
And where was his beautiful wife?
他美丽的妻子在哪里？
Had another serpent beaten them to death?
是另一条蛇把他们打死了吗？
Possibly the mate of the one that had died.
可能是死者的伴侣。
Had they somehow lost the serpent-jewel?
他们是不是因为某种原因丢失了蛇形宝石？
Or had they perhaps visited the upper world?
或者他们可能已经访问过上层世界？
And had they been captured in the upper world?
他们在上层世界被抓了吗？
Such were the reflections of the prince's friend.
这就是王子朋友的想法。
The prince's friend was overwhelmed with grief.
王子的朋友悲痛欲绝。
The waters were quite close to the city.
水域距离城市相当近。
And often the sound of music could be heard.
并且经常可以听到音乐的声音。
He asked passers-by what that music meant.
他向路人询问那首音乐是什么意思。
He was told about the rajah's son.
有人告诉他有关拉贾儿子的事。
And he was told of a wonderful young lady.
有人告诉他有一位非常出色的年轻女士。
And he was told they were going to marry.

有人告诉他他们就要结婚了。
And he was told more about the wonderful lady.
他也了解到了更多关于这位神奇女士的事情。
She had come out of the waters he was waiting by.
她从他等待的水域出来了。
The marriage ceremony was in two days.
婚礼在两天后举行。
The minister's son made the connection.
部长的儿子发现了其中的联系。
The wonderful young lady was the wife of his friend.
这位美丽的年轻女士是他朋友的妻子。
He resolved, therefore, to go into the city.
因此，他决定进城。
And he was going to find out all he could.
他要尽一切可能找出答案。
If he could, he would rescue the princess.
如果可以的话，他要救出公主。
He told the attendants to go home.
他让服务员回家。
And he told them to take the elephants.
他告诉他们把大象带走。
And he told them to take the horses.
他告诉他们把马带走。
And he himself went to the city.
他自己也去了城里。
And he took up his abode in the house of a Brahman.
他住在一位婆罗门家里。
First, he rested from his journey.
首先，他从旅途中休息了一下。
Then the prince's friend had his dinner.
然后王子的朋友吃了晚饭。
And then he spoke to the Brahman.
然后他和婆罗门说话了。
"Throughout the city there are musicians and bands"

"整个城市都有音乐家和乐队"
"What is the cause of all the celebrations?
"所有这些庆祝活动的原因是什么？
The Brahman was rather surprised.
婆罗门颇感惊讶。
"From what part of the world have you come?"
"您从哪里来？"
"What rock have you been living under?"
"你一直生活在什么岩石下面？"
"Have you not heard the wonderful news?"
"你还没听到这个好消息吗？"
"A young lady of heavenly beauty"
"一位美若天仙的年轻女士"
"She rose out of the waters"
"她从水里出来了"
"And she is going to the son of our rajah"
"她要去见我们王公的儿子了。"
The prince's friend wanted to know more.
王子的朋友想知道更多。
The information could be useful.
这些信息可能有用。
"I have not heard of this news"
"我没有听说过这个消息"
"I have come from a distant country"
"我来自遥远的国度"
"The story has not reached us yet"
"我们还没听到这个故事"
"Will you kindly tell me the particulars?"
"您能告诉我详细情况吗？"
The Brahman was happy to relay the story.
婆罗门很高兴地讲述这个故事。
"The rajah's son went out hunting"
"拉贾的儿子出去打猎了"
"It must have been about this time last year"

"那大概是去年这个时候吧"
"They pitched their tents by the waters in the suburbs"
"他们在郊区的水边搭起了帐篷"
"One day, the rajah's son was walking near the water"
"有一天，拉贾的儿子在水边散步"
"On this day, he saw a young woman"
"这一天，他见到了一位年轻女子"
"I have to mention she was of uncommon beauty"
"我不得不说她美貌非凡"
"She had risen from the depth of the waters"
"她从水底升起"
"She gazed about for a minute or two"
"她四处张望了一两分钟"
"And then the beautiful lady disappeared"
"然后这位美丽的女士就消失了"
"The rajah's son, however, had seen her"
"然而，拉贾的儿子却见过她"
"He had been struck by her heavenly beauty"
"她那如天堂般的美貌深深地震撼了他"
"And so he became desperately enamored by her"
"于是他深深地爱上了她"
"Indeed, she had affected him greatly"
"她确实对他影响很大。"
"And his mental faculties gave way to passion"
"他的心智被激情所取代"
"He was carried home as a mad man"
"他被当作疯子抬回家了"
"He spoke no words except a few"
"除了几句话之外，他什么也没说"
"'now here, now gone!' was all he said"
" '一会儿在这里，一会儿又走了！' 他只说了一句
话。"
"The rajah sent for all the best physicians"
"王公派人召集了所有最好的医生"

"They tried to restore his son to reason"
"他们试图让他儿子恢复理智"
"But the physicians were powerless"
"但医生们无能为力"
"At last the rajah made a proclamation"
"最后，拉贾发布了一项声明"
"And he had the drum beat around the kingdom"
"他让整个王国都响起了鼓声"
"There was a reward for anyone who cured his son"
"谁能治好他的儿子，谁就能得到奖励"
"They would become the rajah's son-in-law"
"他们会成为拉贾的女婿"
"And they would get half the kingdom"
"他们将获得半个王国"
"An old woman answered the call of the drum"
"一位老妇人响应了鼓声的召唤"
"All knew her as Phakir's mother"
"大家都知道她是法基尔的母亲"
"She said she could cure the rajah's son"
"她说她能治好王公的儿子"
"She had a hut built outside the town"
"她在城外建了一间小屋"
"In the suburbs, next to the waters"
"位于郊区，毗邻水边"
"An in the hut she took her abode"
"她住在小屋里"
"She also had some huts erected close by"
"她还在附近建了一些小屋"
"And in those huts attendants waited"
"在那些小屋里，侍从们等候着"
"In case she might need their help"
"万一她需要他们的帮助"
"It seems the goddess rose from the waters"
"女神仿佛从水中升起"

"Phakir's mother and the attendants seized her"
"法基尔的母亲和侍从抓住了她"
"And they carried her in a palki to the palace"
"他们用马车把她抬进了宫殿"
"The rajah's son saw the water-nymph"
"王公的儿子看见了水仙女"
"And he was soon restored to his senses"
"他很快就恢复了理智"
"They would have married there and then"
"他们当时就会结婚"
"But the water goddess had made a vow"
"但水女神已经许下誓言"
"She wouldn't look at a man for one year"
"她一年内都不会看一个男人"
"The year of the vow is now over"
"誓言之年已经结束"
"The music is from the rajah's palace"
"音乐来自王公的宫殿"
"This, in brief, is the story"
"简而言之，这就是故事"
The prince's friend could put the story together.
王子的朋友可以把这个故事拼凑起来。
"a truly wonderful story!"
"真是一个精彩的故事！"
"So where is Phakir's mother?"
"那么，法基尔的妈妈在哪里？"
"And where is Phakir-Chand himself?"
"那么帕基尔-昌德本人又在哪里呢？"
"Has he received the hand of the rajah's daughter?"
"他娶了王公的女儿了吗？"
"And has he received half the kingdom?"
"他得到了半个王国吗？"
The Brahman could also answer these questions.
婆罗门也能回答这些问题。

"No, they have not married yet"
"不，他们还没有结婚"
"And he doesn't yet have half the kingdom"
"但他还没有得到半个王国"
"And, I should say, he is a dimwitted lad"
"而且，我应该说，他是个傻小子。"
"In fact, no one knows where the lad is"
"事实上，没人知道这个孩子在哪里"
"He has been away from home for more than a year"
"他已经离家一年多了"
"That is his manner," he explained.
"这就是他的作风，" 他解释道。
"He stays away for a long time"
"他已经很久没有回来了"
"And then suddenly he comes home"
"然后他突然回家了"
"And then suddenly he leaves again"
"然后他又突然离开了"
"I believe his mother expects him to come soon"
"我相信他妈妈希望他快点出生"
This was very useful information.
这是非常有用的信息。
"What is he like?" he asked.
"他是什么样的人？" 他问道。
"And what does he do when he returns home?"
"那他回家后做什么呢？"
These questions the Brahman could also answer.
婆罗门也能回答这些问题。
"Well, he is about your height"
"嗯，他和你差不多高"
"Though he is somewhat younger than you"
"虽然他比你年轻一些"
"He wears a small piece of cloth round his waist"
"他腰上围着一块小布"

"And he rubs his body with ashes"
"他用灰烬擦拭身体"
"He carries the branch of a tree in his hand"
"他手里拿着一根树枝"
"And there is a tune to which he dances"
"他跳舞时有旋律"
"He comes to the door of the hut of his mother"
"他来到母亲的小屋门口"
"And he sings 'dhoop! dhoop! dhoop!'"
"他唱着‘咚！咚！咚！’"
"His articulation is very indistinct"
"他的发音很不清晰"
"'Come, stay with your mother,' she says"
"‘来吧，和你妈妈待在一起。’她说。"
"And he always gives the same answer"
"他总是给出同样的答案"
"'No, I won't remain,' he says unintelligibly"
"‘不，我不会留下来，’他含糊不清地说。"
"You should hear him when he wants to say yes"
"当他想说‘是’的时候你应该听听他的声音"
"To answer in the affirmative he says 'hoom'"
"如果回答是肯定的，他会说‘hoom’"
A flood of light entered the prince's friend.
一道光芒射入了王子的朋友体内。
He now saw very well how matters stood.
现在他已经看清了事情的真相。
The princess must have taken the snake-jewel.
公主肯定拿走了蛇宝石。
And she must have left the palace alone.
她肯定已经独自离开了宫殿。
And she was captured without the king's son.
她被抓获，国王的儿子也未曾到场。
Phakir's mother must have the snake-jewel.
蛇形宝石一定在 Phakir 的母亲手中。

His friend was still below the water.
他的朋友仍在水下。
The prince had no means of escape.
王子已经无路可逃。
He could imagine his friends desolate state.
他可以想象朋友的凄凉状态。
And he could imagine how hopeless he must be.
他可以想象自己有多么绝望。
The prince's friend was filled with grief.
王子的朋友满心悲痛。
But that was not cause to give up hope.
但这并不能成为放弃希望的理由。
Perhaps he could rescue his friend.
也许他可以救他的朋友。
"I must get the jewel from the old woman"
"我必须从老妇人那里得到宝石"
"Can I not do it by personating Phakir-Chand?"
"我不能扮演 Phakir-Chand 来做这件事吗？"
"His mother is expecting him soon"
"他妈妈很快就要生他了"
"Maybe I can rescue the princess the same way"
"也许我可以用同样的方法救出公主"

He resolved to act the role of Phakir-Chand.
他决心扮演 Phakir-Chand 的角色。
In the morning he left the Brahman's house.
早上，他离开了婆罗门的家。
And he went to the outskirts of the city.
他去了城郊。
He divested himself of his usual clothing.
他脱掉了平常的衣服。
Around his waist he put a narrow piece of cloth.
他在腰间围了一块窄布。
The cloth scarcely reached his knees.

布料刚到他的膝盖。
And he rubbed his body well with ashes.
他用灰烬好好擦拭自己的身体。
And finally he broke some twigs off a tree.
最后他从树上折断了一些树枝。
And thus he was ready to play his role.
因此他已准备好扮演他的角色。
He went to the door of the hut of Phakir's mother.
他来到了法基尔母亲的小屋门口。
And he commenced the operation by dancing.
他以舞蹈的方式开始了行动。
He danced in a most violent manner.
他跳舞的样子极其激烈。
And he sung to the tune of"dhoop! dhoop! dhoop!"
他唱的曲调是"噗！噗！噗！"
The dancing attracted the notice of the old woman.
舞蹈引起了老妇人的注意。
The critical moment had come.
关键时刻已经到来。
The old woman looked to her door.
老妇人望向她的门。
"Phakir-Chand, my son, have you come?"
"Phakir-Chand，我的儿子，你来了吗？"
"my darling; the gods have become propitious to us"
"亲爱的，诸神保佑我们"
Her supposed son uttered the monosyllable, "hoom"
她所谓的儿子发出了单音节的"hoom"
And he danced more violent than before.
而且他的舞姿比以前更加狂野。
And he waved the twig in his hand.
他挥动着手中的树枝。
"this time you must not go away"
"这次你不能走"
"you must remain with me"

"你必须留在我身边"

"no, I won't remain," said the prince's friend.

"不，我不会留下来，" 王子的朋友说。

"remain with me," the mother tried again.

"和我在一起，" 母亲再次尝试道。

"i'll get you married to the rajah's daughter"

"我会让你娶王公的女儿"

"will you marry, Phakir-Chand?"

"你愿意结婚吗，Phakir-Chand？"

The minister's son replied—"hoom, hoom"

大臣的儿子回答道： "呼，呼。"

And he danced even more like a madman.

而且他跳舞跳得更加疯狂了。

"will you come with me to the rajah's house?"

"你愿意跟我一起去拉贾的家吗？"

"I'll show you a princess of uncommon beauty"

"我带你见识一位美丽非凡的公主"

"She rose from the waters"

"她从水中升起"

"hoom, hoom," was the answer from his lips.

"呼，呼" ，他这样回答。

And his feet stomped violently to"dhoop! dhoop!"

并用脚猛踩， "咚！咚！"

"Do you wish to see a jewel, Phakir?"

"你想看宝石吗，法基尔？"

"The crest jewel of the serpent"

"蛇之宝石"

"The treasure of seven kings"

"七位国王的宝藏"

"hoom, hoom," was the reply.

"呼，呼。" 回答道。

The old woman went back into the hut.

老妇人回到了小屋。

And she brought out the snake-jewel.

她拿出了蛇形宝石。

She put the jewel into the hand of her supposed son.

她把宝石放到了她所谓的儿子的手中。

The minister's son took the snake-jewel.

大臣的儿子拿走了蛇宝。

He wrapped the jewel up in the piece of cloth.

他用布把宝石包起来。

And he wrapped the cloth around his waist.

他把布裹在腰间。

Phakir's mother was delighted beyond measure.

法基尔的母亲高兴极了。

Her son had come at just the right time.

她的儿子来的正是时候。

She went to the rajah's house.

她去了拉贾的家。

She announced the news of Phakir's appearance.

她宣布了法基尔出现的消息。

And also in order to show Phakir the princess.

同时也为了让法基尔看到公主。

They were given access to the rajah's palace.

他们被允许进入拉贾的宫殿。

And all parts of the palace were open to them.

宫殿的所有部分都向他们开放。

The old woman had saved the rajah's son.

老妇人救了王公的儿子。

So she was the most important person in the kingdom.

所以她是王国里最重要的人物。

She took her supposed son around the palace.

她带着她所谓的儿子参观了宫殿。

And she took him to the princess' room.

她带他去了公主的房间。

Phakir's mother introduced her son to the princess.

法基尔的母亲将她的儿子介绍给了公主。

You can imagine the princess was not best impressed.

你可以想象公主对此印象并不好。
She did not appreciate the company of a madman.
她不喜欢与疯子为伍。
A madman, half naked, and covered in ash.
一个疯子，半裸着，浑身覆盖着灰烬。
And he kept dancing in a wild manner.
并且一直狂野地跳舞。

The three had spent the day together.
三人一起度过了这一天。
It was soon going to be sunset.
很快就要日落了。
The woman asked her son to come with her.
这位妇女叫她的儿子跟她一起去。
But the supposed Phakir-Chand refused to comply.
但所谓的 Phakir-Chand 却拒绝遵守。
He said he would stay there that night.
他说他那天晚上会留在那里。
His mother tried to persuade him to come with her.
他的母亲试图说服他和她一起去。
But he persisted in his determination.
但他坚持自己的决心。
He said he would remain with the princess.
他说他会留在公主身边。
Phakir's mother went home without him.
法基尔的妈妈没有带他回家。
And she told the guards to look after her son.
她告诉警卫要照顾好她的儿子。
Eventually all the palace retired to rest.
最终，整个宫殿都休息了。
The supposed Phakir spoke to the princess again.
所谓的 Phakir 再次与公主交谈。
But this time he spoke in his own voice.
但这次他用自己的声音说话。

"Princess! do you not recognize me?"
"公主！你不认识我了吗？"
"I am the prince's friend"
"我是王子的朋友"
"I am the friend of your princely husband"
"我是你王子丈夫的朋友"
The princess was astonished for a moment.
公主一时愣住了。
"Who? the prince's friend?"
"谁？王子的朋友？"
"Oh, my husband's best friend"
"哦，我丈夫最好的朋友"
"Please rescue me from this terrible captivity"
"请将我从这可怕的囚禁中解救出来"
"This is worse than death"
"这比死亡更糟糕"
"All of this is my own fault"
"这一切都是我的错"
"Rescue me, oh please, thou best of friends!"
"救救我吧，你最好的朋友！"
She then burst into tears.
然后她就哭了起来。
The prince's friend spoke again.
王子的朋友再次开口说话。
"Do not be disconsolate"
"不要忧愁"
"I will try my best to rescue you"
"我会尽力救你"
"I will try to have you out of here tonight"
"今晚我会想办法让你离开这里"
"But you must do whatever I tell you"
"但你必须按照我告诉你的去做"
The princess trusted the prince's friend.
公主信任王子的朋友。

"I will do anything you tell me"
"我会做任何你告诉我的事情"
After this the supposed Phakir left the room.
此后，所谓的 Phakir 离开了房间。
He passed through the courtyard of the palace.
他穿过宫殿的庭院。
Some of the guards challenged him.
一些警卫向他发起挑战。
"hoom hoom!" he replied.
"呼呼！" 他回答道。
"I'm just going out for a minute"
"我只是出去一下"
"And then I will come back again"
"然后我会再回来"
They understood that it was the madcap Phakir.
他们明白，这就是那个疯狂的法基尔。
True to his word he did come back shortly.
他确实信守诺言，很快就回来了。
And again he went to the princess.
他又去见公主。
An hour afterwards he again went out.
一小时后他又出去了。
And again he was challenged by the guards.
他再次受到警卫的质问。
He made the same reply as at the first time.
他做出了和第一次一样的回答。
The guards began to talk among themselves.
警卫们开始互相交谈。
"This Phakir surely has no sense"
"这个法基尔真是毫无常识。"
"He will go out and come in all night"
"他会整夜出去进进出出"
"Let us leave him to do what he likes"
"让他做他喜欢的事吧"

"There's no use guarding him all night"
"整晚守护他是没有意义的"
The minister's son had worn down the guards.
部长的儿子已经把卫兵们打败了。
And he was looking for a way to escape.
他正在寻找逃跑的方法。
He kept going in and out until three at night.
他一直进进出出，直到凌晨三点。
This time there were no guards there.
这次那里没有警卫。
Because all the guards had fallen asleep.
因为所有的守卫都睡着了。
He was overjoyed at the auspicious circumstance.
他为这吉兆而欣喜若狂。
Then he went back to the princess.
然后他回到公主身边。
"Now, princess, is the time for escape"
"公主，现在是逃跑的时候了。"
"The guards are all asleep"
"卫兵们都睡着了"
"You must mount on my back"
"你必须骑在我的背上"
"Tie the locks of your hair round my neck"
"把你的头发系在我的脖子上"
"And keep tight hold of me"
"紧紧抱住我"
The princess did what she was asked of.
公主按照要求做了。
He passed unchallenged through the courtyard.
他顺利地穿过了庭院。
And he had a lovely burden on his back.
他背上还背负着可爱的负担。
Eventually he got to the gate of the palace.
终于，他来到了宫殿的门口。

And he went through without being challenged.
而他却毫无困难地通过了。
Then they went to the outskirts of the city.
然后他们去了城郊。
Eventually he reached the outer suburbs.
最终他到达了远郊。
They reached the water from which the princess had risen.
他们到达了公主浮出水面的地方。
The princess rejoiced at her escape.
公主因自己逃脱而欣喜。
But she was still trembling with fear.
但她还是害怕得浑身发抖。
The prince's friend untied the snake-jewel.
王子的朋友解开了蛇宝石。
And together they ascended into the water.
他们一起浮入水中。
And soon they found back to the subterranean palace.
很快他们就回到了地下宫殿。
You can imagine how happy the prince was.
你可以想象王子有多么高兴。
He had nearly died of grief.
他几乎悲痛欲绝而死。
And you can imagine the princess' happiness too.
你也可以想象公主的幸福。
All the three of them were mad with joy.
三人皆是欣喜若狂。
For three days they remained in the palace.
他们在宫殿里呆了三天。
And they retold the prince the whole story.
他们把整个故事都告诉了王子。
They told of how the princess was seized.
他们讲述了公主被抓获的经过。
They told him of her captivity in the palace.
他们告诉他她被囚禁在宫殿里的情况。

They described the marriage that was planned.
他们描述了计划中的婚礼。
They told him of the old woman.
他们向他讲述了那位老妇人的事。
And they told him all about her Phakir-Chand.
他们把有关她的 Phakir-Chand 的一切告诉了他。
They told him how he had impersonated him.
他们告诉他如何冒充他。
And they told him how he freed the princess.
他们告诉他如何解救公主。
I don't need to tell you how grateful they were.
我不需要告诉你他们有多么感激。
The prince's friend truly was a good friend.
王子的朋友确实是一位好朋友。
They thanked him in the warmest terms.
他们以最热情的言辞向他表示感谢。
And they vowed to always follow his counsel.
他们发誓永远听从他的忠告。

They were all resolved to return home.
他们都决心回家。
They wanted to return to their native country.
他们想回到自己的祖国。
The king's son, the minister's son, and the princess.
国王的儿子、大臣的儿子和公主。
They left the subterranean palace together.
两人一起离开了地下宫殿。
They lighted the passage with the snake-jewel.
他们用蛇形宝石照亮了通道。
And they made their way to the upper world.
他们就前往了上层世界。
They had neither elephants nor horses waiting for them.
没有大象或马匹在等待他们。
So they had no choice but to travel on foot.

所以他们别无选择，只能步行。
The two friends had been bred in the lap of luxury.
这两位朋友都是在奢华的环境中长大的。
Both of them found walking troublesome.
他们俩都觉得走路很麻烦。
But the princess found it infinitely more troublesome.
但公主却发现这更加麻烦。
She was used to even finer treatment.
她已经习惯了更为优厚的待遇。
The stones of the road were too rough for her.
路上的石头对她来说太粗糙了。
And the rough stones wounded her tender feet.
粗糙的石头伤到了她娇嫩的双脚。
Eventually her feet became very sore.
最后她的脚变得非常酸痛。
At times the king's son carried her on his shoulders.
有时国王的儿子会把她扛在肩上。
The load he was carrying was of course lovely.
他所承载的负荷当然是可爱的。
But although lovely, she was heavy to carry.
尽管她很可爱，但她抱起来却很重。
And she could not be carried a great distance.
而且她不能被带走很远的距离。
And therefore she too had to walk often.
因此她也必须经常走路。
One evening they arrived beneath a tree.
一天傍晚，他们来到一棵树下。
There were no visible signs of human habitations.
没有明显的人类居住迹象。
So they decided to make the tree their sleeping place.
因此他们决定把这棵树作为他们的睡觉的地方。
The prince's friend offered to keep guard.
王子的朋友主动提出要守卫。
"Both of you can go to sleep"

"你们两个都可以睡觉了"
"I will keep watch over you both tonight"
"今晚我会守护你们两个"
"In order to prevent any danger"
"为了防止任何危险"
The royal couple soon dozed off.
皇室夫妇很快就打瞌睡了。
And they were locked in the arms of sleep.
他们被困在睡眠的怀抱中。
The faithful friend of the prince did not sleep.
王子的忠实朋友没有睡觉。
He stayed awake and watched for danger.
他时刻保持清醒，警惕危险。
It so happened they camped under a special tree.
碰巧他们在一棵特殊的树下扎营。
In the tree swung the nest of two birds.
树上摇曳着两只鸟的巢。
The immortal birds Bihangama and Bihangami.
不朽的鸟Bihangama和Bihangami。
These birds were endowed with human speech.
这些鸟被赋予了人类的语言能力。
And they could also see into the future.
他们还能预见未来。
The minister's son listened the bird's conversation.
大臣的儿子听着鸟儿的谈话。
He was more than a little astonished at what he heard!
他听到的事情让他非常惊讶！
Bihangama: "The prince's friend risked his own life"
比汉加马："王子的朋友冒着生命危险"
"He did everything for the safety of his friend"
"他所做的一切都是为了朋友的安全"
"But more dangers will befall the king's son"
"但国王的儿子将面临更多危险"
"And he will find it difficult to save the prince"

"而且他很难救出王子。"
Bihangami: "Why is that?"
比杭神： "为什么呢？"
Bihangama: "Many dangers await the king's son"
比汉加马： "国王的儿子面临重重危险"
"The prince's father will hear of his son's approach"
"王子的父亲会听说他儿子的来访"
"He will send for him an elephant and some horses"
"他会派人去取一头大象和一些马。"
"And he will arrange attendants to meet him"
"他会安排侍从来迎接他"
"The king's son will ride the elephant"
"国王的儿子将骑大象"
"But he will fall from the back of the elephant"
"但他会从大象背上掉下来"
"And he will die from his fall from the elephant"
"他会因从大象身上摔下来而死"
Bihangami: "But suppose someone prevented this?"
Bihangami： "但是如果有人阻止了这一切呢？"
"Suppose the king's son is not going to ride on the elephant"
"假设国王的儿子不骑大象"
"What might happen if he rides on a horse instead?"
"如果他骑马的话会发生什么呢？"
"Will he not in that case be saved?"
"这样一来，他就不能得救了吗？"
Bihangama: "Yes, in that case he would escape that fate"
Bihangama： "是的，这样他就能逃脱这种命运了。
"

"But then a fresh danger would await him"
"但随后新的危险又在等着他"
"When the king's son is in sight of his father's palace"
"当国王的儿子看到他父亲的宫殿时"
"When he is in the act of passing through the lion-gate"

"当他穿过狮子门时"
"In that moment the lion-gate will fall upon him"
"那一刻，狮子门将落下"
"And the stones will crush him to death"
"石头会把他压死"
Bihangami: "But suppose someone gets there first"
Bihangami： "但是假设有人先到达那里"
"Suppose someone destroys the lion-gate"
"假设有人摧毁了狮子门"
"If that happens the king's son couldn't go through the lion-gate"
"如果那样的话，国王的儿子就无法穿过狮子门了。"

"Will not the king's son in that case be saved?"
"这样一来，国王的儿子就没救了吗？"
Bihangama: "Yes, in that case he would escape his fate"
Bihangama： "是的，这样他就能逃脱命运了。"
"But then a fresh danger would await him"
"但随后新的危险又在等着他"
"When the king's son reaches the palace"
"当国王的儿子到达宫殿时"
"When he sits at a feast prepared for him"
"当他坐在为他准备的筵席上时"
"The head of a fish will be cooked for him"
"将为他烹制鱼头"
"He will put into his mouth the head of the fish"
"他会把鱼头放进嘴里"
"But the head of the fish will stick in his throat"
"但鱼头会卡在他的喉咙里"
"And he will choke to death on the head of the fish"
"他将被鱼头噎死"
Bihangami: "But suppose someone snatches the fish"
Bihangami： "但是假设有人抢走了鱼"
"Suppose someone takes the head of the fish from his plate"

"假设有人从盘子里拿走了鱼头"
"Suppose he can't put the fish's head in his mouth"
"假设他不能把鱼头放进嘴里"
"Will not the king's son in that case be saved?"
"这样一来，国王的儿子就没救了吗？"
Bihangama: "Yes, in that case he will escape his fate"
Bihangama： "是的，这样他就能逃脱命运了。"
"But a fresh danger would await him"
"但新的危险正在等着他"
"When the prince and princess retire after dinner"
"当王子和公主晚餐后退去时"
"When they go into their sleeping apartment"
"当他们进入卧室时"
"They will lie together in bed"
"他们会一起躺在床上"
"A terrible cobra will come into the room"
"一条可怕的眼镜蛇将会进入房间"
"And the cobra will bite the king's son to death"
"眼镜蛇会咬死国王的儿子"
Bihangami: "But suppose someone was in the room"
Bihangami： "但是假设有人在房间里"
"Suppose this person was waiting for the snake"
"假设这个人正在等蛇"
"And suppose that this person cuts the snake into pieces"
"假设这个人把蛇切成了碎片"
"Will not the king's son in that case be saved?"
"这样一来，国王的儿子就没救了吗？"
Bihangama: "Yes, in that case he will escape his fate"
Bihangama： "是的，这样他就能逃脱命运了。"
"In that case the life of the king's son will be saved"
"这样一来，国王儿子的命就保住了。"
"But he who saves him can't repeat these words"
"但救他的人不能重复这些话"
"If he tells his secret he will be turned into marble"

"如果他说出秘密，他就会变成大理石"
Bihangami: "Can the statue be returned to life?"
比汉加米："雕像能复活吗？"
Bihangama: "Yes, the marble statue can be restored to life"
比汉加马："是的，大理石雕像可以复活。"
"The princess will give birth to a child"
"公主要生一个孩子了"
"They must wash the statue with the blood of the infant"
"他们必须用婴儿的血来清洗雕像"
The prophetical birds had spoken until that point.
预言之鸟已说过这句话。
But then they were interrupted by the craw of crows.
但随后他们被乌鸦的叫声打断了。
The eastern sky tinted in a reddish hue.
东方的天空泛着淡淡的红色。
And the travelers beneath the tree bestirred themselves.
树下的旅人们也都忙碌起来。
The prophetic conversation came to an end.
这场预言性的对话结束了。
But the prince's friend had heard everything.
但王子的朋友听到了一切。

The next morning they continued their journey.
第二天早上他们继续旅程。
The prince, the princess, and the prince's friend.
王子、公主和王子的朋友。
Soon they met the king's procession.
很快他们就遇见了国王的队伍。
There was an elephant, a horse, and a palki.
有一头大象、一匹马和一只帕尔基。
And there was a large number of attendants.
并且还有大量的侍从。
These animals and men had been sent by the king.
这些动物和人都是国王派来的。

The king heard his son was with his friend.
国王听说他的儿子和他的朋友在一起。
And he had heard that his son had married.
他还听说儿子结婚了。
And he heard they were not far from the capital.
他听说他们离首都不远了。
The elephant had been richly caparisoned.
这头大象被装饰得富丽堂皇。
The elephant was intended for the prince.
这头大象是为王子准备的。
The framework of the palki was of silver.
帕尔基的框架是银制的。
The palki was meant for the princess.
这件帕尔基是为公主准备的。
And the horse was for the prince's friend.
这匹马是送给王子的朋友的。
The prince was about to mount on the elephant.
王子正要骑上大象。
But then his friend spoke to him.
但后来他的朋友跟他说话了。
"Allow me to ride on the elephant, please"
"请允许我骑大象。"
"And you can ride back on horseback"
"你可以骑马回去"
The prince was not a little surprised.
王子十分惊讶。
The proposal had been made in a very cold manner.
这个建议是以一种非常冷淡的方式提出的。
Maybe his friend felt a little too entitled.
也许他的朋友觉得自己有点太有资格了。
And the king's son was slightly annoyed.
国王的儿子有点恼火。
But he remembered what his friend had done for him.
但他记得朋友为他所做的一切。

And he remembered how he saved the princess.
他还记得自己是如何拯救公主的。
So he mounted the horse without objecting.
于是他便没有反对，骑上了马。
But his mind became somewhat alienated from him.
但他的思想却变得有些疏远他了。
The procession towards the capital started again.
前往首都的游行队伍再次出发。
After some time they came in sight of the palace.
过了一会儿，他们看见了宫殿。
The lion-gate had been gaily adorned.
狮子门装饰得十分华丽。
There was a grand reception for the prince.
人们为王子举行了盛大的招待会。
And the princess was equally anticipated.
而公主也同样备受期待。
But the prince's friend seemed to have an objection.
但王子的朋友似乎有反对意见。
"I want the lion-gate to be broken down"
"我希望狮子门被打破"
The prince was astounded at the proposal.
王子对这个提议感到很震惊。
The request was very out of the ordinary.
这个请求非常不寻常。
And he had given no reason for his demand.
但他并未说明提出这一要求的理由。
But he remembered all his friend had done for him.
但他记得朋友为他所做的一切。
And he remembered how he saved the princess.
他还记得自己是如何拯救公主的。
So he complied with the wish of his friend.
于是他遵从了朋友的愿望。
And the beautiful lion-gate was torn down.
美丽的狮子门被拆毁了。

But his mind became even more estranged from him.
但他的心灵却变得更加疏远了。
The procession now went into the palace.
游行队伍现在进入宫殿。
The king gave a warm reception to his son.
国王热情地接待了他的儿子。
He welcomed his daughter-in-law equally warmly.
他也同样热情地欢迎自己的儿媳。
And he was very pleased to see the prince's friend.
他见到王子的朋友非常高兴。
The story of their adventures was related.
他们讲述了自己的冒险故事。
The king expressed great astonishment at the tale.
国王对这个故事感到非常惊讶。
And his courtiers were equally impressed.
他的朝臣们也同样印象深刻。
All praised the minister's son's devotion.
大家都对这位大臣儿子的忠诚表示称赞。
And the ladies of the palace praised the princess.
宫中的女官们都对公主赞不绝口。
The connoisseurs of beauty praised the princess.
鉴赏家们对公主赞不绝口。
Her complexion was a mixture of milk and vermilion.
她的肤色是牛奶色和朱红色的混合色。
Her neck was like that of a swan.
她的脖子就像天鹅的脖子。
Her eyes were like those of a gazelle.
她的眼睛就像瞪羚的眼睛。
Her lips were as red as the berry bimba.
她的嘴唇像浆果一样红。
Her cheeks were as lovely as they could be.
她的脸颊美丽极了。
And her nose was straight and high.
她的鼻子又直又高。

Her hair reached down to her ankles.
她的头发一直垂到脚踝。
Her walk was as graceful as that of a young elephant.
她的步态就像一头小象一样优雅。
The princess whom destiny had brought to them.
命运给他们带来的公主。
They sat around her wanting to know everything.
他们围坐在她身边，想知道一切。
And they put to her a thousand questions.
他们向她提出了一千个问题。
They asked her about her parents.
他们询问了她父母的情况。
They asked her about the subterranean palace.
他们向她询问了地下宫殿的情况。
And they asked her all about the serpent.
他们问了她有关蛇的一切事情。
The serpent which had killed all her relatives.
这条蛇杀死了她所有的亲人。
Soon it was time for the new arrivals to dine.
很快就到了新来的人吃饭的时间了。
The dinner was served up in dishes of gold.
晚餐是用金盘子盛放的。
All sorts of delicacies were on the table.
餐桌上摆满了各式各样的美味佳肴。
The most conspicuous dish was the head of a rohita fish.
最引人注目的菜肴是罗希塔鱼头。
The large fish's head was placed in a golden cup.
大鱼的头被放在一个金杯里。
And the cup was placed near the prince's plate.
杯子被放在王子的盘子旁边。
All were eating and retelling the adventure.
大家都一边吃着东西，一边讲述着这次冒险经历。
And suddenly the prince's friend snatched the head.
突然，王子的朋友抢走了头颅。

He took the fish's head from the prince's plate.
他从王子的盘子里拿走了鱼头。
"Let me, prince, eat this rohita's head"
"王子，让我吃掉这个罗希塔的头吧"
The king's son was quite indignant.
国王的儿子非常愤怒。
But he remembered all his friend had done for him.
但他记得朋友为他所做的一切。
And he remembered how he saved the princess.
他还记得自己是如何拯救公主的。
And so he made no objection to the request.
所以他没有反对这个请求。
But he could not hide his terrible rage.
但他无法掩饰他内心的极度愤怒。
Of course the prince's friend noticed this.
王子的朋友当然注意到了这一点。
But there was nothing else he could have done.
但他没有别的选择。
His conduct, however strange, was necessary.
他的行为无论多么奇怪，却是必要的。
It was for the safety of his friend's life.
这是为了他朋友的生命安全。
Nor could he tell his friend the reason.
他也无法告诉他的朋友原因。
Else he would be transformed into a marble statue.
否则他就会变成一座大理石雕像。
Soon the dinner was going to be over.
很快晚餐就结束了。
The prince's friend had one more request.
王子的朋友还有一个请求。
The two friends had spent every night together.
这两个朋友每天晚上都在一起度过。
But tonight he wanted to go to his own house.
但今晚他想回自己的家。

The prince was also shocked at his strange conduct.
王子也对他的奇怪行为感到震惊。
But he remembered all his friend had done for him.
但他记得朋友为他所做的一切。
And he remembered how he saved the princess.
他还记得自己是如何拯救公主的。
And he also agreed to this request of his friend.
而他也答应了朋友的这个请求。
The prince's friend, however, had other plans.
然而，王子的朋友却另有打算。
He had no intentions of going to his own house.
他根本就没打算回自己家。
He was resolved to avert the last peril.
他决心避免最后的危险。
The last thing to threaten the life of his friend.
这绝对不会威胁到他朋友的生命。
Accordingly, he took a sword into his hand.
于是，他拿起了一把剑。
And he stealthily entered the royal room.
他悄悄地进入了王室。
The room of the prince and the princess.
王子和公主的房间。
He ensconced himself under the bedstead.
他安顿在床架下。
The bed was furnished with mattresses of down.
床上配有羽绒床垫。
The mosquito curtains were of the richest silk.
蚊帐是用最华丽的丝绸制成的。
And all the bedding was laced with gold.
所有的床上用品都镶有金边。
Soon the prince and princess came into the bedroom.
不久王子和公主就来到了卧室。
They undressed themselves and went to bed.
他们脱掉衣服然后上床睡觉。

And soon the royal couple were asleep.
很快皇室夫妇就睡着了。

At midnight he heard the slithering of a snake.
半夜时分，他听到了蛇爬行的声音。

The sound was coming from a water passage.
这声音是从水道里传来的。

A snake of gigantic size entered the room.
一条巨大的蛇进入了房间。

The serpent climbed up the frame of the bed.
蛇顺着床架往上爬。

The minister's son rushed out with the sword.
大臣的儿子提着剑冲了出去。

And he killed the serpent with one blow.
他一击就杀死了那条蛇。

And then he cut the snake into smaller pieces.
然后他把蛇切成小块。

He put the pieces in the dish for holding betel-leaves.
他把碎片放在盛槟榔叶的盘子里。

But as he did this, he spilled a drop of blood.
但当他这样做的时候，他洒了一滴血。

The drop of blood fell on the breast of the princess.
一滴血落在公主的胸口上。

Because the mosquito curtains had not been let down.
因为蚊帐还没放下。

He worried for the health of the princess.
他担心公主的健康。

The blood might be of some sort of poison.
血液里可能有某种毒。

So he resolved to lick up the blood.
所以他决心要舔干净血。

But he could not look at the naked princess.
但他不能看赤裸的公主。

It would have been a great sin.
这将是一个巨大的罪孽。

So he blindfolded himself with seven-fold cloth.
于是他用七层布蒙住了自己的眼睛。
And he licked off the drop of blood.
他舔掉了那滴血。
But just at this time the princess awoke.
但就在这时，公主醒了。
Her scream roused her husband from his sleep.
她的尖叫声把睡梦中的丈夫惊醒了。
And he could not believe what he was seeing.
他简直不敢相信自己所看到的一切。
The prince fell into a great rage.
王子勃然大怒。
And he was prepared to kill his friend.
他准备杀死他的朋友。
But he gave his friend a chance to speak.
但他给了朋友说话的机会。
"Please, my friend, restrain your anger"
"我的朋友，请抑制你的愤怒"
"I have done this only to save your life"
"我这么做只是为了救你的命"
The prince was more confused than before.
王子比以前更加困惑了。
"I do not understand what you mean"
"我不明白你的意思"
"From the time we came out of the subterranean palace"
"从我们从地下宫殿出来的时候"
"You have been behaving in a most extraordinary way"
"你的行为举止太特别了"
"First, you insisted on riding my elephant"
"首先，你坚持要骑我的大象"
"The elephant my father had sent for me"
"我父亲派来接我的大象"
"I thought it was vain of you to ask"
"我觉得你问这个问题太无礼了"

"But I remembered what you had done for me"
"但我记得你为我做过的事"
"And I decided to let the matter pass"
"我决定不去管这件事了"
"And instead I rode back on horseback"
"然后我就骑马回去了"
"Secondly, you insisted on destroying the lion-gate"
"其次，你坚持要摧毁狮门。"
"The lion-gate my father had adorned for me"
"我父亲为我装饰的狮子门"
"I thought it was strange of you to ask"
"我觉得你这么问很奇怪。"
"But I remembered what you had done for me"
"但我记得你为我做过的事"
"And I decided to let the matter pass"
"我决定不去管这件事了"
"And I had the lion-gate destroyed"
"我摧毁了狮子门"
"Thirdly, at dinner you behaved most shamefully"
"第三，晚餐时你的行为极其可耻"
"You snatched the rohita's head from my plate"
"你从我的盘子里抢走了罗希塔的头"
"And you insisted on eating the fish head"
"你坚持要吃鱼头"
"I thought you felt too entitled"
"我觉得你觉得自己太有资格了"
"But I remembered what you had done for me"
"但我记得你为我做过的事"
"So I decided to let the matter pass"
"所以我决定不去管这件事"
"You then pretended that you were going home"
"然后你就假装要回家了"
"And I was very glad you were going home"
"我很高兴你要回家了"

"Because you had made yourself very disagreeable"
"因为你让自己变得非常不愉快"
"And now you are actually in my bedroom"
"现在你真的在我的卧室里"
"You are bending over the naked bosom of my wife"
"你正俯身靠近我妻子赤裸的胸部"
"You must have had some evil plan"
"你肯定有什么邪恶的计划"
"And now you pretend you are saving my life"
"现在你假装在救我的命"
"But I don't believe you want to save my life"
"但我不相信你想救我。"
"I believe you want to destroy my wife's chastity"
"我认为你想毁掉我妻子的贞操"
The prince's friend knew how things looked.
王子的朋友知道事情是怎样的。
"Oh, do not harbor such thoughts in your mind"
"哦，别想那么多。"
"Please do not think badly against me"
"请不要对我有不好的想法"
"The gods know what I have done"
"众神知道我做了什么"
"They know I did it to save your life"
"他们知道我这么做是为了救你的命"
"You would see the reasonableness of my conduct"
"你会看到我的行为是合理的"
"But I don't have liberty to state my reasons"
"但我没有自由陈述我的埋由"
The prince asked him to explain himself.
王子要求他作出解释。
"And why are you not at liberty?"
"那你为什么没有自由呢？"
"Who has put a seal upon your mouth?"
"谁封住了你的嘴？"

And the prince's friend answered.
王子的朋友回答道。
"Destiny has put a seal upon my mouth"
"命运已将我的嘴封住"
"If I told you, I would be transformed into marble"
"如果我告诉你，我就会变成大理石"
The prince grew angrier with his friend.
王子对他的朋友越来越生气。
"You should be transformed into a marble statue!"
"你应该变成一座大理石雕像！"
"You must take me to be a simpleton"
"你肯定把我当傻子了"
"You can't expect me to believe this nonsense"
"你不能指望我相信这些胡说八道"
The minister's son made one last request.
部长的儿子提出了最后一个请求。
"Do you wish me then, friend, for me to tell you?
"那么，朋友，你希望我告诉你吗？
"You would make your friend turn into stone?"
"你会让你的朋友变成石头吗？"
The prince wanted to hear the reason.
王子想听听原因。
He did not care about the consequences.
他并不关心后果。
"Tell me, or else you are a dead man"
"告诉我，不然你就死定了"
The prince's friend wanted to clear his name.
王子的朋友想洗清他的罪名。
He wanted no foul accusations brought against him.
他不希望别人对他提出任何不公正的指控。
And he deemed it his duty to reveal the secret.
他认为揭露这个秘密是他的责任。
Even if this would put his life at risk.
即使这会让他的生命处于危险之中。

He again warned the prince not to ask him.
他再次警告王子不要问他。
But the prince remained inexorable.
但王子依然不屈不挠。
The prince's friend then told him his secret.
王子的朋友随后告诉了他自己的秘密。
"While sleeping under a lofty tree one night"
"一天晚上，我在一棵大树下睡觉"
"I overheard a conversation between two birds.
"我无意中听到两只鸟之间的对话。
"The prophesizing birds Bihangama and Bihangami"
"预言鸟 Bihangama 和 Bihangami"
"Bihangama predicted all the dangers in your life"
"Bihangama 预测了你一生中所有的危险"
"First the bird predicted your father would send an elephant"
"首先，这只鸟预言你的父亲会送来一头大象"
"The bird said you would fall from the elephant"
"鸟说你会从大象身上掉下来"
"And the bird said you would die from the fall"
"鸟儿说你会因坠落而死"
At this point the minister's son's legs turned to stone.
这时，牧师儿子的双腿已经僵硬如石。
"See? my legs have already turned to stone"
"看到了吗？我的腿已经变成石头了。"
"Go on with your story," said the prince.
"继续讲你的故事吧，" 王子说。
And the prince's friend continued the story.
王子的朋友继续讲这个故事。
"The bird said the lion-gate would be gaily decorated"
"鸟儿说狮子门会装饰得华丽"
"And the bird said the lion-gate would collapse on you"
"鸟儿说狮子门会倒塌"
"If the lion-gate had fallen on you, you would have died"

"如果狮子门倒塌，你就会死。"

At this point the minister's son's torso turned to stone.

此时，牧师儿子的躯干变成了石头。

But the prince insisted the minister's son continues.

但王子坚持要求大臣的儿子继续干下去。

"Go on with your story," said the prince.

"继续讲你的故事吧，"王子说。

"The bird said there would be the head of a fish"

"鸟说那里会有鱼头"

"And the bird predicted you would choke on the fish"

"那只鸟预言你会被鱼噎住"

Now his head was the only thing not of stone.

现在他的头是唯一不是石头的东西。

"See? my whole body has turned to stone"

"看到了吗？我的整个身体都变成了石头。"

"If I continue, I will become a man of stone"

"如果我继续下去，我就会变成石头人"

"Do you wish me to tell the rest"

"你希望我告诉你剩下的吗？"

"Go on with your story," said the prince.

"继续讲你的故事吧，"王子说。

"Very well, I will go on to the end"

"好吧，我会坚持到底"

"But you may repent after I tell you"

"但我告诉你之后你可能会后悔"

"And you may wish to restore me to life"

"你或许想让我复活"

"I will tell you how to reverse the spell"

"我会告诉你如何解除咒语"

"In a few months the princess will bear a child"

"几个月后公主就会生一个孩子了"

"Wait for the birth of the child"

"等待孩子出生"

"Besmear my statue with the infant's blood"

"用婴儿的血涂抹我的雕像"
"Only then will I be restored back to life"
"只有这样我才能复活"
The last word left his lips, and he turned to stone.
最后一个字从他嘴里出来后，他就变成了石头。
The princess jumped out of bed.
公主从床上跳了起来。
She opened the vessel for betel-leaves and spices.
她打开容器，取出槟榔叶和香料。
And she saw the pieces of a serpent.
她看见了一条蛇的碎片。
The prince and the princess were now convinced.
王子和公主这才相信了。
They saw the good faith of their departed friend.
他们看到了已故朋友的诚意。
They saw the benevolence of his actions.
他们看到了他行为中的仁慈。
They went to the marble statue.
他们去了大理石雕像那里。
But the statue of their friend was lifeless.
但他们朋友的雕像却毫无生气。
They let out a loud cry lamentation.
他们发出一声高声哀号。
But their cries were to no purpose.
但他们的呼喊毫无意义。
Because the statue was not moved by tears.
因为雕像不会被眼泪感动。
The prince and princess knew what they had to do.
王子和公主知道他们必须做什么。
They concealed the marble figure in a safe place.
他们把大理石雕像藏在一个安全的地方。
And they waited for the birth of their child.
他们等待着孩子的出生。
In process of time the hour came.

随着时间的流逝，时刻到来了。
The princess's travail had arrived.
公主的阵痛已经到来。
The princess bore a beautiful boy.
公主生了一个漂亮的男孩。
The child was the perfect image of his mother.
这个孩子和他母亲一模一样。
The beauty of their child was striking.
他们的孩子美貌惊人。
And they were in awe of him.
他们对他充满敬畏。
They would have spared his life.
他们本可以饶他一命。
But they remembered their best friend.
但他们记得他们最好的朋友。
They remembered all he had done for them.
他们记得他为他们所做的一切。
But now he was a lifeless stone.
但现在他只是一块没有生命的石头。
And they remembered the vows they had made.
他们还记得自己许下的誓言。
And they cut the child into two.
他们把孩子切成两半。
They besmeared the statue with the child's blood.
他们把孩子的血涂抹在雕像上。
And their friend became animated back to life.
他们的朋友也恢复了活力。
They were glad to see him alive again.
他们很高兴看到他又活过来了。
But the prince's friend was overwhelmed with grief.
但王子的朋友却悲痛欲绝。
Because he saw the new-born in a pool of blood.
因为他看到新生儿躺在血泊中。
So he picked up the dead infant.

于是他抱起了死婴。
He carefully wrapped the child in a towel.
他小心翼翼地用毛巾包裹孩子。
And he resolved to get the child restored to life.
他决心要让孩子复活。
He consulted all the physicians of the country.
他咨询了全国所有的医生。
They all told him the same thing.
他们都告诉他同样的事情。
A cure can be found for any illness.
任何疾病都可以找到治愈方法。
But life requires the spark of life.
但生命需要生命的火花。
When the spark is gone, it is beyond their jurisdiction.
当火花消失时，它就超出了他们的管辖范围。
And so they had to go on with their lives.
所以他们必须继续他们的生活。

Eventually the prince's friend returned to his wife.
最终王子的朋友回到了他的妻子身边。
She was a devoted worshipper of the goddess kali.
她是女神卡莉的虔诚信徒。
She was the only one who could return life.
她是唯一一个能够让生命重生的人。
His wife was living in a distant town.
他的妻子住在一个遥远的城镇。
So he set out on a journey to the town.
于是他踏上了前往该镇的旅程。
His wife still lived in her father's house.
他的妻子仍然住在她父亲的房子里。
Adjoining the house there was a garden.
房子旁边有一个花园。
And in the garden there was a tree.
花园里有一棵树。

The child had been stored in that tree.
孩子被存放在那棵树里。
His wife was overjoyed to see her husband.
他的妻子见到丈夫非常高兴。
She had not seen him for a long time.
她已经很久没有见到他了。
But she was surprised when she saw him.
但当她看到他时，她很惊讶。
Her husband was very melancholy that day.
那天她的丈夫非常忧郁。
He spoke very little to his wife.
他很少和妻子说话。
And his wife knew that he was not himself.
他的妻子知道他不太对劲。
He was brooding over something in his mind.
他心里正在思索着某件事。
She asked the reason for his melancholy.
她问他忧郁的原因。
But he kept quiet, and wouldn't tell her.
但他保持沉默，不肯告诉她。
One night they were lying together in bed.
一天晚上，他们一起躺在床上。
The wife got up and left the marital bed.
妻子起身离开了婚床。
She opened the door and went into the garden.
她打开门走进了花园。
Her husband had not been able to sleep well.
她的丈夫一直睡不好。
Therefore he awoke from the movement of his wife.
因此他被妻子的动静惊醒了。
He heard her leave in the dead of the night.
他在深夜听到她离开的声音。
And he was determined to follow her.
他决心追随她。

But he was also determined not to be noticed.
但他也决心不被人注意。
She went to a temple of the goddess kali.
她去了一座卡利女神的寺庙。
The temple was at no great distance from her house.
寺庙离她家不远。
She worshipped the goddess with flowers.
她用鲜花来祭拜女神。
And she worshiped the goddess with sandal-wood perfume.
她用檀香香水来崇拜女神。
"Oh mother kali! have mercy upon me"
"哦，卡利母亲！可怜可怜我吧。"
"Deliver me out of all my troubles"
"救我脱离一切苦难"
The goddess replied to the woman.
女神回答了女人。
"Why, what further grievance have you?
"怎么，你还有什么委屈吗？
"You long prayed for the return of your husband"
"你一直祈祷着你的丈夫回来"
"And your prayers have been answered"
"你的祈祷已经得到了回应"
"Your husband has returned to you"
"你的丈夫回来了"
"So then, what ails thee now?"
"那么，你现在有什么不舒服吗？"
The woman answered the goddess.
女人回答了女神。
"True, oh mother, my husband has come to me"
"真的，妈妈，我丈夫来找我了"
"But he has come to me in a melancholy mood"
"但他来找我的时候心情很忧郁"
"He hardly speaks to me when I speak to him"
"当我和他说话时，他几乎不跟我说话"

"He takes no delight in me when he is with me"
"他跟我在一起的时候，并不喜悦我"
"All he does is sit melancholy in a corner"
"他只是忧郁地坐在角落里"
The goddess replied to her devotee.
女神回答了她的信徒。
"Ask your husband why he feels melancholy"
"问问你丈夫为什么感到忧郁"
"When he tells you, let me know the reason"
"当他告诉你的时候，告诉我原因"
The minister's son overheard the conversation.
部长的儿子无意中听到了谈话。
But he stayed unnoticed by the goddess.
但他却没有引起女神的注意。
And his wife did not notice him either.
他的妻子也没有注意到他。
He quietly slunk away before his wife.
他从妻子面前悄悄溜走了。
And he returned back to bed before her.
然后他比她先回到床上。
The following day the wife asked her husband.
第二天妻子问丈夫。
"My dear husband, why are you in a melancholy mood?"
"我亲爱的丈夫，你为什么心情这么忧郁呢？"
Her husband retold the whole story.
她的丈夫复述了整个故事。
He told her about the jewel serpent.
他向她讲述了宝石蛇的事。
He told her about the subterranean palace.
他向她讲述了地下宫殿的情况。
He told her about the princess being captured.
他告诉她公主被俘的事。
He told her how he freed the princess.
他告诉她他是如何解救公主的。

And he told her about Bihangama and Bihangami.

他还向她讲述了 Bihangama 和 Bihangami 的故事。

He told her how he had turned to stone.

他告诉她他是如何变成石头的。

And he told her how he was returned back to life.

他告诉她他是如何复活的。

So he told her also about the killing of the child.

于是他也告诉了她孩子被杀的事。

That night his wife left the bed again.

那天晚上，他的妻子又离开了床。

And she returned to the goddess kali's temple.

她回到了女神卡莉的神庙。

And she told the goddess of her husband's melancholy.

她向女神诉说了她丈夫的忧郁。

The goddess listened intently to what was said.

女神专心地聆听着他们所说的话。

"Bring the child here and I will restore it to life"

"把孩子带过来，我会让他复活。"

The next night she left the marital bed again.

第二天晚上，她又离开了婚床。

She went to the tree in the garden.

她走到花园里的那棵树旁。

And she took the child from the tree.

她就把孩子从树上抱了下来。

And she took the child to the goddess kali.

她把孩子带到了女神卡利那里。

And the goddess kali returned the child back to life.

女神卡利让孩子复活。

The prince's friend was entranced with joy.

王子的朋友欣喜若狂。

He picked up the reanimated child.

他抱起了复活的孩子。

And he ran as fast as he could to his friend.

他尽可能快地跑向他的朋友。

And he gave him his child, alive and well.
他把孩子交给了他，而且活得好好的。
They all rejoiced with exceedingly great joy.
他们全都极其高兴。
And they lived together happily till the day of their death.
他们幸福地生活在一起，直到死去的那一天。

The Indignant Brahman
愤怒的婆罗门

There was once a poor Brahman.
从前，有一个贫穷的婆罗门。
This poor Brahman had a wife.
这个可怜的婆罗门有一个妻子。
And he also had four children.
他还有四个孩子。
He was a very poor man.
他是一个非常贫穷的人。
And he had no resources in the world.
而他在世界上没有任何资源。
He lived from the charity of others.
他靠别人的施舍过活。
During marriages he earned well.
婚姻期间他的收入不错。
And he earned well during funerals.
而且他在葬礼期间赚得不少钱。
But his parishioners did not marry daily.
但他的教区居民并不是每天都结婚。
And they did not die every day either.
而且他们也不是每天都死。
It was difficult to make the two ends meet.
维持生计很困难。
His wife often rebuked him.
他的妻子经常责备他。
"Why can you not support me?"
"你为什么不能支持我？"
"Our children run around naked"
"我们的孩子裸奔"
"And they suffer from hunger"
"他们还饱受饥饿之苦"
Though poor, he was a good man.

虽然贫穷，但他是一个好人。

And he was diligent in his devotions.

他虔诚地信奉宗教。

Every day he said his prayers.

他每天都会祈祷。

He prayed at the same time each day.

他每天在同一时间祈祷。

His tutelary deity was the Goddess Durga.

他的守护神是杜尔迦女神。

She is the consort of Shiva.

她是湿婆的配偶。

She is the creative energy of the universe.

她是宇宙的创造能量。

Every day he wrote the name of Durga.

他每天都会写下杜尔迦的名字。

He wrote the name in red ink.

他用红墨水写下了这个名字。

At least one hundred and eight times.

至少一百零八次。

He did not drink or eat till he did this.

在他做完这件事之前，他没有喝水也没有吃东西。

throughout the day he uttered prayers.

他整天都在祈祷。

"O Durga! have mercy upon me"

"杜尔迦啊！可怜我吧。"

He prayed whenever he felt anxious.

每当他感到焦虑时，他就会祈祷。

And he often felt anxious.

他经常感到焦虑。

Because he lived in poverty.

因为他生活贫困。

He prayed when his worries were too much.

当他忧虑太多时，他就会祈祷。

And there were many things he worried about.

他担心的事情有很多。
He worried about his wife and children.
他担心他的妻子和孩子。
And he worried about supporting them.
他担心无法支持他们。

One day he was very sad.
有一天，他非常伤心。
On this day he went to a forest.
这天他去了一片森林。
The forest was far outside the village.
森林距离村庄很远。
He let out all his grief.
他把所有的悲伤都发泄出来。
And he wept bitter tears.
他流下了痛苦的泪水。
"O Durga! O Mother Bhagavati!"
"杜尔迦啊！巴嘎瓦蒂母亲啊！"
"Please put an end to my misery?"
"请结束我的痛苦吧？"
"I wish I were alone in the world"
"我希望世界上只有我一个人"
"Then my poverty wouldn't worry me"
"这样我就不会为贫穷而烦恼了"
"But thou hast given me a wife"
"但你给了我一个妻子"
"And my wife has given me children"
"我的妻子还给我生了孩子"
"O Mother, I beg of you"
"哦，母亲，我恳求您"
"Give me the means to support them"
"给我办法来支持他们"
Shiva and his wife Durga happened to be there.
湿婆和他的妻子杜尔迦恰巧在那里。

They were taking their morning walk.
他们正在进行晨间散步。
The Goddess Durga saw the Brahman at a distance.
杜尔迦女神远远地看见了婆罗门。
"O Lord of Kailas, do you see that Brahman?"
"噢，凯拉斯之主，你看见那位婆罗门了吗？"
"He is always taking my name on his lips"
"他总是提起我的名字"
"He prays I deliver him from his troubles"
"他祈祷我能帮助他摆脱困境"
"Can we not do something for the poor Brahman?"
"我们能不能为可怜的婆罗门做点什么？"
"He is oppressed with many cares"
"他被许多忧虑压得喘不过气来"
"And he deeply cares for his growing family"
"他非常关心他日益壮大的家庭"
"We should make his life more comfortable"
"我们应该让他的生活更舒适"
"Because the poor man never has enough to eat"
"因为穷人永远吃不饱"
"And his family doesn't have enough to eat either"
"他的家人也吃不饱饭"
"Let us give him a pot"
"我们给他一锅吧"
"A pot with an infinite supply of murukku"
"一锅无限量的murukku"
The divine consort was right.
神妃说得对。
The Lord of Kailas agreed to the proposal.
凯拉斯之王同意了这个提议。
On the spot he created a magical pot.
他当场就做出了一个神奇的罐子。
Durga went to the poor Brahman.
杜尔迦去找可怜的婆罗门。

"O Brahman! My loyal devotee"
"婆罗门啊！我的忠实信徒。"
"I have often thought of your pitiable case"
"我经常想起你那可怜的遭遇"
"Your repeated prayers have moved my compassion"
"你们反复的祈祷让我深受感动"
"Here is a pot for you"
"给你一壶"
"You must turn the pot upside down"
"你必须把锅倒过来"
"And then you must shake the pot"
"然后你必须摇动锅"
"The finest murukku will pour out"
"最优质的穆鲁库即将倾泻而出"
"The murukku will keep pouring out forever"
"穆鲁库将永远喷涌而出"
"Until you put the pot upright again"
"直到你把锅重新竖起来"
"You can eat as much murukku as you like"
"Murukku 想吃多少就吃多少"
"Your wife and children will hunger no more"
"你的妻子和孩子将不再挨饿"
"And you can sell the murukku if you like"
"如果你愿意的话，你可以卖掉murukku。"
The Brahman was delighted beyond measure.
婆罗门非常高兴。
He had received a truly valuable treasure.
他得到了一件真正无价的宝物。
He made his deepest obeisance to the goddess.
他向女神致以最深切的敬意。
And he expressed his eternal gratefulness.
并表达了他永远的感激之情。

The Brahman had started walking home.

婆罗门已经开始往家走。

But first he had to test his magical pot.

但首先他必须测试一下他的魔法锅。

He wanted to see if the pot really worked.

他想看看这个锅是否真的有用。

He turned the pot upside down.

他把锅倒扣过来。

And he shook the pot, as instructed.

然后他按照指示摇晃了锅。

Lo and behold! The pot really did work.

瞧！这锅真的管用了。

The finest murukku fell to the ground.

最精美的穆鲁库掉到了地上。

He tied the sweetmeat in his sheet.

他把糖果绑在床单里。

And he walked on, towards his village.

他继续向他的村庄走去。

By noon the Brahman had gotten hungry.

到了中午，婆罗门已经饿了。

But he could not eat without his ablutions.

但他不洗漱就无法进食。

First, he had to say his prayers.

首先，他必须祈祷。

There was an inn on his way.

途中遇到一家客栈。

Close to the inn there was a water tank.

旅馆附近有一个水箱。

So, he intended to halt there.

所以，他打算就此止步。

In order to bathe and say his prayers.

为了洗澡和祈祷。

After this he could eat all the murukku.

此后他可以吃掉所有的murukku。

The Brahman sat at the innkeeper's shop.

婆罗门坐在旅店老板的店里。
The shopkeeper was smoking tobacco.
店主正在抽烟。
He put the pot near the shopkeeper.
他把锅放在店主附近。
And he asked him to look after the pot.
并请他照看好锅。
"Please take special care of this pot"
"请特别保管这个锅"
"I must bathe and say my prayers"
"我必须洗澡并祈祷"
"Please look after this pot for me"
"请帮我照顾好这个锅"
"Make sure nothing happens to this pot"
"确保这个锅不会出什么问题"
He thought it was a strange request.
他认为这是一个奇怪的要求。
But he agreed to look after the pot.
但他同意照看这个罐子。
And the Brahman gave him the pot.
婆罗门就把罐子给了他。
He besmeared his body with mustard oil.
他把芥子油涂抹在身上。
And he went to do his ablutions.
然后他就去洗漱了。
The innkeeper grew curious about the pot.
旅店老板对这个罐子产生了好奇。
"This pot must have something valuable in it"
"这罐子里肯定有什么值钱的东西"
"Why else would he be so careful?"
"不然他为什么这么小心呢？"
His curiosity had been excited.
他的好奇心被激发了。
So, he opened the pot.

于是，他打开了锅。

To his surprise the pot was empty.
令他惊讶的是，锅是空的。

"What can be the meaning of this?"
"这是什么意思？"

"Why does he care so much for an empty pot?"
"他为什么这么在意一个空锅？"

He began to examine the pot more carefully.
他开始更加仔细地检查这个罐子。

During his inspection he turned the pot upside down.
检查时，他把锅倒过来了。

And then the finest murukku fell out from the pot.
然后最精致的 murukku 从锅里掉了出来。

And the murukku didn't stop falling out.
而 murukku 却不断掉落。

The innkeeper called his wife and children.
旅店老板叫来了他的妻子和孩子。

He wanted them to witness what had happened.
他想让他们见证所发生的一切。

An unexpected stroke of good fortune!
意外的好运！

The pot gave copious showers of sugared paddy.
锅里落下了大片糖粒。

He filled all his pots and jars.
他把所有的罐子和瓶罐都装满了。

He knew he had to have this pot.
他知道他必须得到这个锅。

So, he replaced the pot with another one.
于是，他又换了一个锅。

He had a pot of the same size and color.
他有一个同样大小和颜色的锅。

The Brahman had finished his ablutions.
婆罗门已洗净完毕。

He had performed all of his devotions.
他已履行了他所有的虔诚的信仰。
He came back to the shop in wet clothes.
他穿着湿衣服回到商店。
He was still reciting holy texts of the Vedas.
他仍在吟诵吠陀经的圣典。
He put back on his dry clothes.
他又穿上了干衣服。
In red ink he wrote the name of Durga.
他用红墨水写下了杜尔迦的名字。
He wrote her name one hundred and eight times.
他写了她的名字一百零八次。
After doing this he broke his fast.
做完这些之后，他就停止了斋戒。
And he ate the murukku he had in his sheet.
他把床单里的穆鲁库（murukku）吃掉了。
He was refreshed from the meal.
吃完饭他精神焕发。
Now he could resume his journey home.
现在他可以继续回家了。
So he called to the innkeeper.
于是他叫来了旅店老板。
"Please could I get my pot back"
"请问我可以把我的锅拿回来吗？"
The innkeeper gave him back his pot.
旅店老板把锅还给了他。
"There, sir, here is your pot"
"先生，这是您的锅。"
"The pot is exactly where you had put it"
"锅就在你放的地方"
"Your pot is just as you left it"
"你的锅和你离开时一样"
"I made sure no one has touched your pot"
"我确保没人动过你的锅"

The Brahman didn't suspect a thing.
婆罗门没有怀疑任何事。
He picked up the pot.
他拿起了锅。
And he proceeded on his journey home.
然后他继续回家。

On his journey he had to think.
在旅途中他必须思考。
He congratulated his good fortune.
他祝贺他的好运。
"My wife will be most pleasantly surprised!"
"我的妻子一定会感到非常惊喜！"
"The children will devour the murukku!"
"孩子们会把穆鲁库吃光的！"
"I shall soon become rich"
"我很快就会变得富有"
"I will be able to lift my head up high"
"我将能够昂首挺胸"
The pains of travelling had been reduced.
旅行的痛苦减少了。
Now his problems were much more pleasant.
现在他遇到的问题变得轻松多了。
Only anticipation made the journey difficult.
唯有期待，才让旅途变得艰难。
He finally reached his home again.
他终于又回到了家。
He called to his wife and children.
他呼唤他的妻子和孩子。
"Look at what I have brought"
"看看我带来了什么"
"This pot is an unfailing source of wealth".
"这口锅是取之不尽、用之不竭的财富之源"。
"We will never have to struggle again"

"我们再也不用挣扎了"
"I will turn the pot upside down"
"我要把锅翻过来"
"And then you will see something.
"然后你就会看到一些东西。
"Something you've never seen before"
"你从未见过的东西"
"A stream of the finest murukku will flow"
"最优质的穆鲁库将流淌而出"
You can imagine what his wife was thinking.
你可以想象他的妻子在想什么。
"My husband has gone mad," she thought.
"我的丈夫疯了，" 她想。
She was soon confirmed in her opinion.
她的观点很快就得到了证实。
Nothing fell from the pot, as promised.
正如承诺的那样，锅里什么也没有掉下来。
He turned the pot upside down again and again.
他把锅翻了一遍又一遍。
The Brahman was overwhelmed with grief.
婆罗门悲痛万分。
He realized that he had been tricked.
他意识到自己被骗了。
The innkeeper must have swapped the pot.
旅店老板肯定调换了锅。
He must have stolen Durga's pot.
他肯定偷了杜尔迦的罐子。
And he must have replaced the pot with a normal one.
而且他肯定已经把这个锅换成了一个正常的锅。
He went back to the innkeeper the next day.
第二天他又回到了旅店老板那里。
And he accused him of having changed his pot.
并指责他改变了自己的锅。
At first the innkeeper acted surprised.

起初，旅店老板表现得很惊讶。
Then he pretended to be angry at the accusation.
然后他假装对这一指控感到愤怒。
Finally, he chased him out of his shop.
最后，他把他赶出了商店。

He had no way of getting the pot back.
他没有办法把锅拿回来。
The Brahman knew what he had to do.
婆罗门知道他必须做什么。
He went to see the goddess Durga again.
他又去拜见了女神杜尔迦。
Siva and Durga honored him with their presence.
湿婆和难近母亲临现场向他表示敬意。
Durga spoke to the poor Brahman.
杜尔迦对可怜的婆罗门说话。
"So, you have lost the pot I gave you"
"所以，我给你的那罐子你输了。"
"I take pity on your situation"
"我很同情你的处境"
"Here is another magical pot"
"这又是一个神奇的锅"
"Take this pot, and make good use of it"
"拿着这个锅，好好利用它"
The Brahman was elated with joy.
婆罗门非常高兴。
He made obeisance to the divine couple.
他向这对神圣的夫妇致敬。
And he took the pot with him.
他还把锅带走了。
Again he had to see if the pot worked.
他必须再次检查锅是否能用。
He turned the pot upside down.
他把锅倒扣过来。

And he shook the pot as before.
他又像先前一样摇晃着锅。
And he waited for the murukku to fall out.
他等着穆鲁库掉下来。
But no, horror of horrors!
但事实并非如此，恐怖至极！
Murukku did not fall from the pot.
Murukku 没有从锅里掉下来。
Instead of murukku, demons jumped out.
跳出来的不是 murukku，而是恶魔。
They began to beat the astonished Brahman.
他们开始殴打惊讶的婆罗门。
The Brahman received punches and kicks.
婆罗门遭到拳打脚踢。
But he kept his presence of mind.
但他依然保持着清醒的头脑。
He turned the pot the right way up.
他把锅倒转了方向。
And he covered the pot up again.
他又把锅盖上了。
Fortunately his quick thinking worked.
幸运的是，他的敏捷思维发挥了作用。
The demons disappeared as soon as he did this.
他一这样做，恶魔们就消失了。
The Brahman tried to understand what this meant.
婆罗门试图理解这是什么意思。
It must be to punish the innkeeper!
肯定是为了惩罚客栈老板啊！
So he went to the innkeeper again.
于是他又去找旅店老板。
He gave him the new pot.
他把新锅给了他。
He begged of him to look after the pot.
他恳求他照看好这个锅。

Just like he had done before.

就像他以前做的那样。

He went for his ablutions and prayers.

他去沐浴并祈祷。

The innkeeper was delighted.

旅店老板很高兴。

He had been given a second godsend.

他得到了第二个天赐之物。

He agreed to take the greatest care of the pot.

他同意尽最大努力保管这个罐子。

He waited for the Brahman to go.

他等待婆罗门离开。

And he called his wife and children.

他还叫来了他的妻子和孩子。

"This is another pot from the Brahman"

"这是婆罗门的另一个罐子。"

"This time I hope it is not murukku"

"我希望这次不是murukku"

"I hope this pot is full of sandesa"

"我希望这壶里装满了sandesa"

"Come, be ready with the baskets"

"来，准备好篮子"

"I will turn the pot upside down"

"我要把锅倒扣过来"

"And then I will shake the pot"

"然后我会摇动锅"

And he did what he said he would do.

他确实做到了他所说的一切。

But the room did not fill with food.

但房间里并没有堆满食物。

This time the room filled with demons.

这一次，房间里挤满了恶魔。

The demons caught hold of the innkeeper.

恶魔抓住了旅店老板。

And the demons also caught his family.
而恶魔也抓住了他的家人。
And the demons beat them mercilessly.
而恶魔们却无情地打击了他们。
They would have completely destroyed the shop.
他们会彻底毁掉这家商店。
But the victims ran to the Brahman.
但受害者却跑向了婆罗门。
The Brahman had returned from his ablutions.
婆罗门沐浴完毕回来了。
The Brahman showed mercy to them.
婆罗门对他们表现出了怜悯。
And he accepted their request.
他接受了他们的请求。
But there was one condition to his help.
但他的帮助有一个条件。
"I will only help if I get my pot back"
"只有拿回我的锅我才会帮忙"
The innkeeper didn't have much choice.
旅店老板没有太多选择。
He had to accept the Brahman's conditions.
他必须接受婆罗门的条件。
The Brahman put the pot upright again.
婆罗门又把罐子竖起来。
And he put the lid on the pot.
他把锅盖盖上了。
He took his pot back from the innkeeper.
他从旅店老板手里拿回了他的锅。
And he returned back to his village.
然后他就回到了自己的村庄。
Now the Brahman had two magical pots.
现在婆罗门有两个神奇的罐子。
The Brahman shut the door of his house.
婆罗门关上了家门。

And he called his family again.
他又给家人打了电话。
He turned the murukku-pot upside down.
他把 murukku 锅倒扣过来。
And he shook the murukku-pot as before.
他像先前一样摇晃了穆鲁库罐。
This time the magic pot worked.
这次魔法罐成功了。
An endless stream of the finest murukku.
源源不断的优质 murukku。
The family devoured the sweetmeat.
一家人狼吞虎咽地吃着糖果。
They ate to their hearts' content.
他们吃得很开心。
All the pots and pans were filled.
所有的锅碗瓢盆都装满了。

The next day the Brahman became confectioner.
第二天，婆罗门就成为了糖果师。
He opened a shop in his house.
他在自己家里开了一家商店。
And he sold the best murukku.
他卖的是最好的 murukku。
The whole village came to the Brahman's house.
整个村庄的人都来到婆罗门的家里
They all wanted to buy the wonderful murukku.
他们都想买这美味的 murukku。
They had never seen such murukku in their life.
他们一生中从未见过这样的murukku。
It was the most delicious murukku they ever had.
这是他们吃过的最美味的murukku。
No one had ever made anything like this dessert.
从来没有人制作过类似这种甜点的东西。
The reputation of the Brahman's murukku spread.

婆罗门穆鲁库的名声开始传播。
Soon people from outside the city came.
不一会儿，城外的人就来了。
Cartloads of the sweetmeat were sold every day.
每天都会卖出一车车的糖果。
The Brahman quickly became very rich.
婆罗门很快就变得非常富有。
He built a large brick house.
他建造了一座大砖房。
And he lived like a nobleman of the land.
他过着像当地贵族一样的生活。
Once, however, his luck almost changed.
然而，有一次他的运气几乎发生了改变。
His children had taken the wrong pot.
他的孩子们拿错了罐子。
A large number of demons came out.
大批恶魔涌出。
And they caught hold of the Brahman's wife.
他们抓住了婆罗门的妻子。
And they also caught his children.
他们还抓走了他的孩子。
They were striking them mercilessly.
他们无情地攻击他们。
Fortunately the Brahman came back into the house.
幸运的是，婆罗门回到了屋里。
He turned the pot back to its proper position.
他把锅放回原位。
He wanted to prevent a similar catastrophe.
他想防止类似的灾难再次发生。
So the Brahman had a private room built.
于是婆罗门便命人建造了一间私人房间。
And he put the pot in a secret place.
他把罐子放在一个秘密的地方。
Mortals, however, do not have the luck of Gods.

然而凡人却没有神那样的运气。
Uninterrupted prosperity is not their fortune.
持续不断的繁荣并不是他们的财富。
The demon-pot had been put out of the way.
恶魔罐已被移开。
But why might accident not befall the murukku pot?
但为什么 murukku 锅不会遭遇意外呢？
One day the Brahman and his wife were absent.
有一天，婆罗门和他的妻子不在家。
The children decided to shake the pot.
孩子们决定摇晃锅。
Each of them wanted to do the honors.
他们每个人都想尽一份力。
So there was a fight to get the pot.
因此，为了争夺这个锅，双方发生了争斗。
In the struggle the pot fell to the ground.
争斗中，花盆掉到了地上。
Like any other earthen pot, it broke.
就像其他陶罐一样，它碎了。
Eventually the Braham came back home again.
最终，布拉罕又回到了家。
You can imagine how the news grieved him.
你可以想象这个消息让他多么悲伤。
Of course the children were well cudgeled.
当然，孩子们被狠狠地打了一顿。
But anger could not replace the pot.
但愤怒并不能取代锅。
After some days he went to the forest again.
几天后，他又去了森林。
He offered many a prayer for Durga's favor.
他多次祈祷以求得杜尔迦的恩惠。
At last Siva and Durga appeared to him.
最后，湿婆和难近母出现在他面前。
They listened to how the pot had been broken.

他们听着罐子是如何被打破的。
Durga decided to give him another pot.
杜尔迦决定再给他一罐。
But this pot was accompanied with a caution.
但这锅却伴随着一个警告。
"Brahman, take care of this pot"
"婆罗门，照顾好这个罐子"
"Do not break or lose this pot again"
"别再把这个罐子弄坏或丢掉"
"Next time I will not give you another pot"
"下次我不会再给你一壶了"
The Brahman made obeisance to the Gods.
婆罗门对神明顶礼膜拜。
And he went straight back to his house.
然后他就直接回家了。
This time he did not halt at the innkeepers'.
这次他没有在旅店老板家停留。
He shut the door of his house.
他关上了家门。
He called his family to him.
他把家人叫到身边。
And he turned the pot upside down.
他把锅倒扣过来。
And then he began to shake the pot.
然后他开始摇晃锅。
They were only expecting murukku.
他们只期待 murukku。
But this time it was not murukku.
但这次不是murukku。
A stream of beautiful sandesa poured out.
一股股美丽的桑德萨涌出。
It was the finest sandesa you can imagine.
这是你能想象到的最精致的桑德萨。
It truly was the food of Gods.

这确实是神的食物。
The Brahman set up another shop.
婆罗门又开了一家店铺。
Now he was selling sandesa.
现在他正在销售桑德萨。
The fame of his shop soon drew large crowds.
他的商店很快就出名了，吸引了大批人群。
People came from all over the country.
人们来自全国各地。
At all festivals and marriage feasts.
在所有节日和婚宴上。
And at all funeral celebrations in the area.
以及该地区的所有葬礼。
No one bought any other sandesa.
没有人购买任何其他的 sandesa。
All day long the pot produced sandesa.
锅里一整天都在生产沙子。
Gigantic jars were filled with sweet.
巨大的罐子里装满了糖果。
And the jars were sent all over the country.
这些罐子被送往全国各地。

The Brahman's wealth made the Zemindar jealous.
婆罗门的财富让地主妒忌不已。
In these days all villages had a Zemindar.
那时，每个村庄都有一个地主。
He had heard strange things about the sandesa.
他听说过一些有关桑德萨的奇怪的事情。
He heard the dessert came from a magic pot.
他听说这道甜点是来自一个神奇的锅。
So he devised a plan to get this pot.
于是他想出了一个办法来得到这个罐子。
His son was going to get married.
他的儿子要结婚了。

To celebrate there was a great feast.

为了庆祝，他们举行了一场盛大的宴会。

Many hundreds of people were invited.

数百人受到邀请。

Mountain-loads of sandesa were required.

需要大量的桑德萨。

The Zemindar made a proposal to the Brahman.

地主向婆罗门提出了一个建议。

"Bring the magical pot to my house"

"把神奇的锅带到我家来"

At first the Brahman refused to bring the pot.

起初，婆罗门拒绝带壶来。

But the Zemindar insisted.

但泽明达坚持要这么做。

"I will have hundreds of guests"

"我将有数百位客人"

"I will need mountains of sandesa"

"我需要大量的桑德萨"

"More sandesa than you can carry"

"比你能搬动的还要多的桑德萨"

"Bring the vessel to my house"

"把容器拿到我家来"

"It will be easier for you and me"

"这样对你我来说都会更轻松"

Eventually the Brahman agreed.

最终婆罗门同意了。

Himalayas of sandesa were shaken out.

喜马拉雅山脉的桑德萨被震塌。

But the Zemindar got hold of the pot.

但 Zemindar 却赢得了胜利。

The Zemindar insulted the Brahman.

地主侮辱了婆罗门。

And he chased him out of his house.

并把他赶出了家门。

The Brahman didn't give vent to anger.

婆罗门没有发怒。

Instead, he quietly went back to his house.

相反，他静静地回到了自己的家。

He went to the private room.

他去了包间。

And he took out the demon-pot.

他取出了魔罐。

He came back to the Zemindar's house.

他回到了 Zemindar 的家。

And he went to the door of the Zemindar.

他走到了 Zemindar 的门口。

He turned the pot upside down.

他把锅倒扣过来。

And then shook the magical pot.

然后摇晃魔法罐。

A hundred demons fell out of the pot.

锅里掉出一百个恶魔。

The chaos was impossible to describe.

混乱的程度难以形容。

The unearthly visitors flooded the party.

神秘的访客涌入聚会。

They caught hundreds of the guests.

他们捕获了数百名客人。

And the demons beat them mercilessly.

而恶魔们却无情地打击了他们。

The women were dragged by their hair.

妇女们被拽着头发拖行。

The Zemindar was chased from room to room.

泽明达尔被从一个房间追到另一个房间。

The demons' mischief was getting out of hand.

恶魔们的恶作剧已经失控了。

Someone had to put an end to their mischief.

必须有人制止他们的恶作剧。

Else all the men would have been killed.
否则所有的人都会被杀死。
And the house would have been torn to the ground.
房子就会被夷为平地。
The Zemindar fell at the feet of the Brahman.
地主跌倒在婆罗门的脚下。
And he begged to be shown mercy.
他恳求得到怜悯。
The Brahman showed him great mercy.
婆罗门对他表现出极大的怜悯。
And he put the demons back in the pot.
他把恶魔放回了锅里。
The Zemindar never disturbed the Brahman again.
地主再也没有打扰过婆罗门。
Nor was he disturbed by anyone else.
也没有人打扰他。
And he lived for many happy years.
他过了很多幸福的岁月。

The Story of the Rakshasas
罗刹娑的故事

There was once a poor dimwitted Brahman.
从前，有一个贫穷愚笨的婆罗门。
This dimwitted man had a wife, but no children.
这个愚蠢的男人有妻子，但没有孩子。
But him not having children was probably for the best.
但对他来说，没有孩子或许是最好的。
Because he was barely able to meet his own needs.
因为他几乎无法满足自己的需求。
And he could hardly supply enough for his wife.
而他几乎无法给妻子提供足够的食物。
But his dimwittedness was not even his biggest problem.
但他的愚蠢甚至不是他最大的问题。
This dimwitted man was also a rather lazy man!
这个笨蛋，还是个懒惰的男人！
He was averse to making any long journeys.
他不喜欢进行任何长途旅行。
Had he travelled further he might have had enough.
如果他走得更远，他可能就受够了。
He could have got presents from rich men.
他本可以从富人那里得到礼物。
This would have enabled them to live comfortably.
这将使他们能够过上舒适的生活。
There was a great king in a neighbouring country.
邻国有一位伟大的国王。
The mother of the great king had just died.
这位伟大国王的母亲刚刚去世。
So this king was celebrating the funeral obsequies.
原来这位国王正在举行葬礼。
And the funeral was celebrated with great pomp.
葬礼举行得十分隆重。
Brahmans and beggars were coming from faraway lands.

婆罗门和乞丐从遥远的地方赶来。

They all came expecting to receive rich presents.

他们都期待收到丰厚的礼物。

The Brahman's wife requested him to also go.

婆罗门的妻子请求他也去。

"Seize this opportunity and get us a little money"

"抓住这个机会，帮我们赚点钱"

But his constitutional indolence stood in the way.

但他天生的懒惰却阻碍了他。

The woman, however, gave her husband no rest.

然而，这位妇女却不让丈夫休息。

Finally she extorted from him the promise.

最后她迫使他答应了。

He promised his wife that he would go.

他向妻子保证他会去。

The good woman, accordingly, cut down a plantain tree.

于是，这位好心的女人砍倒了一棵芭蕉树。

And she burnt the plantain tree to ashes.

她把芭蕉树烧成了灰烬。

With the ashes she cleaned the clothes of her husband.

她用灰烬清洗了丈夫的衣服。

And she made his clothes as white as any cleaner could.

她把他的衣服洗得洁白如新。

Her husband was going to the palace of a great king.

她的丈夫要去一位伟大国王的宫殿。

The king could not be approached by men in rags.

衣衫褴褛的人是无法接近国王的。

Besides, Brahman are bound to appear neat and clean.

此外，婆罗门必然显得整洁干净。

At last, one morning the Brahman left his house.

最后，一天早上，婆罗门离开了家。

And he made his way to the palace of the great king.

他来到了伟大国王的宫殿。

I have already mentioned he was a dimwitted man.

我已经提到过他是一个愚蠢的人。

He did not inquire which road he should take.

他没有询问应该走哪条路。

Instead, he walked on and on without directions.

相反，他漫无目的地向前走着。

And he followed wherever his nose pointed him.

无论鼻子指向哪里，他都会跟着走。

I don't need to say he was not on the right road.

我不需要说他走错了路。

The regions he wandered became less and less inhabited.

他游历的地区变得越来越荒凉。

Soon he met no human being for many miles.

很快，他方圆数英里内就再也没有遇见一个人。

But there were many other things he saw there.

但他还在那里看到了许多其他东西。

Things he had never seen in all his life.

他一生中从未见过的东西。

He saw hillocks of cowries on the roadside.

他看到路边有一小堆贝壳。

Cowries were shells used as money in those times.

贝壳是当时用作货币的贝壳。

He kept going and saw hillocks of jewels.

他继续前行，看到了堆积如山的珠宝。

Next, he saw hillocks of four-anna pieces.

接下来，他看到了一堆堆四安娜的金币。

Further along were hillocks of eight-anna pieces.

再往前走，便是堆积如山的八安娜金币。

And further yet were hillocks of rupees.

更远的地方还有成堆的卢比。

But the Brahman's surprise did not end there.

但婆罗门的惊讶还不止于此。

Next there was a hill of burnished gold-mohurs.

旁边有一座磨光的金莫赫山。

The burnished gold-mohurs were shining brightly.

抛光的金饰闪闪发光。

Because the gold-mohurs had been freshly minted.

因为金币是刚刚铸造的。

Close to the hill of gold-mohurs was a large house.

靠近金莫赫山的地方有一座大房子。

The house looked like the palace of a powerful king.

这座房子看上去就像一位强大国王的宫殿。

At the door stood a lady of exquisite beauty.

门口站着一位绝色美女。

The lady, seeing the Brahman, said;

那女人看见婆罗门，说道：

"Come to me, my beloved husband"

"到我这里来吧，我亲爱的丈夫"

"You married me when I was young"

"当我还年轻的时候你就嫁给了我"

"But you never came back after our marriage"

"但我们结婚后你就再也没有回来"

"Though I have been daily expecting you"

"虽然我每天都在盼望你"

"Blessed be this day," said the lady.

"愿今天蒙福，" 女士说道。

"On this day I see the face of my husband"

"今天我看到了我丈夫的脸"

"Come, my sweet, come in," she asked of him.

"来吧，亲爱的，进来吧，" 她向他问道。

"You must be fatigued from your long journey"

"长途旅行你一定很疲惫了。"

"Wash your feet and rest, and eat and drink"

"洗洗脚，休息一下，吃吃喝喝"

"And after that we shall make ourselves merry"

"然后我们会快乐地度过"

The Brahman was astonished beyond measure.

婆罗门惊讶不已。

He had no recollection marrying twice.

他不记得自己结过两次婚。

He remembered marrying the wife he left at home.

他记得自己娶了留在家里的妻子。

But he did not remember marrying this lady.

但他不记得曾娶过这位女士。

But he remembered that he was a Kulin Brahman.

但他记得自己是库林婆罗门。

Perhaps his father got him married as a child.

也许他的父亲在他小时候就让他结婚了。

But what he thought did not matter much.

但他怎么想并不重要。

The woman was certain he was her husband.

女人确信他是她的丈夫。

And he had no reason to say he was not her husband.

他也没有理由说他不是她的丈夫。

Because her beauty was more than he could fathom.

因为她的美貌远超乎他的想象。

As beautiful as the Goddesses of Indra's heaven.

和因陀罗天堂的女神一样美丽。

And he was sure that she was wealthy too.

他确信她也很富有。

These thoughts went through the Brahman's mind.

婆罗门心里闪过这些想法。

But the lady interrupted his flow of thought.

但那位女士打断了他的思路。

"Are you doubting whether I am your wife?"

"你怀疑我是不是你的妻子吗？"

"Have you lost all memories of that happy event?

"那件喜事的记忆你都忘光了吗？

"All the pomp and circumstance of our nuptials"

"我们婚礼的盛况和仪式"

"Come in, beloved; this is your house"

"进来吧，亲爱的；这是你的房子"

"Because whatever is mine is thine also"

"因为凡是我的，也是你的"
The fair lady easily persuaded the Brahman.
美丽的女士很容易就说服了婆罗门。
And he succumbed to her loving entreaties.
他屈服于她充满爱意的恳求。
And he went into the house of the lady.
于是他走进了那位女士的家。
The house was not an ordinary one.
这所房子并不普通。
The house was in fact a magnificent palace.
这座房子实际上是一座宏伟的宫殿。
All the apartments were large and lofty.
所有的公寓都又大又高。
Every room in the palace was richly furnished.
宫殿里的每个房间都装饰华丽。
But one thing surprised the Brahman very much.
但有一件事让婆罗门非常惊讶。
There was no other person in all the house.
整个房子里没有其他人。
The only one there was the lady herself.
那里唯一的人就是那位女士本人。
He could not account for the strange phenomenon.
他无法解释这一奇怪的现象。
They meet anyone on their walks either.
他们在散步时也会遇见任何人。
The fact was that the lady was not a human being.
事实上，这位女士并不是人类。
What the lady really was was a Rakshasi.
这位女士的真实身份是罗刹女。
She had eaten up the king and queen.
她吃掉了国王和王后。
And she had eaten all the members of the royal family.
她把皇室的所有成员都吃掉了。
And gradually she had eaten their servants too.

渐渐地，她也吃掉了他们的仆人。
This was why there were no humans far and wide.
这就是为什么周围没有人类的原因。
The Rakshasi and the Brahman now lived together.
罗刹女与婆罗门现在生活在一起。
After a week the former said to the latter;
一周后，前者对后者说；
"I am very anxious to see my sister"
"我非常想见到我的妹妹"
"As you know, my sister is your other wife"
"你知道的，我妹妹是你的另一个妻子。"
"You must go and fetch my sister; your other wife"
"你必须去把我妹妹叫来，也就是你的另一个妻子。
"

"Then we shall all live together happily"
"那我们就幸福地生活在一起吧"
"You must go to get her early tomorrow"
"你明天必须早点去接她"
"I will give you clothes and jewels for her"
"我会送你衣服和珠宝给她"
Next morning the Brahman set out for his home.
第二天早上，婆罗门就回家了。
He was furnished with fine clothes.
他穿着华丽的衣服。
And he wore around his wrists costly ornaments.
他的手腕上戴着昂贵的饰品。

The poor woman was in great distress.
这位可怜的妇女陷入了极大的痛苦之中。
The funeral ceremony of the king's mother was over.
国王母亲的葬礼结束了。
All the Brahmans and Pandits had returned.
所有的婆罗门和班智达都回来了。
And they were loaded with donations.

他们还收到了大量捐款。

But her husband had not returned.

但她的丈夫还没有回来。

No one could give any news of him.

没有人能提供任何有关他的消息。

Because no one had seen him there.

因为没有人在那里见过他。

The woman therefore could only come to one conclusion.

因此，女人只能得出一个结论。

He must have been murdered on the road by highwaymen.

他肯定是在路上被劫匪杀害了。

She was in this terrible suspense.

她陷入了这种可怕的悬念之中。

But then one day she heard some rumors.

但有一天她听到了一些谣言。

People in her village were talking about her husband.

村里的人们都在谈论她的丈夫。

They said they saw him coming back.

他们说看到他回来了。

And they said he was dressed in fine clothes.

他们说他穿着华丽的衣服。

And they said he had fine jewels for his wife.

他们说他为他的妻子准备了精美的珠宝。

And sure enough the Brahman soon appeared.

果然，婆罗门很快就出现了。

And he was carrying fine jewels for his wife.

他还为妻子携带了精美的珠宝。

On seeing his wife the Brahman thus accosted her;

婆罗门见到他的妻子后，便对她说道：

"Come with me, my dearest wife"

"跟我来吧，我最亲爱的妻子"

"I have found my first wife"

"我找到了我的第一任妻子"

"She lives in a stately palace"

"她住在一座富丽堂皇的宫殿里"
"Near her palace are hillocks of rupees"
"她的宫殿附近有成堆的卢比"
"And there is a large hill of gold-mohurs"
"那里有一座巨大的金山"
"Why should you pine away in wretchedness?"
"你为何要痛苦地消瘦下去？"
"Why would you stay in this horrible place?"
"你为什么要留在这个可怕的地方？"
"Come with me to the house of my first wife"
"跟我去我第一任妻子的家吧"
"There we shall all live together happily"
"在那里，我们将幸福地生活在一起"
At first, she thought her half-witted man had gone mad.
起初，她以为她那个愚蠢的男人疯了。
She could not imagine the hillocks of rupees.
她无法想象卢比堆积成的小山。
And she could not imagine a hill of gold-mohurs.
她无法想象一座金山。
But then she saw how he was beautifully dressed.
但随后她看到他穿着多么漂亮。
Beautiful clothes of exquisite silks and satins.
用精致的丝绸和缎子制成的漂亮衣服。
Ornaments set with diamonds and precious stones.
镶嵌有钻石和宝石的饰品。
Clothes fit for the queen of the land.
适合这片土地上的女王的衣服。
Clothes only princesses were in the habit of putting on.
只有公主才习惯穿的衣服。
She concluded in her mind that something was amiss:
她心里认定有些事情不对劲：
Her stupid husband must have been tricked.
她那个愚蠢的丈夫肯定被骗了。
He must have fallen into the meshes of a Rakshasi.

他肯定是落入了罗刹女的魔网之中了。
The Brahman, however, insisted his wife went with him.
然而，婆罗门坚持要他的妻子和他一起去。
"Feel free to stay here and pine away in poverty"
"请放心留在这里，过着贫困的生活"
"As for me, I will return to the palace of my first wife"
"至于我，我要回我原配的宫殿去。"
The good woman did her best to stop her husband.
这位好心的女人竭尽全力阻止她的丈夫。
But in the end she resolved to go with him.
但最终她还是决定跟他一起去。
Perhaps she could judge the matter better at the palace.
也许她可以在宫里更好地判断此事。

They set out accordingly the next morning.
第二天早上他们就出发了。
They went the same road the Brahman had travelled.
他们走上了婆罗门曾经走过的路。
The woman was not a little surprised by what she saw.
女人看到眼前的景象，十分惊讶。
She saw the hillocks of cowries and of jewels.
她看到了一堆堆的贝壳和珠宝。
And she saw hillocks of eight-anna pieces.
她看到了一堆堆八安娜的金币。
And she saw the hillocks of rupees too.
她还看到了堆积如山的卢比。
And last of all she saw a lofty hill of gold-mohurs.
最后，她看到了一座高耸的金莫赫山。
She saw also an exceedingly beautiful lady.
她还看到了一位极其美丽的女士。
The lady of the palace was hastening towards her.
宫女正急忙朝她走来。
The lady fell on the neck of the Brahman woman.
女士倒在婆罗门女人的脖子上。

And she wept tears of joy, and said:

她喜极而泣，说道：

"Welcome, beloved sister!"

"欢迎你，亲爱的妹妹！"

"This is the happiest day of my life!"

"这是我一生中最快乐的一天！"

"I see the face of my dearest sister again!"

"我又看到我最亲爱的妹妹的脸了！"

The husband and his two wives entered the palace.

丈夫和两个妻子进了宫殿。

Now he was lodged in a stately mansion.

如今他住在一座富丽堂皇的宅邸里。

The most delectable food appeared, as if by enchantment.

最美味的食物仿佛被施了魔法一般出现了。

He was caressed and endeared by his two wives.

他的两位妻子都对他宠爱有加。

Both wives did their best to make him happy.

两位妻子都尽力让他开心。

Both wives did their best to make him comfortable.

两位妻子都尽力让他感到舒服。

His two wives were competing for his love.

他的两个妻子都在争夺他的爱情。

The Brahman had a jolly time of it.

婆罗门度过了一段愉快的时光。

He was steeped in an ocean of enjoyment.

他沉浸在快乐的海洋中。

The Brahman lived in this state of Elysian pleasure.

婆罗门生活在这种极乐快乐的境界中。

Some fifteen or sixteen years he spent this way.

他这样度过了十五、十六年。

During this time his two wives presented him with two sons.

在此期间，他的两位妻子为他生了两个儿子。

The Rakshasi's son was the elder.

罗刹娑的儿子是长子。

He looked more like a god than a human being.

他看上去更像一个神而不是一个人。

He was named Sahasra-Dal.

他的名字是 Sahasra-Dal。

His name meant the thousand-branched.

他的名字的意思是“千枝”。

The son of the Brahman woman was a year younger.

婆罗门女人的儿子小一岁。

He was named Champa-Dal

他的名字叫 Champa-Dal

His name meant the branch of a champaka tree.

他的名字的意思是金木树的树枝。

The two brothers loved each other dearly.

兄弟俩深爱着对方。

They were both sent to the same school.

他们都被送往同一所学校。

The school was several miles distant from the palace.

学校距离宫殿有几英里远。

Every day they rode their two little ponies to school.

他们每天骑着两匹小马去上学。

The Brahman woman had always been suspicious.

婆罗门女一向心存疑虑。

A thousand little circumstances gave her clues.

无数的小事给了她线索。

She knew her sister-in-law was not a human being.

她知道嫂子不是人。

She was sure her sister-in-law was a Rakshasi.

她确信她的嫂子是个罗刹女。

But her suspicion had not yet ripened into certainty.

但她的怀疑尚未确定。

Because the Rakshasi exercised great self-restraint.

因为罗刹女有很强的自我克制力。

She never did anything which human beings did not do.

她从不做人类不会做的事。

But she couldn't hide her demonic nature forever.
但她无法永远隐藏自己的恶魔本性。

Her demonic nature was eventually going to reveal itself.
她的恶魔本性终究会显露出来。

The Brahman had little to keep him busy.
婆罗门没有什么事情可忙。

In order to pass his time he went hunting.
为了消磨时间，他去打猎。

The first day he returned with an antelope.
第一天他带着一只羚羊回来。

The antelope was laid in the courtyard of the palace.
这只羚羊被安放在宫殿的庭院里。

The Rakshasi saw the antelope with great interest.
罗刹女看见这只羚羊，十分感兴趣。

At the sight of the raw meat her mouth began to water.
一看到生肉，她的嘴就开始流口水。

The antelope was never taken to the kitchen.
羚羊从未被带进厨房。

Instead, the Rakshasi took the antelope to another room.
相反，罗刹女将羚羊带往了另一个房间。

In this room she began devouring the antelope.
在这个房间里，她开始吞食羚羊。

The Brahman woman saw everything from a secret room.
婆罗门女在密室中看到了这一切。

Her Rakshasi sister tore a leg off the antelope.
她的罗刹姐妹撕掉了羚羊的一条腿。

She saw how she opened her tremendous jaw.
她看到她张开了巨大的下巴。

And in one mouthful she swallowed up the leg.
她一口就把腿吞了下去。

The other limbs were devoured in the same manner.
其余肢体也以同样的方式被吞噬。

And opening her jaw even further, she swalled the body.
她张开嘴，将尸体吞了下去。
Only a little bit of the meat was kept for the kitchen.
只留下一点点肉给厨房。
On the second day the Brahman caught another antelope.
第二天，婆罗门又抓到了一只羚羊。
On the third day the Brahman caught another antelope.
第三天，婆罗门又抓到了一只羚羊。
The Rakshasi was unable to restrain her appetite.
罗刹女抑制不住自己的食欲。
The raw flesh brought out her demonic nature.
鲜血淋漓的肉体让她的恶魔本性显露出来。
And she devoured each antelope like the last.
她把每一只羚羊都吃掉了，就像最后一只一样。
On the third day the Brahman woman expressed her surprise.
第三天，婆罗门女表示惊讶。
"Nearly three whole antelopes have disappeared"
"近三只羚羊消失了"
"All that is left is a little bit of meat"
"只剩下一点点肉了"
The Rakshasi did not appreciate the accusation.
罗刹女对这个指控很不以为然。
"Do I eat raw flesh?" she asked fiercely.
"我吃生肉吗？" 她凶狠地问道。
"Perhaps you do eat raw flesh," replied the Brahman woman.
"也许你确实吃生肉，" 婆罗门女人回答道。
"I have nothing to prove the contrary"
"我没有任何证据可以证明相反的情况"
The Rakshasi knew she had been discovered.
罗刹女知道她被发现了。
Her eyes became even fiercer than before.
她的目光变得比之前更加凶狠。

And she vowed to get her revenge.

她发誓要报仇。

The Brahman woman concluded her fate was sealed.

婆罗门妇女认定她的命运已成定局。

She thought her husband would meet the same fate.

她以为她的丈夫也会遭遇同样的命运。

She did not expect her son to be spared either.

她也不指望自己的儿子能幸免于难。

That night she hardly slept at all.

那天晚上她几乎根本没睡。

The Rakshasi had prevented her from seeing her husband.

罗刹女阻止她见她的丈夫。

Early next morning Champa-Dal went to school.

第二天一早，Champa-Dal 就去上学了。

Before he went to school she gave her son a golden bottle.

在他上学之前，她给了儿子一个金瓶子。

In the golden bottle was her own breast milk.

金色瓶子里装的是她自己的母乳。

"Carefully watch the colour of the milk"

"仔细观察牛奶的颜色"

"If the milk turns red, your father has been killed"

"如果牛奶变红，那你的父亲就被杀了"

"If the milk turns redder, then I have been killed"

"如果牛奶变得更红，那我就被杀了"

"If the milk turns red you must gallop away"

"如果牛奶变红了你就必须飞奔而去"

"Gallop as fast as your horse can carry you"

"尽你所能，飞奔吧"

"If you do not run away, you will be devoured"

"如果你不逃跑，你就会被吞噬"

That morning the Rakshasi made a suggestion to her husband.

那天早上，罗刹女向她的丈夫提出了一个建议。

"Let us bathe in the river this morning"

"今天早上我们去河里洗澡吧"

She would not take no for an answer.
她不会接受否定的回答。

The river was some distance from the palace.
这条河距离宫殿有一段距离。

The Brahman followed her as meekly as a lamb.
婆罗门像羔羊一样温顺地跟随着她。

The Brahman woman saw that her doom was near.
婆罗门女人看到自己的末日即将来临。

But it was beyond her power to avert the catastrophe.
但她无力扭转这场灾难。

The Brahman and the Rakshasi did indeed reach the river.
婆罗门与罗刹女果然到达了河边。

Soon after the Rakshasi changed into her real dimensions.
不久之后，罗刹女就转变成她真实的面貌。

She tore the Brahman limb from limb.
她把婆罗门的肢体撕成了碎片。

She devoured him like she had devoured the antelope.
她吞噬了他，就像吞噬羚羊一样。

Then she ran back to her palace.
然后她跑回了宫殿。

The wive's fate was the same as the Brahman's.
妻子的命运与婆罗门相同。

Young Champ Dal had done as his mother instructed.
年轻的 Champ Dal 按照母亲的吩咐去做了。

He was diligently observing the golden bottle.
他正认真的观察着那金瓶。

He paid special attention to the colour of the milk.
他特别注意牛奶的颜色。

He was horror-struck to find the milk redden a little.
他惊恐地发现牛奶有点变红了。

"My father has been killed," he cried.
他哭喊道："我父亲被杀了。"

Soon after the milk completely reddened.

不久之后，牛奶就完全变红了。

"Now my mother has been killed too," he cried.

"现在我的母亲也被杀了，"他哭喊道。

Quickly he rushed to mount his pony.

他迅速冲上小马。

His half-brother, Sahasra-Dal, was surprised.

他的同父异母兄弟萨哈斯拉达尔（Sahasra-Dal）感到很惊讶。

"Where are you going, Champa?"

"你要去哪里，Champa？"

"Why are you crying, brother?"

"哥哥，你为什么哭呢？"

"Let me accompany you to wherever you are going"

"无论你去哪里，我都陪你"

But Champa-Dal now feared his brother.

但现在 Champa-Dal 害怕他的兄弟了。

"Oh! do not come to me," he objected.

"哦！别来找我，"他反对道。

"Your mother has devoured my father and mother"

"你妈妈把我爸爸妈妈吃掉了"

"Don't you come and devour me"

"你别来吞噬我"

"I will not devour you," he promised his brother.

"我不会吞噬你，"他向他的兄弟承诺道。

"I'll save you," he promised his brother.

"我会救你的，"他向他的兄弟承诺道。

And he galloped after his brother, Champa-Dal.

他飞奔追赶他的兄弟 Champa-Dal。

Soon his mother, the Rakshasi, appeared at a distance.

不久，他的母亲罗刹女出现在远处。

She demanded Champa-Dal to come to her.

她要求 Champa-Dal 来找她。

But Champa-Dal knew better than to go to the Rakshasi.

但 Champa-Dal 知道不应该去见罗刹女。

"Champa-Dal will not come to you, but I will"

"Champa-Dal 不会来找你，但我会"

And instead, Sahasra-Dal went to his mother.

相反，Sahasra-Dal 去找他的母亲了。

The young prince always carried a sword with him.

年轻的王子总是随身带着一把剑。

With his sword he cut off his mother's head.

他用剑砍下了母亲的头。

Champa-Dal had not stayed to witness this.

Champa-Dal 没有留下来见证这一幕。

He had galloped off as far as his pony could carry him.

他已经飞奔到小马能够载他走的最远的地方了。

Because he was running for his life.

因为他正在逃命。

But Sahasra-Dal soon caught up with his brother.

但萨哈斯拉达尔很快就追上了他的兄弟。

And he told him that his mother was no more.

他告诉他，他的母亲已经不在了。

This was small consolation to Champa-Dal.

这对 Champa-Dal 来说只是一点安慰。

The Rakshasi had already devoured both his parents.

罗刹女已经吞噬了他的父母。

But he could still not trust Sahasra-Dal's friendship.

但他仍然无法相信 Sahasra-Dal 的友谊。

They both rode as fast as their horses could carry them.

他们二人都以马所能承载的速度飞驰。

And their horses could carry them very far.

他们的马可以载他们走很远。

Because their horses were Pakshirajes horses.

因为他们的马是帕克希拉杰斯马。

Pakshirajes horses are the kings of birds.

Pakshirajes 马是鸟类之王。

On their horses they travelled over hundreds of miles.

他们骑马旅行了数百英里。

An hour or two before sundown they reached a village.

日落前一两个小时，他们到达了一个村庄。

Here they became the guests of a respectable family.

在这里，他们成为了一个受人尊敬的家庭的客人。

But the two brothers saw the family was in gloom.

但兄弟俩却看到家里一片愁云惨雾。

Something was agitating the family very much.

有件事让这个家庭非常焦躁。

Some of the family held private consultations.

一些家庭成员举行了私人磋商。

And others in the family were weeping.

家里的其他人也都哭了。

The mother was the eldest lady in the house.

母亲是家里最年长的女性。

"I will go, as I am the eldest," she said.

"我会去，因为我是老大，" 她说。

"I have lived long enough"

"我已经活够了"

"At most my life would be cut short by a year or two"

"最多我的寿命会缩短一两年"

The youngest member of the house was a little girl.

家里最小的成员是一个小女孩。

"I will go, as I am young," she said.

"我会去，因为我还年轻，" 她说。

"I am useless to the family"

"我对这个家庭毫无用处"

"If I die, I shall not be missed"

"如果我死了，人们也不会想念我"

The head of the house was the son of the old lady.

这家的户主是老太太的儿子。

"I am the representative of the family," he said.

"我是这个家庭的代表，" 他说。

"It is but reasonable that I should give up my life"

"我放弃生命是合理的"
He also had a younger brother.
他还有一个弟弟。
"You are the pillar of the family," he said.
他说："你是我们家的顶梁柱。"
"If you go the whole family is ruined"
"如果你去了，整个家庭就毁了"
"It is not reasonable that you should go"
"你去是不合理的"
"I will go, as I shall not be much missed"
"我会去的，因为人们不会太想念我。"
The two strangers listened to all this conversation.
两个陌生人听着这一切谈话。
You can imagine their curiosity was not little.
你可以想象他们的好奇心有多大。
They wondered what the discussion could be about.
他们想知道讨论的内容是什么。
Sahasra-Dal took the risk of being thought meddlesome.
Sahasra-Dal 冒着被认为爱管闲事的风险。
"What is the subject of your consultations?"
"你们磋商的内容是什么？"
"What is the reason for your deep miserable?"
"你为什么这么痛苦？"
"Why are your words full of countenances?"
"你说话怎么都带着表情？"
The head of the house gave the following answer.
户主给出了如下的回答。
"There is something you must know, me worthy guests"
"尊敬的客人，您必须知道一件事。"
"These lands are infested by a terrible Rakshasi"
"这片土地上充满了可怕的罗刹女。"
"This Rakshasi has depopulated all the regions here"
"这个罗刹娑已经让这里所有地区人口减少。"
"This town, too, would have been depopulated"

"这个镇也会变得人口稀少"
"But that our king became suppliant to the Rakshasi"
"但我们的国王却向罗刹婆祈求。"
"He begged her to show mercy to us his people"
"他恳求她怜悯我们这些他的人民"
The Rakshasi replied to the king.
罗刹婆回答国王。
"I will consent to show mercy to your subjects"
"我同意对你的臣民仁慈。"
"But there is one condition for my mercy"
"但我的仁慈有一个条件"
"Every night I demand one human being"
"每天晚上我都需要一个人"
"I don't mind if it is a male or a female"
"我不介意它是男性还是女性"
"Put the human being in a temple for me to feast"
"把人类放在寺庙里供我享用"
"If I get a human being every night I will rest satisfied"
"如果每天晚上都能遇到一个人，我就会安心休息"
"Promise me this and I will commit no further depredations"
"答应我，我就不会再进行掠夺了。"
"Your subjects will be spared from my ravenous hunger"
"你的臣民将免受我饥荒的折磨"
"Our king had no other alternative than to agree"
"我们的国王别无选择，只能同意"
"What human can ever hope to contend against a Rakshasi?"
"人类又有谁能与罗刹女抗衡呢？"
"From that day the king made a new law"
"从那天起，国王颁布了一条新法律"
"Every family has to send one member to the temple"
"每个家庭都要派一名成员去寺庙"
"To appease the wrath of the terrible Rakshasi"
"为了平息可怕的罗刹女的愤怒"

"To satisfy the endless hunger of the Rakshasi"
"为了满足罗刹女无尽的饥饿"
"All the families in this neighbourhood have had their turn"
"这个街区的所有家庭都轮到了"
"This night it is the turn of our family"
"今晚轮到我们家了"
"One of us is to devote ourself to destruction"
"我们之中有一个人要致力于毁灭"
"We are therefore discussing who should go to the Rakshasi"
"因此，我们正在讨论谁应该去罗刹婆。"
"You can now perceive the cause of our distress"
"现在你应该明白我们痛苦的原因了吧"
The two friends consulted together for a few minutes.
两个朋友一起商量了几分钟。
After this time they concluded their consultation.
此后，他们结束了磋商。
Sahasra-Dal was the spokesman for the brothers.
萨哈斯拉·达尔（Sahasra-Dal）是兄弟俩的发言人。
"Most worthy host, do not any longer be sad"
"尊贵的主人，请不要再悲伤了。"
"You have been very kind to us"
"你对我们太好了"
"We have resolved to requite your hospitality"
"我们决心报答您的热情款待"
"We will go to the temple instead of you"
"我们代替你去寺庙"
"We shall go as your representatives"
"我们将作为你们的代表前往"
"We will become the food of the Rakshasi"
"我们会成为罗刹女的食物"
The whole family protested against the proposal.
全家人都反对这个提议。
They declared that guests were like gods.

他们宣称客人就像神一样。
"The host must ensure the comfort of the guests"
"主人必须确保客人的舒适"
"The guests must not suffer for the host"
"客人不能为主人受苦"
But the two strangers could not be persuaded.
但这两个陌生人却无法被说服。
"We will stand as proxies for your family"
"我们将代表您的家人"
There was a great deal of objection to the proposal.
该提议遭到了强烈反对。
But eventually the guests persuaded their hosts.
但最终客人们说服了主人。
Finally the hosts consented to the arrangement.
最终主人同意了这一安排。

Sahasra-Dal and Champa-Dal rode off on their horses.
Sahasra-Dal 和 Champa-Dal 骑着马离开了。
Immediately after candle light they reached the temple.
烛光一亮，他们就到了寺庙。
They went into the temple, and shut the door.
他们走进寺庙，关上了门。
Sahasra told his brother to go to sleep.
萨哈斯拉让他的弟弟去睡觉。
"I will guard over your sleep"
"我会守护你的睡眠"
"I will watch out for the terrible Rakshasi"
"我会警惕可怕的罗刹女。"
Champa was soon in a fine sleep.
查姆帕很快就进入了梦乡。
Sahasra lay awake, waiting for the Rakshasi.
萨哈斯拉醒着，等待着罗刹女。
Nothing happened during the early hours of the night.
夜半时分，什么事也没有发生。

But then the gong of the king's bell sounded.
但就在这时，国王的钟声响了。
It was midnight, the dead hour of the night.
当时正是午夜，夜深人静的时刻。
Sahasra heard the sound as of a rushing tempest.
萨哈斯拉听到的声音就像是暴风雨来临的声音。
He used the knowledge he had of Rakshasas.
他运用了自己对罗刹的了解。
He concluded the Rakshasi was nigh.
他断定罗刹女已经临近了。
A thundering knock was heard at the door.
门口传来一阵雷鸣般的敲门声。
The following words accompanied the knock at the door:
敲门声响起：
"How, mow, khow! A human being I smell"
"嗬，嗬！我闻到的是人味儿。"
"Who keeps guard inside this temple?"
"这座寺庙里是谁守卫的？"
To this question Sahasra-Dal made the following reply:
对于这个问题，Sahasra-Dal 做出了如下回答：
"Sahasra-Dal keeps guard inside this temple"
"Sahasra-Dal 守护着这座寺庙"
"Champa-Dal keeps guard inside this temple"
"Champa-Dal 守护着这座寺庙"
"Two winged horses keep guard inside this temple"
"两匹有翼的马守卫着这座寺庙"
Rakshasa blood flowed through Sahasra-Dal's veins.
萨哈斯拉-达尔的血管里流淌着罗刹血。
The Rakshasi knew Sahasra-Dal was not human.
罗刹知道萨哈斯拉-达尔不是人类。
And so the Rakshasi turned away with a groan.
于是罗刹女呻吟一声，转身离去。
After an hour the Rakshasi returned to the temple.
一个小时后，罗刹女返回寺庙。

The Rakshasi thundered at the door again.

罗刹女再次对着门怒吼。

"How, mow, khow! A human being I smell"

"嗬，嗬！我闻到的是人味儿。"

"Who keeps guard inside this temple?"

"这座寺庙里是谁守卫的？"

To this question Sahasra-Dal again replied:

对于这个问题，Sahasra-Dal 再次回答道：

"Sahasra-Dal keeps guard inside this temple"

"Sahasra-Dal 守护着这座寺庙"

"Champa-Dal keeps guard inside this temple"

"Champa-Dal 守护着这座寺庙"

"Two winged horses keep guard inside this temple"

"两匹有翼的马守卫着这座寺庙"

The Rakshasi again groaned and went away.

罗刹女再次哀嚎一声，转身离去。

At two o'clock the Rakshasi appeared once more.

两点钟时，罗刹女再次出现。

And at three o'clock the Rakshasi came again.

三点钟的时候，罗刹女又来了。

Each time the Rakshasi made the same inquiry.

每次罗刹婆都会提出同样的询问。

And each time the Rakshasi left with a groan.

每次罗刹女都呻吟着离开。

After three o'clock, however, Sahasra-Dal felt very sleepy.

然而，三点之后，Sahasra-Dal 感到非常困倦。

He could not any longer keep awake.

他再也无法保持清醒了。

He therefore roused Champa.

因此他唤醒了 Champa。

And he told him to keep guard over the temple.

并吩咐他要看守圣殿。

"The Rakshasi will come again in an hour"

"罗刹女一小时后会再来。"

"The Rakshasi will ask who keeps guard here"
"罗刹女会问是谁守卫这里"
"You must mention Sahasra's name first"
"你必须先提到萨哈斯拉的名字"
Having given these instructions he went to sleep.
给出这些指示后，他就去睡觉了。
At four o'clock the Rakshasi again made her appearance.
四点钟时，罗刹女再次出现。
The Rakshasi thundered at the door, and said:
罗刹娑对着门吼叫道：
"How, mow, khow! A human being I smell"
"嗬，嗬！我闻到的是人味儿。"
"Who keeps guard inside this temple?"
"这座寺庙里是谁守卫的？"
Champa-Dal was in a terrible fright.
昌帕达尔惊恐万分。
He had forgotten the instructions of his brother.
他忘记了哥哥的指示。
"Champa-Dal keeps guard inside this temple"
"Champa-Dal 守护着这座寺庙"
"Sahasra-Dal keeps guard inside this temple"
"Sahasra-Dal 守护着这座寺庙"
"Two winged horses keep guard inside this temple"
"两匹有翼的马守卫着这座寺庙"
The Rakshasi uttered a shout of exultation.
罗刹娑发出一声欢呼。
And the Rakshasi laughed how only demons can laugh.
罗刹女发出了只有恶魔才能发出的笑声。
With a dreadful noise the door broke open.
随着一声可怕的响声，门被打开了。
The noise roused Sahasra from his sleep.
这噪音把萨哈斯拉从睡梦中惊醒。
Within a moment he sprung to his feet.
不一会儿他就跳了起来。

He had his sword with him not only by day.
他不仅在白天随身带着剑。
He had his sword with him by night too.
晚上他也带着剑。
His sword was as supple as a palm-leaf.
他的剑像棕榈叶一样柔软。
And he cut off the head of the Rakshasi.
他砍下了罗刹鬼的头。
The huge mountain of a body fell to the ground.
一座座巨大的身躯，坠落到了地面上。
The body made a great noise when it fell.
尸体倒下时发出很大的声音。
And the body covered many surrounding acres.
尸体覆盖了周围数英亩的土地。
Sahasra-Dal kept the severed head of the Rakshasi.
萨哈斯拉-达尔保留着罗刹女被砍下的头颅。
And he slept again with the head near him.
然后他又把头靠在他身边睡觉了。

Early in the morning some wood-cutters came.
一大早，就来了一些伐木工人。
The wood-cutters were passing near the temple.
樵夫们正经过寺庙附近。
The wood-cutters saw the huge body on the ground.
樵夫们看见地上有一具巨大的尸体。
So they walked towards the temple.
于是他们向寺庙走去。
Soon they saw that it was a carcass.
很快他们就发现那是一具尸体。
The carcass of the terrible Rakshasi.
可怕的罗刹女的尸体。
The Rakshasi that had nearly depopulated the land.
罗刹娑几乎让这片土地上的人口绝迹。
There had been a bounty for this Rakshasi.

这名罗刹婆曾获悬赏。
The king offered the hand of his daughter.
国王向她求婚。
And the king had offered half the kingdom.
国王献出了半个王国。
He would trade it all for the head of the Rakshasi.
他愿意用这一切来换取罗刹鬼的头颅。
The wood-cutters saw no claimant at hand.
伐木工们发现周围没有人认领木材。
So they went to get the reward.
于是他们就去领取奖励。
Each wood-cutter cut off a limb from the Rakshasi.
每个伐木工人都从罗刹女身上砍下一根树枝。
And each wood-cutter went to the king.
于是每个伐木工人都去见国王。
And each wood-cutter tried to claim the reward.
每个伐木工人都想获得奖励。
"I am the destroyer of the great man eater"
"我是大食人魔的毁灭者"
"I have come to claim my reward"
"我来领取我的奖励"
The king knew there could only be one hero.
国王知道只能有一个英雄。
So he made an inquiry with his minister.
于是他向大臣询问。
"What family's turn was it last night?"
"昨晚轮到哪一家了？"
"And who is the head of that family?"
"那这个家族的族长是谁？"
The king's minister set out to find the family.
国王的大臣出发去寻找这个家庭。
He brought the head of the family to the king.
他把一家之主带到国王面前。
And the head of the family told of his guests.

于是一家之主讲述了他的客人的情况。
"Last night two youthful travelers came to me"
"昨晚有两个年轻的旅行者来找我"
"We offered to be their hosts for the night"
"我们主动提出当晚接待他们"
"Soon they discovered the problem we had"
"他们很快就发现了我们的问题"
"And they volunteered to take our place"
"他们自愿接替我们"
"They went to the temple, instead of one of us"
"他们去了圣殿，而不是我们"
The king took his men to the temple.
国王带着他的士兵来到寺庙。
The door of the temple was broken open.
神殿的门被撞开了。
They found the two brothers sleeping.
他们发现兄弟俩正在睡觉。
And the horses were safe in the temple too.
寺庙里的马匹也很安全。
And the head of the Rakshasi was there too.
罗刹鬼的首领也在那里。
There was no doubt about who had killed the monster.
毫无疑问是谁杀死了怪物。
The real hero had been discovered.
真正的英雄已被发现。
And the king kept true to his word.
国王履行了自己的诺言。
He gave the hand of his daughter to Sahasra-Dal.
他将女儿嫁给了 Sahasra-Dal。
And he gave him half his kingdom too.
并且还将自己的半个王国赐给了他。
Champa-Dal remained with his friend.
Champa-Dal 和他的朋友在一起。
And he rejoiced in Sahasra-Dal's prosperity.

他为 Sahasra-Dal 的繁荣而高兴。
And they lived together happily for some time.
他们幸福地一起生活了一段时间。

But one day a misunderstanding arose between them.
但有一天，他们之间产生了误会。
The queen-mother had a certain maid-servant.
太后有一位婢女。
This maid-servant was the most useful domestic.
这个女仆是最有用的佣人。
She could turn her hand to any task.
她可以承担任何任务。
And she had uncommon strength for a woman.
作为一个女人，她拥有非凡的力量。
Her intelligence was not lacking either.
她的智力也并不缺乏。
And she had a remarkable amount of energy.
她精力充沛。
She would have been quickly missed in the palace.
宫殿里很快就会失去她。
The zenana was completely dependent on her.
这位女士完全依赖她。
Hence her services were highly valued.
因此她的服务受到高度重视。
The queen-mother appreciated her very much.
太后非常赏识她。
And the ladies of the palace valued her too.
而宫中的女官们也都很看重她。
But this valuable woman was not a woman.
但这位可贵的女人并不是一个女人。
What this woman was was a Rakshasi.
此女子乃是罗刹女。
She had put on the appearance of a woman.
她已经表现出女人的外表。

She had her own nefarious reasons for doing this.
她这样做有她自己的邪恶目的。
And then she took service in the royal household.
随后她在皇室任职。
At night she used to assume her own real form.
到了晚上，她就会恢复原来的形态。
When everyone in the palace was asleep.
当宫殿里的所有人都睡着的时候。
And then she went about in search of food.
然后她就出去寻找食物。
Because her hunger was not satisfied at the palace.
因为在宫殿里她的饥饿没有得到满足。
A Rakshasi needs much more food than a man or woman.
罗刹女比男人或女人需要更多的食物。
At this time Champa-Dal had no wife.
当时 Champa-Dal 还没有妻子。
So he often slept outside the zenana.
所以他经常睡在修道院外面。
He was not far from the outer gate of the palace.
他距离宫殿的外门不远。
And from there he could observe her.
从那里他可以观察她。
He saw her devouring sundry goats and sheep.
他看见她正在吞食各种山羊和绵羊。
And he saw her devouring horses and elephants.
他看到她正在吞食马和大象。
This of course was not good for the maid-servant.
这对于婢女来说，当然不是好事。
Champa-Dal was in the way of her supper.
昌帕达尔（Champa-Dal）妨碍了她吃晚饭。
So she was determined to get rid of him.
所以她决心要除掉他。
One day she went to the queen-mother.
有一天，她去拜访王太后。

"Queen-mother," she said to her.
"太后，"她对她说。
"I can no longer work in the palace"
"我不能再在宫里工作了"
"Why?" asked the queen-mother.
"为什么？"王太后问。
"What is the matter, Dasi" she wanted to know.
"发生什么事了，达西？"她想知道。
"How can I go on without you?"
"没有你我该怎么活下去？"
"Tell me your reasons for leaving"
"告诉我你离开的原因"
The maid-servant explained her situation.
婢女說明了自己的情況。
"I am but a poor woman in this palace"
"我只是这座宫殿里的一个可怜女人"
"A woman like me can't preserve her honour here"
"像我这样的女人在这里无法维护自己的荣誉"
"Your son-in-law has a friend, Champa-Dal"
"你女婿有个朋友，Champa-Dal"
"He always cracks indecent jokes with me"
"他总是跟我讲一些下流的笑话"
"I would rather beg for my rice than to lose my honour"
"我宁愿乞讨我的米饭，也不愿失去我的荣誉"
"If Champa-Dal remains in the palace I must go away"
"如果 Champa-Dal 继续留在宫里，我就必须离开"
The maid-servant was irreplicable in the palace.
宫女是宫中无人可比的。
The queen-mother knew what sacrifice to make.
王太后知道该做出什么样的牺牲。
Champa-Dal was going to have to leave the palace.
昌帕达尔（Champa-Dal）不得不离开宫殿。
And she told Sahasra-Dal all her reasons.
她把所有的理由都告诉了 Sahasra-Dal。

"Champa-Dal is a bad man"
"Champa-Dal是个坏人"
"His character and morals are loose"
"他的性格和道德都很放荡"
"He must leave this palace at once"
"他必须立刻离开这座宫殿。"
Sahasra-Dal did his best to persuade her otherwise.
Sahasra-Dal 尽力劝说她改变主意。
He earnestly pleaded on behalf of his friend.
他恳切地为他的朋友恳求。
But his efforts were in vain.
但他的努力是徒劳的。
The queen-mother had made up her mind.
太后已经下定了决心。
He had to be driven out of the palace.
他不得不被赶出宫殿。
Sahasra-Dal had not the courage to tell his friend.
Sahasra-Dal 没有勇气告诉他的朋友。
He therefore wrote a letter to him.
因此他给他写了一封信。
In the letter he was vague about the reason.
在信中他并未明确说明原因。
But either way, he was going to have to leave.
但无论如何，他都必须离开。
Champa-Dal went to have a bath.
Champa-Dal 去洗澡了。
And the letter was put in his room.
这封信被放在了他的房间里。
Champa-Dal was grieved upon reading the letter.
读完这封信后，Champa-Dal 感到非常悲痛。
He mounted his fleet of horses.
他骑上了他的马队。
And on his horses he left the palace.
他骑马离开了宫殿。

Champa's horses were uncommonly fleet.

占婆的马匹异常敏捷。

Soon he had traversed thousands of miles.

很快，他便行走了数千英里。

And eventually he reached a new city.

最终他到达了一座新城市。

He stood at the gateway of a magnificent palace.

他站在一座宏伟宫殿的门口。

He dismounted from his horse.

他下了马。

And he entered the palace.

然后他就进入了宫殿。

But in the palace he met not a single creature.

但在宫殿里他没有遇见任何生物。

He went from apartment to apartment.

他从一个公寓走到另一个公寓。

All the rooms were richly furnished.

所有房间都装饰华丽。

But none of the rooms were lived in.

但所有房间均无人居住。

But in the end he came to a different room.

但最终他却来到了另外一个房间。

In this room there was a young lady.

这个房间里有一位年轻的女士。

The young lady was of heavenly beauty.

这位年轻女士有着天籁般的美貌。

And she was lying down on a splendid bedstead.

她正躺在一张华丽的床上。

The beautiful young lady was asleep.

美丽的年轻女士正在睡觉。

Champa-Dal looked upon the sleeping beauty.

昌帕达尔看着这位睡美人。

He was captivated by what he was seeing.

他被眼前的景象迷住了。

He had not seen any woman so beautiful.

他从未见过如此美丽的女人。

Upon the bed there were two sticks.

床上有两根棍子。

The two sticks were near the woman's head.

两根棍子就在女人头部附近。

One of the sticks was made of silver.

其中一根棍子是银做的。

And the other stick was made of gold.

另一根棍子是金子做的。

Champa took the silver stick into his hand.

查姆帕把银棍拿在手里。

And with the stick he touched the body of the lady.

他用棍子触碰了那位女士的身体。

But no change was perceptible to her sleep.

但她的睡眠没有出现任何变化。

He then took up the gold stick.

然后他拿起了金棒。

And with the stick he touched the body of the lady.

他用棍子触碰了那位女士的身体。

This time the young lady did awake.

这次小姐确实醒了。

Eyeing the stranger, she inquired who he was.

她看着陌生人，询问他是谁。

"I am Champa-Dal," he told her.

"我是 Champa-Dal，" 他告诉她。

"There was once a poor dimwitted Brahman"

"从前有一个贫穷愚昧的婆罗门"

"This dimwitted man had a wife, but no children"

"这个愚蠢的男人有妻子，但没有孩子"

"But him not having children was probably for the best"

"但他不生孩子或许是最好的选择"

"Because he was barely able to meet his own needs"

"因为他几乎无法满足自己的需求"
"And he could hardly supply enough for his wife"
"他几乎无法养活他的妻子"
"But his dimwittedness was not even his biggest problem"
"但他的愚蠢甚至不是他最大的问题"
And he continued the story as we have followed it.
他继续讲述我们所关注的故事。
"My mother concluded her fate was sealed"
"我母亲认为她的命运已成定局"
"And she thought my father would meet the same fate"
"她以为我父亲也会遭遇同样的命运"
"And she did not expect me to be spared either"
"她也没指望我能幸免于难。"
"That night she hardly slept at all"
"那天晚上她几乎没睡"
"The Rakshasi had prevented her from seeing my father"
"罗刹女阻止她见我的父亲"
"Early next morning I went to school"
"第二天一早我就去上学了"
"Before I went to school she gave me a golden bottle"
"在我上学之前，她给了我一个金瓶子"
"In the golden bottle was her own breast milk"
"金瓶里装的是她自己的母乳"
"I was told to carefully watch the colour of the milk"
"我被告知要仔细观察牛奶的颜色"
And he continued the story as we have followed it.
他继续讲述我们所关注的故事。
"We will stand as proxies for your family"
"我们将代表您的家人"
"There was a great deal of objection to our proposal"
"我们的提议遭到了很多人反对"
"But eventually we persuaded our hosts"
"但最终我们说服了主人"
"Finally the hosts consented to the arrangement"

"最终主人同意了这个安排"

And he continued the story as we have followed it.

他继续讲述我们所关注的故事。

"So I often slept outside the zenana"

"所以我经常睡在修道院外面"

"I was not far from the outer gate of the palace"

"我当时离宫殿的外门不远。"

"And from there I could observe her"

"从那里我可以观察她"

"I saw her devouring sundry goats and sheep"

"我看到她吞食了各种各样的山羊和绵羊"

"And I saw her devouring horses and elephants"

"我看到她吞食马和大象"

And he continued the story as we have followed it.

他继续讲述我们所关注的故事。

"One day a letter was put in my room"

"有一天，有人把一封信放到我的房间里"

"I was grieved upon reading the letter"

"读了这封信我感到很难过"

"I mounted my fleet of horses"

"我骑上了我的马队"

"And on my horses he left the palace"

"他骑着我的马离开了宫殿"

"My horse are uncommonly fleet"

"我的马跑得异常快"

"Soon I had traversed thousands of miles"

"很快我就走完了千里路"

"And eventually I reached a new city"

"最终我到达了一座新城市"

And he continued the story as we have followed it.

他继续讲述我们所关注的故事。

"I took the silver stick into his hand"

"我把银杖拿到他手里"

"And with the stick I touched your body"

"我用棍子触碰了你的身体"
"But no change was perceptible to your sleep"
"但你的睡眠没有察觉到任何变化"
"I then took up the gold stick"
"然后我拿起了金棒"
And with the stick he touched your body.
他用棍子触碰了你的身体。
"This time you did awake from your sleep"
"这次你确实从睡梦中醒来了"
The young lady had listened to Champa-Dal's story.
这位年轻女士听了 Champa-Dal 的故事。
The young lady was in fact a princess.
这位年轻的女士实际上是一位公主。
"Unhappy man! why have you come here?"
"不幸的人！你为什么来这里？"
"This is the country of Rakshasas"
"这里是罗刹国。"
"No less than seven hundred Rakshasas live here"
"这里居住着至少七百个罗刹。"
"Every morning the Rakshasas leave"
"每天早晨罗刹们都会离开"
"They go to the other side of the ocean"
"他们去了大洋彼岸"
"And they search for provisions there"
"他们在那里寻找食物"
"And before dusk they return again"
"黄昏前它们又回来了"
"My father was king in these regions"
"我的父亲是这些地区的国王"
"His kingdom had millions of subjects"
"他的王国有数百万臣民"
"They lived in flourishing towns and cities"
"他们生活在繁荣的城镇"
"But some years ago the Rakshasas invaded"

"但几年前罗刹族入侵了"
"And they devoured all the subjects of the kingdom"
"他们吞噬了王国的所有臣民"
"The Rakshasas devoured my father and my mother"
"罗刹娑吞噬了我的父亲和母亲"
"The Rakshasas devoured my brothers and sisters"
"罗刹娑吞噬了我的兄弟姐妹"
"And they devoured all the cattle of the country"
"他们吃掉了该国所有的牲畜"
"There is no living human being in these regions"
"这些地区没有活着的人类"
"I am the last human living left"
"我是最后一个活着的人"
"I too would have been devoured long ago"
"我早就被吞噬了"
"But an old Rakshasi took a liking to me"
"但一位老罗刹女喜欢我"
"She prevents the other Rakshasas from eating me"
"她阻止其他罗刹吃掉我"
"Do you see those sticks of silver and gold?"
"你看到那些金银棒子了吗？"
"Every morning she kills me with the silver stick"
"每天早上她都会用银棍杀死我"
"Every evening she re-animates me with the gold stick"
"每天晚上她都会用金棒让我重新活跃起来"
"I do not know how to advise you"
"我不知道该如何建议你"
"If the Rakshasas see you, you are a dead man"
"如果罗刹看到你，你就死定了"
Then they talked in a very affectionate manner.
然后他们非常亲热地交谈。
And they laid their heads together.
然后他们把头靠在一起。
And they thought to devise a means of escape.

他们想办法逃跑。

Some way to get out of the hands of the Rakshasas.

想办法摆脱罗刹魔爪。

The hour of the return of the Rakshasas was coming.

罗刹娑回归的时刻即将到来。

The seven hundred flesh-eaters were soon returning.

七百名食肉者很快就回来了。

Keshavati called out to Champa-Dal.

凯沙瓦蒂（Keshavati）向 Champa-Dal 呼喊。

(Because that was the name of the princess)

（因为那是公主的名字）

"Hide yourself in the heaps of the sacred trefoil"

"把自己藏在神圣的三叶草堆里"

But first Champ Dal picked up the silver stick.

但 Champ Dal 首先拿起了银棍。

He touched Keshavati with the silver stick.

他用银棒触碰了凯沙瓦蒂（Keshavati）。

And as soon as he touched her, she died.

他一碰到她，她就死了。

Then he went to the center of the temple of Siva.

然后他来到了湿婆神庙的中心。

And he hid beneath the heaps of sacred trefoil.

他藏身于神圣的三叶草堆下。

From his hiding place he heard the sound of wind rushing.

他从藏身之处听到了风呼啸的声音。

Then he heard terrible noises in the palace.

然后他听到宫殿里传来可怕的声音。

The Rakshasas had come home from their hunt.

罗刹娑们狩猎完毕回家了。

They had filled their stomachs with meat.

他们已经吃饱了肉。

Sundry goats, sheep, cows, horses, buffaloes.

各种山羊、绵羊、牛、马、水牛。

And they had devoured elephants too.
它们也吞食大象。
The old Rakshasi returned to the palace too.
老罗刹娑也回宫了。
She went to the room of the sleeping princess.
她来到了正在睡觉的公主的房间。
And she woke her with the stick made of gold.
她用金杖唤醒了她。
"Hye, mye, khye! A human being I smell"
"喂，喵，喵！我闻到人的味道了。"
"I am the only human being here," said the princess.
"我是这里唯一的人类，"公主说。
"Eat me if you like," added Keshavati.
"如果你愿意的话就吃我吧，"凯沙瓦蒂补充道。
To this the Rakshasi replied:
对此，罗刹娑回答道：
"Let me eat up your enemies"
"让我吃掉你的敌人"
"Why should I eat you?" she asked the princess.
"我为什么要吃你？"她问公主。
She laid herself down on the ground.
她躺在地上。
She was as long and high as the Vindhya Hills.
她和温迪亚山一样长，一样高。
And in this position she fell asleep.
她就以这个姿势睡着了。
The other Rakshasas and Rakshasis soon fell asleep too.
其他的罗刹娑和罗刹女也很快睡着了。
Because they were tired from their gigantic labour.
因为他们因繁重的劳动而疲惫不堪。
Keshavati also composed herself to sleep.
凯沙瓦蒂也安心入睡。
But Champa did not dare to come out from under the leaves.
但 Champa 不敢从树叶下面出来。

And he tried his best to pray to the god of repose.
并尽力向安息之神祈祷。

At daybreak all seven hundred Rakshasas got up again.
天一亮，七百罗刹众人都起来了。
They went on their usual predatory excursion.
它们继续进行惯常的掠食活动。
And along with them went the old Rakshasi.
和他们一起去的还有老罗刹婆。
But first the old Rakshasi picked up the silver stick.
但老罗刹女首先拿起了银杖。
And she touched Keshavati with the silver stick.
她用银棒触碰了凯沙瓦蒂。
Soon the coast was clear for Champa-Dal.
很快，Champa-Dal 的海上安全就恢复了。
And he dared to come out from under the pile of leaves.
他敢从树叶堆下面走出来。
He walked back into the room of the princess.
他走回公主的房间。
And he touched her with the golden stick.
他用金棍子碰了她一下。
And the princess revived from her death again.
公主又死而复生了。
They sauntered about in the gardens.
他们在花园里闲逛。
They enjoyed the cool breeze of the morning.
他们享受着清晨凉爽的微风。
They bathed in a lucid pool of water.
他们在清澈的水池中沐浴。
And they ate and drank food in the palace.
他们在宫里吃喝。
And they spent the day in sweet converse.
他们愉快地交谈了一整天。
And they concocted a plan for their deliverance.

他们制定了一个拯救计划。
Keshavaity was going to speak to the old Rakshasi.
凯沙瓦提 (Keshavaity) 正要和老罗刹女
(Rakshasi) 谈话。
She was going to ask on what a Rakshasa's life depended.
她要问罗刹女的性命，是靠什么维持的。
And with that secret they were going to act accordingly.
他们会根据这个秘密采取相应的行动。

The hour of the return of the Rakshasas was coming again.
罗刹娑归来的时辰又要到了。
And events unfolded as they had the evening before.
事情的发展和前一天晚上一样。
The seven hundred flesh-eaters were returning to the palace.
七百名食肉者正在返回宫殿。
Champ Dal touched Keshavati with the silver stick.
尚普·达尔 (Champ Dal) 用银棒触碰了凯沙瓦蒂
(Keshavati)。
She died like the had died the night before.
她死去了，就像前一天晚上死去一样。
Champa-Dal went to the centre of the temple of Siva.
昌帕达尔 (Champa-Dal) 来到了湿婆神庙的中心。
He hid beneath the heaps of sacred trefoil again.
他又躲进了神圣的三叶草堆下面。
He heard the sound of wind rushing.
他听到了风呼啸的声音。
And he heard terrible noises in the palace.
他听到宫殿里传来可怕的声音。
The Rakshasas had come home from their hunt.
罗刹娑狩猎完毕回家了。
They had filled their stomachs with meat.
他们已经吃饱了肉。
Sundry goats, sheep, cows, horses, buffaloes.
各种山羊、绵羊、牛、马、水牛。

And they had devoured elephants too.
它们也吞噬大象。
The old Rakshasi returned to the palace too.
老罗刹女也回宫了。
She went to the room of the sleeping princess.
她来到了正在睡觉的公主的房间。
And she woke her with the stick made of gold.
她用金杖唤醒了她。
"Hye, mye, khye! A human being I smell"
"喂，喵，喵！我闻到人的味道了。"
"I am the only human being here," said the princess.
"我是这里唯一的人类，" 公主说。
"Eat me if you like," added Keshavati.
"如果你愿意的话就吃我吧，" 凯沙瓦蒂补充道。
To this the Rakshasi replied:
对此，罗刹婆回答道：
"Let me eat up your enemies"
"让我吃掉你的敌人"
"Why should I eat you?" she asked the princess.
"我为什么要吃你？" 她问公主。
She laid herself down on the ground.
她躺在地上。
And she looked like a part of the Himalaya mountains.
她看起来就像喜马拉雅山脉的一部分。
Keshavati had a phial of heated mustard oil.
凯沙瓦蒂 (Keshavati) 有一小瓶加热的芥子油。
And she approached the foot of the Rakshasi.
她便来到了罗刹女的脚下。
"Mother, your feet are sore from walking"
"妈妈，你的脚走路很酸痛"
"Let me rub your sore feet with oil"
"让我给你酸痛的脚抹点油"
And she began to rub with oil the Rakshasi's feet.
她开始用油擦拭罗刹女的脚。

Then a few tear-drops fell from the eyes of the princess.

这时，几滴泪珠从公主的眼里落了下来。

And the tear-drops landed on the monster's legs.

泪珠落在了怪物的腿上。

The Rakshasi tasted the tear-drops with her lips.

罗刹女用嘴唇尝了尝泪珠的味道。

And she found the tear-drops tasted briny.

她发现泪珠尝起来有咸味。

"Why are you weeping, darling?" asked the Rakshasi.

"亲爱的，你为什么哭？"罗刹女问道。

"What aileth thee?" she wanted to know.

"你怎么了？"她想知道。

The princess tried to stop herself from crying.

公主强忍着不让自己哭出来。

"Mother, I am weeping because you are old"

"妈妈，我哭是因为您老了"

"When you die one of the Rakshasas will devour me"

"你死了，罗刹女就会吞噬我"

"When I die?! Don't be foolish, girl"

"当我死的时候？！别傻了，姑娘。"

"Don't you know that Rakshasas never die?"

"你不知道罗刹婆是永远不会死的吗？"

"We are not naturally immortal"

"我们并非天生不朽"

"There is a secret to our strength"

"我们的力量有一个秘密"

"But no human can unravel this secret"

"但没有人能够解开这个秘密"

"But let me tell you the secret"

"但让我告诉你这个秘密"

"So that you are comforted a little"

"这样你们可以稍微得到安慰"

"Do you see the pool of water in the palace?"

"你看到宫殿里的水池了吗？"

"In that pool of water is a Sphatikasthamba"
"那水池里有一尊 Sphatikasthamba"
"The Sphatikasthambha is deep in the water"
"Sphatikasthambha 河水很深"
"And on the Sphatikasthambha are two bees"
"Sphatikasthambha 上有两只蜜蜂"
"A human being would have to dive into the water"
"人类必须潜入水中"
"The human being would have to bring the bees onto dry land"
"人类必须把蜜蜂带到陆地上"
"Then the human being would have to kill the two bees"
"那么人类就必须杀死这两只蜜蜂"
"But not a drop of their blood must touch the ground"
"但他们的血一滴都不能沾到地上"
"Only then can a human kill a Rakshasa"
"只有这样，人类才能杀死罗刹。"
"But if the blood touches the ground, a thousand Rakshasas will rise"
"但只要鲜血沾到地上，就会有一千个罗刹鬼出现。"

"But what human will find out this secret?"
"但是哪个人类会发现这个秘密呢？"
"And what human can achieve this feat?"
"哪个人类能实现这一壮举？"
"No human knows the secret to the life of a Rakshasa"
"没有人知道罗刹娑生活的秘密"
"And no human can achieve such a feat"
"没有人能够实现这样的壮举"
"So there is no reason to be sad, my darling"
"所以没有理由悲伤，亲爱的"
"I am practically immortal," she confirmed.
"我实际上是不朽的，" 她证实道。
Keshavati treasured the secret in her memory.

凯沙瓦蒂将这个秘密珍藏在记忆中。
And then she went back to sleep.
然后她又睡着了。

Next morning the Rakshasas, as usual, went away.
第二天早上，罗刹娑们像往常一样走了。
Champa came out of his hiding-place.
恰姆帕从藏身之处走了出来。
And he roused Keshavati from her sleep.
他把凯沙瓦蒂从睡梦中唤醒。
The princess told him the secret she had learnt.
公主告诉了他她所知道的秘密。
Champa-Dal immediately started to prepare himself.
Champa-Dal 立刻开始做准备。
He brought to the pool a knife.
他带着一把刀来到游泳池。
And he brought a quantity of ashes.
他还带来了大量的灰烬。
He took off his heavy clothes.
他脱掉了厚重的衣服。
He put a drop or two of mustard oil into each ear.
他往每只耳朵里滴了一两滴芥子油。
To prevent water from entering into his ears.
以防止水进入他的耳朵。
He swam out into the middle of the water.
他游到了水中央。
And from there he dove down into the pool.
然后他就从那里跳入了水池。
Soon he reached the top of the crystal pillar.
很快他就到达了水晶柱的顶端。
And on Sphatikasthambha were the two bees.
而在 Sphatikasthambha 上有两只蜜蜂。
He caught hold of the two bees he found there.
他抓住了在那里发现的两只蜜蜂。

And he swam up again in a singular breath.

他一口气又游了上来。

He took the knife he had left at the edge of the water.

他拿起留在水边的刀。

And over the ashes he cut up the bees.

他在灰烬上把蜜蜂切碎。

A drop or two of the blood fell from the bees.

一两滴血从蜜蜂身上滴下来。

But their blood did not touch the ground.

但他们的血没有沾到地上。

Instead, their blood landed on the ashes.

相反，他们的血落在了灰烬上。

A terrible scream was heard at a distance.

远处传来一声可怕的尖叫。

The scream was the wailing of the Rakshasas.

这尖叫声是罗刹婆的哀嚎。

They were all running home as fast as they could.

他们都尽可能快地跑回家。

They wanted to prevent the bees from being killed.

他们想防止蜜蜂被杀死。

But they could not reach the palace in time.

但他们没能及时到达宫殿。

Because the bees had already perished.

因为蜜蜂已经灭绝了。

The moment the bees were killed, all the Rakshasas died.

蜜蜂被杀死的瞬间，罗刹婆全部死去。

Their carcases fell on the very spot they were standing.

他们的尸体就倒在他们站立的地方。

Their carcases now blocked the gateway of the palace.

他们的尸体现在堵住了宫殿的大门。

In this manner the seven hundred Rakshasas were
destroyed.

就这样，七百罗刹被消灭了。

Afterwards Champa-Dal and Keshavati got married.
后来，Champa-Dal 和 Keshavati 结婚了。
They made the traditional exchange of garlands of flowers.
他们按照传统交换了花环。
The princess had never been out of the house.
公主从未离开过家。
So she naturally expressed a desire to see the outer world.
所以她很自然地表达了想去看看外面世界的愿望。
Every morning and evening they went on long walks.
每天早晚他们都出去散步。
There was a large river Keshavati wished to bathe in.
有一条大河，Keshavati 希望在其中沐浴。
As she bathed one of Keshavati's hairs came off.
当她洗澡时，Keshavati 的一根头发掉了。
There was a special custom in those times.
那个时候有一个特殊的习俗。
A woman never threw away a hair away by itself.
女人从来不会自己丢掉一根头发。
A sea-shell was floating in the water.
一个贝壳漂浮在水面上。
So Keshavati tied the strand of hair to the sea-shell.
于是，Keshavati 将这缕头发绑在了贝壳上。
And then the couple returned to the palace.
然后这对夫妇就返回了宫殿。
Meanwhile the sea-shell floated down the stream.
与此同时，贝壳顺着溪流漂流而下。
And in due time the sea-shell reached another bathing spot.
不久之后，贝壳就到达了另一个沐浴地点。
This was the bathing spot Sahasra-Dal went to.
这是 Sahasra-Dal 去的沐浴地点。
Here Champa-Dal's brother performed his ablutions.
在这里，Champa-Dal 的兄弟进行了沐浴。
On this day Sahasra-Dal was in the water.
这一天，Sahasra-Dal 在水中。

He was bathing and swimming with his friends.
他正在和朋友们一起洗澡和游泳。
And so the sea-shell floated past the men.
就这样，贝壳从人们身边漂了过去。
The men were in a playful mood that day.
那天，男人们的心情很愉快。
"Whoever gets to the sea-shell first wins"
"谁先拿到贝壳谁就赢了"
And so they all swam towards the sea-shell.
于是它们全都向贝壳游去。
Sahasra-Dal was the strongest swimmer among his friends.
Sahasra-Dal 是朋友中游泳最厉害的。
And so he was the first the reach the sea-shell.
因此他是第一个到达贝壳的人。
Examining the seashell, he found a hair tied to it.
检查贝壳时，他发现上面绑着一根头发。
But it was a hair of extraordinary length.
但这是一根非常长的头发。
He had never seen such a long hair.
他从来没有见过这么长的头发。
The strand of hair was exactly seven cubits long.
这缕头发正好有七肘长。
"This strand of hair must belong to a woman"
"这缕头发一定是女人的"
"And this woman must be very remarkable"
"这个女人一定非常了不起"
"I must see who this remarkable woman is"
"我一定要看看这位非凡的女士是谁"
Sahasra-Dal was determined to find the remarkable woman.
Sahasra-Dal 决心找到这位非凡的女子。
He went home from the river in a pensive mood.
他心想事成，从河边回家。
And he did not proceed to the zenana for breakfast.
他没有去后屋吃早餐。

Instead he remained in the outer part of the palace.
相反，他留在了宫殿的外围。
The queen-mother heard about Sahasra-Dal's meloncholy.
王太后听说了萨哈斯拉·达尔的忧郁症。
And she heard he had not come to breakfast.
她听说他还没有来吃早餐。
So she went to him and asked the reason.
于是她去找他并询问原因。
He showed her the strand of hair he had found.
他向她展示了他发现的那缕头发。
"I must see the woman who's head this strand of hair adorned"
"我必须见见头上戴着这缕头发的女人"
The queen-mother was happy to help her son-in-law.
太后很乐意帮助自己的女婿。
"Very well," she said to him.
"很好，" 她对他说。
"You shall soon have that lady in the palace"
"你很快就会把那位女士带进宫里。"
"I promise you to bring her here"
"我答应你带她来这里"
The queen mother already had a plan.
太后早有打算。
Her favourite maid-servant would be good at the job.
她最喜欢的女仆会很擅长这份工作。
Because this maid-servant was very resourceful.
因为这丫鬟很有办法。
Of course the queen-mother did not really know her maid.
当然，太后并不真正了解她的侍女。
She did not know her favourite maid was a Rakshasi.
她不知道自己最喜爱的侍女是罗刹女。
"Please find the owner of this strand of hair," she asked.
"请找出这根头发的主人。" 她问道。
And her maid-servant more than politely agreed.

她的女仆非常有礼貌地同意了。
"It would my pleasure to find this woman"
"我很高兴能找到这个女人"
"I will soon bring her to the palace"
"我很快就会带她进宫。"
"I will need a boat build from Hajol wood"
"我需要一艘用 Hajol 木材建造的船"
"The oars of the boat must be made from Mon-Paban wood"
"船桨必须用孟巴班木材制成"
The boat makers soon made the boat.
造船工人很快就把船造好了。
And the boat was launched on the stream.
于是船就开进了河里。
The maid-servant went on board of the boat.
婢女上了船。
With her she took some baskets of wicker.
她带着一些柳条篮子。
The baskets of wicker were of curious workmanship.
这些柳条篮子做工十分精巧。
She also took with her some sweetmeats.
她还带了一些甜食。
Into the sweetmeats some poison had been mixed.
糖果里混入了一些毒药。
She snapped her fingers thrice.
她打了三次响指。
And then she uttered the following charm:
然后她念出了以下咒语：
"Boat of Hajol! Oars of Mon Paban!"
"哈卓尔之船！蒙帕班之桨！"
"Take me to the Ghat,"
"带我去河坛，"
"The Ghat in which Keshavati bathes"
"凯沙瓦蒂沐浴的河坛"
The boat heeded to her command.

船听从了她的指挥。
And the boat flew like lightning over the waters.
小船像闪电一样在水面上飞驰。
And the boat left many towns and cities behind.
船儿驶过了许多城镇。
At last the boat stopped at a bathing-place.
最后，船停在一个浴场边。
The Rakshasi maid-servant had reached her goal.
罗刹婢女的目的已经达到了。
She concluded it was the bathing ghat of Keshavati.
她断定这就是凯沙瓦蒂的沐浴场所。
She landed with the sweetmeats in her hand.
她落地时，手里拿着糖果。
She went to the gate of the palace, and cried aloud:
她走到宫门口，高声喊道：
"Oh Keshavati! Keshavati! I am your aunt"
"哦，凯沙瓦蒂！凯沙瓦蒂！我是你的阿姨。"
"Oh Keshavati, I am your mother's sister"
"哦，Keshavati，我是你妈妈的姐妹"
"I have come to see you, my darling"
"我来看你了，亲爱的"
"I have come after so many years"
"这么多年我终于来了"
"Are you home, Keshavati?" she asked.
"你在家吗，凯沙瓦蒂？" 她问道。
The princess heard the words of the false-aunt.
公主听到了假姑妈的话。
She came out of her room and to the entrance of the palace.
她走出房间，来到宫殿的入口处。
She had no doubt that it was really her aunt.
她毫不怀疑那确实是她的姑姑。
And she embraced and kissed her aunt.
她拥抱并亲吻了她的姑姑。
They both wept rivers of joy.

他们俩都喜极而泣。
Although you should know the Rakshasi wept first.
虽然你应该知道罗刹女先哭了。
Keshavati wept with her out of empathy.
凯沙瓦蒂因同情她而与她一起哭泣。
Champa-Dal also believed the Rakshasi to be her aunt.
昌帕达尔（Champa-Dal）也相信罗刹女（Rakshasi）
是她的姑姑。
They all ate and drank and enjoyed the happy occasion.
大家吃吃喝喝，享受这快乐的时光。
And then they took rest in the middle of the day.
然后他们在中午休息。
And they celebrated again in the evening.
晚上他们又再次庆祝。

The next day the celebrations continued at breakfast.
第二天早餐时庆祝活动继续进行。
Champa-Dal had a habit of sleeping after breakfast.
Champa-Dal 有吃完早餐后睡觉的习惯。
Towards afternoon, the supposed aunt said to Keshavati:
下午时分，这位所谓的阿姨对凯沙瓦蒂说道：
"Let us both go to the river and wash ourselves:
"我们俩去河边洗洗吧：
Keshavati replied, "How can we go now?"
凯沙瓦蒂回答说："我们现在怎么走呢？"
"My husband is sleeping," she explained.
"我丈夫正在睡觉，"她解释道。
"Do not worry about your husband's sleep," said the aunt.
"不用担心你丈夫的睡眠，"阿姨说。
"Let him sleep as much as he likes"
"让他想睡多久就睡多久"
"Let me put these sweetmeats near his bedside"
"让我把这些糖果放在他的床边"
"That way, when he awakes, he has something to eat"

"这样，当他醒来时，他就可以吃东西了。"
Then they then went to the river-side.
然后他们就去了河边。
They went close to the spot where the boat was.
他们走近了船所在的地方。
From a distance Keshavati saw the baskets of wicker-work.
从远处，凯沙瓦蒂看到了柳条编织的篮子。
"Aunt, what beautiful things are those!"
"阿姨，那些东西多漂亮啊！"
"I wish I could get some of those wicker baskets"
"我希望我能得到一些这样的柳条篮"
Her aunt happily obliged her.
她的姑姑很高兴地答应了她。
"Come, my child, and look at the wicker baskets"
"孩子，来看这些柳条筐"
"You can have as many baskets as you like"
"你可以拥有任意数量的篮子"
Keshavati at first refused to go into the boat.
起初，Keshavati 拒绝上船。
But her aunt was very persuasive.
但她的姑姑很有说服力。
And finally she went onto the boat.
最后她登上了船。
But once on the boat her aunt did a strange thing.
但有一次在船上，她的姑姑做了一件奇怪的事。
The aunt snapped her fingers thrice and said:
姑姑打了三次响指，说道：
"Boat of Hajol! Oars of Mon-Paban!"
"哈卓尔之船！蒙帕班之桨！"
"Take me to the Ghat,"
"带我去河坛，"
"The Ghat in which Sahasra-Dal bathes"
"萨哈斯拉·达尔沐浴的河坛"
And the boat heeded to her command.

船听从了她的指挥。

And the boat flew like an arrow over the waters.

小船像箭一样在水面上飞驰。

Keshavati was frightened and began to cry.

凯沙瓦蒂（Keshavati）被吓坏了，开始哭泣。

But the boat went on despite her crying.

尽管她哭泣，船还是继续前行。

And the boat left behind many towns and cities.

船儿驶过了许多城镇。

In a trice the boat reached its destination.

不一会儿，船就到达了目的地。

The ghat where Sahasra-Dal was in the habit of bathing.

萨哈斯拉-达尔（Sahasra-Dal）习惯沐浴的河坛。

Keshavati was taken to the palace.

凯沙瓦蒂被带进了宫殿。

Sahasra-Dal admired her beauty and the length of her hair.

Sahasra-Dal 欣赏她的美貌和她的头发的长度。

And the ladies of the palace tried their best to comfort her.

宫中的女官们也尽力安慰她。

But she set up a loud cry of protest.

但她却大声抗议

And she wanted to be taken back to her husband.

她想回到丈夫身边。

Finally she saw that she had been taken captive.

最后她发现自己已经被俘虏了。

So she spoke to the ladies of the palace.

于是她对宫里的女士们说了这些话。

"Upon marriage I made a vow to my husband"

"结婚时我向丈夫许下誓言"

"I promised not to look upon the face of any other man"

"我答应过不看其他男人的脸"

"I promised to uphold this vow for six months"

"我承诺六个月内履行这个誓言"

She was then lodged away from the others in the palace.

然后她被安置在宫殿里，远离其他人。
And she was given a small house to live in.
她被分配到一间小房子居住。
The window of the house overlooked the road.
房子的窗户俯瞰着道路。
There she spent the livelong day.
她在那里度过了漫长的一天。
And there she spent the livelong night.
她在那里度过了一整夜。
Because she had very little sleep.
因为她睡眠很少。
Because her time was spent in sighing and weeping.
因为她的时间都花在叹息和哭泣上了。

In the meantime Champa-Dal awoke from his sleep.
与此同时，Champa-Dal 从睡梦中醒来。
He was distracted with the grief of not finding his wife.
他因找不到妻子而悲痛不已，心烦意乱。
His suspicions turned to the aunt of Keshavati.
他开始怀疑凯沙瓦蒂的姑姑。
He knew she was a cheat and an impostor.
他知道她是个骗子、冒名顶替者。
It must have been her who carried away Keshavati.
肯定是她带走了 Keshavati。
He did not eat the sweetmeats left for him.
他没有吃给他留下的甜食。
Because he suspected the sweets to have been poisoned.
因为他怀疑糖果里有毒。
He threw one of the sweets to a crow.
他把一颗糖果扔给了一只乌鸦。
The moment the crow ate the sweet, it dropped down dead.
乌鸦一吃糖果，就倒地死了。
This confirmed his suspicion of the pretend aunt.
这更加证实了他对这位假阿姨的怀疑。

Maddened with grief, he rushed out of the house.

他悲痛欲绝，冲出了家门。

He was determined to go wherever his feet took him.

他决心跟随自己的脚步去往任何地方。

Like a madman he blubbered, "Oh Keshavati! Oh Keshavati!"

他像疯子一样哭泣着，"哦，凯沙瓦蒂！哦，凯沙瓦蒂！"

He travelled on foot day after day.

他日复一日地步行出行。

And he followed whatever way his feet took him.

无论他的脚步引领他走向何方，他都会跟随。

Six months he spent travelling in this wearisome manner.

他就这样疲惫地旅行了六个月。

After six month he reached the capital of Sahasra-Dal.

六个月后，他到达了萨哈斯拉达尔的首都。

He passed by the gate of the palace.

他路过了宫殿的大门。

And from the road he could see a small house.

从路上他可以看到一座小房子。

And from in the house he could hear sighs.

他能听到屋里传来的叹息声。

Champa-Dal instantly recognized his wife.

Champa-Dal 立刻认出了他的妻子。

And Keshavita instantly recognized her husband.

凯沙维塔立刻就认出了她的丈夫。

Keshavita told her husband everything that had happened.

凯沙维塔把发生的一切告诉了她的丈夫。

"The woman asked to go bathing after breakfast"

"女人要求吃完早餐后去洗澡"

"At the river there was a boat"

"河边有一艘船"

"The woman persuaded me onto the boat"

"那个女人说服我上了船"

"And then the boat took us to this place"
"然后船把我们带到了这个地方"
"I realized that I had been made captive"
"我意识到自己已经被俘虏了"
"So I told them of my vows to you"
"所以我告诉他们我对你的誓言"
"But tomorrow will be the end of six month"
"但明天就是六个月的结束"
There was a custom in those days.
那时候有一个习俗。
The fulfilments of vows were publicly recited.
誓言的履行被公开宣读。
This was normally fulfilled by a learned Brahman.
这通常由博学的婆罗门来完成。
They planned for Champa-Dal to take on this role.
他们计划让 Champa-Dal 担任这一角色。
And so that evening the palace drum was beat.
于是那天晚上，宫鼓敲响了。
The king wanted a learned Brahman to make a recitation.
国王请一位博学的婆罗门来诵读。
The story of Keshavati on the fulfilment of her vow.
凯沙瓦蒂（Keshavati）履行誓言的故事。
Champa-Dal touched the drum and volunteered.
Champa-Dal 摸着鼓自愿参加。
"I will make the recitation of Keshavita's vows"
"我将诵念Keshavita的誓言"
The next morning all assembled in the courtyard.
第二天早上，大家都聚集在院子里。
The old king and the queen mother.
老国王和王太后。
Sahasra-Dal and his wife were there.
Sahasra-Dal 和他的妻子在那里。
All the courtiers and the learned Brahmans of the country.
全国的臣子和博学的婆罗门。

All royalty was under a huge canopy of silk.
所有皇室成员都处于巨大的丝绸华盖之下。
Kashavati was also there, but behind a veil.
卡沙瓦蒂（Kashavati）
也在那里，但她躲在面纱后面。
So that she wouldn't be exposed to the rude gaze of people.
以免她暴露在人们粗鲁的目光之下。
Champa-Dal, the reciter, sat on a dais.
朗诵者 Champa-Dal 坐在讲台上。
And he began to tell the story of Keshavati.
他开始讲述凯沙瓦蒂的故事。
"There was once a poor dimwitted Brahman"
"从前有一个贫穷愚昧的婆罗门"
"This dimwitted man had a wife, but no children"
"这个愚蠢的男人有妻子，但没有孩子"
"But him not having children was probably for the best"
"但他不生孩子或许是最好的选择"
"Because he was barely able to meet his own needs"
"因为他几乎无法满足自己的需求"
"And he could hardly supply enough for his wife"
"他几乎无法养活他的妻子"
"But his dimwittedness was not even his biggest problem"
"但他的愚蠢甚至不是他最大的问题"
And he continued the story as we have followed it.
他继续讲述我们所关注的故事。
And sometimes he turned around to Keshavati.
有时他会转身面向凯沙瓦蒂。
And he asked her if he was telling the story correctly.
他问她他讲述的故事是否正确。
And she told him he was telling the story correctly.
她告诉他，他讲述的故事是正确的。
"The Brahman woman concluded her fate was sealed"
"婆罗门女人认定自己的命运已成定局"
"And she thought her husband would meet the same fate"

"她以为她的丈夫也会遭遇同样的命运"
"And she did not expect her son to be spared either"
"她也不指望自己的儿子能幸免于难"
"That night she hardly slept at all"
"那天晚上她几乎没睡"
"The Rakshasi had prevented her from seeing her husband"
"罗刹女阻止她见她的丈夫"
"Early next morning Champa-Dal went to school"
"第二天一早，Champa-Dal 就去上学了。"
"Before he went to school, she gave her son a golden bottle"
"在儿子上学前，她给了他一个金瓶子"
"In the golden bottle was her own breast milk"
"金瓶里装的是她自己的母乳"
"Carefully watch the colour of the milk"
"仔细观察牛奶的颜色"
During the recitation the Rakshasi maid-servant grew pale.
念诵期间，罗刹婢女脸色变得苍白。
She perceived that her real character was going to be discovered.
她意识到她的真实性格即将被发现。
And Sahasra-Dal was astonished at the knowledge of the reciter.
萨哈斯拉·达尔对朗诵者的知识感到惊讶。
The reciter clearly told the history of the prince's life.
朗诵者清晰地讲述了王子的一生的故事。
"A drop or two of the blood fell from the bees"
"蜜蜂滴了一两滴血"
"But their blood did not touch the ground"
"但他们的血没有沾到地上"
"Instead, their blood landed on the ashes"
"相反，他们的血落在了灰烬上"
"A terrible scream was heard at a distance"
"远处传来一声可怕的尖叫"
"The scream was the wailing of the Rakshasas"

"那尖叫声是罗刹娑的哀嚎"
"They were all running home as fast as they could"
"他们都尽可能快地跑回家"
"They wanted to prevent the bees from being killed"
"他们想防止蜜蜂被杀死"
"But they could not reach the palace in time"
"但他们没能及时到达宫殿"
"Because the bees had already been killed"
"因为蜜蜂已经被杀死了"
"The moment the bees were killed, all the Rakshasas died"
"蜜蜂被杀死的那一刻，所有的罗刹娑都死了。"
"Their carcasses fell on the very spot they were standing"
"他们的尸体就倒在他们站立的地方"
"Their carcasses now blocked the gateway of the palace"
"他们的尸体现在堵住了宫殿的大门"
"In this manner the seven hundred Rakshasas were destroyed"
"就这样，七百罗刹被消灭了。"
All where enthralled by the story of the Rakshasas.
所有人都被罗刹娑的故事迷住了。
Because the story was being told by a true storyteller.
因为这个故事是由一位真正的讲故事的人讲述的。
All enjoyed the story except for the maid-servant.
除了女仆以外，大家都很喜欢这个故事。
Because her real character was bound to be discovered.
因为她的真实性格必然会被发现。
"Champa-Dal touched the drum and volunteered.
"Champa-Dal 触摸了鼓并自愿参加。
"I will make the recitation of Keshavita's vows"
"我将诵念Keshavita的誓言"
"The next morning all assembled in the courtyard"
"第二天早上，大家都聚集在院子里"
"The old king and the queen mother"
"老国王和王太后"

"Sahasra-Dal and his wife were there"
"Sahasra-Dal 和他的妻子在场"
"All the courtiers and the learned Brahmans of the country"
"全国的朝臣和博学的婆罗门们"
"All royalty was under a huge canopy of silk"
"所有皇室成员都身处巨大的丝绸华盖之下"
"Kashavati was also there, but behind a veil"
"Kashavati 也在那里，但她被面纱遮住了。"
"So that she wouldn't be exposed to the rude gaze of people"
"这样她就不会暴露在人们粗鲁的目光之下"
"Champa-Dal, the reciter, sat on a dais"
"诵经者 Champa-Dal 坐在讲台上"
"And he began to tell the story of Keshavati"
"他开始讲述凯沙瓦蒂的故事"
Sahasra-Dal jumped up from his seat.
萨哈斯拉-达尔从座位上跳了起来。
And he embraced the reciter of the story.
他拥抱了故事的朗诵者。
"You can be none other than my brother Champa-Dal"
"你就是我的兄弟 Champa-Dal"
Then the prince was inflamed with rage.
王子听后勃然大怒。
He ordered the maid-servant to come into his presence.
他吩咐女仆来到他面前。
A hole the height of a man was dug in the ground.
地面上被挖出了一个一人高的洞。
And the maid-servant was put into the hole, standing.
于是，那女仆站着被放进了洞里。
Prickly thorns were heaped around her.
她的周围堆满了带刺的荆棘。
Up to the crown of her head she was covered in thorns.
她的头顶上长满了荆棘。
In this way the maid-servant was buried alive.
就这样，婢女被活埋了。

After this all lived happily together for many years.
此后，大家幸福地生活了很多年。
Sahasra-Dal and his princess, and Champa-Dal and Keshavati.
Sahasra-Dal 和他的公主，还有 Champa-Dal 和 Keshavati。

The Story of Swet and Bachanta
斯威特和巴坎塔的故事

There was once upon a time a rich merchant.
从前，有一位富商。
This rich merchant had only one son.
这位富商只有一个儿子。
And he loved his only son very much.
他非常爱他的独子。
He gave to his son whatever he wanted.
他儿子想要什么他就给什么。
Of course his son wanted a beautiful house.
他的儿子当然想要一栋漂亮的房子。
And he also wanted to have a large garden.
他还想要一个大花园。
So a beautiful house was built for him.
于是人们为他建造了一座漂亮的房子。
And a fine garden was made for him too.
还为他建造了一座美丽的花园。
The merchant's son was pleased with the garden.
商人的儿子对这个花园很满意。
And he enjoyed walking in the garden.
他喜欢在花园里散步。
One day a bird's nest caught his attention.
有一天，一个鸟巢引起了他的注意。
This bird happens to be called Toontooni.
这只鸟恰好被称为 Toontooni。
He put his hand into the small bird's nest.
他把手伸进了小鸟巢里。
And in the nest he found an egg.
他在鸟巢里发现了一颗蛋。
He took the egg out of its nest.
他把蛋从窝里拿出来。
There was an almirah in the wall of his house.

他家的墙上有一个衣柜。
So he put the egg in the almirah.
于是他把鸡蛋放进了衣柜里。
He closed the door of the almirah.
他关上了衣柜的门。
And then he thought no more of the egg.
然后他就不再想那个蛋了。
The merchant's son had a house of his own.
商人的儿子有自己的房子。
But he had a house without a household.
但他有房子，却没有家人。
So in his house there was no cook.
所以他家里没有厨师。
But he had no need for his own cook.
但他不需要自己的厨师。
Because his mother regularly sent him food.
因为他的母亲定期给他送食物。
In the morning she sent him breakfast.
早上她给他送来了早餐。
And every day she had dinner sent to him.
她每天都会送晚餐给他。
One day the egg in the almirah burst.
有一天，衣柜里的鸡蛋破了。
But it was not a bird that came out of the egg.
但它并不是从蛋里出来的鸟。
Out of the egg came a beautiful infant.
从蛋里出来了一个美丽的婴儿。
The infant was not a bird, but a human girl.
这个婴儿不是一只鸟，而是一个人类女孩。
But the merchant's son knew nothing of the event.
但商人的儿子对此事一无所知。
He had forgotten everything about the egg.
他已经忘记了有关那颗蛋的一切。
The door of the wall-almirah had been kept closed.

壁橱的门一直处于关闭状态。
However, the merchant's son did not lock the door.
然而商人的儿子却没有锁门。
The child grew up within the wall-almirah.
孩子在壁橱里长大。
She had no knowledge of the merchant's son.
她对这位商人的儿子一无所知。
Nor did she know of anyone else.
她也不认识其他任何人。
When the child could walk it grew curious.
当孩子学会走路时，他变得好奇。
And out of curiosity she opened the door.
出于好奇，她打开了门。
That day, too, the mother had sent breakfast.
那天，母亲也送来了早餐。
And the breakfast had been put on the floor.
早餐被放在了地板上。
The child saw the food that was on the floor.
孩子看到了地板上的食物。
Of course the child ate from the food.
当然，孩子吃了食物。
And then the child returned into the wall.
然后孩子又回到了墙里。
The merchant's mother always made a lot of food.
商人的母亲总是做很多食物。
It was more food than he could possibly eat.
他吃不完那么多食物。
So he didn't notice that any food was missing.
所以他没有注意到食物丢失了。
The girl of the wall-almirah came out every day.
衣柜里的女孩每天都会出来。
And every day she ate a part of the food.
每天她都会吃一部分食物。
After eating the food she returned to the almirah.

吃完饭后，她回到了衣柜。

But with time the girl got older and older.

但随着时间的流逝，女孩越来越老了。

And with age she got bigger and bigger.

随着年龄的增长，她变得越来越大。

And the bigger she got the hungrier she got.

她越长大就越饿。

And she began to eat more of the food each day.

她开始每天吃更多的食物。

Eventually the merchant's son noticed the missing food.

最终，商人的儿子发现了食物丢失了。

But he had no way of knowing where the food went.

但他不知道食物去了哪里。

The last thing he suspected was a girl from inside the almirah.

他最不怀疑的就是衣柜里有一个女孩。

And so he came to a very different conclusion.

因此他得出了一个截然不同的结论。

"Why is mother sending such a small quantity of food?".

"妈妈为什么送来的食物这么少？"

And he had a message sent to his mother.

他还给他妈妈发了一条信息。

"Why am I being sent insufficient food?".

"为什么给我送来的食物不够？"

"And why is the dish served so slovenly?".

"而且菜怎么上得这么马虎？"

Of course we know why the food was insufficient.

我们当然知道为什么食物不够。

And we know why the food was presented slovenly.

我们也知道为什么食物呈现得如此粗糙。

The girl from in the wall ate from his food.

墙里的女孩吃了他的食物。

And as she ate she fingered the rice and curry.

她一边吃，一边用手指触摸米饭和咖喱。

And she always hurried back into her cell in the wall.
她总是匆匆忙忙地回到墙里的牢房里。
So that she would not be seen by anyone.
以免被任何人看见。
She had no time to put the rice in proper order.
她没有时间把米饭摆放整齐。
The mother was astonished at her son's complaint.
母亲对儿子的抱怨感到十分惊讶。
She gave him more than he could eat.
她给他的食物多得他吃不完。
The food was served up on a silver plate.
食物盛在银盘里。
And she neatly arranged the food herself.
她亲自把食物摆放得整整齐齐。
But her son repeated the same complaint again.
但她的儿子又重复了同样的抱怨。
Day after day he complained of the small portions.
他日复一日地抱怨食物分量太少。
Day after day he complained of the messy food.
他日复一日地抱怨食物太乱。
And so his mother began to suspect foul play.
因此他的母亲开始怀疑有谋杀。
She told her son to watch over the food.
她告诉儿子要注意食物。
"See if anyone is eating your food".
"看看有没有人吃你的食物"。
The next day a servant brought the food.
第二天，一个仆人送来了食物。
The servant laid the food in a clean place.
仆人把食物放在干净的地方。
Normally the merchant's son took a bath.
通常商人的儿子会洗澡。
But this day he did not go for a bath.
但这天他没有去洗澡。

Instead, on this day he hid himself nearby.

相反，这天他躲在附近。

From his hiding place he could see the food.

从他的藏身之处他可以看到食物。

The merchant's son did not have to wait for long.

商人的儿子并没有等待太久。

Soon he saw the wall-almirah open.

很快他就看到壁橱打开了。

And he saw a beautiful damsel step out.

他看见一位美丽的少女走了出来。

She could not have been more than sixteen.

她最多不过十六岁。

She sat on the carpet by the breakfast.

她坐在早餐旁边的地毯上。

And she began to eat from the food left on the floor.

她开始吃掉地板上剩下的食物。

The merchant's son came out of his hiding-place.

商人的儿子从藏身之处走了出来。

And the damsel could not escape from him.

而少女却无法逃脱他的追捕。

"Who are you, beautiful creature?".

"你是谁，美丽的生物？"

"You do not seem to be earth-born".

"你看起来不像是土生土长的。"

"Are you one of the daughters of the gods?".

"你是神的女儿之一吗？"

The girl replied, "I do not know who I am".

女孩回答说："我不知道我是谁。"

"But there is one thing I do know," the girl continued.

"但有一件事我确实知道，" 女孩继续说道。

"One day I found myself in the almirah in the wall".

"有一天，我发现自己身处墙内的衣柜里"。

"And since then I have been living in the wall".

"从那时起我就一直住在墙里。"

The merchant's son thought her story was strange.
商人的儿子认为她的故事很奇怪。
But then he thought a bit more about the story.
但后来他对这个故事又想了想。
And he remembered what happened sixteen years ago.
他还记得十六年前发生的事。
He remembered the nest of the toontoori bird.
他记得香椿鸟的巢穴。
And he remembered finding an egg in the nest.
他还记得在鸟巢里发现了一颗蛋。
And he remembered putting the egg in the almirah.
他还记得把鸡蛋放在了衣柜里。
The wall-almirah girl was of uncommon beauty.
壁橱里的女孩有着非凡的美貌。
And the merchant's son was struck by her beauty.
商人的儿子被她的美貌所吸引。
Her beauty made a deep impression on his mind.
她的美貌给他留下了深刻的印象。
And he resolved in his mind to marry her.
他下定决心要娶她。
From then on the girl didn't stay in the almirah.
从此以后女孩就不再呆在衣橱里了。
She was given a room in the merchant's son's house.
商人儿子的房子里给了她一间房间。
The next day the merchant's son wrote a message.
第二天，商人的儿子写了一条消息。
And he had the message sent to his mother.
他还把这条信息发给了他的母亲。
You can guess the general theme of the message.
您可以猜出该消息的大致主题。
The merchant's son said he would like to get married.
商人的儿子说他想结婚。
The mother of the merchant's son reproached herself.
商人儿子的母亲自责道。

She had not tried to find a wife for his son.
她没有尝试为他的儿子找一个妻子。
She felt she should have thought of his marriage.
她觉得她应该考虑他的婚姻。
And so she promptly replied to her son's message.
于是她立即回复了儿子的信息。
She and her father were going to send out ghataks.
她和她的父亲正要送出 ghatak。
The ghataks were going to go to different countries.
这些 ghatak 将会前往不同的国家。
There they were going to look for suitable brides.
他们将在那里寻找合适的新娘。
But the merchant's son said there would be no need.
但商人的儿子说没有必要。
He had secured himself a lovely young lady.
他已经娶到了一位可爱的年轻女士。
If they had no objection, he would introduce her to them.
如果他们不反对的话，他会把她介绍给他们认识。
And so the young lady was taken to the merchant's house.
于是这位年轻女士被带到了商人的家里
The merchant and his wife welcomed the stranger.
商人和他的妻子欢迎了陌生人。
And they were also struck by her unmatched beauty.
他们也被她无与伦比的美貌所震撼。
The girl was of perfect loveliness and grace.
这个女孩非常可爱、优雅。
The parents made no questions to her birth.
父母对她的出生没有提出任何疑问。
And the nuptials were celebrated there and then.
婚礼就在那里举行了。

In the course of time the merchant's son had two sons.
随着时间的推移，商人的儿子有了两个儿子。
The elder of the sons he named Swet.

他给长子起名叫斯韦特 (Swet)。
And the younger son he named Basanta.
他给小儿子起名叫巴桑塔。
After the passing of more time the old merchant died.
又过了一段时间，老商人去世了。
So the merchant's son now became the merchant.
于是商人的儿子就成了商人。
And after some time his mother died too.
过了一段时间，他的母亲也去世了。
Swet and Basanta grew up to be fine lads.
斯威特和巴桑塔长大后成为了优秀的小伙子。
And the elder son was in due time married.
大儿子也到了结婚的年龄。
Sometime after Swet's marriage his mother also died.
斯韦特结婚后不久，他的母亲也去世了。
The girl from in the wall was no more.
墙里的那个女孩已经不复存在了。
The widower lost no time in marrying again.
鳏夫立即又娶了人。
And he had a new young and beautiful wife.
他有了一位年轻漂亮的新妻子。
Swet's wife was older than his stepmother.
斯韦特的妻子比他的继母年纪还大。
So his wife became the mistress of the house.
于是他的妻子就成了这个家的女主人。
The stepmother was like all stepmothers are.
这位继母就和所有的继母一样。
She hated Swet and Basanta with a perfect hatred.
她对斯威特和巴桑塔恨之入骨。
And the two ladies also couldn't stand each other.
而且两位女士也互相看不顺眼。
It so happened one day that a fisherman came.
有一天，碰巧来了一位渔夫。
The fisherman brought to the merchant a fish.

渔夫给商人带了一条鱼。
This fish was of singular and remarkable beauty.
这条鱼美丽非凡。
It was unlike any other fish that had been seen.
它与我们见过的其他鱼都不一样。
And the fish had other qualities too.
而且这种鱼还具有其他特性。
The fisherman explained the wonders of the fish.
渔夫讲解了鱼的奇妙之处。
"Two things will happen if you eat this fish".
"如果你吃了这条鱼，就会发生两件事"。
"When you laugh maniks will drop from your mouth".
"当你笑的时候，咒语就会从你的嘴里掉下来"。
"And when you weep pearls will drop from your eyes".
"当你哭泣时，珍珠会从你的眼中掉落"。
The merchant was astounded by what he had heard.
商人听到后大吃一惊。
And he wanted the wonderful properties of the fish.
他想要鱼的奇妙特性。
And so he bought the fish at one thousand rupees.
于是他以一千卢比的价格买下了这条鱼。
And he put the fish into the hands of Swet's wife.
他把鱼放到了斯韦特妻子的手里。
Because Swet's wife was the mistress of the house.
因为斯威特的妻子是这个家的女主人。
He strictly instructed her to cook the fish well.
他严格指示她把鱼煮好。
And he told her to give the fish to him alone to eat.
他让她把鱼给他一个人吃。
The house-mother however knew the fish's secret.
然而，女舍监知道这条鱼的秘密。
She had overheard what the fisherman had said.
她无意中听到了渔夫说的话。
Secretly she made a different plan in her mind.

她心里暗暗制定了一个不同的计划。
She was going to cook the fish for her husband.
她正要为她的丈夫做鱼。
And she was going to share the fish with his brother.
她要和他的兄弟分享这条鱼。
For her father-in-law she was going to prepare a frog.
她准备为公公准备一只青蛙。
Soon she had finished cooking the marvelous fish.
很快她就把这条美味的鱼烹好了。
And she had finished cooking a frog too.
她还煮完了一只青蛙。
But from the kitchen she could hear a squable.
但她听见厨房里传来争吵声。
She could hear who it was that was arguing.
她听得出来是谁在争吵。
Her stepmother-in-law and her husband's brother.
她的继母和她丈夫的兄弟。
And she understood the cause of the argument.
她也明白争论的原因。
Basanta was still but a young lad.
巴桑塔还只是个年轻人。
But he was passionately fond of his pigeons.
但他非常喜爱他的鸽子。
And he tamed his pigeons very well.
他非常善于驯服他的鸽子。
Nonetheless, one of his pigeons had escaped.
尽管如此，他的一只鸽子还是逃走了。
And the pigeon flew into his stepmother's room.
鸽子飞进了他继母的房间。
His stepmother hid the pigeon in her clothes.
他的继母把鸽子藏在衣服里。
Basanta rushed after the pigeon into the room.
巴桑塔追着鸽子冲进了房间。
And he loudly demanded to have the pigeon back.

他大声要求把鸽子归还。
His stepmother denied having the pigeon.
他的继母否认拥有这只鸽子。
Swet, however, did know she had the pigeon.
然而，斯威特确实知道她有这只鸽子。
And the older brother forcibly took the bird.
而哥哥则强行把鸟拿走了。
And he freed the pigeon from her clothes.
他把鸽子从她的衣服里放了出来。
And he gave the pigeon back to his brother.
他把鸽子还给了他的兄弟。
The stepmother cursed and swore, and added;
继母咒骂着，并补充道；
"Wait until the head of the house comes home".
"等到一家之主回家"。
"He will get no water till he sheds your blood".
"除非他流出你的血，否则他将得不到水。"
Swet's wife called her husband and said to him;
斯威特的妻子打电话给她的丈夫并告诉他；
"My dearest lord, that woman is a most wicked woman".
"我最亲爱的大人，那个女人是一个极其邪恶的女人。"
"And she has boundless influence over my father-in-law".
"她对我岳父的影响力是无穷的。"
"She will make him do what she has threatened".
"她会让他履行她所威胁的义务。"
"All our lives are in imminent danger".
"我们所有人的生命都处于迫在眉睫的危险之中"。
"But let us first eat a little," she added.
"但我们先吃一点东西吧，"她补充道。
"And then let us all three run away from this place".
"那么我们三个就逃离这里吧。"
Swet forthwith called Basanta to him.
斯威特立即把巴桑塔叫到身边。

And he told him what he had heard from his wife.
他把从妻子那里听到的事情告诉了丈夫。
They resolved to run away before nightfall.
他们决定在天黑之前逃跑。
The woman placed before her husband the fish.
女人把鱼放在丈夫面前。
And her brother-in-law ate of the fish too.
她的姐夫也吃了鱼。
And they ate of the fish heartily.
他们尽情地吃着鱼。
The woman packed up all her jewels in a box.
女人把她所有的珠宝都装进了一个盒子里。
There was only one horse in the stables.
马厩里只有一匹马。
But the horse was of uncommon fleetness.
但这匹马却异常敏捷。
They could all sit on the horse together.
他们可以一起坐在马上。
Swet held the reins of the horse.
斯威特握着马缰绳。
The woman sat in the middle of the horse.
女人坐在马的中间。
And she had the jewel-box in her lap.
她的腿上放着珠宝盒。
And Basanta sat on the rear of the horse.
巴桑塔则坐在马后座上。
The horse galloped with the utmost swiftness.
这匹马飞奔得飞快。
They passed through many a plain and noted town.
他们穿过了许多平原和著名的城镇。
After midnight they found themselves in a forest.
午夜过后，他们发现自己身处一片森林。
And they were not far from the banks of a river.
他们距离河岸不远。

Here the most untoward event took place.
最不幸的事情就在这里发生了。
Swet's wife began to feel the pains of child-birth.
斯韦特的妻子开始感受到分娩的痛苦。
They dismounted from the horse without delay.
他们立即下了马。
And within an hour Swet's wife gave birth to a son.
不到一小时，斯韦特的妻子就生下了一个儿子。
What were the two brothers to do in this forest?
两兄弟要在这片森林里做什么呢？
They knew that a fire had to be kindled.
他们知道必须点燃一把火。
The mother and the new-born baby needed warmth.
母亲和新生儿需要温暖。
But from where was there fire to be gotten?
但是火从哪里来呢？
There were no human habitations visible.
看不到任何人类居住的地方。
Nonetheless, a fire had to be procured.
尽管如此，还是必须生火。
And it was the winter month of December.
当时正值冬季十二月。
The mother and the baby would certainly perish.
母亲和婴儿必定会死去。
Swet told Basanta to sit beside his wife.
斯韦特让巴桑塔坐在他妻子旁边。
And he set out in the darkness of the night.
于是他在漆黑的夜里出发了。
And he went in search of wood to make a fire.
他出去寻找木柴来生火。
Swet walked many a mile through the darkness.
斯威特在黑暗中走了好几英里。
But despite the distance he saw no human habitations.
但尽管距离很远，他却没有看到人类居住的地方。

But eventually his eyes were given some help.
但最终他的眼睛得到了一些帮助。
The genial light of Sukra somewhat illumined his path.
苏克拉的和煦光芒多少照亮了他的道路。
And he saw at a distance what seemed a large city.
他远远地看见一座看似很大的城市。
He was congratulating himself on his journey's end.
他正在为旅程的结束而庆贺。
And he congratulated himself for finding fire.
他为自己找到了火而感到庆幸。
The fire that was going to benefit his poor wife.
这场火灾原本是为了造福他可怜的妻子。
His wife that was lying cold in the forest.
他的妻子正躺在森林里，浑身冰冷。
The fire that was going to save his new-born child.
这场大火将要拯救他刚出生的孩子。
The new-born baby born into the coldness.
寒冷中诞生的新生婴儿。
Suddenly an elephant shot across his path.
突然，一头大象冲到他的路上。
The elephant was gorgeously caparisoned.
大象装扮得十分华丽。
And the elephant gently picked him with his trunk.
大象用鼻子轻轻地把他挑了起来。
He placed him on the rich howdah on its back.
他把他放在华丽的象轿上。
The elephant then walked rapidly towards the city.
大象便快步向城市走去。
Swet was quite taken aback by the events.
斯威特对这一事件感到非常吃惊。
He did not understand the elephant's actions.
他不理解大象的行为。
And he wondered what was in store for him.
他不知道自己将会面临什么。

A crown is that which was in store for him.
为他准备的就是一顶王冠。
He was being taken to the chief city of a kingdom.
他被带到了一个王国的首府。
In this kingdom every morning a king was elected.
在这个王国里，每天早上都会选举一位国王。
Because the kings of this city lasted but a day.
因为这座城的国王只存在了一天。
Every night the new king joined the queen in her room.
每天晚上，新国王都会来到王后的房间。
And every morning the previous king was found dead.
每天早上都会有人发现前任国王死了。
No one knew what caused the deaths of the kings.
没有人知道导致国王死亡的原因。
Not even the queen knew what caused their death.
甚至连女王都不知道他们的死因。
So this kingdom had its own king-maker.
所以这个王国有自己的造王者。
The elephant who suddenly took hold of Swet.
大象突然抓住了斯威特。
Early in the morning the elephant roamed about.
清晨，大象四处游荡。
Sometimes the elephant went to distant places.
有时大象会去很远的地方。
And every evening the elephant returned with a man.
每天傍晚，大象都会带着一个人回来。
The man on the elephant's became their king.
骑在大象身上的人成为了大象的国王。
The elephant majestically marched through the streets.
大象威风凛凛地在街道上行进。
A crowd of people welcomed their new king.
一大群人欢迎他们的新国王。
But Swet did not yet understand their cheers.
但斯威特还不明白他们的欢呼声。

The elephant entered the kingdom's palace.

大象进入了王国的宫殿。

And the elephant placed Swet on the throne.

大象把斯威特安置在了王座上。

Amid much rejoicing he was proclaimed king.

在一片欢腾声中，他被拥立为国王。

But there were lamentations in the crowd too.

但人群中也传来哀叹声。

In the course of the day he heard of the curse.

那天他听说了这个诅咒。

The nightly death of every newly elected king.

每位新当选的国王每晚都会去世。

But Swet was possessed of great discretion.

但斯威特非常谨慎。

And he had the courage not to try an escape.

他有勇气不去尝试逃跑。

He took every precaution that he could take.

他采取了一切可能采取的预防措施。

But he did not know how to avert the catastrophe.

但他不知道如何避免这场灾难。

And he knew not what expedients to adopt.

他不知道该采取什么办法。

Because he didn't know the nature of the danger.

因为他不知道危险的性质。

He resolved, however, upon two things;

然而，他决定做两件事；

He was going to go armed into the bedchamber.

他正要带着武器走进卧室。

And he was going to stay awake the whole night.

他将整晚不睡觉。

The queen was young and of exquisite beauty.

女王年轻且美丽绝伦。

Guileless and benevolent was the expression of her face.

她脸上的表情真诚而仁慈。

It was impossible to attribute her any malice.
不可能将任何恶意归咎于她。
No one believed she caused all the kings' deaths.
没有人相信她导致了所有国王的死亡。
In the queen's chamber Swet spent an agreeable evening.
斯威特在王后的房间里度过了一个愉快的夜晚。
As the night advanced the queen fell asleep.
夜幕降临，女王睡着了。
But Swet kept awake, and was on the alert.
但斯威特始终保持清醒，并保持警惕。
He looked at every creek and corner of the room.
他查看了房间的每条小溪和角落。
And he expected every minute to be murdered.
他预料到每一分钟都会被浪费掉。
But the queen did not rise to murder him.
但女王并没有起身去谋杀他。
And no one entered the room to murder him either.
也没有人进入房间谋杀他。
Nor did he feel anything other than sleepiness.
除了困倦之外，他没有任何其他感觉。
But in the dead of night he perceived something.
但在深夜里他察觉到了一些东西。
A thread was coming out the queen's nostril.
一根线从女王的鼻孔里出来了。
The thread was so thin that it was almost invisible.
线非常细，几乎看不见。
Slowly the thread reached several yards in length.
线慢慢地长到了几码长。
And eventually all the thread came out.
最后所有的线索都出来了。
Only then did the thread begin to grow thicker.
这时线才开始变粗。
Soon the thread took on its real shape.
很快，线就呈现出了它的真实形状。

The thread was in fact a huge serpent.
这根线其实是一条巨大的蛇。
Immediately Swet cut off the head of the serpent.
斯威特立即砍掉了蛇的头
The body of the serpent wriggled violently.
大蛇身躯剧烈的蠕动着。
He sat quiet in the room, expecting other adventures.
他静静地坐在房间里，期待着其他的冒险。
But nothing else happened the rest of the night.
但那天晚上剩下的时间没有发生其他事情。
The queen slept longer than usual.
女王睡得比平时久。
Because she had been relieved of the huge snake.
因为她已经摆脱了那条巨蛇。
Early next morning the ministers came.
第二天一早，大臣们就来了。
They were expecting to hear of the king's death.
他们期待听到国王去世的消息。
The ladies of the bedchamber knocked at the door.
寝宫里的女士们敲了敲门。
But to their astonishment Swet come out.
但令他们惊讶的是，Swet 出现了。
The folk learned the mystery of all the kings' deaths.
民众得知了所有国王死亡的秘密
And now the country rejoiced their permanent king.
现在，全国人民都为他们的永久国王而欢欣鼓舞。
There is a strange thing you probably noticed.
您可能注意到了一件奇怪的事情。
Swet did not remember his wife he left behind.
斯威特不记得他留下的妻子。
It is a strange thing, nevertheless it is true.
这是一件很奇怪的事情，但这是事实
Nor did he remember the defenceless new-born babe.
他也不记得那个毫无防御能力的新生婴儿。

And he did not remember his brother either.
他也不记得他的兄弟了。
He had no time to remember when the elephant came.
他没有时间记住大象什么时候来的。
On the first night he had to worry for his own life.
第一天晚上，他不得不担心自己的生命安全。
And now the crown brought on his forgetfulness.
如今，王冠却让他忘记了一切。
But he had entrusted his wife and child to Basanta.
但他已将妻子和孩子托付给了巴桑塔。
And his brother sat waiting for many weary hours.
他的哥哥坐着等了好几个小时，非常疲惫。
Every moment he expected to see Swet return with fire.
他时刻盼望着看到斯威特带着火回来。
But the whole night passed away without his return.
但一整夜过去了，他还没有回来。
At sunrise he went to the bank of the river.
日出时，他来到河岸。
There he anxiously looked about for his brother.
他在那里焦急地寻找他的兄弟。
But his waiting and searching were all in vain.
但他的等待和寻找都是徒劳的。
Distressed beyond measure, he wept at the riverside.
他悲痛万分，在河边哭泣。
As he was weeping a boat was passing by.
当他哭泣的时候，有一艘船经过。
In the boat a merchant was returning from business.
船上有一位商人做完生意回来。
The boat was not far from the shore.
船离岸边不远了。
So the merchant could see Basanta weeping.
所以商人可以看到巴桑塔在哭泣。
Something struck the attention of the merchant.
有一件事引起了商人的注意。

By the weeping man appeared to be a pile of pearls.
哭泣的男人旁边似乎是一堆珍珠。
The merchant requested the boatman to halt.
商人请求船夫停下来。
And the merchant went to the weeping man.
于是商人走向了哭泣的男人。
By the weeping man was in fact a pile of pearls.
哭泣的男人身边其实有一堆珍珠。
And the pearls were of the highest quality.
而且这些珍珠的品质都是最高品质的。
And another thing astonished the merchant.
还有一件事让商人大吃一惊。
The pile of pearls grew larger every second.
珍珠堆每秒都在变大。
Because the man was crying, but not tears.
因为那个男人在哭，但哭的不是眼泪。
Because his tears turned to pearls on the ground.
因为他的眼泪落到地上，变成了珍珠。
The merchant stowed away the pearls into his boat.
商人把珍珠收进他的船里。
Then the merchant got his servants to help him.
于是商人叫仆人来帮助他。
And together they captured the crying man.
他们一起抓住了那个哭泣的男人。
They put him on board of the vessel.
他们把他送上了船。
And he tied him to one of the ship's masts.
然后他把他绑在船的一根桅杆上。
Basanta, of course, tried his best to resist.
巴桑塔当然竭力抵抗。
But what could he do against so many sailors?
但是面对这么多水手他能做什么呢？
He thought of his brother who never returned.
他想起了再也没有回来的哥哥。

He thought of his sister-in-law in the forest.
他想起了森林里的嫂子。
And he thought of his newly born niece.
他又想到了自己刚出生的侄女。
And he cried even more bitterly than before.
而且哭得比刚才更伤心了。
His weeping mightily pleased the merchant.
他的哭泣让商人非常高兴。
Because even more pearls were falling to the ground.
因为有更多的珍珠掉落到地上。
And the merchant became richer and richer.
商人变得越来越富有。
Eventually the merchant reached his native town.
最终，商人到达了他的家乡。
When they got there he confined Basanta in a room.
当他们到达那里时，他把巴桑塔关在一个房间里。
At stated hours every day he had him whipped.
每天在规定的时间，他都会鞭打他。
In order to make him shed yet more tears.
为了让他流下更多的眼泪。
And every tear converted into a bright pearl.
每一滴泪水都化作一颗璀璨的珍珠。
The merchant one day said to his servants;
有一天，商人对他的仆人说；
"The fellow is making me rich by his weeping".
"这家伙的哭泣让我变得富有。"
"Let us see what he gives me by laughing".
"让我们看看他笑了会给我带来什么。"
Accordingly, he began to tickle his captive.
于是，他开始挠他的俘虏的痒痒。
Upon being tickled Basanta began to laugh.
巴桑塔被挠痒痒后开始大笑。
Of course he was not laughing out of happiness.
当然，他并不是因为高兴而笑。

But none the less maniks dropped from his mouth.
但尽管如此，咒语还是从他的嘴里冒了出来。
After this Basanta was not just whipped anymore.
从此以后，巴桑塔就不再只是被鞭打了。
Now he was alternately whipped and tickled.
现在他被交替鞭打和挠痒痒。
All day and far into the night he was exploited.
他整天都在遭受剥削，直到深夜。
The merchant's wealth increased day and night.
商人的财富日夜增加。
Soon he became the wealthiest man in the land.
很快他就成为了这个国家最富有的人。
But let us return to Basanta's subjugation later.
但我们稍后再讨论巴桑塔的征服。
Now let us turn our attention to Swet's wife.
现在让我们把注意力转向斯韦特的妻子。

Swet's abandoned wife was still in the forest.
斯威特被抛弃的妻子仍在森林里。
She had just given birth to her child.
她刚刚生下孩子。
But now she was alone in the forest.
但现在她独自一人在森林里。
First her husband had abandoned her.
首先，她的丈夫抛弃了她。
And now her brother-in-law abandoned her too.
现在她的姐夫也抛弃了她。
Imagine how overwhelmed with grief she felt.
想象一下她感到多么悲痛欲绝。
Alone, and in a forest, far from civilization.
独自一人，在森林里，远离文明。
Her case was indeed deserving of sympathy.
她的情况确实值得同情。
She wept rivers of sad and lonely tears.

她悲伤而孤独地哭成了河。

Excessive grief, however, brought her relief.

然而，过度的悲伤却给她带来了解脱。

She fell asleep with the new-born in her arms.

她抱着新生儿睡着了。

While she was deep in sleep another tragedy took place.

当她沉睡时，另一起悲剧发生了。

It so happened that the Kotwal was passing by.

碰巧的是，科特瓦尔（Kotwal）正好路过这里。

He had recently suffered his own misfortune.

他最近也遭遇了不幸。

But his misfortune was of a different nature.

但他的不幸却有着不同的性质。

The children his wife bore died shortly after birth.

他妻子所生的孩子出生后不久就死了。

And he was now going to bury the last infant.

现在他要埋葬最后一个婴儿。

He was heading to the banks of the river.

他正朝河岸走去。

The place where the other infants were buried.

其他婴儿被埋葬的地方。

But then he saw the woman sleeping in the forest.

但随后他看到那个女人正在森林里睡觉。

And in her arms he saw her holding a baby.

他看到她怀里抱着一个婴儿。

The infant was a lively and beautiful boy.

这个婴儿是一个活泼漂亮的男孩。

IIis liveliness did not disturb his mother's sleep.

他的活泼并没有打扰母亲的睡眠。

The Kotwal wanted the lovely infant very much.

Kotwal 一家非常想要这个可爱的婴儿。

He quietly took the child from his mother.

他悄悄地把孩子从母亲身边抱走。

And in her arms he placed his own dead child.

他将自己死去的孩子放在了她的怀里。
Of course this is not what he could tell his wife.
当然这不是他能告诉妻子的。
"We both thought that our son had died".
"我们都以为我们的儿子已经死了"。
"And I carried his body to the river bank".
"我把他的尸体抬到了河岸边"。
"And that was when a miracle occurred".
"就在那时，奇迹发生了。"
"Once more our son opened his young eyes".
"我们的儿子再次睁开了他幼小的眼睛"。
"And now we have a beautiful and lively boy".
"现在我们有了一个漂亮又活泼的男孩。"
But Swet's wife did not know the true events.
但斯韦特的妻子并不知道事情的真相。
When she woke she held the dead child in her arms.
当她醒来时，她怀里抱着死去的孩子。
And she thought it was her child that had died.
她以为是她的孩子死了。
The distress of her mind may easily be imagined.
她的内心有多么痛苦是可想而知的。
The whole world became dark to her.
整个世界对她来说都变得黑暗了。
She was distracted by the loss of her child.
失去孩子使她心烦意乱。
And in her distraction she formed a resolution.
在心烦意乱的时候，她下定了决心。
She had resolved to take her own life.
她已决心自杀。
The river was not far from where she had slept.
这条河距离她睡觉的地方不远。
And she determined to drown herself in the river.
她决心投河自尽。
She took in her hand the bundle of jewels.

她手里拿着那捆珠宝。
And then she proceeded to the river-side.
然后她继续向河边走去。
An old Brahman was at no great distance.
一位老婆罗门就在不远处。
The Brahman was performing his morning ablutions.
婆罗门正在进行晨间沐浴。
He noticed the woman going into the water.
他注意到那个女人正走进水里。
Naturally he thought that she was going to bathe.
他自然而然地以为她要去洗澡。
But then he saw her going into the deep waters.
但随后他看到她走进了深水区。
Something akin to suspicion arose in his mind.
他心中升起一丝类似怀疑的情绪。
The Brahman discontinued his devotions.
婆罗门不再继续他的虔诚信仰。
He too waded out towards the river's depth.
他也向河深处涉水而去。
And he ordered the woman to come to him.
他命令那女人到他面前来。
Swet's wife heard the old man calling her.
斯威特的妻子听到老人在呼唤她。
So she retraced her steps to the old man.
于是她沿着原路返回，来到了老人身边。
"What were your intentions?" asked the Braham.
"你的意图是什么？" 布拉罕问道。
And the woman confirmed his suspicions.
而这位女士证实了他的怀疑。
"I was going to put an end to my life".
"我打算结束我的生命" 。
And she thanked the Brahman for saving her.
她感谢婆罗门救了她。
"Accept these jewels as a sign of appreciation".

"接受这些珠宝作为感谢的象征"。

The Brahman accepted the sign of appreciation.

婆罗门接受了这个感谢之意。

But he was more interested in her story.

但他对她的故事更感兴趣。

And at his request she related her story.

在他的请求下，她讲述了自己的故事。

She had escaped from her stepmother in law.

她从继婆那里逃了出来。

In the forest she gave birth to a child.

她在森林里生了一个孩子。

First her husband went looking for fire.

首先，她的丈夫去寻找火。

But her husband never came back to her.

但她的丈夫再也没有回到她身边。

Then her brother-in-law looked for her husband.

然后她的姐夫来找她的丈夫。

But her brother-in-law did not return either.

但她的姐夫也没有回来。

Eventually she fell asleep with her child.

最后她和孩子一起睡着了。

But when she woke her child was dead.

但当她醒来时，她的孩子已经死了。

And that's when she decided to drown herself.

就在那时，她决定投河自尽。

She felt the relieve of telling her fate.

告诉了自己的命运后，她感到如释重负。

The Brahman invited the woman to his house.

婆罗门邀请这名女子到他家里做客。

And the woman was accepted into his family.

而这个女人也被接纳进了他的家庭。

The Brahman's wife treated her like a daughter.

婆罗门的妻子待她如同女儿一样。

And she spent years with her new family.

她与新家庭一起度过了数年。
Swet spend those years in his kingdom.
斯威特在他的王国里度过了那些年。
Basanta spent those years being tortured.
巴桑塔那些年一直饱受折磨。
And the adopted son of the Kotwal grew up.
科特瓦尔的养子长大了。
The Brahman's house was not far from the Kotwal's.
婆罗门的房子离科特瓦尔家不远。
So the Kotwal's son met the Brahman's adopted daughter.
于是，科特瓦尔的儿子遇见了婆罗门的养女。
And the lad thought he fell in love with her.
小伙子以为自己爱上了她。
He spoke to his father about the woman.
他向父亲谈论了那个女人。
And the father spoke to the Brahman about the woman.
父亲便向婆罗门讲述了这个女人的事。
The Brahman's rage knew no bounds.
婆罗门的愤怒是无止境的。
"What is this insolence!" the Brahman protested.
"这是什么傲慢行为！" 婆罗门抗议道。
"Your son is the son of an infidel".
"你的儿子是异教徒的儿子" 。
"How can he aspire to the hand of a Brahman's daughter!?".
"他怎么能向往婆罗门的女儿呢？！"
"A dwarf may as well aspire to catch hold of the moon!".
"矮人也想抓住月亮！"
But the Kotwal's son determined to have her by force.
但科特瓦尔的儿子决心用武力夺取她。
One day he scaled the wall of the Brahman's house.
有一天，他爬上了婆罗门家的墙。
He got upon the thatched roof of the cow-house.
他爬上了牛棚的茅草屋顶。
And from that lofty position he reconnoitered.

他从那个高处进行侦察。

And he saw two young calves below him.

他看见下面有两只小牛犊。

And he overheard the conversation of two young calves.

他无意中听到了两头小牛犊的谈话。

"Men accuse us of brutish ignorance and immorality".

"人们指责我们愚昧无知、不道德。"

"But in my opinion men are fifty times worse".

"但在我看来，男人要糟糕五十倍。"

"What makes you say so, brother?" the calf asked.

小牛问道："兄弟，你为什么这么说呢？"

"Have you witnessed instances of human depravity?".

"你见过人类堕落的例子吗？"

"Who is a greater monster than the Kotwal's son?".

"谁比科特瓦尔的儿子更可怕？"

"The same lad standing on the thatched roof".

"同一个少年站在茅草屋顶上"。

"The roof of this hut above our heads".

"我们头顶上这间小屋的屋顶"。

"I thought he was just the son of our Kotwal".

"我以为他只是我们科特瓦尔的儿子。"

"I never heard that he was exceptionally vicious".

"我从未听说他特别凶恶"。

"You may have never heard of his wickedness".

"你可能从未听说过他的邪恶行为"。

"But now you will hear of his wickedness from me".

"但现在你会从我口中得知他的恶行"。

"This wicked lad is now making immoral plans".

"这个邪恶的小伙子现在正在制定不道德的计划"。

"He is trying get married to his own mother!".

"他想和自己的母亲结婚！"

The First Calf then related the whole story.

第一头小牛随后讲述了整个故事。

And the inquisitive Second Calf listened.

好奇的第二头小牛听着。

And the calf told Swet's and Basanta's story.

小牛讲述了斯韦特和巴桑塔的故事。

"A merchant built a house for his son"

"一位商人为他的儿子建造了一栋房子"

"In the garden of the house was a Toontooni bird"

"房子的花园里有一只 Toontooni 鸟"

"In the nest of the Toontooni bird was an egg"

"Toontooni 鸟的巢里有一枚蛋"

"The merchant's son put the egg in a almirah"

"商人的儿子把鸡蛋放进了衣柜里"

"Out of the egg came a beautiful girl"

"从蛋里出来了一个美丽的女孩"

"Eventually the merchant's son married this beautiful girl"

"最终商人的儿子娶了这位美丽的女孩"

"Together they had two children; Swet and Basanta"

"他们有两个孩子：Swet 和 Basanta"

"Some time later the grandfather of the children died"

"过了一段时间，孩子们的祖父去世了"

"Some time later again their grandmother died too"

"过了一段时间，他们的祖母也去世了。"

"At the right time, the oldest son, Swet, got married"

"时机成熟时，大儿子斯威特结婚了"

"His mother, the Toontooni woman, died sometime later"

"他的母亲，那个图托尼女人，后来去世了。"

"Soon after their father married a younger woman"

"不久之后，他们的父亲就娶了一位年轻女子"

"But their new stepmother hated her stepsons"

"但他们的新继母讨厌她的继子"

"And she also hated her new stepdaughter-in-law"

"而且她也讨厌她的新继儿媳"

"One day a fisherman happened to visit the merchant"

"有一天，一位渔夫碰巧拜访了商人"

"The Fisherman had sold the merchant a magical fish"

"渔夫卖给了商人一条神奇的鱼"
"Whoever ate the fish would laugh maniks"
"吃这条鱼的人都会大笑"
"And whoever ate the fish would weep pearls"
"吃鱼的人会哭出珍珠"
"The same day there was an argument over some pigeons"
"同一天，有人因为几只鸽子而发生了争吵"
"The stepmother was terribly vengeful to her stepsons"
"继母对继子们怀有极强的报复心"
"And she swore revenge on her stepsons"
"她发誓要向她的继子们复仇"
"That day Swet, his wife, and Basanta escaped"
"那天，斯韦特和他的妻子以及巴桑塔逃走了"
"But before leaving they ate the magical fish"
"但在离开之前，他们吃了那条神奇的鱼"
"On their journey Swet's wife gave birth to a baby boy"
"在旅途中，斯韦特的妻子生了一个男孩"
"Swet went to look for wood to make a fire"
"斯威特去找木柴生火"
"But he was carried away by an elephant"
"但他被大象叼走了"
"He was taken to a Queen haunted by a snake"
"他被带到了一位被蛇缠身的女王那里"
"But he succeeded in killing the serpent"
"但他成功杀死了蛇"
"And so he became king of the land""Basanta went looking for his brother"
"于是他成为了这片土地的国王。"
"巴桑塔去寻找他的兄弟了。"
"But he was captured by a merchant"
"但他被一个商人抓住了"
"And now he's flogged and tickled daily"
"现在他每天都要挨鞭子、挨搔痒"
"And he cries pearls and laughs maniks"

"他哭的是珍珠，笑的是怪物"
"The Kotwal's son had died that night"
"科特瓦尔的儿子那天晚上死了"
"So the Kotwal exchanged the two babies"
"所以科特瓦尔人交换了两个婴儿"
"The mother couldn't bear the loss of her child"
"母亲无法承受失去孩子的痛苦"
"So she made the decision to drown herself"
"所以她决定投河自尽"
"But there was a Brahman that saved her life"
"但有一位婆罗门救了她的命"
"And this Brahman took her into his home"
"这位婆罗门就把她带回了自己的家。"
"The Kotwal's son grew up a hardy boy"
"科特瓦尔的儿子长大后是个坚强的孩子"
"And he fell in love with the woman"
"他爱上了这个女人"
"And now he stands on the roof"
"现在他站在屋顶上"
"And he's intent on having the woman"
"他一心想得到这个女人"
All this the Kotwal's son heard.
这一切都被科特瓦尔的儿子听到了。
And he was struck with horror.
他感到十分恐惧。
He forthwith got down from the thatch.
他立刻从茅草屋顶上下来。
And he went home to his father.
然后他就回家去见他父亲了。
And he said he must speak with the king.
他说他必须和国王谈谈。
The father protested against the request.
父亲对这一要求提出抗议。
But he got an interview with the king.

但他得到了与国王的面谈机会。
He told the king about the two calves.
他向国王讲述了这两头小牛的故事。
And he repeated the whole story.
他又把整个故事讲了一遍。
The king now remembered his poor wife.
国王这才想起了他可怜的妻子。
So a servant was sent to the Brahman.
于是，一个仆人被派去见婆罗门。
And the Brahman was richly rewarded.
婆罗门得到了丰厚的回报。
And his wife was brought back to the palace.
他的妻子被带回了宫殿。
His wife was put in her proper position.
他的妻子被安置在了她应有的位置上。
And she became queen of the kingdom.
她成为了王国的王后。
The reputed son of the Kotwal was readopted.
科特瓦尔 (Kotwal)
的名声显赫的儿子被重新收养了。
And he was proclaimed heir to the throne.
他被宣布为王位继承人。
Basanta was brought out of the dungeon.
巴桑塔被带出了地牢。
And the wicked merchant was buried alive.
而这个邪恶的商人则被活埋了。
And thorns were put in his burying-place.
他的埋葬处被荆棘所覆盖。
And all lived together happily for many years.
大家幸福地生活了很多年
Swet, his wife and son, and Basantas.
斯韦特、他的妻子和儿子，还有巴桑塔斯。

The Evil Eye of Sani
萨尼的邪恶之眼

Once upon a time Sani and Lakshmi fell out with each other.

很久以前，萨尼（Sani）和拉克希米（Lakshmi）吵架了。

Sani, also known as Saturn, is the God of bad luck.

萨尼，又称土星，是厄运之神。

And Lakshmi is the Goddess of good luck.

拉克希米（Lakshmi）是吉祥女神。

And these two Gods fell out with each other in heaven.

这两位神在天堂里互相吵翻了。

Sani said he was higher in rank than Lakshmi.

萨尼称他的级别比拉克希米高。

And Lakshmi said she was higher in rank than Sani.

拉克希米说她的级别比萨尼高。

But there were just as many Gods as there were Goddesses.

但男神的数量和女神的数量是一样的。

Therefore the dispute could not be settled in heaven.

因此，争端无法在天堂得到解决。

The contending deities agreed to refer the matter to humans.

争执的神灵同意将此事提交人类处理。

The humans had a name for wisdom and justice.

人类以智慧和正义命名。

There lived at that time upon earth a man named Sribatsa.

当时地球上住着一位名叫斯里巴察（Sribatsa）的人。

(Sri is another name of Lakshmi).

（Sri 是 Lakshmi 的另一个名字）。

(And"batsa" is another word for child).

（"batsa" 是孩子的另一个意思）。

(so Sribatsa literally means"the child of fortune").

（因此 Sribatsa 的字面意思是 "幸运之子"）。

Sribatsa had as much wisdom as he had wealth.

Sribatsa 的智慧与财富一样多。

And he was as fair as he was rich, too.

他不仅富有，而且公正。

He was therefore a good judge for the dispute.

因此，他是这一争议的优秀裁判者。

And the God and Goddess agreed he could judge their case.

男神和女神同意他来审判他们的案件。

One day, accordingly, Sribatsa was contacted.

因此，有一天，有人联系了 Sribatsa。

He was told that Sani and Lakshmi would come to him.

有人告诉他，萨尼（Sani）和拉克希米（Lakshmi）将会来找他。

And he was told they wished for him to settle their dispute.

并告诉他，他们希望他能解决他们的争端。

This put Sribatsa in a delicate situation.

这使得斯里巴查陷入了微妙的境地。

He could say Sani was higher in rank than Lakshmi.

他可以说萨尼的地位比拉克希米高。

But then she would be angry with him and forsake him.

但随后她就会对他生气并抛弃他。

He could say Lakshmi was higher in rank than Sani.

他可以说拉克希米的地位比萨尼高。

But then Sani would cast his evil eye upon him.

但萨尼却会用邪恶的目光看着他。

He made up his mind not to say anything directly.

他决定不直接说任何话。

The god and the goddess had to observe his actions.

男神和女神必须观察他的举动。

And from his actions they could gather their opinions.

他们可以从他的行为中得出自己的意见。

Sribatsa ordered two chairs to be made.

Sribatsa 下令制作两把椅子。

One of the chairs was made from gold.

其中一把椅子是用金子做的。

And the other chair was made from silver.
另一把椅子是用银制成的。
And he placed the two chairs beside himself.
他把两把椅子放在自己身边。
The day came when Sani and Lakshmi visited Sribatsa.
萨尼（Sani）和拉克希米（Lakshmi）拜访斯里巴查（Sribatsa）的那一天到来了。
He told Sani to sit upon the silver chair.
他让萨尼坐在银椅子上。
And he told Lakshmi to sit upon the gold chair.
他让拉克希米坐在金椅子上。
Sani became mad with rage, and spoke angrily;
萨尼勃然大怒，愤怒地说道；
"You consider me lower in rank than Lakshmi"
"你认为我的地位比拉克希米低"
"I will cast my eye on you for three years"
"我会注视你三年"
"We shall see how you fare at the end of that period"
"我们将看看你在这段时间结束时的表现如何"
The god then went away in great anger.
然后神就愤怒地走了。
Lakshmi, before she went away, said to Sribatsa;
拉克希米在离开之前对斯里巴查说道；
"My child, do not fear. I'll befriend you"
"孩子，别害怕。我会和你做朋友。"
The god and the goddess then went away.
男神和女神随后就离开了。
Sribatsa spoke to his wife, Chantamani;
Sribatsa 与他的妻子 Chantamani 交谈；
"Dearest, the evil eye of Sani will be upon me"
"亲爱的，萨尼的邪恶之眼将会注视着我"
"I had better go away from the house"
"我最好离开这所房子"
"If I stay evil will befall you and me"

"如果我留下来，你我都会遭殃"
"But if I go, evil will overtake me only"
"但如果我走了，邪恶只会降临到我头上"
Chintamani said, "it cannot be that way"
Chintamani 说："不可能。"
"Wherever you go, I will go with you"
"无论你去哪里，我都会陪你"
"Your good luck shall be my good luck"
"你的好运就是我的好运"
"And your bad luck shall be my bad luck"
"你的厄运也将是我的厄运"
The husband tried hard to persuade his wife to stay.
丈夫竭力劝说妻子留下来。
But all his efforts were of no use.
但他的一切努力都无济于事。
She refused to abandon her husband.
她拒绝抛弃她的丈夫。
Sribatsa told his wife to make an opening in their mattress.
Sribatsa 让他的妻子在床垫上开一个口。
And he told her to stow away all their money and jewels.
他让她把所有的钱和珠宝都收起来。
On the eve of leaving their house, Sribatsa invoked Lakshmi.
在离开家的前一天晚上，斯里巴察祈求了拉克希米。
Upon being invoked, Lakshmi forthwith appeared.
一经召唤，拉克希米便立即出现。
"Mother Lakshmi, the evil eye of Sani is upon us"
"拉克希米妈妈，萨尼的邪恶之眼正注视着我们"
"We are going away into exile"
"我们要被掳了"
"Please befriend us, and take care of our property"
"请与我们友善，并照顾好我们的财产"
The goddess of good luck answered.
幸运女神回答道。

"Do not fear; I'll befriend you"
"别害怕，我会和你做朋友"
"In the end all will be right"
"最终一切都会好起来"
They then set out on their journey.
然后他们就踏上了旅程。
Sribatsa rolled up the mattress and put it on his head.
Sribatsa 将床垫卷起来并放在他的头上。
They had not gone many miles when they saw a river.
他们没走多远就看到了一条河。
There was a canoe with a man sitting in it.
有一艘独木舟，里面坐着一个人。
The travelers requested the ferryman to take them across.
旅人们请求渡船者带他们过河。
The ferryman said he could only take one at a time.
船夫说他一次只能载一个人。
"Tere are three of you," he objected.
"你们有三个人，" 他反对道。
"There is you, your wife, and your mattress"
"有你、你的妻子和你的床垫"
Sribatsa proposed in what order they should ferry over the river.
Sribatsa 建议他们应该按照什么顺序渡过这条河。
"First my wife should be taken across the river"
"首先应该把我的妻子带过河"
"After my wife, take the mattress across the river"
"跟在我老婆后面，把床垫带过河"
"And then you can take me across the river"
"然后你就可以带我过河了"
But the ferryman would not hear of it.
但船夫不肯听。
"Only one at a time," he repeated.
"一次只能一个，" 他重复道。
"First let me take across the mattress"

"首先让我把床垫拿过来"
Sribatsa saw no reason to object to the proposal.
Sribatsa 认为没有理由反对该提议。
The ferryman started taking the mattress across the river.
摆渡人开始把床垫运过河。
He had reached halfway across the river.
他已经走到河的一半了。
But then, from nowhere, a fierce gale arose.
但就在这时，不知从何而来，一阵狂风骤起。
The ferryman lost control of his canoe.
渡船夫失去了对独木舟的控制。
The mattress was blown into the river.
床垫被吹进了河里。
The river carried everything away with it.
河水卷走了一切。
And the ferrymen, canoe, and mattress were never seen again.
从此，渡船者、独木舟和床垫就再也没有出现过。
But that was not even the strangest events.
但这还不是最奇怪的事件。
Because the river also disappeared into thin air.
因为那条河也消失得无影无踪了。
Where there was water there was now dry ground.
以前有水的地方现在变成了干地。
Sribatsa knew the evil eye of Sani had been watching.
斯里巴察知道萨尼的邪恶之眼一直在注视着他。

Sribatsa and his wife had not a pice in their pockets.
Sribatsa 和他的妻子口袋里没有一分钱。
Together, impoverished, they went to a nearby village.
他们一贫如洗，一起去了附近的一个村庄。
The village was dwelt in mostly by wood-cutters.
该村的居民大多是樵夫。
At sunrise the woodcutters went to cut wood.

日出时分，樵夫们就出去砍柴。
And the wood they cut they sold in a faraway town.
他们砍伐的木材被卖到遥远的城镇。
Sribatsa asked to work with the wood-cutters.
Sribatsa 请求与伐木工一起工作。
And the wood-cutters agreed to let him cut wood.
于是樵夫们就同意让他砍柴。
He could fell trees as well as the best of them.
他能和他们当中最优秀的人一样砍树。
But Sribatsa was different from the wood-cutters.
但斯里巴查与樵夫不同。
The wood-cutters cut any and every sort of wood.
伐木工人可以砍伐各种木材。
But Sribatsa cut only the precious types of wood.
但 Sribatsa 只砍伐珍贵的木材。
His efforts were focused on cutting down sandal-wood.
他的努力主要集中在砍伐檀香木上。
The wood-cutters brought to market large loads of common wood.
伐木工人把大量的普通木材运到市场上。
Sribatsa brought only a few pieces of sandal-wood to the market.
Sribatsa 只带了几块檀香木到市场。
He was paid a great deal more money than the others.
他的薪水比其他人高得多。
Things went on this way for some days.
事情就这样持续了几天。
And the wood-cutters became jealous of Sribatsa.
樵夫们开始嫉妒斯里巴查。
In their jealousy they plotted against Sribatsa.
他们出于嫉妒，密谋反对斯里巴查。
And finally they drove Sribatsa and his wife from the village.
最后他们把斯里巴查和他的妻了赶出了村子。

Sribatsa and his wife made their way to another village.
斯里巴查和他的妻子前往另一个村庄。
In this village there were many women that weaved.
这个村子里有很多从事纺织的妇女。
Here Chintamani made herself useful by spinning cotton.
在这里，Chintamani
通过纺棉花来发挥自己的作用。
Chintamani was an intelligent and skillful woman.
Chintamani 是一位聪明且技艺娴熟的女性。
So she spun finer thread than the other women.
因此她纺出的线比其他女人更细。
And she got paid more money than the other women.
而且她的薪水比其他女性更高。
This roused the envy of the native women of the village.
这引起了村里当地妇女的羡慕。
But the envy of the other women was not all.
但其他女人的羡慕还不是全部。
Sribatsa wanted to gain the good grace of the weavers.
Sribatsa 想要赢得织工们的青睐。
So he invited the women that spun cotton to a feast.
于是他邀请纺棉的妇女们来参加宴会。
The dishes of the feat were all cooked by his wife.
这次盛宴的菜肴均由他的妻子烹制。
Chintamani was a good weaver, and an excellent in cook.
Chintamani
是一位优秀的织工，也是一位出色的厨师。
She placed the delicacies before the women.
她把美味佳肴摆在了女人们面前。
And the barbarous weavers were quite charmed.
而那些野蛮的织工们却十分着迷。
The men went to their homes with their bellies full.
男人们吃饱喝足回家了。
But when they got home, they reproached their wives.

但当他们回到家时，他们却责备自己的妻子。
"Why do you not cook like the wife of Sribatsa"
"你为什么不像 Sribatsa 的妻子那样做饭呢？"
And the men called their wives good-for-nothing women.
而男人则骂自己的妻子是没用的女人。
This made the women hate Chintamani the more.
这使得妇女们对如意宝珠的憎恨更加强烈。

One day Chintamani went to the river-side.
有一天，Chintamani 来到河边。
She wanted to bathe along with the other women of the village.
她想和村里的其他妇女一起洗澡。
A boat had been lying on the bank, stranded on the sand.
一艘船搁浅在岸边，搁浅在沙滩上。
The boat had been stranded there for many days.
这艘船已在那里搁浅多日了。
They had tried to move the boat, but in vain.
他们曾试图移动这艘船，但是徒劳无功。
It so happened that Chintamani touched the boat.
碰巧的是，Chintamani 碰到了船。
It was an accident, for she did not mean to touch the boat.
这是一次意外，因为她并不是故意去碰那艘船。
But whether she meant to or not, the boat moved.
但不管她是否有意，船还是动了。
And soon the boat was heading off to the river.
很快，船就驶向了河边。
The boatmen were astonished by what they had seen.
船夫们对他们所看到的景象感到震惊。
They thought that the woman had uncommon power.
他们认为这个女人拥有非凡的力量。
And so they thought she might be useful in future.
所以他们认为她将来可能会有用。
They therefore caught hold of her, against her will.

因此，他们违背她的意愿抓住了她。

And they put her in the boat, and rowed off.

他们把她放到船上，然后划走了。

The women of the village were present for this kidnapping.

村里的妇女们都目睹了这次绑架事件。

But they did not offer Chintamani any assistance.

但他们没有向 Chintamani 提供任何帮助。

Because Chintamani had put them in a bad light.

因为 Chintamani 让他们的形象变得不好。

Sribatsa heard how his wife had been carried away by boatmen.

斯里巴察听说了他的妻子被船夫带走的经过。

I will let you imagine how he became mad with grief.

我让你想象一下他是如何因悲伤而发疯的。

He left the village and went to the river-side.

他离开村庄，来到河边。

And he resolved to follow the course of the stream.

他决定顺着溪流走。

Along the stream he was sure to meet the kidnappers' boat.

沿着小河，他肯定会遇见绑匪的船。

He travelled on and on, along the side of the river.

他沿着河边不停地旅行。

And he travelled till it eventually became dark.

他一直旅行直到天色渐渐暗下来。

Where he was there were no huts to be seen.

他所在的地方没有看到任何小屋。

So he climbed into a tree to sleep for the night.

于是他爬到一棵树上睡觉。

In the next morning he got down from the tree.

第二天早上他从树上下来。

At the foot of the tree he saw a Kapila-cow.

在树脚下，他看见了一头卡皮拉牛。

A Kapila-cow never has any calves of her own.

卡皮拉母牛从来不会生下自己的小牛。
But she can be milked at all hours of the day.
但她可以在一天中的任何时间挤奶。
Sribatsa milked the cow without her objecting.
Sribatsa 没有反对就挤了奶。
And he drank the milk to his heart's content.
他尽情地喝着牛奶。
And then he noticed something else about the cow.
然后他注意到了这头牛的其他一些事情。
The dung of the cow was of a bright yellow color.
牛粪呈亮黄色。
In fact, the dung of the cow was made of pure gold.
事实上，牛粪是由纯金制成的。
The golden cow dung was still in a soft state.
金色的牛粪还处于松软的状态。
So he was able to write his name in the golden dung.
因此他能够在金粪上写下自己的名字。
During the course of the day the dung hardened.
一天下来，粪便就变硬了。
And finally the dung looked like a brick of gold.
最后，粪便看起来就像一块金砖。
The tree he had slept in grew on the river-side.
他睡觉的那棵树长在河边。
And the Kapila-cow supplied him with milk all day.
卡皮拉牛整天为他提供牛奶。
So Sribatsa decided to wait there for the boat.
因此 Sribatsa 决定在那里等船。
In the morning the cow deposited the precious article.
早上，母牛产下了珍贵的物品。
And at night the cow deposited the precious article.
晚上，母牛就把这件珍贵的物品产了下来。
So the gold bricks increased every day.
于是金砖每天都在增加。
And on each golden brick he had engraved his name.

每块金砖上都刻上了他的名字。

He stacked the bricks on top of each other.
他把砖块一块一块地摞起来。
From a distance it looked like a hillock of gold.
从远处看，它就像一座金色的小山丘。

But now we must leave Sribatsa to stack his gold.
但现在我们必须让 Sribatsa 去堆放他的黄金。
And we must turn our attention to Chintamani.
我们必须把注意力转向如意宝珠。
Chintamani was a graceful woman of great beauty.
钦塔玛尼是一位美丽而优雅的女性。
She had worried her beauty might be her ruin.
她曾担心自己的美貌会毁了她。
So she offered a prayer as she was being kidnapped.
因此，她在被绑架时进行了祈祷。
"Lakshmi, O Mother Lakshmi! have pity upon me"
"拉克希米，拉克希米妈妈！可怜可怜我吧。"
"Thou hast made me beautiful, you have"
"你让我变得美丽，你"
"But now my beauty will undoubtedly be my ruin"
"但现在我的美貌无疑会毁了我"
"I am bound to loss my honor and my chastity"
"我注定要失去我的荣誉和贞洁"
"I therefore beseech thee, gracious Mother;"
"因此，我恳求您，仁慈的母亲；"
"Take my beauty from me, and make me ugly"
"夺走我的美貌，让我变得丑陋"
"Cover my body with some loathsome disease"
"用某种令人厌恶的疾病覆盖我的身体"
"That way the boatmen might not touch me"
"这样船夫就不会碰我了"
Chintamani was in the arms of the boatmen.
奇塔玛尼被船夫们抱在怀里。

But the Goddess of good fortune heard her prayer.
但幸运女神听到了她的祈祷。
In the twinkling of an eye her form changed.
转眼间，她的身影就变了。
Her naturally beautiful form faded away.
她天生美丽的身躯已消失殆尽。
And she was turned into a vile carcass.
她变成了一具丑陋的尸体。
The boatmen were putting her down in the boat.
船夫们正把她放到船上。
They found her body was covered with loathsome sores.
他们发现她的身上布满了令人厌恶的疮疡。
And the sores were giving out a disgusting stench.
伤口处散发着令人作呕的恶臭。
They therefore threw her into the hold of the boat.
于是他们把她扔进了船舱。
And they left her amongst the cargo of the ship.
他们把她留在船上的货物中。
Morning and evening they sent her some food.
他们每天早晚都会给她送来一些食物。
A little boiled rice, and some water to drink.
一点煮熟的米饭和一些喝的水。
Chintamani was miserable in the hull of the ship.
Chintamani 在船舱里感到很痛苦。
But she greatly preferred misery to the alternative.
但她宁愿忍受痛苦，也不愿接受其他选择。
She would rather be miserable than loss her chastity.
她宁愿痛苦，也不愿失去贞洁。

The boatmen had gone to some port to sell cargo.
船夫们去某个港口卖货物了。
While sailing back they caught sight something.
当他们返回时，他们看到了一些东西。
By the river-side there seemed to be a hillock of gold.

河边好像有一座金子般的小山丘。
Sribatsa had been keeping watch by the river.
斯里巴查一直在河边守望。
So he was delighted to see a boat approach him.
因此，当他看到一艘船向他驶来时，他很高兴。
Because he fondly imagined his wife might be on board.
因为他满怀深情地想象着他的妻子可能也在船上。
The boatmen went greedily to the hillock of gold.
船夫们贪婪地向金丘走去。
Of course Sribatsa told them the gold was his.
当然，斯里巴查告诉他们黄金是他的。
But that didn't help Sribatsa very much.
但这并没有给斯里巴察带来多大帮助。
The sailors took him prisoner on the boat.
水手们把他俘虏在船上。
And they loaded the gold onto their vessel.
他们将黄金装上船。
They happened to imprison him close to the ugly woman.
他们恰好将他囚禁在丑陋女人附近。
Of course the husband and wife recognized each other.
夫妻二人当然认出了对方。
In spite of the change Chintamani had undergone.
尽管 Chintamani 已经发生了变化。
And despite their excitement they kept their composure.
尽管他们很激动，但他们还是保持了镇定。
And they thought it prudent not to speak to each other.
他们认为最好不要互相说话。
Instead they communicated their ideas through gestures.
相反，他们通过手势来传达他们的想法。
There is something you should know about the boatmen.
关于船夫，有一些事情你应该了解。
These boatmen were very fond of playing at dice.
这些船夫非常喜欢玩骰子。
Sribatsa appeared to them to be a respectable man.

在他们看来，斯里巴察是一位值得尊敬的人。
So they always asked him to join in the game.
所以他们总是邀请他参加比赛。
Sribatsa happened to be an expert dice player.
Sribatsa 恰好是一位掷骰子高手。
Despite their efforts he won almost every game.
尽管他们付出了很大努力，但他几乎赢得了每一场比赛。
You can imagine how the sailors felt about losing.
你可以想象水手们失败后的感受。
And in jealousy the boatmen threw him overboard.
船夫们嫉妒地将他扔下了海。
Chintamani saw the men throw her husband overboard.
钦塔玛尼亲眼看到那些人把她的丈夫扔下海。
Fortunately for Sribatsa, his wife had great presence of mind.
幸运的是，斯里巴察的妻子非常冷静。
The boatmen had allowed her a pillow to rest her head.
船夫给了她一个枕头让她休息。
And she simultaneously threw this pillow into the water.
同时她还把这个枕头扔进了水里。
Sribatsa was able to grab hold of the pillow.
Sribatsa 成功抓住了枕头。
And the pillow helped him float down the stream.
枕头帮助他顺流而下。
Up until nightfall the river carried him downstream.
直到夜幕降临，河水才顺流而下。
At nightfall he arrived at what seemed to be a garden.
夜幕降临时，他来到了一个看似花园的地方。
Because it was dark there was nothing he could do.
因为天色已暗，他什么也做不了。
So all night he stayed in the garden, cold and wet.
于是他整晚都呆在花园里，又冷又湿。
I should tell you who this garden belonged to.

我应该告诉你这个花园属于谁。

This was the garden of an old widowed woman.

这是一位老寡妇的花园。

This woman used to supply flowers for the king.

这位妇女曾经为国王供应鲜花。

But one day some blight had come over her garden.

但有一天，她的花园遭遇了枯萎病。

Almost all the trees and plants ceased flowering.

几乎所有的树木和植物都停止了开花。

She had therefore given up the business she had.

因此她放弃了自己的生意。

And she was no longer the royal flower supplier.

她不再是皇家鲜花供应商了。

However, Sribatsa's arrival had rejuvenated her garden.

然而，斯里巴莎的到来让她的花园恢复了生机。

She could scarcely believe her eyes in the morning.

早上她简直不敢相信自己的眼睛。

The whole garden was ablaze with flowers again.

整个花园再次鲜花盛开。

There was no plant that was not in bloom.

没有一株植物不开花。

And every tree she had was begemmed with flowers.

她拥有的每棵树上都开满了鲜花。

She had no way of knowing the cause of the miracle.

她无法知道奇迹发生的原因。

And so she took a walk through the garden.

于是她在花园里散步。

But she soon found the cause of all the flowers.

但她很快就找到了所有这些花开的原因。

At the edge of her garden was a cold, wet man.

在她的花园边缘有一个又冷又湿的男人。

He was shivering and almost dead from hypothermia.

他浑身发抖，几乎因体温过低而死亡。

She immediately brought the man into to her cottage.

她立即把那个男人带进了她的小屋。
And she lighted a fire to give him some warmth.
她点燃了一堆火，让他感到温暖。
She nursed him and showed him every attention.
她悉心照料他，对他关怀备至。
And she ascribed the miracle to his presence.
她将这个奇迹归功于他的存在。
She made him as comfortable as she could.
她尽力让他感到舒服。
And then she ran to the king's palace.
然后她跑向国王的宫殿。
She asked to speak to the king's chief servant.
她请求与国王的首席仆人谈话。
And she told him the good fortune she had had.
她向他讲述了自己的好运。
"I can again supply the palace with flowers"
"我可以再次向宫殿提供鲜花"
Her flowers had been very much missed at the palace.
宫殿里的人都非常怀念她的花。
So she was immediately restored to her former position.
于是她立即被恢复原职。
She was again the flower-woman of the royal household.
她再次成为皇室的宠臣。

Sribatsa spent a few more days recovering his health.
斯里巴查又花了几天时间恢复健康。
And eventually he had all his vitality back.
最终他恢复了全部活力。
He asked the woman if he could speak with a minister.
他问那位女士是否可以和一位牧师谈谈。
So the woman took him to the palace with her.
于是女人就带着他进了宫殿。
One of the king's ministers gave him an appointment.
国王的一位大臣任命了他。

And he was at once found to be a man of intelligence.
人们立刻发现他是一个聪明人。
So was offered a position in the king's service.
因此被授予了为国王服务的职位。
In fact, he was allowed to choose what job he wanted.
事实上，他可以选择自己想要的工作。
He asked to be collector of tolls on the river.
他请求担任河上的通行费征收员。
The minister was happy to give Sribatsa the job.
部长很高兴给予斯里巴查这份工作。
The kingdom needed someone to collect river-tolls.
王国需要有人来征收河流通行费。
And Sribatsa immediately started his new job.
而 Sribatsa 也立即开始了他的新工作。
It wasn't long before his plan came to fruition.
不久之后，他的计划就实现了。
The boat his wife was on was coming down the river.
他妻子所乘的船正顺流而下。
Under the king's authority he detained the boat.
他奉国王之命扣留了这艘船。
And he charged the boatmen with the theft of gold-bricks.
他还指控船夫偷窃金砖。
The king liked the sound of a boat full of gold.
国王喜欢满载金子的船的声音。
So the king himself came to the river-side.
于是国王亲自来到了河边。
Even he was amazed by the quantity of gold they had.
就连他自己也对他们拥有的黄金数量感到惊讶。
And every gold brick had Sribatsa's inscription.
每一块金砖上都刻有斯里巴查的铭文。
At the same time he rescued his wife from the boatmen.
同时他还从船夫手中救出了他的妻子。
Back on dry land she returned to her previous beauty.
回到陆地后，她又恢复了以前的美丽。

He told the king the story of their misfortune.

他向国王讲述了他们的不幸遭遇。

And the king had them as a guest in his palace.

国王把他们当作宾客请到宫中。

The king gave them presents of horses and elephants.

国王送给他们马和大象作为礼物。

And on the horses and elephants they rode to their country.

他们骑着马和大象回到了自己的国家。

The evil eye of Sani was now turned away from Sribatsa.

萨尼的邪恶之眼现在已经从斯里巴查身上移开了。

And he again became what he formerly was.

他又恢复了原来的样子。

He was again Sribatsa; the Child of Fortune.

他再次成为了斯里巴察（Sribatsa），幸运之子。

The Boy whom Seven Mothers Suckled
七个母亲哺育的男孩

Once on a time there reigned a king who had seven queens.
从前，有一位国王，他有七位王后。
He was very sad, for the seven queens were all barren.
他非常伤心，因为七位王后都不孕。
One day, however, he met a holy mendicant.
然而有一天，他遇见了一位圣僧。
The holy mendicant told the king about a certain forest.
圣僧向国王讲述了一片森林的有关情况。
In this forest there grew a special kind of tree.
这片森林里生长着一种特殊的树。
On a branch of this tree hung seven mangoes.
这棵树的树枝上挂着七个芒果。
These mangos could restore the fertilities of his queens.
这些芒果可以恢复蜂后的生育能力。
But the king had to pluck the mangoes himself.
但国王必须亲自采摘芒果。
The king followed the advice of the mendicant.
国王听从了乞丐的建议。
And he set off to go to the forest with the mango tree.
于是他出发去芒果树所在的森林。
Soon he had found the tree the mendicant spoke of.
很快他就找到了乞丐所说的那棵树。
And he plucked the seven mangoes that grew upon one branch.
他摘下了长在一根枝子上的七个芒果。
He gave a mango to each of the queens to eat.
他给每位王后一个芒果吃。
In a short time the king's heart was filled with joy.
不一会儿，国王的心里充满了喜悦。
He was told that the seven queens were all with child.
有人告诉他，七位王后都怀孕了。

One day the king was out hunting.
有一天，国王出去打猎。
On his path he saw a young lady of peerless beauty.
在路上，他遇见了一位绝世美人。
He instantly fell in love with the beautiful woman.
他立刻爱上了这位美丽的女人。
And he brought her to his palace, and married her.
他把她带回宫殿并娶了她。
This lady was, however, not a human being.
然而，这位女士并不是人类。
But what this woman was was a Rakshasi.
但这名女子，却是罗刹女。
But the king of course did not know this.
但国王当然不知道这一点。
The king became dotingly fond of her.
国王非常宠爱她。
And he did whatever she told him to do.
她让他做什么他就做什么。
One day she made a very particular request of the king.
有一天，她向国王提出了一个非常特殊的请求。
"You say that you love me more than anyone else"
"你说你比任何人都更爱我"
"Let me see whether you really love me as much as you say"
"让我看看你是否真的像你说的那样爱我"
"If you love me, make your seven other queens blind"
"如果你爱我，就让你的其他七个王后都失明"
"And once they are blind, let them be killed"
"一旦他们失明，就让他们被杀死"
The king became very sad at the terrible request.
国王听到这个可怕的要求后变得非常悲伤。
He was especially sad because the queens were all pregnant.
他特别伤心，因为王后们都怀孕了。
But he had no choice but to comply with her request.

但他别无选择，只能答应她的要求。

The eyes of the queens were plucked out of their sockets.
女王的眼睛被挖出了眼窝。
And the queens were delivered up to the chief minister.
王后们被交给了首席大臣。
It was up to the chief minister to destroy the queens.
消灭女王的任务由首席大臣承担。
But the chief minister was a merciful man.
但首席部长是一位仁慈的人。
In the side of the hill there was secret a cave.
山坡上有一个秘密的洞穴。
Instead of killing the queens, the minister hid them.
大臣没有杀死女王，而是将她们藏了起来。
In course of time the eldest of the seven queens gave birth.
随着时间的推移，七位王后中最年长的一位生下了孩子。
"What shall I do with the child," said she.
"我该怎么处置这个孩子呢？"她问道。
"we are blind and are dying for want of food?"
"我们是瞎子，而且因为缺乏食物而快要死了？"
"Let me kill the child," she proposed.
"让我杀了这个孩子，"她提议道。
"let us all eat of the child's flesh" she added.
她补充道："让我们都吃这个孩子的肉吧。"
Just as she said she would, she killed the infant.
正如她所说的那样，她杀死了婴儿。
She gave to each of her sister-queens a part of the child.
她把孩子的一部分分给了她的每位姐妹王后。
And the sister queens ate their part of the child.
姐妹王后们吃掉了孩子身上属于她们的那一部分。
But the youngest queen did not eat her share.
但最年轻的女王没有吃掉她的那一份。
Instead, she laid her part of the child beside her.

相反，她把孩子的身体部分放在了自己身边。
In a few days the second queen also was delivered of a child.
几天后，第二任王后也生了一个孩子。
She did with her child as her eldest sister had done with hers.
她对待她的孩子就像她大姐对待她的孩子一样。
So did the third, the fourth, the fifth, and the sixth queen.
第三、第四、第五、第六位女王也同样如此。
Eventually the seventh queen gave birth to a son.
最终第七位王后生了一个儿子。
But she did not follow the example of her sister-queens.
但她并没有效仿她的姐妹王后们。
Instead, she resolved to raise the child.
相反，她决心抚养这个孩子。
The other queens demanded their portions of the newly-born.
其他女王要求得到新生儿的份额。
But she still had the portions she had not eaten.
但她还有一些没吃完的。
And she gave her sister-queens back their children's parts.
她把姐妹王后们的子女的身体部位归还给了她们。
The other queens at once perceived that their portions were dry.
其他女王立刻发现她们的那份食物已经干了。
Therefore the parts could not be of the newly born child.
因此这些部位不可能属于新生儿。
"I have decided not to kill me child," she explained.
"我决定不杀死我的孩子，" 她解释道。
"I will not eat him, but try to raise him instead"
"我不会吃掉他，而是试着养育他"
The others were glad to hear this news.
其他人听到这个消息都很高兴。
They all said that they would help her in nursing the child.
他们都表示会帮助她照顾孩子。

And so the child was suckled by seven mothers.
因此，这个孩子由七位母亲哺育。
And the child became the hardiest and strongest boy that ever lived.
这个孩子成为了有史以来最坚强、最坚强的男孩。

In the meantime the Rakshasi-queen was doing infinite mischief.
与此同时，罗刹女王也在做着无尽的恶作剧。
And she got the royal household into all sorts of trouble.
她给王室带来了各种麻烦。
What she ate at the royal table did not fill her capacious stomach.
她在皇家餐桌上吃的食物根本填不满她那宽大的肚子。

She therefore, in the darkness of night, went hunting.
因此，她在夜幕降临时出去打猎。
Gradually she ate up all the members of the royal family.
渐渐地，她吃掉了所有皇室成员。
She ate all the king's servants, and his attendants.
她吃掉了国王的所有仆人和侍从。
She ate all his horses, elephants, and cattle.
她吃掉了他所有的马、大象和牛。
And eventually only her royal consort and the king were left.
最后只剩下她的王妃和国王了。
After that she used to go out in the evenings into the city.
此后，她常常在晚上去城里。
And she ate up stray human beings wherever she found any.
无论她发现什么流浪人类，她都会吃掉它们。
The king was left without any servants.
国王失去了所有仆人。
There was no person left to cook for him.
没有人给他做饭。

Because no one would accept this job.
因为没有人会接受这份工作。
But at last someone volunteered their services.
但最终还是有人自愿提供服务。
The boy who had been suckled by seven mothers.
这个男孩曾被七位母亲哺育。
He had now grown up to be a stalwart youth.
如今他已经长成了一名伟岸的青年。
He attended on the king and prepared his food.
他侍奉国王并为他准备食物。
But he took every care while with the queen.
但他与女王相处时十分小心。
And he made sure that she did not swallow him up.
并且他确保她不会把他吞噬。
The Rakshasi-queen seized her victims only at night.
罗刹女王只在夜间捕获受害者。
So the boy he went home long before nightfall.
因此，男孩早在天黑之前就回家了。
So she had to find another way to get rid of the boy.
所以她必须想其他办法摆脱这个男孩。

The boy always boasted that he could do any work.
这个男孩总是夸口说他能做任何工作。
So the queen invented a disease for herself.
于是女王就给自己发明了一种疾病。
She said that there was a cure for her disease.
她说她的病有药可治。
But she said the cure was not easy to get.
但她表示，这种治疗方法并不容易。
This made the boy even more interested in the task.
这让男孩对这项任务更加感兴趣。
She said there was a melon which cured her disease.
她说有一种瓜治好了她的病。
The melon was twelve cubits in length.

这个西瓜长十二肘尺。
But the stone of the lemon was thirteen cubits long.
但柠檬的果核却有十三肘长。
The fruit could only be gotten from her mother.
这种水果只能从她母亲那里得到。
And her mother lived on the other side of the ocean.
她的母亲住在大洋彼岸。
She gave him a letter of introduction to her mother.
她给了他一封给她母亲的介绍信。
But actually the note told her to eat the boy.
但实际上纸条上却告诉她要吃掉这个男孩。
The boy had suspected there was some foul play.
男孩怀疑其中有不法行为。
So he tore up the letter and proceeded on his journey.
于是他撕毁了这封信并继续上路。
The dauntless youth passed through many lands.
这位无畏的年轻人走遍了许多土地。
After much travel he stood on the shore of the ocean.
经过长途跋涉后，他站在了海边。
On the other side of the ocean was the country of the Rakshasis.
大洋彼岸，是罗刹女的国度。
He then bawled as loud as he could, and said;
然后他尽可能大声地喊道；
"Granny! granny! come and save your daughter"
"奶奶！奶奶！快来救救你的女儿！"
"Your daughter, my mother, is dangerously ill"
"你的女儿，我的母亲，病情危急"
On the other side of the ocean an old Rakshasi heard him.
在海洋的另一边，一位年老的罗刹女听到了他的声音
。

The old Rakshasi crossed the ocean to the boy.
老罗刹女跨越海洋来到了男孩身边。
The boy told her the message of the queen.

男孩告诉了她女王的信息。
And the Rakshasi took the boy on her back.
于是罗刹婆便将男孩背在了背上。
She re-crossed the ocean to the land of the Rakshasi.
她再次跨越海洋，来到罗刹女的国度。
And the boy was at once given the medicinal melon.
于是男孩就立即得到了药瓜。
The Rakshasi told him to hurry back to her daughter.
罗刹女叫他赶紧回到女儿身边。
But the boy said he was too tired to keep travelling.
但男孩说他太累了，无法继续前行。
And he begged to be allowed to rest one day.
他请求允许他休息一天。
The old Rakshasi consented to her grandson's wishes.
老罗刹女答应了孙子的愿望。

The boy noticed interesting things in the Rakshasi's room.
男孩注意到罗刹女房间里有一些有趣的东西。
There was a stout club and a rope hanging in the room.
房间里挂着一根粗壮的棍棒和一根绳子。
The boy inquired what the stout club and rope were for.
男孩问这根粗棒子和绳子是干什么用的。
"Child, with that club and rope I cross the ocean"
"孩子，用这根棍子和绳子，我可以渡过大海"
"One just has to take the club and the rope in his hands"
"你只需要手里拿着棍棒和绳子"
"And then you have to say the following magical words:"
"然后你必须说出以下神奇的话语："
"O stout club! O strong rope!"
"好结实的棍棒！好结实的绳子！"
"Take me at once to the other side"
"立即带我去另一边"
"Then they will take him to the other side of the ocean"
"然后他们会把他带到大洋彼岸"

The boy noticed another interesting thing in the room.
男孩注意到房间里另一件有趣的东西。
There was a bird in a cage in the corner of the room.
房间角落里的笼子里有一只鸟。
The boy also wanted to know what this bird was for.
男孩还想知道这只鸟是做什么用的。
"The bird contains a secret, my child"
"这只鸟有一个秘密，我的孩子"
"But that secret must not be disclosed to mortals"
"但这个秘密不能向凡人透露。"
"But how can I hide this secret from my own grandchild?"
"但是我怎么能向我自己的孙子隐瞒这个秘密呢？"
"That bird, child, contains the life of your mother.
"孩子，那只鸟蕴含着你母亲的生命。
"If the bird is killed, your mother will at once die"
"如果鸟被杀了，你的母亲就会立刻死去"
Armed with these secrets, the boy went to bed that night.
带着这些秘密，男孩那天晚上就去睡觉了。

Next morning the old Rakshasi went to distant countries.
第二天早上，老罗刹婆去了遥远的国家。
Together with all the other Rakshasis, she went to forage.
她和所有其他的罗刹女一起出去觅食。
The boy took down the bird-cage from the ceiling.
男孩把鸟笼从天花板上取下来。
And the boy took the club and the rope.
男孩拿走了棍棒和绳子。
And then he spoke the magic words to the club and rope.
然后他对着棍棒和绳子念出了咒语。
"O stout club! O strong rope!"
"好结实的棍棒！好结实的绳子！"
"Take me at once to the other side"
"立即带我去另一边"

In the twinkling of an eye the boy was put on this side of the ocean.
转眼间，男孩就被送到了大洋的这边。
He then retraced his steps, back to the queen.
然后他沿着原路返回，回到女王身边。
To her astonishment he really had the medicinal lemon.
令她惊讶的是，他真的有药用柠檬。
But the bird in the cage he kept carefully concealed.
但他却把笼中的鸟小心地隐藏起来。

In the course of time the people of the city came to the king.
随着时间的推移，城里的人们来到了国王面前。
And they told the king of their troubles.
他们便向国王诉说了自己的苦恼。
"A monstrous bird comes from the palace every evening"
"每天傍晚，宫殿里都会飞来一只怪鸟"
"The bird seizes the people in the streets"
"鸟儿在街上抓人"
"And the bird swallows the people up whole"
"鸟儿把人们整个吞了"
"This has been going on for a long time"
"这种情况已经持续很长时间了"
"And now the city has become almost desolate"
"现在这座城市几乎荒无人迹"
The king did not know what this monstrous bird was.
国王不知道这只怪鸟是什么。
But the king's servant, the boy, said he knew.
但国王的仆人，那个男孩，说他知道。
"I will kill the monstrous bird," he offered.
"我要杀死这只怪鸟，" 他提议道。
"But the queen has to stand beside us," he added.
"但女王必须站在我们身边，" 他补充道。
The king saw no reason to object to the proposal.
国王认为没有理由反对该提议。

And so the queen was made to stand beside the king.
于是王后就被安排站在国王身边。
The boy then took the bird out from its cage.
然后男孩把鸟从笼子里拿出来。
On seeing the bird she fell into a fainting fit.
一看到这只鸟，她就昏了过去。
Then the boy turned to the king, and spoke.
然后男孩转向国王并说道。
"King, you will soon perceive who the monstrous bird is"
"国王，你很快就会知道这只怪鸟是谁了。"
"You will see what devours your people every evening"
"你每晚都会看到什么吞噬你的人民"
"I tear off each limb of this bird"
"我把这只鸟的四肢都撕下来了"
"The corresponding limb of the man-eater will fall off"
"食人兽的相应肢体将会脱落"
The boy then tore off one leg of the bird in his hand.
然后男孩撕下了手中鸟的一条腿。
All assembled were astonished at what happened next.
所有在场的人都对接下来发生的事情感到惊讶。
One of the legs of the queen fell off.
女王的一条腿掉了。
Then the boy squeezed the throat of the bird.
然后男孩捏住了鸟的喉咙。
And as he squeezed the bird, the queen gave up the ghost.
当他挤压这只鸟时，女王就断气了。
The boy then retold his history to the king.
男孩便向国王讲述了他的故事。
"You used to have seven barren wives"
"你曾经有七个不育的妻子"
"To treat their barrenness, you gave them each a mango"
"为了治疗他们的不孕不育，你给了他们每人一个芒果"
"And each of your wives fell pregnant with a child"

"你们的妻子都怀了孕"

"However, you then married an eighth wife"

"然而，你后来又娶了第八个妻子。"

"This wife ordered you to blind your other wives"

"这个妻子命令你弄瞎你的其他妻子"

"And she ordered you to have your other wives killed"

"她命令你杀死你的其他妻子"

"Your minister blinded your seven wives"

"你的大臣弄瞎了你的七个妻子"

"But he was too good hearted to kill your wives"

"但他心地善良，不会杀死你的妻子"

"Your seven wives were taken to a hiding place"

"你的七个妻子被带到了一个藏身之处"

"And in this hiding place they each gave birth"

"在这个藏身之处，她们各自生下了孩子"

"But they were forced to eat their newly born children"

"但他们被迫吃掉自己刚出生的孩子"

"Only my mother did not let me be eaten"

"只有我妈妈不让我被吃掉"

"Instead, I was suckled by seven mothers"

"相反，我是由七个母亲哺育的"

"And I grew up strong and capable"

"我变得坚强而有能力"

"Eventually I came to work in your palace"

"最终我来到了你的宫殿工作"

"Your wife, my stepmother, sent me on a mission"

"你的妻子，我的继母，派我去执行一项任务"

"She sent me to her mother for a medicine"

"她让我去她妈妈那里买药"

"However, her mother was a Rakshasi"

"但她的母亲是罗刹女。"

"From her I found the secret of your wife's life"

"我从她身上发现了你妻子生活的秘密"

"And so I brought the bird that held your wife's life"

"所以我把那只抓住你妻子生命的鸟带来了"
The king had listened to the story his son told him.
国王听了儿子讲的故事。
The seven queens were brought back to the palace.
七位王后被带回宫中。
And their eyes were miraculously restored.
他们的眼睛奇迹般地恢复了。
The boy that was suckled by seven mothers was crowned.
由七位母亲哺育的男孩被加冕。
And he was recognized by the king as his rightful heir.
国王承认他是合法的继承人。
And they lived together happily.
他们幸福地生活在一起。

The Story of Prince Sobur
索伯王子的故事

Once upon a time there lived a merchant.
从前，有一位商人。
This merchant had seven daughters.
这个商人有七个女儿。
One day the merchant asked them a question.
有一天，商人问了他们一个问题。
"From whose fortune do you live?"
"你靠谁的财产生活？"
The eldest daughter answered first.
大女儿第一个回答。
"Papa, I live from your fortune"
"爸爸，我靠你的财富生活"
The second daughter gave the same answer.
二女儿也给出了同样的答案。
The same answer was given by the third daughter.
三女儿也给出了同样的答案。
His fourth daughter also lived from his fortune.
他的第四个女儿也靠他的财产生活。
His fifth daughter was no different.
他的第五个女儿也不例外。
And his sixth daughter was like the rest.
他的第六个女儿也和其他女儿一样。
But his youngest daughter surprised him.
但他的小女儿却让他大吃一惊。
She had a very different answer.
她的答案截然不同。
"I live from my own fortune"
"我靠自己的财富生活"
He did not like this answer.
他不喜欢这个答案。
Her answer made the merchant very angry.

她的回答让商人非常生气。

"You are very ungrateful," he told her.

他告诉她：“你太忘恩负义了。”

"See how well you do on your own"

“看看你自己做得怎么样”

"I am kicking you out of my house"

“我要把你赶出我家”

"You will not have a rupee in your pocket"

“你的口袋里将一文不值”

He called his palanquins to come.

他召集轿子过来。

And he ordered them to take the girl away.

并命令他们把女孩带走。

"Leave her in the midst of a forest"

“把她留在森林里”

The girl begged to be allowed one thing.

女孩请求允许做一件事。

"Please let me take my work-box"

“请让我带上我的针线盒”

"In the box are my needles and threads"

“盒子里是我的针和线”

Her father allowed her to take her box.

她的父亲允许她带走她的盒子。

She got into the seat of the palanquins.

她坐进了轿子里。

And the bearers lifted her up.

于是抬轿的人把她抬了起来。

And they put her onto their shoulders.

他们把她扛在肩上。

As the bearers ran they chanted.

轿夫们一边奔跑，一边高呼口号。

"hoon! hoon! hoon! hoon! hoon!"

“勋！勋！勋！勋！勋！”

But they didn't get very far.

但他们并没有走太远。

An old woman stood in their way.

一位老妇人挡住了他们的路。

She came up to the carriage.

她走到马车跟前。

"Where are you taking my daughter?"

"你要带我女儿去哪儿？"

She was the maid of the child.

她是这个孩子的女佣。

"We have been given orders by the merchant"

"商人给我们下了命令。"

"He told us to take her away"

"他让我们把她带走"

"We will leave her in a forest"

"我们会把她留在森林里"

"We are going to do his bidding"

"我们将执行他的命令"

"I must go with her," said the old woman.

"我必须和她一起去，" 老妇人说。

But the bearers were not sure.

但抬轿的人并不确定。

Bearers run when they carry a sedan chair.

轿夫抬轿子时，会跑动。

"How will you be able to keep pace with us?"

"你怎么能跟上我们的步伐呢？"

The old woman was not deterred.

老妇人并没有被吓倒。

"It does not matter how I do it"

"我怎么做并不重要"

"I must go where my daughter goes"

"我必须跟随我女儿的脚步"

The youngest daughter begged the bearers.

小女儿向轿夫们恳求。

"Please carry my mother with me"

"请把我妈妈带走"
And the bearers gracefully agreed.
轿夫们也欣然同意了。
They carried mother and child to the forest.
他们把母子俩抬进了森林。
"hoon! hoon! hoon! hoon! hoon!"
"勋！勋！勋！勋！勋！"
In the afternoon they reached a dense forest.
下午他们到达了一片茂密的森林。
They went deeper and deeper into the forest.
他们越走越深入森林。
Towards sunset they reached their goal.
日落时分，他们到达了目的地。
They stopped at the foot of an old tree.
他们在一棵老树下停了下来。
They lowered the girl and the old woman.
他们把女孩和老妇人放下来。
And they left them in the forest.
然后他们就把他们留在了森林里。
Then they retraced their steps home.
然后他们原路返回。

The merchant's youngest daughter looked around.
商人的小女儿环顾四周。
You would not have wanted to be in her shoes.
你不会想处于她的境地。
Her situation was truly pitiable.
她的处境实在令人怜悯。
She was hardly fourteen years old.
她还不到十四岁。
She had grown up in luxury.
她在富裕的环境中长大。
But now there was no luxury for her.
但现在她已经没有奢侈的享受了。

She was in the heart of a dark forest.

她身处一片黑暗森林的中心。

She had not a rupee in her pocket.

她口袋里没有一卢比。

And she had nothing for protection.

而她却没有任何保护措施。

Nothing except an old, decrepit, woman.

除了一个年老体衰的女人外，什么也没有。

Even the trees of the forest pitied her.

就连森林里的树木也同情她。

The young girl and old woman sat together.

小女孩和老妇人坐在一起。

They were at the foot of an old tree.

他们在一棵老树的脚下。

And together they cried over their situation.

他们一起为自己的处境哭泣。

I should say this all happened long ago.

我应该说这一切都是很久以前发生的。

In these times the trees could talk.

在这些时候，树木会说话。

And the old tree spoke to the girl.

老树对女孩说了话。

"Unhappy women, I much pity you"

"不幸的女人，我很同情你们"

"There are wild beasts in this forest"

"这片森林里有野兽"

"Soon they will come out of their lairs"

"他们很快就会从巢穴里出来"

"They will roam about for prey"

"它们会四处游荡寻找猎物"

"And they are sure to devour you two"

"他们肯定会把你们两个吃掉。"

"But I can help you, if you want"

"但如果你想要的话我可以帮你"

"I will make an opening for you"
"我会为你打开一个机会"
"When you see the opening, go into it"
"当你看到开口时，就进去"
"And then I will close the opening up"
"然后我将关闭开口"
"As long as you are in me you'll be safe"
"只要你在我体内，你就会安全"
"This way the wild beasts can't touch you"
"这样野兽就无法伤害你了"
And then the tree split itself in two.
然后树就裂成了两半。
The two women went inside the tree.
两个女人走进了树里。
And the old tree resumed its natural shape.
老树又恢复了自然的形状。

The shade of night darkened the forest.
夜色笼罩了森林。
Everything the tree had said was true.
树说的一切都是真的。
The wild beasts came out of their lairs.
野兽们从巢穴里出来了。
The fierce tiger came out at night.
凶猛的老虎在夜间出来了。
The wild bear left his lair.
野熊离开了它的巢穴。
The rhinoceros roamed the forest.
犀牛在森林里漫步。
The bushy bear was there that night.
那天晚上，那只毛茸茸的熊就在那里。
The great elephant could be heard.
可以听到大象的声音。
And there was the horned buffalo.

还有一头长角水牛。
They all growled as they circled the tree.
它们绕着树转圈，发出咆哮声。
They had gotten the scent of human blood.
他们闻到了人血的气味。
They could hear the growls of the beasts.
他们可以听到野兽的咆哮声。
The beasts came dashing against the tree.
野兽们向树猛冲过来。
They broke the old tree's branches.
他们折断了老树的树枝。
Their horns pierced the tree's trunk.
它们的角刺穿了树干。
They scratched its bark with their claws.
它们用爪子抓挠树皮。
But all their efforts were in vain.
但他们的一切都是徒劳的。
The girl and woman were safe in the tree.
女孩和女人安全地待在树上。
Towards dawn the wild beasts went away.
黎明时分，野兽们都走了。
After sunrise the good tree spoke again.
日出之后，好树又说话了。
"The wild beasts have gone back"
"野兽已经回去了"
"They are in their lairs again"
"他们又回到巢穴了"
"But they did their best to torment me"
"但他们却竭尽全力折磨我"
"The sun has risen up again"
"太阳又升起来了"
"So you can come out now"
"所以你现在可以出来了"
The tree split itself into two again.

树又裂成了两半。
The girl and the old woman came out.
女孩和老妇人走了出来。
They saw the extent of the damage.
他们看到了损坏的程度。
The tree's branches had been broken off.
树枝已被折断。
The tree's trunk had been pierced.
树干已被刺穿。
The bark had been stripped off.
树皮已被剥去。
"Good mother, we thank you"
"好妈妈，我们感谢您"
"You have been very kind to us"
"你对我们太好了"
"You gave us shelter from the beasts"
"您为我们提供了躲避野兽的庇护所"
"But it was at a great cost to yourself"
"但这对你来说代价太大了"
"You have many wounds from the wilds beasts"
"你身上多处被野兽咬伤"
"You must be in great pain?"
"你一定很痛苦吧？"
Close by there was a flowing river.
附近有一条流淌的河流。
The young girl went to the river bank.
小女孩走到了河岸边。
At the bank of the river she found mud.
她在河岸边发现了泥土。
She covered the tree with the mud.
她用泥土盖住了树。
She especially covered the damaged parts.
她特别遮盖了受损的部分。
The tree thanked her for the treatment.

树木感谢她的治疗。

"My good girl, I thank you"

"我的好姑娘，谢谢你"

"I am greatly relieved of my pain"

"我的痛苦减轻了很多"

"I am, however, more concerned for you"

"但我更关心你"

"You must be hungry"

"你肯定饿了"

"You have not eaten since yesterday"

"你从昨天开始就没吃过东西"

"But what can I give you?"

"但是我能给你什么呢？"

"I have no fruit of my own"

"我没有自己的果实"

"But I do have some advice"

"但我确实有一些建议"

"Give the old woman whatever money you have"

"把你所有的钱都给老妇人"

"Let her go into the city"

"让她进城去"

"In the city she can buy some food"

"在城里她可以买到一些食物"

They explained their situation to the tree.

他们向树解释了他们的情况。

"We have been sent out with no money"

"我们被派出去的时候没钱"

But she searched through her work-box anyway.

但她还是搜查了她的工作箱。

And in the box she found five cowries.

她在盒子里发现了五个贝壳。

The tree continued to give its advice.

树木继续给出它的建议。

"Go with your cowries to the city"

"带着你的宝贝去城里"
"Use the cowries to buy some fried rice"
"用贝壳买点炒饭"
So the old woman went to the city.
于是老妇人就去了城里。
Fortunately the city was not far away.
幸运的是，这座城市并不遥远。
She went to the first shopkeeper she found.
她去找了她找到的第一个店主。
"Please give me five cowries worth of rice"
"请给我五枚贝壳的米"
The shopkeeper laughed at her.
店主嘲笑她。
"Where can rice be had for five cowries?"
"哪里可以买到五个贝壳的大米？"
"Be off, you old hag," he told her.
"走开，你这个老巫婆，" 他告诉她。
So she tried to barter at another shop.
因此她尝试在另一家商店进行易货交易。
This shopkeeper could see her distress.
这位店主看得出她的苦恼。
And the shopkeeper took pity on her.
店主很可怜她。
She gave her a large quantity of rice.
她给了她大量的米。
The old woman returned with the rice.
老妇人带着米回来了。
And the tree gave further instructions.
树木给出了进一步的指示。
"Eat less than half of the rice"
"少吃一半的米饭"
"Go to the embankments of the river bank"
"去河岸边的堤岸"
"Cast the remaining rice on the river bank"

"把剩下的米撒在河岸上"
They did not understand the sense of it.
他们不理解这句话的意思。
"Why sow the riverbank with rice?"
"为什么要在河岸边种水稻？"
But they did as they were advised.
但他们按照建议做了。
And they threw their rice onto the ground.
他们把米撒在地上。

They spent the day lamenting their fate.
他们整天都在哀叹自己的命运。
Just as before the beasts came out at night.
就像以前野兽在夜间出来一样。
The tree housed them inside of its trunk again.
树木又将它们安置在树干内。
Again they mutilated and tortured the tree.
他们再次肢解并折磨这棵树。
But that night something else happened.
但那天晚上又发生了另一件事。
The women only saw it the next day.
妇女们直到第二天才看到它。
The rice had attracted hundreds of peacocks.
这些大米吸引了数百只孔雀。
The peacocks competed for the rice.
孔雀们争相争夺大米。
And their feathers fell on the floor.
它们的羽毛掉落在地板上。
The tree had known what would happen.
这棵树知道会发生什么。
And the tree advised them what to do next.
树告诉他们下一步该做什么。
"Go back to the bank of the river"
"回到河岸去"

"Go to where you cast the rice"
"去你种稻子的地方"
"There you will see many feathers"
"在那里你会看到许多羽毛"
"Collect all the feathers you can find"
"收集所有你能找到的羽毛"
"Use the feathers to make a beautiful fan"
"用羽毛做一把漂亮的扇子"
"And take the feather-fan to the city"
"把羽毛扇带进城去"
The two women did as they were advised.
两名女子按照她们的建议去做了。
It was good the girl had taken her work-box.
幸好女孩带走了她的针线盒。
In her work-box was some string.
在她的针线盒里有一些绳子。
The tied the feathers together.
他们将羽毛绑在一起。
And she had made a fan from the feathers.
她用羽毛做了一把扇子。
She took the feather fan to the city.
她拿着羽毛扇去了城里。
The son of the king happened to be there.
国王的儿子恰巧在那里。
He admired the feathers greatly.
他非常欣赏这些羽毛。
He paid a large sum of money for the feathers.
他为这些羽毛付了一大笔钱。
Each morning a quantity of feathers was collected.
每天早上都会收集一定量的羽毛。
And each day a feather fan was made and sold.
每天都会制作并出售一把羽毛扇。
Within a short time the two women got rich.
不久之后，这两个女人就变得富有了。

The tree then advised them to build a house.
然后树建议他们建造一座房子。
"Employ men to burn bricks for you"
"雇人给你烧砖"
"Get them to cut beams and rafters"
"让他们砍梁和椽子"
"Make them plaster the walls with lime"
"让他们用石灰抹墙"
In a few months a stately house was built.
几个月后，一座富丽堂皇的房子建成了。
The tree was pleased for the women.
树为女人感到高兴。
"You should add a garden to your house"
"你应该给你的房子加一个花园"
"And you want to be able to store water"
"你还想储存水"
"Dig a water tank in your garden"
"在你的花园里挖一个水箱"

The girl had not had much time.
女孩已经没有多少时间了。
So she didn't think of her family.
所以她没有想到她的家人。
The merchant's luck had taken a turn.
这位商人的运气突然转变了。
The goddess of wealth frowned upon him.
财富女神对他皱起了眉头。
He was struck by a sudden misfortune.
他突然遭遇不幸。
All at once he lost all of his money.
一下子，他失去了所有的钱。
He was forced to sell his house.
他被迫卖掉了房子。
But he made a great loss on the property.

但他的财产却遭受了巨大损失。
He and his family were left penniless.
他和他的家人变得身无分文。
So they were forced to live elsewhere.
因此他们被迫到别处居住。
They happened to move to a nearby village.
他们恰巧搬到了附近的一个村庄。
The palace was not far from their new house.
宫殿离他们的新家不远。
But the merchant was not rich anymore.
但商人不再富有了。
And he still had to support his family.
而且他还得养家糊口。
He had been reduced to doing manual labour.
他被迫从事体力劳动。
He applied for the job at the palace.
他申请了宫廷里的职位。
He was going to dig the hole for the water.
他正要挖一个洞来取水。
His wife also offered to work with him.
他的妻子也愿意和他一起工作。
But they got there too late to work.
但他们到达那里已经太晚了，无法工作。
The water tank had already been finished.
水箱已经完工了。
And they did not know whose house it was.
他们不知道那是谁的房子。
The merchant's daughter was looking out the window.
商人的女儿正望着窗外。
She happened to see her parents in the garden.
她偶然在花园里看到了她的父母。
She could see the rags they were wearing.
她看见他们穿着破烂的衣服。
Her eyes filled with tears at the sight.

看到这一幕，她的眼里噙满了泪水。
She could not believe what she saw.
她简直不敢相信自己所看到的。
Her parents had come to her for work.
她的父母来找她工作。
She immediately called her servants.
她立即叫来仆人。
"Outside in the garden are my parents"
"外面花园里有我的父母"
"Please offer them these fine clothes"
"请把这些漂亮的衣服送给他们"
"And ask them to come into the palace"
"并请他们进宫。"
Her servants did as they were told.
她的仆人按照吩咐去做了。
But her parents were frightened beyond measure.
但她的父母却惊恐万分。
They had seen that the tank was finished.
他们看到坦克已经完工了。
There used to be a strange tradition.
曾经有一个奇怪的传统。
In those days human sacrifices were offered.
在那些日子里，人们会献上活人祭品。
One of those occasions was after digging a pool.
其中一次是在挖完一个游泳池之后。
You can imagine her parents' fear.
你可以想象她父母的恐惧。
They had come to dig the water tank.
他们是来挖水箱的。
But now servants were calling them.
但现在仆人们正在呼唤他们。
They thought they going to be sacrificed.
他们以为自己将被牺牲。
"Throw away your rags" they said.

他们说："把你的破布扔掉。"

"Here, wear these fine clothes"

"来，穿上这些漂亮的衣服"

And their fears increased even more.

他们的恐惧感更加强烈了。

But they did not have to fear for long.

但他们不必担心太久。

Their rich daughter came out to meet them.

他们的富家女儿出来迎接他们。

She hugged and kissed her parents.

她拥抱并亲吻了她的父母。

And she told them everything that had happened.

她把发生的一切告诉了他们。

The father felt that she had been right.

父亲觉得她说得对。

"You do live from your own fortune"

"你确实靠自己的财富生活"

The daughter did not blame her father.

女儿没有责怪父亲。

And she gave him a large fortune.

她给了他一大笔财产。

With the money he moved back to the city.

他用这笔钱搬回了城里。

Soon he became a merchant again.

不久他又成为一名商人。

And he went to distant countries for trade.

他到遥远的国家去进行贸易。

One day he got ready for another business venture.

有一天，他准备进行另一项商业冒险。

But that day something strange happened.

但那天发生了一件奇怪的事。

The ship was ready to leave the port.

该船已准备好离开港口。

But for some reason the ship did not move.
但不知为何，船却没有移动。
No one could explain what was happening.
没有人能够解释到底发生了什么。
But the merchant had an idea.
但商人有一个主意。
"Perhaps my daughters would like presents"
"也许我的女儿们会喜欢礼物"
"I need to ask them what they would like"
"我需要问问他们想要什么"
He went to see his daughters.
他去看望他的女儿们。
He asked them what they would like.
他问他们想要什么。
And he promised to bring them presents.
他还答应给他们带礼物。
But the ship would still not move.
但船还是不动。
He had not asked all his daughters.
他并没有询问过他所有的女儿。
His youngest daughter was not there.
他的小女儿不在那里。
She was living in a different city.
她住在另一个城市。
So he ordered his servants go to her palace.
于是他命令仆人前往她的宫殿。
The messenger came at the wrong time.
信使来的不是时候。
The young girl was engaged in devotions.
这个年轻女孩正在做礼拜。
But the messenger asked her anyway.
但信使还是问了她。
She just told him"sobur"
她只是告诉他 "sobur"

The meaning of this was"wait"

这句话的意思是 “等待”

But the messenger didn't know this.

但信使并不知道这一点。

He thought she wanted something called"sobur"

他以为她想要一种叫做 “sobur” 的东西

So he went back to the city of the merchant.

于是他又回到了商人的城市。

And he delivered the message he received.

他传达了他收到的信息。

“Your daughter wants something called 'sobur'"

“你女儿想要一种叫 ‘sobur’ 的东西”

This time the ship could move again.

这次船又能开动了。

So the merchant started on his travels.

于是商人开始了他的旅行。

He visited many ports on his journey.

他在旅途中访问了许多港口。

And he made good profits from his trades.

他从交易中获得了丰厚的利润。

Finding the presents was not difficult.

找到礼物并不难。

He found everything his oldest daughters wanted.

他找到了大女儿们想要的一切。

But his youngest daughter's wish was difficult.

但他的小女儿的愿望却很难实现。

He could not find the thing called"sobur"

他找不到那个叫做 “sobur” 的东西

He asked at every port he came to.

他每到一处港口都会询问。

“Do you have something called 'sobur'?"

“你们有叫 ‘sobur’ 的东西吗？”

But the merchants all shook their heads.

但商人们却都摇了摇头。

"We've never heard of 'sobur'"
"我们从未听说过‘sobur’"
His voyage had almost come to its end.
他的航行即将结束。
He was soon going to head back home.
他很快就要回家了。
But he wanted"sobur" for his daughter.
但他希望女儿也能获得"sobur"的待遇。
So he went calling through the streets.
于是他就走遍大街小巷去呼吁。
"Sobur, does anyone have sobur?!"
"Sobur，有人有sobur吗？！"
The son of the King was in his castle.
国王的儿子在他的城堡里。
He happened to be looking out the window.
他恰巧正看着窗外。
And the calls attracted his attention.
这些电话引起了他的注意。
Because his name happened to be Sobur.
因为他的名字恰好是索伯（Sobur）。
He came to the merchant to speak with him.
他来到商人那里想和他谈话。
"I have the Sobur that you want"
"我有你想要的 Sobur"
"Take this box, but be careful with it"
"拿着这个盒子，但要小心"
"In the box is a magical feather fan and mirror"
"盒子里有一把神奇的羽毛扇和一面镜子"
"This is the Sobur your daughter wishes for"
"这就是你女儿想要的索伯尔"
The merchant thanked the prince for the box.
商人向王子表达了对这个盒子的感谢。
And he returned back to his country.
然后他就回国了。

He gave the box to his daughter.
他把盒子给了他的女儿。
But the daughter didn't think about it.
但女儿却没有想到这一点。
She thought it was just a common box.
她以为这只是一个普通的盒子。
She had forgotten about the messenger.
她已经忘记了信使的存在。
But one day she decided to open the box.
但有一天她决定打开这个盒子。
Inside the box she found a beautiful fan.
她在盒子里发现了一把漂亮的扇子。
In the feather fan there was a beautiful mirror.
羽毛扇里有一面漂亮的镜子。
She waved the feather fan to cool herself.
她挥动着羽毛扇，给自己乘凉。
And Prince Sobur appeared before her.
于是索布尔王子出现在她面前。
"You called me, so here I am," he said.
他说："你打电话给我，所以我就来了。"
"What is it you wish for?" he asked.
"你的愿望是什么？"他问。
She was astonished at what she saw.
她对所见的景象感到十分惊讶。
A handsome prince had suddenly appeared!
一位英俊的王子突然出现了！
"Who are you?" she asked the prince.
"你是谁？"她问王子。
"And how did you suddenly appear?"
"那你是怎么突然出现的？"
The Prince explained what had happened.
王子解释了所发生的事。
"Your father was looking for 'sobur'"

"你父亲正在寻找 'sobur' "
"I am prince Sobur," he explained.
"我是索布尔王子，" 他解释道。
"I gave your father a box"
"我给了你父亲一个盒子"
"In this box there is a feather fan and mirror"
"这个盒子里有一把羽毛扇和一面镜子"
"When you shake the feather fan I will appear"
"当你摇动羽毛扇时我就会出现"
She asked the prince to stay as a guest.
她请求王子留下来做客。
And for two days the prince stayed with her.
王子和她一起待了两天。
And she entertained him in her palace.
她在宫殿里招待他。
During that time the two fell in love.
那段时间，两人坠入了爱河。
They made their vows to each.
他们互相许下誓言。
And they became husband and wife.
他们就结为夫妻。
After this the prince returned to his father.
此后王子回到了父亲身边。
He told him that he had selected a wife.
他告诉他，他已经选好了妻子。
The day for the wedding was decided.
婚礼的日子已经决定了。
All the family was invited.
全家人都受到了邀请。
And they had a beautiful wedding.
他们举行了一场美丽的婚礼。

But there was a death in the marriage bed.
但婚床上却发生了一起死亡事件。

The six daughters of the merchant were envious.
商人的六个女儿都很羡慕。
They were jealous of their sister's success.
他们嫉妒姐姐的成功。
So they decided to destroy her happiness.
所以他们决定毁掉她的幸福。
They broke several glass bottles.
他们打破了几个玻璃瓶。
And they ground the glass into fine powder.
他们将玻璃磨成细粉。
Then they scattered the powder on the bed.
然后他们把粉末撒在床上。
The prince suspected no danger.
王子没有怀疑任何危险。
He laid himself down in the bed.
他躺在床上。
Soon he felt an acute pain.
很快他就感到一阵剧痛。
All of his whole body ached.
他全身都酸痛。
The powder had gone through his skin.
粉末已经渗入他的皮肤。
The prince became restless through pain.
王子因疼痛而变得焦躁不安。
And he started to kick and scream.
他开始又踢又叫。
He was taken away to his own country.
他被带回了自己的国家。
The king and queen were very worried.
国王和王后非常担心。
They consulted all the kingdom's physicians.
他们咨询了王国里所有的医生。
But their efforts were in vain.
但他们的努力都是徒劳的。

Day and night the young prince was screaming.
年轻的王子日夜都在尖叫。
No one could ascertain the disease.
没人能确定这种疾病。
So they had no way of knowing the remedy.
所以他们无法知道解决办法。
You can imagine the grief of his wife.
你可以想象他的妻子有多么悲伤。
The marriage knot had only just been tied.
他们的婚事才刚刚结。
She thought a terrible disease had attacked him.
她以为他患上了可怕的疾病。
Then he was carried hundreds of miles away.
然后他被带到了数百英里之外。
She had never been to his country.
她从未去过他的国家。
But she was determined to go there.
但她决心要去那里。
And she was determined to nurse him better.
她决心更好地照顾他。
She put on the garb of a Sannyasi.
她穿上了桑雅士的服装。
And she carried a dagger in her hand.
她手里拿着一把匕首。
And then she set out on her journey.
然后她就踏上了旅程。

The princess was still relatively young.
公主还比较年轻。
She was unaccustomed to long journeys.
她不习惯长途旅行。
And she wasn't used to walking so far.
而且她还不习惯走这么远。
She soon got weary of walking.

她很快就走累了。
So she sat under a tree to rest.
于是她坐在一棵树下休息。
On the top of the tree there was a nest.
树顶上有一个鸟巢。
It was the nest of two divine birds.
那是两只神鸟的巢穴。
Bihangami and Bihangama lived here.
Bihangami和Bihangama住在这里。
They were not in their nest at the time.
当时它们并不在巢穴里。
But two of their chicks were in the nest.
但其中两只雏鸟仍在巢中。
Suddenly the chicks gave a scream.
突然，小鸡们发出一声尖叫。
This roused the half-drowsy princess.
这惊醒了半睡半醒的公主。
The little birds had seen huge serpent.
小鸟们看见了一条大蛇。
The snake was about to climb the tree.
蛇正要爬树。
This would have been the end of the birds.
这可能是鸟类的末日。
But the Sannyasi took out her dagger.
但桑雅西拔出了她的匕首。
And she cut the serpent in two.
她把蛇砍成了两半。
Of course even this frightened the young birds.
当然，即使这样，也会吓到小鸟。
And they flew from the nest screaming.
它们尖叫着飞出了鸟巢。
Bihangama and Bihangami were on their way back.
Bihangama 和 Bihangami 正在返回的路上。
They came sailing through the air.

它们从空中飞来。
They thought they already knew what had happened.
他们以为自己已经知道发生了什么事。
"I don't expect to see our children"
"我不指望见到我们的孩子"
"The nest will be empty again"
"鸟巢又会空了"
"All our previous children were eaten"
"我们以前的孩子都被吃掉了"
"They were eaten by our great enemy the serpent"
"他们被我们的大敌——蛇吃掉了"
"They will have met the same fate"
"他们也会遭遇同样的命运"
"I do not hear the cries of my young ones"
"我听不到孩子们的哭声"
The two birds got to their nest.
两只鸟回到了巢穴。
And as predicted, the nest was empty.
正如所料,鸟巢是空的。
This seemed to confirm their suspicions.
这似乎证实了他们的怀疑。
But soon the young birds returned.
但不久,幼鸟就回来了。
The divine birds were pleasantly surprised.
神鸟们惊喜不已。
The young birds told them what had happened.
小鸟们把发生的事情告诉了他们。
"There was a young Sannyasi under the tree"
"树下有一位年轻的桑雅士"
"He destroyed the serpent"
"他消灭了蛇"
"He cut the snake in two with his dagger"
"他用匕首把蛇砍成了两半"
The parents went to foot of the tree.

父母走到树下。
Two halves of the snake were still there.
蛇的两半仍在那里。
"The young Sannyasi has saved our offspring"
"年轻的桑雅士拯救了我们的后代"
"I wish we could do him some service in return"
"我希望我们能为他提供一些帮助作为回报"
The divine bird Bihangama replied.
神鸟比汉加玛回答道。
"We shall do our service to HER"
"我们将竭诚为她服务"
"The Sannyasi under the tree is not a man"
"树下的桑雅士不是男人"
"The Sannyasi under the tree is a woman"
"树下的桑雅士是个女人"
"Last night she got married to Prince Sobur"
"昨晚她和索伯王子结婚了"
"Shortly after their marriage he was poisoned"
"他们结婚后不久他就被毒死了"
"His skin was pierced with small shards of glass"
"他的皮肤被小玻璃碎片刺破了"
"His sisters-in-law envied his wife"
"他的嫂子们羡慕他的妻子"
"Her sisters spread the powder over the bed"
"她的姐妹们把粉末撒在床上"
"He is still suffering from his pain"
"他仍然痛苦不堪"
"But he is in his native land"
"但他在自己的祖国"
"And now he is at the point of death"
"现在他已经濒临死亡"
"Beneath the tree is his heroic bride"
"树下是他英勇的新娘"
"She is wearing the garb of a Sannyasi"

"她穿着桑雅士的服装"
"And she is going to nurse him"
"她要照顾他"
The Bihangami asked the Bihangama.
比汉加米问比汉加米。
"Is there no cure for the prince?"
"王子没有解药吗？"
"Yes, there is a cure" replied the Bihangama.
"是的，有办法。" 比汉加玛回答道。
"There is hardened dung lying on the ground"
"地上还有硬邦邦的粪便"
"She must take this hardened dung"
"她必须吃下这块硬化的粪便"
"Then she must reduce the dung to powder"
"然后她必须把粪便磨成粉末"
"And then she must bathe the prince"
"然后她必须给王子洗澡"
"She must bathe him in seven jars of water"
"她必须用七罐水给他洗澡"
"Then she must bathe him in seven jars of milk"
"然后她必须用七罐牛奶给他洗澡"
"Then she must apply the powder to his body"
"那么她必须把粉末涂到他的身上"
"After this Prince Sobur will get well"
"这样索布尔王子就会康复了"
"I have no doubts about this remedy"
"我对这个疗法毫不怀疑"
The Bihangami saw a problem though.
然而，Bihangami 发现了一个问题。
"The princess is but a young girl"
"公主还只是个小女孩"
"She cannot walk such a distance"
"她走不了这么远的距离"
"The journey would take her many days"

"这趟旅程要花很多天"
"By that time the poor prince will have died"
"到那时可怜的王子就死了"
"I can," replied the Bihangama.
"我可以，" 比汉加玛回答道。
"I will take the young lady on my back"
"我会把这位小姐背上"
"I will fly her to Prince Sobur's city"
"我会带她飞往索布尔王子的城市"
"If she takes no presents, I will fly her back"
"如果她不接受礼物，我就让她飞回去"
The merchant's daughter heard this conversation.
商人的女儿听到了这段对话。
She begged the Bihangama to take her on his back.
她恳求比汉加玛把她背在背上。
And of course the bird willingly consented.
当然，小鸟欣然同意了。
First she gathered some of the birds dung.
首先，她收集了一些鸟粪。
And then she reduced the dung to fine powder.
然后她将粪便磨成细粉。
She was armed with this potent drug.
她拥有这种强效药物。
And she got on the back of the kind bird.
她骑上了这只善良的鸟的背。

The Bihangama flew as fast as lightning.
比汉加玛飞行速度快如闪电。
They soon reached Prince Sobur's city.
他们很快就到达了索布尔王子的城市。
The young Sannyasi went up to the palace.
年轻的桑雅士走进了宫殿。
And she spoke to the guards at the gate.
她对门口的守卫说了话。

"Send word to the king that I have a drug"
"去告诉国王我有一种药"
"This drug will save the prince's life"
"这药能救王子的命"
"Within hours I will have cured the prince"
"几个小时内我就能治好王子"
The king had tried all the best doctors.
国王已经试遍了所有最好的医生。
But no doctor had been able to cure his son.
但没有医生能够治愈他的儿子。
So he didn't believe the Sannyasi's words.
所以他不相信沙尼亚西的话。
But his councilors advised him otherwise.
但他的顾问却建议他不要这么做。
The Sannyasi ordered for seven jars of water.
桑雅士订购了七罐水。
And seven jars of milk were ordered.
并订购了七罐牛奶。
He poured a jar of water on the prince.
他把一罐水倒在王子身上。
And he poured a jar of milk on the prince.
他把一罐牛奶倒在王子身上。
He had a feather from the divine bird.
他有一根神鸟的羽毛。
And he used the feather to apply the powder.
他用羽毛涂抹粉末。
All of the prince's body was covered.
王子的整个身体都被覆盖了。
This was repeated another six times.
此事又重复了六次。
The last treatment did the magic.
最后的治疗产生了神奇的效果。
The prince started to feel well again.
王子又开始感觉好起来了。

The king was happier than words can describe.
国王的幸福难以言表。
"Give the Sannyasi the finest treasures"
"给桑雅士们最好的宝藏"
But the Sannyasi refused to take presents.
但桑雅士拒绝接受礼物。
"Let me have the ring on the prince's finger"
"把王子手指上的戒指给我吧"
The king and the prince were happy.
国王和王子都很高兴。
And they gave him what he wanted.
他们给了他想要的东西。
The merchant's daughter hastened back.
商人的女儿赶紧回来了。
The Bihangama was waiting at the sea-shore.
比汉加玛正在海边等候。
They reached the tree of the divine birds.
他们到达了神鸟树。
The young bride walked back to her palace.
年轻的新娘走回了她的宫殿。

The following day she shook the magical feather fan.
第二天她摇动了那把神奇的羽毛扇。
Just as before, her husband appeared.
正如之前一样，她的丈夫出现了。
Of course he was happy to see his wife.
他当然很高兴见到他的妻子。
But he was infinitely surprised.
但他却无限惊讶。
She had his ring on her finger.
她的手指上戴着他的戒指。
His own wife was his doctor.
他的妻子就是他的医生。
It was his wife that had cured him!

是他的妻子治愈了他！
The prince took his bride to his palace.
王子带着新娘回到了宫殿。
He forgave his sisters-in-law.
他原谅了他的嫂子们。
They lived happily for many years.
他们幸福地生活了很多年。
And they were blessed with children.
他们有幸有了孩子。

The Origins of Opium
鸦片的起源

Once upon on a time there lived a Rishi.
从前，有一位圣人。
He lived on the banks of the holy Ganges.
他住在神圣的恒河岸边。
This Rishi was a very religious man.
这位圣人是一位非常虔诚的人。
He spent his days performing religious rites.
他每天都在进行宗教仪式。
From sunrise to sunset he sat on the river bank.
从日出到日落，他一直坐在河岸上。
For the whole time he sat engaged in devotion.
他始终坐着，虔诚地祈祷。
At night he took shelter in his hut.
晚上，他躲进了自己的小屋。
His hut was made from palm-leaves.
他的小屋是用棕榈叶做成的。
The palms he had grown from saplings.
他从树苗培育出来的棕榈树。
There was no one around for miles.
方圆数英里内空无一人。
However, in the hut there was a mouse.
然而，小屋里有一只老鼠。
She lived from what the Rishi left for her.
她靠圣贤给她留下的东西生活。
The Rishi was a kind-hearted man.
圣人是一位心地善良的人。
He would not hurt any living thing.
他不会伤害任何生物。
So our mouse never ran away from him.
所以我们的老鼠从来没有从他身边跑过。
In fact, our mouse went to him.

事实上，我们的老鼠已经去找他了。
She touched his feet when he was sitting.
当他坐着的时候，她触摸了他的脚。
And she enjoyed playing with him.
她很喜欢和他一起玩。
The Rishi also liked the little mouse.
圣人也很喜欢这只小老鼠。
So he wanted to be kind to her.
所以他想善待她。
And he wanted someone to talk to.
他想找个人聊聊。
So he gave her the power of speech.
于是他赋予了她说话的能力。

One night the mouse stood up.
一天晚上，老鼠站了起来。
She got onto her hind legs.
她用后腿站立起来。
And she stood in front of the Rishi.
她站在圣人的面前。
And she put her front paws together.
她把前爪并拢。
"Holy Sage, you have been kind to me"
"圣贤，你对我太好了。"
"And you have given me human language"
"你赐给我人类的语言"
"I hope it doesn't displease your reverence"
"我希望这不会令尊贵的您不悦。"
"But I have one more boon to ask"
"但我还有一个请求"
The Rishi listened to his mouse.
圣人听着老鼠的话。
"What is it?" asked the Rishi.
"什么事？" 圣人问道。

"Say what you want, little mouse"
"小老鼠，你想说什么就说什么"
The mouse answered the Rishi.
老鼠回答了圣人。
"By day your reverence goes to the river"
"白天，尊敬的先生们去河边"
"And there you practice your devotions"
"在那里，你们践行你们的虔诚"
"During this time a cat comes to the hut"
"这时，一只猫来到小屋"
"This cat has been trying to catch me"
"这只猫一直想抓我"
"She still has some fear of your reverence"
"她仍然对你的崇敬感到有些恐惧"
"Otherwise she would have eaten me long ago"
"不然她早就把我吃了"
"But I fear the cat will eat me someday"
"但我担心有一天猫会吃掉我"
"So I have one prayer to ask of you"
"所以我想请你祈祷"
"Please may I be changed into a cat!"
"请让我变成一只猫吧！"
"Then I would be a match for my foe"
"那我就能与我的敌人匹敌了"
The Rishi understood the mouse's plight.
圣人了解老鼠的困境。
He threw some holy water on the mouse.
他向老鼠身上泼了一些圣水。
And the mouse instantly turned into a cat.
老鼠瞬间变成了一只猫。

She had lived as a cat for some days.
她已经作为一只猫生活了好几天了。
One night she went to the Rishi again.

一天晚上，她又去见了圣人。
And the Rishi spoke to his pet.
圣人对他的宠物说话了。
"Well, little kitty, how are you!"
"嗯，小猫咪，你好吗！"
"How do you like your present life!"
"你喜欢现在的生活吗！"
The cat thought about what to say.
猫想了想该说什么。
But she didn't have to say anything.
但她什么也不用说。
The Rishi could tell by her expression.
圣人从她的表情就能看出来。
"Why don't you like it?" asked the sage.
"你为什么不喜欢它？" 圣人问道。
"Are you not as strong as the other cats!"
"你难道不如其他猫那么强吗！"
"Yes, I am strong enough," answered the cat.
"是的，我足够强壮，" 猫回答道。
"Your reverence has made me a strong cat"
"您的尊敬使我成为一只坚强的猫"
"As strong as any cat in the world"
"和世界上任何一只猫一样强壮"
"Now I do not fear cats anymore"
"现在我不再怕猫了"
"But now I have got a new foe"
"但现在我遇到了一个新的敌人"
"By day your reverence goes to the river"
"白天，尊敬的先生们去河边"
"During this time dogs come to the hut"
"这段时间，狗会来小屋"
"These dogs have been barking at me"
"这些狗一直冲我叫"
"And I have been frightened for my life"

"我担心自己的生命安全"
"So I have one more prayer to ask of you"
"所以我还有一个祷告要请你"
"Please may I be changed into a dog!"
"请让我变成一只狗吧！"
The Rishi understood the cat's plight.
圣人了解猫的困境。
He threw some holy water on the cat.
他向猫身上泼了一些圣水。
And the cat instantly became a dog.
猫立刻变成了狗。

She lived as a dog for some days.
她像狗一样生活了几天。
But one night she spoke to the Rishi.
但一天晚上，她与圣人交谈。
"I cannot thank your reverence enough"
"我非常感谢您的尊敬"
"You have been most kind to me"
"你对我太好了"
"I was but a poor mouse"
"我只是一只可怜的老鼠"
"You not only gave me speech"
"你不仅给了我演讲的机会"
"But you also turned me into a cat"
"但你也把我变成了一只猫"
"And your kindness didn't end there"
"你的善意还不止于此"
"Then you changed me into a dog"
"然后你就把我变成了一只狗"
"As a dog, however, I suffer greatly"
"然而，作为一条狗，我却很痛苦"
"I do not get enough to eat"
"我吃不饱"

"My only food is what you leave me"
"我唯一的食物就是你留给我的东西"
"That was fine when I was a mouse"
"当我还是一只老鼠的时候，这很好"
"But you have made me much larger"
"但你让我变得更强大了"
"And it is not enough to fill my mouth"
"但这还不够我吃"
"OH your reverence, how I envy those monkeys"
"哦，尊敬的先生，我真羡慕那些猴子。"
"They jump about from tree to tree"
"它们在树间跳来跳去"
"They eat all sorts of delicious fruits!"
"它们吃各种美味的水果！"
"Please may reverence not get angry"
"请您不要生气"
"I pray to be changed into an monkey"
"我祈求变成一只猴子"
The sage was a very understanding man.
这位圣人是一位非常通情达理的人。
His heart was filled with patience.
他心里充满了耐心。
He was happy to grant his pet's wish.
他很高兴能满足宠物的愿望。
He threw some holy water on the dog.
他向狗泼了一些圣水。
And the dog instantly became an monkey.
狗立刻变成了猴子。

Our monkey was at first wild with joy.
我们的猴子一开始高兴得发狂。
She leaped from one tree to another.
她从一棵树跳到另一棵树。
She sucked every luscious fruit.

她吮吸着每一个美味的水果。
But her joy was short-lived again.
但她的喜悦又短暂了。
Summer had brought with it its drought.
夏季带来了干旱。
Monkeys find it hard to climb down.
猴子很难爬下来。
So she couldn't drink from the river.
所以她不能喝河里的水。
She saw how the wild boars lived.
她看到了野猪的生活方式。
All day they splashed in the water.
他们整天都在水里嬉戏。
She envied their life now.
她很羡慕他们现在的生活。
"Oh how happy those wild boars are!"
"哦，那些野猪多么高兴啊！"
"All day their bodies are cooled"
"他们的身体一整天都处于冷却状态"
"All day they are refreshed by water"
"他们整天都喝水，精神焕发"
"How I wish I were a wild boar"
"我多么希望自己是一头野猪"
That night she went to the Rishi.
那天晚上她去了圣人那里。
She recounted her troubles to him.
她向他诉说了自己的苦恼。
She told him all about the wild boars.
她把有关野猪的一切告诉了他。
"Oh how pleasant their lives must be"
"他们的生活一定很幸福。"
And she begged to be changed again.
她又恳求换衣服。
"I pray to be changed into a wild boar"

"我祈求变成一头野猪"
The sage's kindness knew no bounds.
圣人的仁慈是无止境的。
and he complied with his pet's request.
他满足了宠物的请求。
He threw some holy water on the monkey.
他向猴子泼了一些圣水。
And the monkey instantly became a wild boar.
猴子瞬间变成了一头野猪。

Our boar was now very content.
我们的野猪现在非常满足。
She kept her body soaking wet.
她的身体一直湿透。
Every day she went to the river.
她每天都去河边。
She splashed about in her favorite element.
她在她最喜欢的元素中嬉戏。
But life is not safe for wild boars.
但野猪的生活并不安全。
One day the king was out hunting.
有一天，国王出去打猎。
He was riding on an adorned elephant.
他骑着一头装饰华丽的大象。
Only by luck did our wild boar escape.
我们的野猪侥幸逃脱了。
She thought a lot about her experience.
她对自己的经历想了很多。
She dwelt on the dangers of her life.
她反复思考着自己生活中的危险。
And she envied the stately elephant.
她很羡慕这头威严的大象。
The elephant was more fortunate than her.
大象比她幸运得多。

He got to carry the king on his back.
他必须把国王背在背上。
Now she longed to be an elephant.
现在她渴望成为一头大象。
And at night she besought the Rishi.
晚上，她向圣人祈求。

Our elephant was roaming the wilderness.
我们的大象正在荒野中漫步。
On her adventures she saw the king.
在她的冒险中她见到了国王。
Our elephant went towards the king's suite.
我们的大象走向国王的套房。
She had every intention of being caught.
她完全有被抓住的意图。
The king saw the elephant from a distance.
国王从远处看到了大象。
He couldn't help but admire her beauty.
他禁不住赞叹她的美貌。
He gave his orders to his servants.
他向仆人们发出了命令。
"Catch and tame this elephant"
"抓住并驯服这头大象"
Our elephant was easily caught.
我们的大象很容易就被抓住了。
She was taken into the royal stables.
她被带进了皇家马厩。
And she was tamed without any trouble.
她没有费什么力气就被驯服了。

One day the queen had a wish.
有一天，女王许了一个愿望。
She wished to go to the holy Ganges.
她希望前往神圣的恒河。

She wished to bathe in the holy waters.
她希望在圣水中沐浴。
The king wanted to accompany his wife.
国王想陪伴他的妻子。
So he made his orders to his servants.
于是他吩咐仆人。
"Bring us the newly caught elephant"
"把刚抓到的大象带给我们"
The king and queen mounted on her back.
国王和王后骑仕她的背上。
Our elephant had gotten her wish.
我们的大象实现了她的愿望。
Well... she seemed to have gotten her wish.
嗯……看来她的愿望已经实现了。
The king had mounted on her back.
国王已经骑在了她的背上。
But no, the elephant didn't get her wish.
但没有，大象没有实现她的愿望。
She looked upon herself as a lordly beast.
她视自己为高贵的野兽。
She could not a woman riding on her back.
她不能让女人骑在她的背上。
It wasn't enough that she was a queen.
她是一位女王，但这还不够。
She could not bear the idea of it.
她无法忍受这个想法。
She felt she had been degraded.
她感觉自己受到了侮辱。
She jumped up as violently as elephants can.
她像大象一样猛烈地跳了起来。
Both the king and queen fell to the ground.
国王和王后都倒在了地上。
The king carefully picked up the queen.
国王小心翼翼地抱起王后。

He took the queen in his arms.
他将女王拥入怀中。
He asked her whether she had been hurt.
他问她是否受伤了。
He wiped off the dust from her clothes.
他擦掉了她衣服上的灰尘。
And he tenderly kissed her a hundred times.
他温柔地吻了她一百次。
Our elephant witnessed the king's caresses.
我们的大象见证了国王的爱抚。
And she scampered off to the woods.
然后她就跑进了树林。
She ran as fast as her legs could carry her.
她拼尽全力奔跑。
As she ran, she thought within herself;
她一边跑，一边心里想着；
"I have experienced many different lives"
"我经历过很多不同的人生"
"And I have experienced different happiness"
"我也体会到了不一样的幸福"
"But those lives cannot be compared"
"但那些生命无法相比"
"A queen is the happiest creature of all"
"女王是世界上最幸福的人"
"Of what infinite regard is she the object of!"
"她是多么令人敬佩啊！"
"The king lifted her off the ground"
"国王把她从地上抱了起来"
"And he carefully took her in his arms"
"他小心翼翼地把她抱在怀里"
"He made many tender inquiries to her"
他温柔地问她许多问题
"And he wiped off the dust from her clothes"
"他擦去了她衣服上的灰尘"

"And he kissed her a hundred times!"
"他还吻了她一百次！"
"Oh, the happiness of being a queen!"
"哦，成为女王真幸福！"
"I must ask the Rishi to make me a queen!"
"我必须请求圣贤立我为王后！"

The sun was just about to set.
太阳即将落山。
Our elephant made it back to the hut.
我们的大象回到了小屋。
The Rishi had just finished his devotions.
圣人刚刚结束他的祈祷。
She fell on the ground at his feet.
她倒在他的脚下。
She was still the little mouse.
她还是那只小老鼠。
And he was still the holy sage.
而他，依然是圣贤。
"What's the news?" inquired the Rishi.
"有什么消息吗？" 圣人询问。
"Why have you left the king's palace!"
"你为什么离开王宫？"
Our elephant thought about her words.
我们的大象思考了她的话。
"What shall I say to your reverence!"
"我该对尊者说什么呢？"
"You have been very kind to me"
"你对我很好"
"You have granted every wish of mine"
"你满足了我的所有愿望"
"I was a mouse and you gave me speech"
"我是一只老鼠，你让我开口说话"
"But as a mouse my life was in danger"

"但作为一只老鼠，我的生命处于危险之中"
"You saved me by turning me into a cat"
"你把我变成了一只猫，救了我"
"But as a cat my life was no safer"
"但作为一只猫，我的生活也并不安全"
"And you helped me become a dog"
"你帮我变成了一只狗"
"But as a dog I had not enough to eat"
"但作为一条狗，我没有足够的食物"
"You provided for me again"
"你又供给我了"
"And you turned my into a monkey"
"你把我变成了猴子"
"I had all I could wish to eat"
"我吃饱了"
"But I had no way of cooling my body"
"但我没有办法冷却我的身体"
"You helped me with this too"
"你也帮我做了这件事"
"And you turned me into a wild boar"
"你把我变成了一头野猪"
"Wild boars have a comfortable life"
"野猪过着舒适的生活"
"But they don't live without danger"
"但他们的生活并非没有危险"
"And again you protected me"
"你又一次保护了我"
"And you turned me into an elephant"
"你把我变成了一头大象"
"Being an elephant has increased my bulk"
"成为大象让我的体型变大了"
"But being an elephant has not increased my happiness"
"但成为大象并没有增加我的幸福感"
"I have one more boon to ask of you"

"我还想请求你再做一件事"
"It will be the last boon I ask for"
"这将是我祈求的最后一个恩惠"
"I see now who the happiest creature is"
"我现在知道谁是最幸福的人了"
"A queen is the happiest in the world"
"女王是世界上最幸福的人"
"Holy father, please make me a queen"
"圣父，请让我成为女王吧"
"Silly child," answered the Rishi.
"傻孩子，" 圣人回答道。
"How can I make you a queen!"
"我怎样才能让你成为女王呢？"
"Where can I get a kingdom for you!"
"我到哪里去给你弄一个王国啊！"
"Where would I find a royal husband!"
"我上哪儿去找一位皇室丈夫啊！"
But the Rishi was still patient.
但圣人仍然很有耐心。
"There is one thing I can do for you"
"有一件事我可以为你做"
"I can change you into a beautiful girl"
"我可以把你变成一个美丽的女孩"
"You will be as beautiful as a queen"
"你会像女王一样美丽"
"You will possess all the charms you need"
"你将拥有你所需要的一切魅力"
"Your charms can captivate a prince's heart"
"你的魅力可以俘获王子的心"
"But you must wait for what the gods decide"
"但你必须等待神的决定。"
"They will grant you an interview"
"他们会给你面试机会的"
"Tou will have your chance with a prince!"

"你将有机会遇到一位王子！"
Our elephant agreed to the change.
我们的大象同意了这个改变。
The beast was transformed by the Rishi.
这只野兽被圣人改变了。
And now she was a beautiful young lady.
现在她是一位美丽的年轻女士。
The holy sage named her Postomani.
圣贤给她取名为波斯托玛尼（Postomani）。
Her name meant 'the poppy-seed lady'.
她的名字的意思是"罂粟籽女士"。

Postomani lived in the Rishi's hut.
波斯托玛尼（Postomani）住在圣人的小屋里。
She spent her time tending the flowers.
她花时间照料花朵。
And she watered the plants in the garden.
她还给花园里的植物浇水。
One day she was sitting at the hut.
有一天，她坐在小屋里。
The Rishi was at the holy Ganges.
圣人来到了神圣的恒河。
A richly dressed man came towards the cottage.
一位衣着华丽的男子向小屋走来。
She stood up to welcome the man.
她站起身去迎接那位男士。
And she asked the stranger who he was.
她问陌生人他是谁。
"What have you come for?" she asked.
"你来干什么？"她问。
"I have been on a hunt"
"我一直在追捕"
"But we chased the deer in vain"
"但我们徒劳地追赶鹿"

"Now I am thirsty from the heat"
"现在我热得口渴"
"I thought that a Rishi lives here"
"我以为这里有一位圣贤住着"
"I had come to ask him for water"
"我来向他要水"
"But now I see you live here"
"但现在我看到你住在这里"
Postomani answered the stranger.
波斯托马尼回答了陌生人。
"Look upon this hut as your own"
"把这间小屋当成你自己的"
"I am sorry, but we are poor"
"很抱歉，我们很穷"
"We cannot offer you any entertainment"
"我们无法为您提供任何娱乐活动"
"But let me make your visit comfortable"
"但我会让您的访问舒适"
"Because, I believe you are a king"
"因为，我相信你是一位国王"
"If I am not mistaken," she added.
"如果我没记错的话，" 她补充道。
The stranger smiled in recognition.
陌生人认出了我，并微笑着。

Postomani then brought a pot of water.
然后，波斯托马尼拿来一壶水。
She went to wash her royal guest's feet.
她去为她的贵宾洗脚。
But the visitor did not let her do this.
但来访者并没有让她这么做。
"Holy maid, do not touch my feet"
"圣女，别碰我的脚"
"I am only a Kshatriya," he confessed.

"我只是一个刹帝利，" 他承认道。

"And you are the daughter of a holy sage"

"而你是一位圣贤的女儿。"

"Noble sir;" Postomani begun to confess.

"尊贵的先生；" 波斯托马尼开始忏悔。

"I am not the daughter of the Rishi"

"我不是圣贤的女儿"

"And am I not a Brahmani girl either"

"我也不是婆罗门女子吗？"

"There is no harm in me touching your feet"

"我摸摸你的脚也没什么坏处"

"Besides, you are my guest"

"再说，你是我的客人。"

"And I am bound to wash your feet"

"我有责任给你洗脚"

"Forgive my impertinence," the king wished.

"请原谅我的无礼，" 国王希望道。

"What caste do you belong to?" he asked.

"你属于什么种姓？" 他问道。

"I only know what the sage told me"

"我只知道圣人告诉我的事"

"I heard my parents were Kshatriyas"

"我听说我的父母是刹帝利"

The stranger wanted to know more.

陌生人想知道更多。

"May I ask whether your father was a king!"

"请问您的父亲是不是一位国王！"

"You have an uncommon beauty," he said.

"你有一种非凡的美貌，" 他说。

"And you possess a stately demeanor"

"而且你举止庄重"

"These qualities cannot be worked for"

"这些品质是无法通过努力获得的"

"It shows that you were born a princess"

"这表明你生来就是一位公主"
Postomani avoided answering the question.
波斯托马尼回避回答这个问题。
Instead she went inside the hut.
相反，她走进了小屋。
She brought out a tray of delicious fruits.
她端出一盘美味的水果。
And she set the fruits before the king.
她把水果摆在国王面前。
The king, however, did not touch the fruits.
然而，国王并没有碰这些水果。
He waited until his question was answered.
他一直等到他的问题得到解答。
"I only know what the holy sage says"
"我只知道圣贤说了什么"
"He says that my father was a king"
"他说我父亲是一位国王"
"But he was overcome in a battle"
"但他在战斗中被击败了"
"So he, with my mother, fled into the woods"
"于是他和我母亲逃进了树林"
"My poor father was eaten by a tiger"
"我可怜的父亲被老虎吃掉了"
"My mother closed her eyes as I opened mine"
"我睁开眼睛的时候，妈妈却闭上了眼睛"
"There was a bee-hive on the tree"
"树上有一个蜂巢"
"I lay at the foot of that tree"
"我躺在那棵树下"
"Drops of honey fell into my mouth"
"几滴蜂蜜落进我的嘴里"
"The honey maintained the spark inside me"
"蜂蜜让我内心的火花得以延续"
"And then the kind Rishi found me"

"然后善良的Rishi找到了我"
"The holy sage brought me into his hut"
"圣贤带我进入他的小屋"
"This is the simple story of this wretched girl"
"这就是这个可怜女孩的简单故事"
"The girl who now stands before the king"
"现在站在国王面前的女孩"
"Call not yourself wretched," replied the king.
"别说你自己可怜，" 国王回答道。
"You are the most beautiful of women"
"你是最美丽的女人"
"And you are the loveliest of women"
"你是最可爱的女人"
"You would adorn the grandest palaces"
"你会装饰最宏伟的宫殿"

Postomani had gotten her interview.
波斯托玛尼已经接受了采访。
She fell in love with the king.
她爱上了国王。
And the king fell in love with her.
国王爱上了她。
The Rishi joined them in marriage.
圣人让他们结为夫妻。
Postomani became the king's favourite queen.
波斯托玛尼成为了国王最喜爱的王后。
And the former queen was in disgrace.
而前任女王则蒙羞。
But Postomani's happiness was short-lived.
但波斯托马尼的幸福并没有持续太久。
One day as she was standing by a well.
有一天，她站在一口井边。
She was overcome by a moment of giddiness.
她感到一阵眩晕。

Fortune had her fall into the water.
命运让她落入水中。
And she died in the water of the well.
她就死在井水中。
The Rishi then came to the king.
然后圣人来到国王面前。
"O king, grieve not over the past"
"国王啊，不要为过去而悲伤"
"What is fixed by fate must come to pass"
"命中注定的事，必然发生"
"The queen drowned in your well"
"女王淹死在你的井里了"
"But she was not of royal blood"
"但她不是皇室血统"
"She was born to a family of mice"
"她出生在一个老鼠家庭"
"Each evening she came to my hut"
"每天晚上她都会来我的小屋"
"And I gave her the power of speech"
"我赋予她说话的能力"
"With speech she could express her wishes"
"她可以通过言语表达自己的愿望"
"I changed her according to her wishes"
"我按照她的意愿改变了她"
"As a mouse she feared the cat"
"她就像老鼠一样害怕猫"
"And so I changed her into a cat"
"所以我把她变成了一只猫"
"As a cat she feared the dogs"
"作为一只猫，她害怕狗"
"And so I changed her into a dog"
"所以我把她变成了一只狗"
"As a dog she had not enough to eat"
"她像条狗一样，连饭都吃不饱"

"And so I changed her into a monkey"
"所以我把她变成了一只猴子"
"As a monkey she couldn't bear the heat"
"作为一只猴子，她无法忍受炎热"
"And so I changed her into a wild boar"
"所以我把她变成了一头野猪"
"As a boar her life was not safe"
"作为一头野猪，她的生命没有安全感"
"And so I changed her into an elephant"
"所以我把她变成了一头大象"
"That was the elephant you caught"
"这就是你抓到的大象"
"But as an elephant she was not loved"
"但作为一头大象，她并不被人喜爱"
"And so I changed her one last time"
"所以我最后一次改变了她"
"I changed her into a beautiful girl"
"我把她变成了一个美丽的女孩"
"That is the girl that you married"
"这就是你娶的女孩"
"And that is the girl that drowned"
"这就是溺水的女孩"
"Take into favor your former queen"
"照顾你的前任女王"
"And don't worry for my daughter"
"不用担心我的女儿"
"I will make her name immortal"
"我要让她的名字永垂不朽"
"Let her body remain in the well"
"让她的尸体留在井里"
"Fill the well up with earth"
"用土填满井"
"In her flesh there is a seed"
"她的肉体里有一颗种子"

"From her bones a tree will grow"
"她的骨头将长成一棵树"
"We will name this tree after her"
"我们将以她的名字命名这棵树"
"The tree shall be called 'Posto'"
"这棵树应该被称为 'Posto'"
"This means 'the Poppy tree'"
"这意味着 '罂粟树'"
"From this tree there will come a drug"
"这棵树上会长出药来"
"This drug will be called opium"
"这种药将被称为鸦片"
"Opium will be a powerful medicine"
"鸦片将成为一种强效药物"
"People will consume opium in every epoch"
"每个时代都会有人吸食鸦片"
"Opium will either be swallowed or smoked"
"鸦片要么吞下去，要么吸下去"
"And opium will be a wonderful narcotic"
"鸦片将是一种极好的麻醉剂"
"Opium will be used till the end of time"
"鸦片将永远被使用"
"You will recognize the opium smoker"
"你会认出那个吸鸦片的人"
"He will have many different qualities"
"他将拥有许多不同的品质"
"One quality for each of the animals"
"每种动物都有一种品质"
"The animals which Postomani had lived as"
"波斯托马尼曾经生活的动物"
"He will be mischievous, like a mouse"
"他会像老鼠一样淘气"
"He will be fond of milk, like a cat"
"他会像猫一样喜欢牛奶"

"He will be quarrelsome, like a dog"

"他会像狗一样吵闹"

"He will be filthy, like a monkey"

"他会变得很脏，就像猴子一样"

"He will be savage, like a boar"

"他会变得野蛮，像一头野猪"

"He will be confident, like an elephant"

"他会像大象一样自信"

"And he will be high-tempered, like a queen"

"他会脾气暴躁，就像女王一样"

Strike, but Listen First
先出击，但先听取意见

There was once a king who had three sons.
从前有一位国王，他有三个儿子。
His royal subjects came to him one day and said;
有一天，他的皇室臣民来找他并说道；
"Oh incarnation of justice! hear our plea"
"正义的化身啊！请听我们的恳求。"
"The kingdom is infested with thieves and robbers"
"王国里盗贼猖獗"
"Our property is not safe from their thievery"
"他们的盗窃行为危及我们的财产安全"
"We pray your majesty to catch hold of these thieves"
"我们祈求陛下抓住这些小偷。"
"We beg you punish them to the full extent of the law"
"我们恳求你们依法严惩他们"
The king said to his sons, "Oh, my sons, I am old"
国王对他的儿子们说："噢，我的儿子们，我老了"
"But you are all in the prime of manhood"
"但你们都正值壮年"
"How is it that my kingdom is full of thieves?"
"我的王国怎么到处都是小偷？"
"I look to you to catch hold of these thieves"
"我希望你能抓住这些小偷"
The three princes then made up their minds.
三位王子这才下定了决心。
They were going to patrol the city every night.
他们每晚都要在城里巡逻。
They set up a watch out in the outskirts of the city.
他们在城市郊区设立了哨所。
The early part of the night had arrived.
夜幕已近黄昏。
So the eldest prince took on his duties.

于是大皇子就承担起了自己的职责。

He rode upon his horse through the whole city.

他骑着马穿过了整个城市。

But did not see a single thief anywhere he looked.

但他四处张望，没有发现一个小偷。

He came back to the policing station.

他回到了警察局。

The middle part of the night had arrived.

已是深夜了。

So the second prince took on his duties.

于是二皇子便承担起了自己的职责。

And he too rode through every part of the city.

他也骑马走遍了城市的每个角落。

But he did not see or hear of a single thief.

但他没有看到或听说任何一个小偷。

He came also back to the policing station.

他也回到了警察局。

The latter part of the night had arrived.

夜幕已经降临。

So the youngest prince took on his duties.

于是最小的王子承担了他的职责。

He went near the gate of his father's palace.

他走到他父亲宫殿的门口。

There he saw a beautiful woman leaving the palace.

在那里，他看到一位美丽的女子走出宫殿。

The prince asked the woman, "who are you?"

王子问女人：“你是谁？”

"Where are you going at this hour of the night?"

“这么晚了你要去哪儿？”

The woman answered the young prince.

女人回答了年轻的王子。

"I am Rajlakshmi, the guardian deity of this palace"

“我是拉贾拉克希米，这座宫殿的守护神。”

"The king will be killed this night"

"国王今晚将被杀死"
"I am therefore not needed here"
"因此这里不需要我"
"And that is why I am going away"
"这就是我要离开的原因"
The prince did not know what to make of this message.
王子不知道该如何理解这个消息。
After a moment's reflection he said to the goddess;
经过片刻的思考后，他对女神说道；
"But, suppose the king is not killed tonight"
"但是，假设国王今晚没有被杀"
"Have you any objection to return to the palace?"
"你不反对回宫吗？"
"I have no objection," replied the goddess.
"我没有异议，" 女神回答道。
The prince then begged the goddess to go back.
王子于是恳求女神回去。
And he promised to do his best to protect the king.
并承诺会尽全力保护国王。
Then the goddess entered the palace again.
女神又回到了宫殿。
Within a moment she disappeared into the palace.
不一会儿，她就消失在宫殿里了。

The prince went straight into the palace too.
王子也直接进了宫殿。
And he went into the bedroom of his royal father.
他走进了他父亲的卧室。
There his father lay immersed in deep sleep.
他的父亲躺在那里，沉沉地睡着了。
The king had a second, younger wife.
国王有第二位更年轻的妻子。
This woman was the stepmother of our prince.
这个女人是我们王子的继母。

She was sleeping in another bed in the room.

她正在房间的另一张床上睡觉。

There was a light that was burning dimly.

有一盏昏暗的灯亮着。

But then the prince saw something that surprised him!

但随后王子看到了令他惊讶的事情！

A huge cobra going round and round the golden bedstead.

一条巨大的眼镜蛇绕着金色的床架转来转去。

The bedstead on which his father was sleeping.

他父亲睡觉的床架。

The prince with his sword cut the serpent in two.

王子用剑把蛇砍成了两半。

But he was not satisfied with killing the cobra.

但他并不满足于杀死眼镜蛇。

So he cut the cobra up into a hundred pieces.

于是他把眼镜蛇砍成了一百段。

And he put the pieces of the cobra inside a pan.

他把眼镜蛇的碎片放进平底锅里。

But while cutting the cobra a misfortune happened.

但在切割眼镜蛇时不幸发生了。

A drop of blood fell on the breast of his stepmother.

一滴血落在继母的胸口上。

The prince was in great distress by what had happened.

所发生的事让王子非常苦恼。

"I have saved my father, but killed my stepmother"

"我救了我的父亲，却害死了我的继母"

How could he remove the drop of blood from her breast?

他怎样才能除去她胸口的那滴血呢？

He wrapped round his tongue a piece of cloth sevenfold.

他用一块布将舌头缠了七圈。

And with the cloth he licked up the drop of blood.

他用布舔掉了那滴血。

But his stepmother's sleep was not so deep.

但他的继母睡得就没那么沉了。

And in his attempt to save her he awoke her.

为了救她，他唤醒了她。

When opening her eyes she saw it was her stepson.

当她睁开眼睛时，她发现那是她的继子。

The young prince rushed out of the room.

年轻的王子冲出了房间。

The queen, hated her stepson, the youngest prince.

女王非常讨厌她的继子，最小的王子。

And she had every intention to ruin his reputation.

她一心想毁掉他的名誉。

She called out to her husband, "My lord, my lord"

她向丈夫喊道："我的主，我的主。"

"Are you awake? are you awake? Rouse yourself up"

"你醒了吗？你醒了吗？快起来！"

"Here is a nice piece of news for you"

"有个好消息告诉你"

The king on awaking inquired what the matter was.

国王醒来后询问发生了什么事。

"What the matter is, my lord, let me tell you"

"大人，请让我来告诉你。"

"Your worthy son was just here in this room"

"你的儿子刚才就在这房间里。"

"The youngest prince, of whom you speak so highly"

"您称赞的最年轻的王子。"

"I caught him in the act of touching my breast"

"我发现他正在摸我的胸部"

"I don't doubt he came with wicked intents"

"我毫不怀疑他是带着恶意来的"

The king was horror-struck by what he heard.

国王听到后大为震惊。

The prince went back to where his brothers kept watch.

王子回到了哥哥们守望的地方。

But he told them nothing of what had happened.

但他没有告诉他们发生了什么事。

Early in the morning the king called his eldest son.
清晨，国王召集了他的长子。
"I entrust my life and my honor to men"
"我将我的生命和荣誉托付给人类"
"But what if one of these men prove faithless?
"但如果其中有一个人不忠怎么办？
"How should such a man be punished?"
"这样的人该受到怎样的惩罚？"
The eldest prince replied to his father, the king.
大王子回答他的父亲国王。
"Doubtless such a man's head should be cut off"
"毫无疑问，这种人的头应该被砍掉"
"But first you should establish the facts"
"但首先你应该确定事实"
"You must see whether the man is really faithless"
"你必须看看这个人是否真的不忠。"
"What do you mean?" inquired the king.
"你是什么意思？" 国王问道。
"Let your majesty be pleased to listen"
"陛下乐意聆听"
Once upon on a time there lived a goldsmith.
从前，有一位金匠。
This goldsmith had a son who had a wife.
这位金匠有一个儿子，他有一个妻子。
His wife had the rare faculty of understanding beasts.
他的妻子具有罕见的了解野兽的能力。
But she never told anyone about her uncommon gift.
但她从未告诉任何人她的非凡天赋。
Not even her husband knew she could understand animals.
甚至连她的丈夫都不知道她能听懂动物的语言。
One night she was lying in bed beside her husband.
一天晚上，她躺在丈夫身边。
From the river by their house she heard a jackal howl.

她听到从他们家附近的河边传来一声豺狼的嚎叫。
"There goes a carcass floating on the river"
"河里漂浮着一具尸体"
"There's a diamond ring on the dead man's finger"
"死者的手指上戴着一枚钻戒"
"Will anyone take the ring and give me the corpse?"
"有人能拿走戒指并把尸体给我吗？"
The woman understood the jackal's language.
女人听懂了豺狼的语言。
She got up from bed and went to the river-side.
她从床上起身，走到河边。
The husband had not been in deep sleep.
丈夫并没有睡得很熟。
So with his wife's movements he woke up too.
于是随着妻子的动作他也醒了。
And he followed his wife to see where she went.
他跟着妻子看她去了哪里。
But he kept his distance, so that he could observe her.
但他还是保持着距离，以便能够观察她。
The woman went into the water next to their house.
这名女子跳入了他们家旁边的水中。
She tugged the floating corpse towards the shore.
她把漂浮的尸体拖向岸边。
And she saw the diamond ring on the finger.
她看到了手指上的钻戒。
She was unable to loosen the ring with her hand.
她无法用手松开戒指。
Because the fingers of the dead body had swelled.
因为尸体的手指已经肿了。
So she bit off the finger with her teeth.
于是她用牙齿咬掉了手指。
And she put the dead body upon land, for the jackal.
她把尸体放到岸上，给豺狼吃。
Then she returned to bed, where her husband already was.

然后她回到床上，她的丈夫已经在那里了。
The young goldsmith lay almost petrified with fear.
年轻的金匠吓得几乎瘫倒在地。
He was convinced he was lying next to a Rakshasi.
他确信自己正躺在罗刹女的旁边。
He spent the rest of the night tossing in his bed.
那天晚上他一直在床上辗转反侧。
And early in the morning spoke to his father.
一大早他就和父亲谈话。
"The woman thou hast given me is not a real woman"
"你给我的女人不是一个真正的女人"
"The woman thou hast given me to wife is a Rakshasi"
"你赐给我的女人是罗刹女"
"Last night I was lying in bed with her"
"昨晚我和她一起躺在床上"
"By the river I heard the howl of a jackal"
"在河边我听到了豺狼的嚎叫"
"My wife too, heard the howl of the jackal"
"我的妻子也听到了豺狼的嚎叫"
"Thinking I was asleep; she went towards the howl"
"她以为我睡着了，就朝着嚎叫声走去。"
"I was surprised to see her go out of bed alone"
"看到她独自起床，我很惊讶"
"Suspecting some sort of evil, I followed her outside"
"我怀疑有什么不祥之兆，就跟着她出去了。"
"But she could not see that I had followed her"
"但她没发现我跟踪了她"
"What did she do, do you think? O horror of horrors!"
"你觉得她做了什么？太可怕了！"
"From the stream she dragged a dead body out"
"她从溪里拖出一具尸体"
"And what do you think she did with the dead body?"
"那你认为她对尸体做了什么？"
"She wasted no time devouring the dead man!"

"她毫不犹豫地吞噬了死者！"
"All this I had the misfortune to see with my own eyes"
"我很不幸亲眼目睹了这一切"
"While she feasted on the carcass I went back to bed"
"当她吃尸体的时候，我回去睡觉了"
"In a few minutes she also returned to bed"
"几分钟后她也回到了床上"
"She bolted the door shut, and lay beside me"
"她把门闩上，躺在我旁边"
"Oh my father, how can I live with a Rakshasi?"
"哦，父亲，我怎么能和一个罗刹女一起生活呢？"
"She will certainly kill me and eat me up one night"
"她肯定会在某天晚上杀了我然后把我吃掉"
You can imagine the shock of the old goldsmith.
你可以想象老金匠的震惊。
Both father and son agreed about what should be done.
父子俩对于应该做的事情达成了一致。
The woman should be taken deep into the forest.
应该把这个女人带到森林深处。
And she should be left for wild beasts to devoured.
她应该被留给野兽去吞噬。
Accordingly, the young goldsmith spoke to his wife.
于是，年轻的金匠对他的妻子说。
"My dear love," he said to his wife.
"我的亲爱的，"他对妻子说。
"You had better not cook much this morning"
"你今天早上最好不要做太多饭"
"Boil a little rice and burn a brinjal"
"煮一点米饭，烧一个茄子"
"Because today we are going to see your parents"
"因为今天我们要去见你的父母"
"Your mother and father are dying to see you"
"你的父母非常想见到你"
The woman was full of joy at the unexpected news.

听到这个意外的消息，女人满心欢喜。
She loved returning to her father's house.
她喜欢回到父亲的家。
And she finished the cooking in no time.
她很快就把饭做好了。
The husband and wife snatched a hasty breakfast.
夫妻俩匆匆吃完早餐。
And soon after breakfast they started their journey.
早餐后不久，他们就开始了旅程。
The way to her father's house was through dense jungle.
去她父亲家的路要穿过茂密的丛林。
It was the perfect place to abandon his wife.
这是抛弃妻子的最佳地点。
She was bound to be eaten up by wild beasts there.
她注定会被那里的野兽吃掉。
But while they were walking the woman heard a snake.
但当他们走路的时候，女人听到了蛇的声音。
"Oh passer-by, in yonder hole there is a frog"
"哦，路人，那边的洞里有一只青蛙"
"How thankful I would be if you caught the frog"
"如果你能抓住这只青蛙，我会非常感激的。"
"And the hole is full of gold and precious stones"
"洞里满是金子和宝石"
"Give me the frog, and take the treasure for yourself"
"把青蛙给我，宝藏你自己拿去"
The woman forthwith went to the frog's hole.
女人立即来到了青蛙洞边。
And she began digging the hole with a stick.
她开始用一根棍子挖洞。
The young goldsmith was now quaking with fear.
年轻的金匠现在吓得浑身发抖。
He thought his Rakshasi-wife was about to kill him.
他以为他的罗刹妻子要杀死他。
And then his wife called for him to help her.

然后他的妻子叫他来帮忙。
"Take all this gold and these precious stones"
"把这些黄金和宝石都拿去"
The goldsmith did not understand her request.
金匠不明白她的请求。
Timidly he went to where she had dug the hole.
他胆怯地走到她挖洞的地方。
But he was infinitely surprised by what he saw.
但他所看到的景象却让他无限惊讶。
The hole was full of gold and precious stones.
洞里满是金子和宝石。
"How did you know there was a treasure here?"
"你怎么知道这里有宝藏？"
And finally his wife told him of her gift.
最后他的妻子告诉了他她的礼物。
"I can understand all the beasts in the forest"
"我能理解森林里所有野兽的声音"
"Just over there, there is a snake coiled up"
"就在那里，有一条蛇盘绕着"
"She had told me there was a treasure here"
"她告诉我这里有宝藏"
The husband now felt very blessed with his wife.
丈夫现在觉得有了妻子就非常幸福。
"My love, it has gotten very late today"
"亲爱的，今天已经很晚了"
"I don't think we will reach your father's house"
"我觉得我们到不了你父亲的家"
"Nightfall will catch us before we get there"
"我们还没到达目的地，夜幕就降临了"
"If we stay we might be devoured by wild beasts"
"如果我们留下来，可能会被野兽吞噬"
"I propose therefore that we both return home"
"因此我建议我们一起回家"
You can imagine the wife's disappointment.

你可以想象妻子的失望。
But she agreed with her husband's assessment.
但她同意丈夫的评价。
It took them a long time to reach home.
他们花了很长时间才到家。
They were laden with a large quantity of gold.
他们装载了大量黄金。
And they were carrying many precious stones.
他们带着许多宝石。
But eventually the got close to their home.
但最终他们还是接近了他们的家。
"My dear, go by the back door," said the goldsmith.
"亲爱的，从后门走吧，" 金匠说。
"I will go by the front door and see my father"
"我要从前门去见我的父亲"
"And I will show him all this treasure"
"我会把这些宝藏都给他看"
So she entered the house by the back door.
于是她从后门进了房子。
But the old goldsmith had reason to be there too.
但老金匠也有理由去那里。
He had gone there to collect a hammer.
他去那里取一把锤子。
The old goldsmith saw his Rakshasi daughter-in-law.
老金匠见到了自己的罗刹女儿媳。
He concluded she had swallowed up his son.
他断定她已经把他的儿子吞噬了。
And he therefore struck her with the hammer.
于是他用锤子打了她。
The blow immediately killed his daughter-in-law.
这一击直接导致其儿媳死亡。
At that moment the son came into the house.
就在这时，儿子走进了屋子。
But it was too late for him to explain.

但他解释已经太晚了。

And so the eldest prince's story concluded.

大王子的故事就这样结束了。

"You might have to cut a man's head off"

"你可能得砍掉一个人的头"

"But first you should establish the facts"

"但首先你应该确定事实"

"You must see whether the man is really faithless"

"你必须看看这个人是否真的不忠。"

The king then called his second son to him.

于是国王叫他的次子过来。

"I entrust my life and my honor to men"

"我将我的生命和荣誉托付给人类"

"But what if one of these men prove faithless?

"但如果其中有一个人不忠怎么办？

"How should such a man be punished?"

"这样的人该受到怎样的惩罚？"

The second prince replied to his father, the king.

二皇子回答自己的父亲国王。

"Doubtless such a man's head should be cut off"

"毫无疑问，这种人的头应该被砍掉"

"But first you should establish the facts"

"但首先你应该确定事实"

"What do you mean?" inquired the king.

"你是什么意思？" 国王问道。

"Let your majesty be pleased to listen"

"陛下乐意聆听"

Once upon a time there reigned a king.

从前，有一位国王。

This king was very fond of going out hunting.

这位国王非常喜欢外出打猎。

One day his horse took him into a dense forest.

有一天，他的马把他带进了一片茂密的森林。

He went far from his followers, deep into the woods.
他远离了追随者，深入了森林。
He rode on and on through the endless, quiet forest.
他骑马继续前行，穿过无边无际、寂静无声的森林。
He saw neither villages nor towns, only trees.
他没有看到村庄，也没有看到城镇，只有树木。
On the long, lonely journey he became very thirsty.
在漫长而孤独的旅途中，他变得非常口渴。
He could see no pond, nor lake, nor stream.
他看不到池塘、湖泊或溪流。
But then he saw something dripping from a tree.
但随后他看到有东西从树上滴下来。
He concluded it was rainwater resting in a cavity.
他断定这是雨水在洞穴中积聚的结果。
He stood on horseback beneath the tree, cup in hand.
他骑在马上，站在树下，手里拿着杯子。
He caught the drops slowly dripping into the small cup.
他接住了慢慢滴入小杯中的水滴。
The water, however, was not rain from the sky.
然而，这些水并不是天上的雨。
A huge cobra sat on top of the tall tree.
一条巨大的眼镜蛇蹲在高大的树顶上。
The snake had struck the tree in rage with its sharp fangs.
蛇愤怒地用锋利的毒牙攻击树木。
The snake's poison came out and fell downward in heavy drops.
蛇的毒液流了出来，大颗大颗地落了下来。
The king thought the falling liquid was simple rainwater.
国王以为落下的液体只是普通的雨水。
The horse sensed the danger and tried to warn him.
马感觉到了危险并试图警告他。
The cup was nearly filled with the deadly snake-poison.
杯子里几乎装满了致命的蛇毒。
The king raised the cup and prepared to drink.

国王举起杯子，准备喝酒。

But the horse moved wildly, with the king on its back.

但国王骑在马背上，马儿疯狂地奔跑。

The cup fell from his hand, and the poison spilled.

杯子从他手中掉落，毒药洒了出来。

The king became angry and struck the horse's neck.

国王非常生气，打了马的脖子。

The blow from the sword immediately killed his horse.

这一剑，立刻就将他的马砍死了。

And so the second prince's story concluded.

二皇子的故事就这样结束了。

"You might have to cut a man's head off"

"你可能得砍掉一个人的头"

"But first you should establish the facts"

"但首先你应该确定事实"

"You must see whether the man is really faithless"

"你必须看看这个人是否真的不忠。"

The king then called to him his third youngest son.

于是国王叫来了他的第三个小儿子。

"I entrust my life and my honor to men"

"我将我的生命和荣誉托付给人类"

"But what if one of these men prove faithless?

"但如果其中有一个人不忠怎么办？

"How should such a man be punished?"

"这样的人该受到怎样的惩罚？"

"Doubtless such a man's head should be cut off"

"毫无疑问，这种人的头应该被砍掉"

"But first you should establish the facts"

"但首先你应该确定事实"

"What do you mean?" inquired the king.

"你是什么意思？" 国王问道。

"Let your majesty be pleased to listen"

"陛下乐意聆听"

Once long ago there reigned a wise and noble king.
很久以前，有一位睿智而高贵的国王。
In his palace he kept a bird of Suka species.
他在宫殿里养了一只苏卡鸟。
One day the bird went out flying into the fields.
有一天，这只鸟飞进了田野。
There he saw his father and mother calling from above.
在那里，他看到他的父母在上面呼唤他。
They asked him to come visit them in their nest.
他们请他到他们的窝里来拜访他们。
The nest was far away in a distant hidden land.
巢穴位于遥远的隐秘之地。
The Suka said, "I'll come if I get king's leave"
苏卡说："如果得到国王的许可，我就来。"
"I'll speak to the king today and return tomorrow"
"我今天会和国王谈谈，明天再回来。"
"Please wait at this same spot in the morning"
"请明早在此地点等候"
That very day, Suka spoke with the gentle, kind king.
就在那一天，苏卡与这位温柔、善良的国王进行了交谈。
The king gave permission for the bird to leave.
国王允许这只鸟离开。
Although he was sad to part with his bird.
尽管他很伤心要与他的鸟儿分离。
The next morning, Suka met his parents again.
第二天早上，苏卡又见到了他的父母。
He flew with them to their nest on a tall tree.
他和它们一起飞到高高的树上的巢穴。
The three birds lived together happily in peaceful joy.
三只鸟平安快乐地生活在一起。
They stayed like this for a fortnight of lovely days.
他们就这样度过了两个星期美好的日子。
But even those quiet and pleasant days had to end.

但即使是这样平静而愉快的日子也不得不结束。
Suka said, "Beloved parents, the king gave me two weeks"
苏卡说：“亲爱的父母，国王给了我两周的时间。”
"That time is now over, so I must return tomorrow"
“那段时间已经过去了，明天我一定要再来。”
His father and mother agreed and blessed his decision.
他的父母同意并祝福他的决定。
They told him to carry a gift for the king.
他们让他给国王带一份礼物。
After some talk, they chose some fruit as a gift.
经过一番交谈，他们选择了一些水果作为礼物。
The fruit had grown from the Immortality Tree.
这颗果实是从长生树上长出来的。
Early the next morning, Suka went to the tree.
第二天一大早，苏卡就来到了那棵树旁。
And he plucked a magical glowing fruit.
他摘下一颗发光的魔法果实。
He held the fruit gently in his beak, full of care.
他小心翼翼地用嘴叼着水果，满怀关切。
The fruit was heavy and slowed his swift flying pace.
水果很重，减慢了他快速飞行的速度。
He could not reach the city before night arrived.
天黑之前他无法到达这座城市。
Suka stopped to rest in a tree along the way.
苏卡在路上的一棵树上停下来休息。
He feared the fruit might drop while he slept.
他担心水果会在他睡觉时掉下来。
If he kept the fruit in his beak, it could fall.
如果他把水果含在嘴里，水果就会掉下来。
But he saw a hole in the trunk of the tree.
但他看到树干上有一个洞。
He placed the fruit safely inside the dark tree.
他把果实安全地放在了黑暗的树里。
But inside the hole, there lived a poisonous black snake.

但洞里却住着一条黑色的毒蛇。
In the night, the snake bit the fruit with venom.
夜里，蛇用毒液咬了水果。
And the fruit became smeared with deadly poison.
水果上沾满了致命的毒药。
At dawn Suka took the fruit back in his beak.
黎明时分，苏卡用嘴叼回了水果。
He flew again on his journey to the king's palace.
他再次飞翔，前往国王的宫殿。
As he reached the palace the king was sitting with ministers.
当他到达宫殿时，国王正与大臣们坐在一起。
The king was overjoyed to see Suka return once more.
国王看到苏卡再次归来，欣喜若狂。
He greatly admired the beautiful, shining fruit gift.
他非常欣赏这份美丽、闪亮的水果礼物。
The fruit was lovely to look at and admire.
这些水果看上去很可爱，令人赏心悦目。
It was the finest fruit found across the earth.
这是地球上最优质的水果。
And anyone who ate the fruit was granted immortality.
任何吃了这种水果的人都会获得永生。
The king was about to eat the beautiful fruit.
国王正要吃掉这颗美丽的水果。
But his ministers warned him the fruit might be poisoned"
但他的大臣们警告他，这种水果可能有毒。"
"It would be better to test the fruit before you eat it"
"吃水果之前最好先尝一下"
He threw the fruit to a crow sitting on the wall.
他把水果扔给了坐在墙上的一只乌鸦。
The crow ate from the fruit, and dropped dead instantly.
乌鸦吃了水果后立即死去。
The king, thinking Suka tried to kill him, grew furious.
国王以为苏卡想要杀死他，非常愤怒。
He seized the bird and killed him with his bare hands.

他抓住了那只鸟并徒手杀死了它。
He ordered the seed to be planted outside the city.
他下令将种子种在城外。
The seed became a tree with the same glowing fruit.
种子长成了一棵树，结出了同样闪亮的果实。
The king feared the fruit would bring more death.
国王担心这种水果会带来更多的死亡。
So he had the tree fenced off and guarded.
因此他用栅栏围住了这棵树并派人看守。

There lived in that city an old, poor Brahman man.
那个城市里住着一位年老贫穷的婆罗门。
He and his wife survived only on the town's charity.
他和妻子仅靠镇上的施舍维持生计。
One day the Brahman mourned his long, miserable, life.
有一天，婆罗门哀叹自己漫长而悲惨的一生。
He said, "Instead of begging, I will eat poison fruit."
他说："与其乞讨，我宁愿吃毒果。"
"I'll end my life beneath that deadly tree in silence."
"我将在那棵致命的树下默默地结束我的生命。"
That very night, he rose quietly and left his home.
那天晚上，他悄悄起床，离开了家。
His wife suspected and followed behind in silence.
他的妻子怀疑，默默地跟在后面。
She had decided to die too, alongside her sad husband.
她也决定与她悲伤的丈夫一起死去。
She loved him deeply and didn't wish to stay behind.
她深爱着他，不愿留下。
The palace guard was asleep that night, unaware of visitors.
那天晚上，宫廷卫兵正在睡觉，没有注意到有访客。
The Brahman reached the garden and plucked a hanging fruit.
婆罗门来到花园，摘下了一枚悬挂的果实。
He looked at it once and ate the entire fruit.

他看了一眼就把整个水果吃掉了。

His wife cried, "If you die, my life becomes nothing"

他的妻子哭喊道："如果你死了，我的生活就没了。
"

"I will also eat and die here with you now"

"我现在也要和你一起在这里吃饭和死去"

So saying she plucked a fruit and ate it.

说完她就摘下一个果子吃了。

They thought the poison would act slowly through the night.

他们以为毒药会在夜间慢慢起作用。

So they both went home and quietly lay down in bed.

于是他们俩都回家了，静静地躺在床上。

They believed they would never again rise from sleep.

他们相信自己永远不会再从睡梦中醒来。

To their surprise, they woke up feeling full of life.

令他们惊讶的是，他们醒来后感觉充满活力。

Not only were they alive, but they were young again.

他们不仅活着，而且又年轻了。

And they were strong and had new found energy.

他们很坚强，并且拥有新的活力。

Neighbors hardly recognized them, so changed they looked.

邻居们几乎认不出他们了，所以他们的外表也变了。

The old Brahman was now handsome and full of youth.

昔日的婆罗门如今英俊潇洒，充满青春气息。

His grey hair vanished, and had colour again.

他的白发消失了，又恢复了颜色。

His wrinkled cheeks turned smooth, and his skin shone.

他布满皱纹的脸颊变得光滑，皮肤闪闪发光。

And as for his wife, she became extremely beautiful.

而他的妻子则变得极其美丽。

She looked as beautiful as any lady of the kingdom.

她看上去和王国里的任何一位女士一样美丽。

The king heard of their miraculous transformation.

国王听说了他们的神奇转变。

He asked his guards to send the Brahman to him.
他要求卫兵把婆罗门送到他身边。

And he asked the Brahman the source of his youth.
他向婆罗门询问他的青春之源。

The Brahman told the king every detail of the story.
婆罗门把事情的经过详细地告诉了国王。

The king then wept for his poor, loyal pet bird.
国王为他可怜的、忠诚的宠物鸟哭泣。

He deeply regretted killing his faithful bird.
他深深后悔杀死了他忠实的鸟。

And he wished he had known the bird's loyalty.
他希望自己能了解这只鸟的忠诚。

And so the second prince's story concluded.
二皇子的故事就这样结束了。

"You might have to cut a man's head off"
"你可能得砍掉一个人的头"

"But first you should establish the facts"
"但首先你应该确定事实"

"You must see whether the man is really faithless"
"你必须看看这个人是否真的不忠。"

"I know Your Majesty suspects me of evil last night"
"我知道陛下昨晚怀疑我做了坏事。"

"Please allow me to explain myself before punishing me"
"在惩罚我之前，请允许我解释一下。"

"While making rounds I saw a woman leave the palace"
"巡视时，我看到一个女人离开了宫殿"

"I stopped her, and she said her name was Rajlakshmi"
"我拦住了她，她说她叫 Rajlakshmi"

"She claimed to be the guardian deity of the palace"
"她自称是宫殿的守护神。"

"She said she was leaving because death was near"
"她说她要离开，因为死亡临近了"

"The king," she said, "would be killed later that night"

"国王，" 她说， "那天晚上就会被杀。"
"I begged her to go back into the palace"
"我求她回宫去"
"And I promised to do my best to protect you."
"而且我承诺会尽我所能保护你。"
"I ran quickly into Your Majesty's chamber without delay."
"我毫不迟疑地跑进了陛下的房间。"
"There I saw a cobra circling your golden bedstead."
"我看到一条眼镜蛇在你的金床架上盘旋。"
"I fought the snake and killed it with my blade."
"我与蛇搏斗并用我的刀杀死了它。"
"I chopped the body into many exactly one hundred pieces."
"我把尸体砍成了整整一百块。"
"I placed those pieces inside the pan for proof."
"我把那些碎片放在锅里作为证据。"
"But something occurred as I was cutting up the snake."
"但当我切开蛇的时候发生了一些事情。"
"A drop of blood fell onto the breast of your wife."
"一滴血滴在你妻子的胸口上。"
"I feared I had saved my father, but killed my stepmother."
"我担心我救了我的父亲，却害死了我的继母。"
"I wrapped my tongue tightly with cloth seven times."
"我用布紧紧地缠住我的舌头七次。"
"Then I licked up the drop of venomous blood."
"然后我舔掉了那滴毒血。"
"While I was licking the blood, my stepmother awoke."
"当我正在舔血的时候，我的继母醒了。"
"She saw me and opened her eyes with confusion."
"她看到我，困惑地睁开了眼睛。"
"This is the truth of what I did last night."
"这就是我昨晚所做的事情的真相。"
"If Your Majesty commands, then cut off my head now."
"陛下若有吩咐，就现在就砍下我的头吧。"
The king, full of love and joy, embraced his son.

国王满怀爱意和喜悦地拥抱了他的儿子。
From that moment, he loved him more than ever before.
从那一刻起，他比以往任何时候都更爱他。

国王满怀爱意和喜悦地拥抱了他的儿子。
From that moment, he loved him more than ever before.
从那一刻起，他比以往任何时候都更爱他。